THE TENSION IS MOUNTAIN!

"Listen! It doesn't matter what the police and the rest of them think! Someone was killed right under my nose, and I feel a personal obligation to help find out who murdered her! I don't care if everybody in this whole fancy, ritzy, glitzy, world-class resort looks at me like I'm some dopey freeloader from the wrong part of town. A woman has been murdered, there's a killer out there, and I'm going to do my damnedest to find out who it is! You got it?"

"I think so." Renie's voice was unnaturally meek.

"Good!" Judith gestured with her head. "You see those mountains?" Renie replied that she certainly did. "I'm like those climbers. Why do I have to solve the mystery? *Because it's there!* That's why!"

Renie waited for Judith to turn her back. Only then did she dare roll her eyes.

MARY DAHEIM

MURDER, MY SUITE

A BED-AND-BREAKFAST MYSTERY

AVON BOOKS

An Imprint of HarperCollins*Publishers*

This is a work of fiction. Names, characters, places, and incidents are products of the author's imagination or are used fictitiously and are not to be construed as real. Any resemblance to actual events, locales, organizations, or persons, living or dead, is entirely coincidental.

AVON BOOKS
An Imprint of HarperCollins*Publishers*
10 East 53rd Street
New York, New York 10022-5299

Copyright © 1995 by Mary Daheim
Inside cover author photo by Tim Schlecht
Library of Congress Catalog Card Number: 95-90096
ISBN: 0-380-77877-7
www.avonmystery.com

First Avon Books printing: October 1995

Avon Trademark Reg. U.S. Pat. Off. and in Other Countries, Marca Registrada, Hecho en U.S.A.
HarperCollins® is a trademark of HarperCollins Publishers Inc.

Printed in the U.S.A.

10 9

MURDER,
MY
SUITE

ONE

JUDITH GROVER MCMONIGLE Flynn stared in horror at the slashed beige drapes, the shredded down comforter, and the tattered petit-point chair. Hillside Manor's choice bedroom was a shambles. Judith understood why her current guest had been thrown out of the Cascadia Hotel.

"It's that awful bitch," Judith groaned to her husband over the telephone a few minutes later. "She's wrecked the place. She even piddled on one of Grandma Grover's braided rugs."

Joe Flynn's voice was seemingly sympathetic. "So what's your mother doing in the guest rooms? I thought she was getting used to her apartment in the old toolshed."

Judith gritted her teeth. "You know I'm not talking about Mother. I mean the awful dog that belongs to Dagmar Delacroix Chatsworth. That woman and her wrecking crew haven't been here twenty-four hours, and they've already put me out of pocket. I'm going to have to charge for damages."

"Is that legal?" Joe now sounded serious, his policeman's mind obviously at work.

Leaning against the kitchen sink, Judith ran a nervous hand through her silver-streaked black hair. It was noon, straight up, on a muggy Wednesday in August. She felt short of breath, and on the verge of a sneezing spell. During the five and a half years that Judith had been running the

1

bed-and-breakfast on Heraldsgate Hill, the old family home
had suffered occasional misadventures. Soiled carpets, broken
dishes, clogged drains, even a minor flood, had all cost Judith
money, but she'd never yet asked a guest to pay for damages.
She had insurance, although the deductible was two hundred
dollars.

"Mother did the petit point on the chair years ago, when
her eyes were still sharp," Judith said with regret as her cleaning woman, Phyliss Rackley, stomped into the kitchen. "The
needlework is irreplaceable."

"But your mother isn't," Joe went on ingenuously. "Why
don't we trade her in on a nice recliner?"

"Joe . . ." It was hopeless, Judith knew, to discuss her
mother with her husband. Or vice versa. Joe Flynn and Gertrude Grover didn't like each other. They never had: not in
the beginning, almost thirty years earlier, when Judith and Joe
had met; not when they had become engaged a few years later;
certainly not when Joe had run off with another woman; and
definitely not after the pair had finally reunited and married
the previous summer. Gertrude had announced she wouldn't
live under the same roof as Joe. Compromises were attempted,
but proved unworkable. For a time, Gertrude had lived with
her sister-in-law, Deborah Grover, but that situation also had
turned out to be untenable. So for the past ten months Judith's
mother had been living in the renovated toolshed next to the
garage. It was the most feasible arrangement so far. While
Judith was elated at finally becoming Joe's wife, the incessant
wrangling between her husband and her mother was a constant
irritant, like a bunion.

"Hey," Joe said, his usually mellow voice suddenly
brusque, "I've got to run. I just got a call for the My Brew
Heaven Tavern over on Polk Street, possible homicide. See
you tonight."

Wearily, Judith hung up the phone. Joe was doing his job,
which was that of a homicide detective with the metropolitan
police force. He had better ways to spend his time than con-
soling his wife about her marauding guests and their vicious
dog. Judith should never have allowed anyone to bring a pet
into Hillside Manor in the first place. Ordinarily, it was against
her rules. But Dagmar Chatsworth's secretary, Agnes Shay,

had begged so piteously that Judith had given in. And now she was very sorry.

"The Lord didn't like dogs, either," Phyliss Rackley asserted, waggling her dust mop. "Have you ever seen a picture of Him holding a cocker spaniel?"

Judith gave a faint nod of agreement. She was used to her cleaning woman's skewed theology. "I'll take the braided rug to the dry cleaner's," Judith said, stifling a sneeze and adding the errand to her list of afternoon duties. "I've got some old drapes in the basement that'll have to do until the August white sales. Will you have time to help me hang them before the guests get back?"

"I'd hang the guests, if I were you," huffed Phyliss, her gray sausage curls bobbing in time with her dust mop. "They're an ungodly lot, and not fit company for that nice couple from Idaho and those nurses from Alberta."

Judith didn't argue. Dagmar Delacroix Chatsworth might be a nationally syndicated gossip columnist who had become as much of a celebrity as the people she parboiled in her thrice-weekly articles, but she was also a world-class pain in the neck. By contrast, Dagmar's secretary, Agnes Shay, was a meek, mousy woman with an appallingly put-upon manner. The third member of the party, Freddy Whobrey, was Dagmar's nephew. A former jockey, Freddy was small, dark, and feral, with a prominent overbite. Judith was reminded of a weasel. Or maybe a guinea pig. His nickname was Freddy Whoa, for reasons Judith could only guess.

But the most exasperating member of the Chatsworth entourage was Dagmar's fuzzy black-and-white Pomeranian. At the moment, the nasty little animal was locked in the bathroom that adjoined the front bedroom where Dagmar was staying. All of Judith's guests were out. Dagmar was signing her new book, *Chatty Chatsworth Digs the Dirt*, at a downtown bookstore. Freddy and Agnes had accompanied her. The couple from Idaho and the nurses from Alberta were sightseeing.

"If only the Carlsons hadn't canceled," Judith lamented, "I wouldn't have had an opening for these creeps." The Carlsons were annual visitors from Alaska who always brought along their two grown children and spouses; they all would have filled the three rooms required by the Chatsworth party.

But Mr. Carlson had had an unfortunate run-in with an elk and wasn't able to sit down. The family had rescheduled for the week after Labor Day.

Phyliss volunteered to find the old drapes on her next laundry mission to the basement. Judith grabbed her list, her handbag, and a handful of tissues. She still felt like sneezing. From upstairs the two women could hear Dagmar's dog, yipping its head off.

"Buy a muzzle," Phyliss urged. "That mutt is driving me crazy. I've asked the Lord for extra strength, but I think He's putting me through another test. As if my ingrown toenail wasn't enough. Say, did I tell you what happened Sunday at church when I tried to raise my arms after Pastor Polhamus told us to give the Devil the heave-ho? Well, there I was, standing in between . . ."

Judith braced herself and listened patiently to Phyliss's latest diatribe about her alleged ill health and ongoing search for salvation. Five minutes later, Judith was en route to the garage, feeling the oppressive heat and the muggy summer air. The grass in the backyard was turning yellow; the rhododendrons and azaleas drooped; even the small statue of St. Francis looked as if it could use a few swipes of sunscreen. The Pacific Northwest was suffering from drought, with water restrictions in force. Sprinklers could be used only for short periods on specified days of the week. Plants and shrubs were in danger of dying. Consumers were urged to cut back on using water-related appliances, including the shower and the toilet. A hefty surcharge would be added for anyone in violation. With the B&B full every night through the summer, Judith couldn't impose such regulations on her guests, but she knew she would pay a high price for her thoughtfulness when the water bill arrived in September.

Passing the garage, Judith approached the converted toolshed. She wondered why her mother didn't keep the door and the windows open on such a hot day. Gertrude greeted her daughter's knock with a scowl. She was wearing a heavy sweater over her leopard-print housecoat.

"Well? You here to get your damned cat?" Gertrude demanded.

"No, Mother," Judith replied, her voice now husky. "I

can't take Sweetums into the house with that dog there. Don't fuss, it'll only be until tomorrow. Then the Chatsworths will be gone.''

Gertrude leaned on her walker, barring the door. ''Dumb. That's what you are, Judith Anne. *Dumb.* Why would you agree to take in guests with a dog? You know better.''

Judith was forced to allow that her mother was right. For once. ''It was just for two nights, and they were in a bind. I was, too, with the Carlsons canceling. This is summer, and if I don't keep the B&B full every night, I'll lose money. I'd have been out almost six hundred dollars.''

''Six hundred dollars!'' Gertrude all but spit at Judith's feet. ''What's that, these days? The way you blow money—how much did you spend on that Collar Idea?''

Trying to ignore that she was perspiring under the midday sun and that her breathing was constricted and that she wanted to sneeze and that her mother was being unreasonable, Judith reined in her patience. ''It's not Collar Idea. It's Caller I.D. I'm trying it out, because it's a way to keep track of people who don't leave phone messages on the answering machine. Some people won't cooperate with modern technology, which is fine, but I lose reservations that way. With Caller I.D., I can figure out if they're from out of town and get back to them. It's costing me about eleven bucks to try it for a month.''

''Dumb,'' Gertrude muttered. ''They can't call back?''

''Sometimes they don't.'' Judith jumped as Sweetums angled between Gertrude's feet and the walker. ''I'm going to the top of the Hill. Is there anything you want?'' She felt Sweetums rub against her bare ankles.

Gertrude snorted. ''Is there anything I want? Are you kidding? How about new legs? New eyes? New ears? How about living in my own house where I belong instead of in this shipping crate of a so-called apartment? How about you dumping that shanty Irishman? How about,'' she raged on, though her voice suddenly dropped a notch, ''bringing back your father?''

Judith winced. ''Mother, you know I'd like . . .''

Her head down, Gertrude turned away. ''Skip it,'' she ordered in her raspy old voice. ''Get me some chocolate-covered peanuts and a birthday card for Uncle Win in Nebraska.''

Judith started to protest that Uncle Win's birthday wasn't until September, but she knew that her mother liked to be prepared. "I'm making open-faced smoked salmon sandwiches for dinner tonight," Judith said as Sweetums shook his orange and yellow fur, then scampered off to the small patio. "How does that sound?" She was accustomed to Gertrude routinely rejecting her menus and preparing meals in the toolshed's small kitchen.

But Gertrude inclined her head to one side, her small bright eyes uncharacteristically moist. "Huh? Sandwiches? For supper? What with?"

"Uh . . . fresh sliced peaches? A green salad? Ambrosia?" Out of the corner of her eye Judith saw Sweetums poised to pounce on a robin.

"Sounds good," Gertrude replied, starting to close the door. "All of 'em."

Judith trudged to her blue Japanese compact. The robin had eluded Sweetums, who was now batting a paw at the small stone birds which surrounded St. Francis. For good measure, Sweetums slugged St. Francis, too. Judith got into her car and headed for the top of Heraldsgate Hill.

As Dairy turned into Deli, Judith paused, considering her larder. Resting her statuesque figure on the sturdy grocery cart, she visualized her crisper drawers. Dagmar Delacroix Chatsworth had consumed eight rashers of bacon, three pieces of toast, and four scrambled eggs for breakfast. Freddy also ate like a horse, while Agnes pecked like a bird. Judith picked up two pounds of bacon, not on sale, and moved on to Beer. She was rounding the end of Aisle 2B at Falstaff's Market when she almost collided with another cart.

"Yikes!" cried Cousin Renie, pulling up short. "Coz! I was going to call you when I got home. How's Dagmar and Company?"

Judith shook her head. "They're a mess. Thank God they'll be gone tomorrow."

Renie started to nod, then eyed Judith curiously. "Hey, what's wrong with your voice? Have you got a cold?"

Judith blinked several times. "No . . . I don't think so. But

I do feel all choked up and sneezy. Do you suppose I'm allergic to that damned dog?''

Renie shrugged. She was wearing one of her most disreputable summer costumes, a short-sleeved flowered frock with both pockets partly ripped off. No doubt she had caught them on doorknobs or drawer handles. Renie's wardrobe never ceased to amaze Judith. On the one hand, it consisted of elegant and expensive designer clothes that she wore for her career as a graphic designer; on the other, it was a deplorable collection of sloppy sweatshirts, baggy pants, and tattered dresses. Judith, in her trim navy slacks and red pocket-T, felt like a fashion goddess by comparison.

''You're allergic,'' Renie said simply. ''You always were, to both cats and dogs. You must have gotten over your allergy to cats, since you've been around Sweetums for so long, but I'll bet you still can't tolerate dogs. Take some Benadryl when you get home.''

''Good idea.'' Judith nodded, then jumped as a woman with steel-gray hair tried to get past the cousins, who were blocking the bakery aisle.

Renie pulled her cart to one side. ''Say, coz, are you interested in getting out of town for a couple of days? Bill and I have a freebie for a condo up at Bugler Ski Resort next week. He can't go because he's got a couple of big faculty meetings at the university, and then he heads north for his Alaska fishing trip.''

Sadly, Judith shook her head. ''I can't take off in August. What about a month from now? Things slow down for me in September.''

''No good.'' Renie paused to nod vaguely at a fellow parishioner from Our Lady, Star of the Sea parish. Judith smiled, though the only thing she could remember about the woman was that she always wrung her hands during the consecration of the Host. ''It's a freebie, I told you,'' Renie continued, sounding a bit testy. ''It's only good for midweek, late August. It's off-season, and what they're trying to do is sell condos. I've got a lull, since everybody in the corporate world goes on vacation during August. But Bill can't change his Alaska reservation because the salmon are supposed to be in.''

"What about taking one of your kids?" Judith asked as an elderly man pushed past them and mumbled to himself.

Renie tossed her chestnut hair, which she'd recently had cut into a short, not particularly becoming, pageboy. "The kids! I want a rest, not responsibility! You know perfectly well that Tom, Anne, and Tony all have been home this summer—I was looking forward to a brief break. They won't go back to college until late September. And none of them will ever graduate."

Judith couldn't help but feel slightly smug. Her only child, Mike, was gainfully employed with the U.S. Forest Service at Nez Percé National Historical Park in Idaho. He would be home for Thanksgiving and Christmas, probably with his girlfriend, Kristin, in tow. But in the meantime, Judith was enjoying her sabbatical from motherhood.

"Sorry, coz," Judith apologized. "I can't. I'd like to, though."

Renie was looking miffed. "Right, right. As my mother would say, 'Don't worry about me.' I'll put off succumbing to heat prostration while I trudge from shop to shop, then go home and fix dinner for five, plus whichever light-o'-loves the young ones have dragged in. Afterward, I'll wave Anne and her friends off to the Ice Dreams show. They'll have a wonderful time while I clean up and do the laundry."

Judith brightened. "Ice Dreams? Starring Mia Prohowska, the Olympic Gold Medalist?"

Dolefully, Renie nodded. "Mia doesn't do laundry, I'll bet. She and her coach, Nat Linski, have made so much money from her skating that she probably wears an outfit once and gives it to somebody poor—like me."

Judith reached for a baguette. "You like to wear rags when you're not out hustling your graphic-design work." She put two loaves of sliced white bread into her cart. "The rest of your wardrobe makes me drool."

"The bakery section does likewise to me," Renie replied, selecting an epi loaf and a package of bagels. "If I didn't have so many mouths to feed, I, too, could afford to see Mia Prohowska skate. They had to add an extra show, a matinee this afternoon. This is the end of the tour for Ice Dreams, so Anne is hoping they'll do something special."

Judith's gaze fixed on a loaf of Russian rye. "Mia's amazing, all right. About a month ago, I saw her skate in some exhibition on TV. She's every bit as graceful as a ballet dancer and even more athletic."

"Beautiful, too." Renie was growing increasingly morose. "Some people have it all. We have our mothers."

Judith's mouth twitched in a smile. "Courage." She patted Renie's arm. "We also have Joe and Bill and our kids."

Renie shot Judith a sardonic look. "And you have Dagmar Chatsworth. Serves you right for turning down my offer. Maybe I'll call Madge Navarre," she said in a tight voice, referring to their longtime mutual friend who had the advantage of being single and unencumbered. "I've got to scoot. This is my afternoon for errands."

Judith said it was hers, too, as most of them were. While she was responsible only for feeding her guests breakfast and an early-evening appetizer with sherry—or punch, in the summer—running a B&B as well as a household seemed to require an inordinate amount of time racing from store to store and spending unbudgeted monies. After the tour of Falstaff's, she headed for the liquor store, the bakery, the pharmacy, and, finally, Risqué, the local card-and-gift shop.

Judith was browsing in the birthday section when a head bobbed around the corner. "Coz!" Judith exclaimed. "You again?"

Renie made a face. "My mother sent me to get a card for Uncle Win's birthday. Jeez, it's not for over a month!"

Judith laughed. "You know our mothers," she said, thinking of how the two sisters-in-law scrapped and yapped at each other, yet had so much in common. "The Depression-era mentality. They don't want to be caught short."

Selecting a card that depicted the sun setting over the ocean, Renie nodded. "That's why they save everything. Like blue baloney and furry cheese and four thousand rubber bands."

"Exactly. That's also why neither of them will believe that greeting cards cost more than a quarter. I've been subsidizing my mother for years. Postage, too. She's still in denial over the three-cent stamp." Judith picked up a card that showed a cute, cuddly dog, then slapped it back into the display rack.

"Yipes! I've had enough of dogs. I'll go for this mountain scene. It's very tranquil."

Renie arched her eyebrows. "So is Bugler. You've never been there. Bill and I took the kids about six years ago, when it was just getting under way. You'd love it, coz. The weather will be cooler in the mountains. It's so secluded up there in British Columbia, and the facilities are absolutely top-notch. Terrific restaurants, too." Renie licked her lips.

"Knock it off," Judith warned. "I can't go, and that's final." She jammed the mountain scene back into the rack, and grabbed a card that featured a grinning chimpanzee playing the banjo. "I've got to run. Phyliss needs help."

"True," Renie replied. The expression on her round face was puckish as she watched Judith's long-legged strides to the cashier's counter. But Renie didn't say another word to her cousin. Not yet.

Dagmar Delacroix Chatsworth was not ugly, nor was she pretty. If asked, Judith would have struggled to describe her current guest. Publicly claiming to be fiftyish, Dagmar could have been ten years older. She was rather short, slightly stocky, and had a widow's peak of reddish-brown hair that Judith guessed was probably dyed. Still, Dagmar disguised her age and flaws quite well: Despite the warm weather, she wore draped wool crepe, with a matching turban and a scarf that was carefully wrapped around her neck. Crepe on crepe, Judith reflected, then chastised herself for being catty. Dagmar's small feet were encased in four-inch, open-toed pumps. She carried a lacy beige shawl, though there was no need for it with the temperature in the high eighties. Her jewelry was gold, handsome, and studded with diamonds. It occurred to Judith that Dagmar had done very well for herself by doing in others.

"Did you read my column today?" Dagmar demanded upon entering Hillside Manor at precisely five o'clock. She had arrived by limousine; Agnes and Freddy were returning on a city bus. According to Dagmar, they had errands to run for her. And for Rover. While they slaved, she raved: "I made a chump of Trump and slam-dunked Michael Jordan. Princess

Di will die of mortification, and Pavarotti will perforate his pasta. Am I hot or what?''

Grudgingly, Judith admitted that she had read Dagmar's latest installment of "Get Your Chat's Worth" in the morning paper. She always did. The barbs were irresistible, the style irreverent, the gossip irrefutable—if only because Dagmar was so vague when it came to facts and sources. The thrice-weekly column was perfect over the second cup of coffee, especially, in Judith's case, when she had already been coping with a houseful of guests for breakfast. There had been mornings in her career as a B&B hostess when Judith actually considered "Chat's Worth" therapeutic. She could take out her frustrations on the rich and famous, rather than on her own not-so-rich and rarely famous, yet aggravating, guests.

"You were at the top of your form today," Judith admitted, smiling weakly at Dagmar. "I really liked the paragraph where you insinuated that a certain aging rocker was no longer stoned, but merely rolling along on his past glory. Especially in bed."

Dagmar shook a well-manicured finger at Judith. "Innuendo, my dear. That's the trick. Hints, allusions, the slightest of slurs." She waved her hand like a conjurer. "It's all in the wrists. The typing, you know."

Judith nodded, also weakly. "Very . . . clever. What about those cryptic comments you made the last week or two about athletes' pasts catching up with them? You've been very coy."

Dagmar chuckled. "Naturally. So many celebrities have secrets. All this big money for people who play games—in more ways than one. Stadiums and arenas reek with greed and perfidy. What piqued your interest most? The hint of perverse puckishness? The men who do more than play with their balls? The club that's not just a club? The talent scout for underage groupies?"

Judith blanched as Dagmar leered. "It was the turncoat-redcoat item. I didn't get it. In conjunction with Cinderella?"

Again Dagmar chortled. "Nor should you. Yet. Did you understand the part about cold storage?"

Judith hadn't. She tried to remember the series of insinuations. Someone was a turncoat and/or a redcoat, which seemed unlikely, since the Revolutionary War was long forgotten. Unless, of course, Dagmar had been referring to the British in general. And Cinderella was being kept in cold storage. The deep freeze was thawing, though. Royalty was getting the boot. Judith remembered that phrase.

"Does it have something to do with soccer?" she asked innocently.

Now Dagmar's mirth was unbridled. "Soccer! My dear! Does anyone in this country care about *soccer*? Only children under twelve and their rabid parents! Think again! Major sports! Major money! Major *readership*!"

Judith was at a loss. She abandoned guessing at Dagmar's veiled intentions. "You certainly cover everybody's peccadilloes. Do you ever get threatened with lawsuits?"

For a brief moment Dagmar's high forehead clouded over under the turban. "Threatened?" Her crimson lips clamped shut; then she gave Judith an ironic smile. "My publishers have superb lawyers, my dear. Libel is surprisingly hard to prove with public figures."

The phone rang, and Judith chose to pick it up in the living room. She was only mildly surprised when the caller asked for Dagmar Chatsworth. The columnist already had received a half-dozen messages since arriving at Hillside Manor the previous day.

While Dagmar took the call, Judith busied herself setting up the gateleg table she used for hors d'oeuvres and beverages. At first, Dagmar sounded brisk, holding a ballpoint pen poised over the notepad Judith kept by the living room extension. Then her voice tensed; so did her pudgy body.

"How dare you!" Dagmar breathed into the receiver. "Swine!" She banged the phone down and spun around to confront Judith. "Were you eavesdropping?"

"In my own house?" Judith tried to appear reasonable. "If you wanted privacy, you should have gone upstairs to the hallway phone by the guest rooms."

Lowering her gaze, Dagmar fingered the swatch of fabric at her throat. "I didn't realize who was calling. I thought it was one of my sources."

"It wasn't?" Judith was casual.

"No." Dagmar again turned her back, now gazing through the bay window that looked out over downtown and the harbor. Judith sensed the other woman was gathering her composure, so she quietly started for the kitchen.

She had got as far as the dining room when the other two members of Dagmar's party entered the house. Agnes Shay carried a large shopping bag bearing the logo of a nationally known book chain; Freddy Whobrey hoisted a brown paper bag which Judith suspected contained a bottle of liquor. Another rule was about to be broken, Judith realized: She discouraged guests from bringing alcoholic beverages to their rooms, but a complete ban was difficult to enforce.

The bark of Dagmar's dog sent the entire group into a frenzy. Clutching the shopping bag to her flat breast, Agnes started up the main staircase. Freddy waved his paper sack and shook his head. Dagmar put a hand to her turban and let out a small cry.

"Rover! Poor baby! He's been neglected!" She moved to the bottom of the stairs, shouting at Agnes. The telephone call appeared to be forgotten. "Give him his Woofy Treats. Extra, for now. They're in that ugly blue dish on the dresser."

Judith blanched. She knew precisely where the treats reposed, since she had discovered them earlier in the day, sitting in her mother's favorite Wedgwood bowl. Anxiously, Judith watched the obedient Agnes disappear from the second landing of the stairs. Rover continued barking.

"I thought the dog was a female," Judith said lamely.

Dagmar beamed. "That's because he's so beautiful. Pomeranians are such adorable dogs. Rover is five, and still acts like the most precious of puppies. Would you mind if he came down for punch and hors d'oeuvres?"

Judith did mind, quite a bit. On the other hand, the dog would be under supervision. "Well, as long as he stays in the living room." Judith's smile was now strained.

Out in the kitchen, Phyliss Rackley was finishing her chores for the day. Usually she was gone by three, but Rover's destructive habits had provided more work for the cleaning woman, as well as for Judith.

"All those feathers from the down comforter," Phyliss

grumbled as she gave the counters a last swipe with a wet rag. "Now my allergies are acting up. I found one of your old quilts to cover the bed."

Judith, in the act of taking a bottle of Benadryl from the windowsill above the sink, snatched her hand away. She wasn't about to get into a discussion of allergic reactions with Phyliss.

"That's fine, Phyliss," Judith said with an appreciative smile. "I'm sorry things were in such a mess today. Let's hope they keep that blasted dog under control until they leave tomorrow morning."

Phyliss was rummaging in her large straw shopping bag. "What's with the strongbox upstairs? It's heavy. I had to move it to get under the nightstand next to the bed. The dog did something truly nasty there."

Judith shook her head. "I've no idea. Dagmar's got a typewriter, too. I'd figure her for using a laptop, but apparently she's the old-fashioned sort."

"Filth," Phyliss declared, removing an Ace bandage from her straw bag and deftly wrapping it around her right ankle. "The woman writes filth. I don't know why a family newspaper runs such trash. Decent people wouldn't read it." On her way out, she banged the screen door for emphasis.

Judith grabbed the Benadryl just as Agnes Shay crept into the kitchen.

"We're out of bottled water," Agnes said in her wispy, anxious voice. "I'm so sorry . . . Do you have any in the refrigerator, or should I walk up to the grocery store?"

Judith had no qualms about drinking from the tap, and did so before answering Agnes. Since many of her guests preferred a more purified form of water, she always kept a supply on hand.

"There's both plain and flavored," she replied after swallowing her allergy pill. "It's too hot to walk up to the top of the Hill. Take what you need." Judith gestured at the refrigerator with her glass.

"Oh . . . thank you!" Agnes's round face glowed with gratitude. Like her employer's, Agnes's age was difficult to guess. Thirties, Judith figured, but with a naive air that made her seem younger. On the other hand, her appearance added extra years. Agnes was small, with drab brown hair, a smattering of freckles across her plain face, and a shapeless figure. "You're so kind!" she exclaimed, turning to face Judith. She clutched at least a half-dozen bottles against her insignificant bosom.

Judith gaped. "Ah . . . do you really need *all* of those?" It looked to Judith as if Agnes had commandeered the entire inventory.

But Agnes nodded. "Oh, yes. They'll last only until morning. It's this warm weather, you see. Rover gets so thirsty." On scurrying feet, Agnes padded out of the kitchen.

Judith grimaced and went to the phone. Maybe she could catch Joe before he left work. She was sure he wouldn't mind stopping to pick up more bottled water. Using the phone on the kitchen wall, she was about to punch in her husband's number when she heard a voice on the line.

". . . and the dawn comes up like thunder . . ."

It was a man. Judith hung up, carefully. The living room was vacant. Someone was using the phone in the upstairs hallway. After a five-minute wait, she gently lifted the receiver. Now she heard a woman, speaking in a lilting yet singsong voice:

". . . will be different when Crown Colony is no more . . ."

Judith sighed. Unless she went all the way up to the third floor and used the private family line, she'd never reach Joe in time. The water could wait. No doubt she'd have more errands to run the following day.

A few minutes later, Judith was dividing her purchase of smoked salmon between the hors d'oeuvres platter and the open-faced sandwiches when Freddy Whobrey breezed into the kitchen.

"Rocks," he said, then planted himself expectantly next to the sink. He had been wearing snakeskin cowboy boots upon his arrival at Hillside Manor; now his feet were shod in alligator shoes. Judith suspected that they contained lifts. Freddy probably wasn't more than five feet two in his stocking feet.

"Rocks?" Judith used the back of her hand to wipe the perspiration off her forehead.

"Ice." Freddy's beady black eyes were fixed on the refrigerator door. "I could use a glass, too."

"I'm making punch," Judith responded a bit crossly. "It'll be ready in about twenty minutes."

"Punch!" Freddy guffawed, revealing very sharp teeth. "That's for old ladies like Dagmar and old maids like Agnes! I never drink anything but the real McCoy."

Judith eyed him with distaste, then remembered her manners as a hostess and forced a smile. "I prefer that guests don't drink upstairs," she said, keeping her voice pleasant.

"No problem," he retorted. "Downstairs, outside, inside—you name it, sweetie. Where's the rocks?"

Resignedly, Judith got out a highball glass and shoved it under the ice dispenser. "Here," she said. "To your health."

Freddy gazed up at her with admiration. "Say, you're a big one! Nice. I like tall women. Got some curves, too." Apparently noticing Judith's black eyes snap, Freddy held up the hand that didn't hold the highball. "No offense—I'm giving you a sincere compliment. I may be small, but I'm perfectly formed. You got good features, I can see that. Strong, even, all of a piece. I'll bet you can go the distance. A mile and a sixteenth wouldn't bother you at all, huh?"

Judith favored Freddy with an arch little smile. She noted that he was beginning to bald on top, though he had carefully combed his dark hair over the offending spot. "It wouldn't bother me," she replied, looking over his head to the back door, "but it'd make my husband mad as hell. Hi, Joe. Shoot anybody today?"

"Only one," Joe replied. "He's in intensive care." Joe threw his summer-weight jacket on the peg in the entryway by the back stairs and unfastened his holster. "Hi, Freddy," he said, putting out his free hand. "How about a game of William Tell? If you've got the apple, I've got the gun."

Freddy ran out of the kitchen. The swinging door rocked behind him. Rover barked and a woman screamed. A hissing sound followed. Furniture fell. More voices were raised in alarm. Judith started for the living room, but Joe caught her by the waist.

"Relax," he said, his round, faintly florid face close to hers. "These people are crazy. I'm not. How about a hug?"

Judith obliged. With gusto.

TWO

PUNCH AND HORS D'OEUVRES were late. The couple from Idaho and the nurses from Alberta didn't linger in the living room. Both parties had seven o'clock dinner reservations. The Chatsworth ménage planned on being fashionably late for an eight-thirty table at a waterfront bistro.

Upon arriving with the punch bowl and the appetizer tray around six-fifteen, Judith learned the reason for the scream: Rover had cornered Sweetums under the baby grand piano. The dog had barked, the cat had clawed, and Dagmar had reacted with anguish. Sweetums had wisely fled via the open French doors. Rover didn't try to follow.

"Your cat is undisciplined," Dagmar announced angrily when Judith finally appeared. "He attacked my precious."

"Gosh, that's terrible," Judith said, feigning dismay. "I can't think what got into him. Normally, he's such a sweet-tempered little guy." *Like Hitler*, Judith thought to herself, but for once, she blessed her pet's rotten disposition.

Sitting on one of Judith's matching beige sofas, Dagmar fanned herself with her hand. She was now wearing a yellowish-orange crepe dress with another matching turban and scarf. The famous columnist reminded Judith of a large cheese.

"I thought the Pacific Northwest was cool and damp," Dagmar complained. "What's with all this heat? And sunshine."

Judith retained her sweet smile. "Some years we actually have a summer. This is one of them. Trout pâté? Pickled herring? Smoked salmon?" She proffered the tray to Dagmar.

Dagmar recoiled. "Fish! *Herring!* I was raised on all this in Minneapolis! What's wrong with Brie and stuffed mushrooms?"

"Ohhh!" Judith tried to appear disappointed. "I feel awful! If you were going to be here for another night, I'd serve you your favorites. I feel so remiss."

Seemingly assuaged, Dagmar sampled the smoked salmon. "This is an improvement over the Cascadia Hotel. You can be sure they'll get an unflattering mention in an upcoming column. How dare they ask me to leave! No one in his right mind could blame Rover for biting the concierge!"

At present, Rover was cowering on the hearth. Dagmar gave him the rest of her smoked salmon. Judith cringed.

Freddy had added something of an amber hue to his highball glass. Judging from his somewhat unsteady gait, he'd probably added it two or three times since his visit to the kitchen.

"That was *after* we got tossed," he said, leaning against the grandfather clock for support. "It was the Grand Ballroom that caused the real problem."

Judith eyed Freddy curiously, but it was Dagmar who answered the unspoken question: "Well, where else could you walk a dog in a place like that? How did we know they were hosting the Japanese ambassador that night? Rover didn't care much for the raw fish, but he thought those little strips of beef were delicious."

Agnes returned to the living room with a sterling silver bowl, which she placed in front of Rover. Judith noticed that some of her bottled water was in the bowl. Rover lapped it up like a lush at an open bar.

"Good puppy," said Agnes in her soft, mushy voice. Shyly, she smiled at Judith. "Pets are such endearing creatures. Like babies. They break down barriers and allow human beings to become acquainted."

Judith tried not to look askance. "A hello and a handshake often serve as well." Seeing Agnes all but recoil at the suggestion of such social aggressiveness, Judith gave a little shrug. "It depends upon the situation, of course. And the people involved."

Agnes, who was still on her knees watching Rover slurp, darted a diffident look at Dagmar. "Mia made friends with Rover, didn't she? Before the accident?"

Dagmar's visage was stern. "Mia Prohowska doesn't care for animals. Unless you count Nat Linski. As for the alleged 'accident,' Rover merely nipped two of the skaters in the Ice Dreams supporting cast. They shouldn't have tried to interfere with his swim in the hotel pool. Attempting to drown my adorable poochy-woochy was hardly civilized behavior."

Judith couldn't conceal her curiosity. "Mia Prohowska and Nat Linksi are staying at the Cascadia Hotel? My cousin's daughter and her friends are going to . . ."

Freddy was smirking in his tipsy, rodentlike way. Judith envisioned a drunken gerbil, trying to cope with a runaway Rollo-Ball. "Skaters! Ice! Skimpy costumes! I love it! Talk about T&A! 'Cept those skaters don't have much T."

"You're referring to the men, I trust." Dagmar's expression was one of reproof. She favored Judith with a cool gaze. "Yes, Mia and Nat and their troupe were at the Cascadia. A revolting group, by and large. Mia feigns an interest in freedom and democracy. Frankly, all she cares about is money. And Nat sees that she makes plenty of it." With a vicious stab, Dagmar attacked a slice of pickled herring. "That will end soon, of course. As all bad things must."

Startled, Judith was about to ask why when the phone rang. She picked it up on the second ring, but Joe had already answered in the kitchen.

"So what's your problem?" Joe asked, sounding dangerously mild.

Whoever had called hung up. Judith frowned and did likewise. "Wrong number," she remarked with a fatuous smile. Her guests appeared indifferent. Except, Judith thought, for Dagmar, whose forehead wrinkled slightly before she flounced about on the sofa in an exaggerated manner.

"Have you bought my book yet?" she asked, feeding Rover another serving of smoked salmon. "It's terribly shocking. You'd be amazed how badly famous people behave."

"No, I wouldn't," Judith replied promptly as Rover shook himself and leaped up to settle next to his mistress on the sofa. "I'll be sure to put in a reserve for the book at the library."

Dagmar was aghast. "The *library*?" She made it sound like a dirty word. "Why don't you buy it, like real people do?"

Still trying to control her patience, Judith gave Dagmar a self-deprecating smile. "I used to be a librarian. That's what I majored in at the university. Besides, hardcover books are so expensive these days."

Dagmar dismissed Judith's attempt at economy with a sneer. "It's people like you who undermine authors. What's twenty-four-ninety-five? You can't get a facial that cheap."

Since Judith hadn't had a facial in almost thirty years, the argument fell flat. But she felt it was unwise to say so. "I'll try to stop at the Heraldsgate Bookstore in the next couple of days," she lied.

"I should think so." Dagmar's crepe-clad body shuddered. "The library! How pedestrian!"

Judith ignored the comment. Ordinarily, she stayed at the appetizer hour only long enough to make sure that her guests had everything they needed for their relaxation and enjoyment. The hands on the grandfather clock showed that it was now almost seven. Joe would be hungry, and Gertrude was no doubt in a tizzy. Judith's mother preferred eating at five o'clock, and only under duress had she given in to waiting an extra hour.

Excusing herself, Judith went back to the kitchen to dish up the family meal. She wasn't surprised to find Gertrude and her walker positioned by the stove. Sweetums was sitting in front of the refrigerator.

"Are you joining us tonight?" Judith asked, wondering if her mother's appearance in the house indicated an unexpected change of heart toward Joe.

"Are you kidding?" Gertrude rasped. "I came to see if you were dead. Supper's almost an hour late. What's going on?"

The kitchen seemed even warmer than the living room. Judith again mopped perspiration from her brow. Her breathing was better, but the Benadryl had made her sleepy. She wasn't up to coping with her mother's complaints. Swiftly she began dishing up the sliced peaches, the green salad, and the open-faced sandwich. She also grabbed a can of seafood banquet for Sweetums.

"Come on, Mother, I'll take this stuff to your apartment right now. I got a little behind this afternoon." Judith didn't look Gertrude in the eye.

Gertrude, however, didn't budge. "Your behind's not so little. Where's my dessert?"

Judith hadn't planned on dessert. It was too hot for a heavy meal. "I'll bring you a dish of ice cream later," she promised.

Seemingly appeased, Gertrude steered her walker toward the back door. With both hands full, Judith had to move quickly to keep the screen from hitting her in the face. She had crossed the threshold when Sweetums flew past, his great plume of a tail swishing against her calves.

"Open-faced sandwiches aren't my favorite, you know, kiddo," said Gertrude, clumping down the walk. "They're fine for bridge-club lunches, but supper ought to be hearty. When was the last time you fixed a pot roast?"

"April," Judith answered without hesitation. "The weather's been too warm to have the oven on all day to cook a pot roast. Nobody feels like stuffing themselves in this kind of heat. That's why I've been serving lighter menus."

"Lighter!" Gertrude turned to give her daughter a disgusted look. "If they were any lighter, I'd float away! What happened to the ambrosia?"

"I didn't have time to make it," Judith responded, feeling her crankiness return. "Besides, you've got peaches and—"

At that moment Rover came bounding out of the house, heading straight for Sweetums, who was chasing a yellow-and-black butterfly in the vicinity of Judith's phlox. Sensing danger, the cat froze, orange and yellow fur on end. Rover moved in to attack.

The animals streaked around the backyard, past the laurel hedge, the rose bushes, the rhododendrons, the Shasta daisies, and the gladioli. Rover barked and barked. Sweetums leaped from a lawn chair to the barbecue. Rover followed; Sweetums fled in the direction of Judith's prized dahlias, which were about to bloom.

"Hey," yelled Gertrude, "knock it off!"

Her cries went unheeded. Judith made an end run around

her mother so that she could deposit the food in the former toolshed. But not only was Gertrude's door closed, it was locked.

"Mother!" Judith called., "Open this sucker! Why did you lock it in the first place?"

Gertrude was still making her laborious way to the toolshed. "Are you nuts? With the kind of guests you get, I wouldn't trust 'em an inch!"

Sweetums was now back on the porch, vainly trying to open the screen door with his paw. Rover was upon him. The two animals tumbled and whirled in a blur of color. Judith and Gertrude both yelled.

Judith set Gertrude's supper down on the walk and raced to separate cat and dog. Trying to grab both of their collars, Judith felt Sweetums's claws rake her arm and Rover's teeth sink into her leg. Fighting the pain, she finally managed to pull the warring animals apart. Giving Rover a sharp boot, she sent him back into the house. Sweetums's furious little yellow eyes regarded Judith with distress and contempt. She picked him up in her arms and held on tight as he tried to struggle free.

"Open your door!" Judith screamed at Gertrude. "Sweetums is hurt!"

A torn ear, a missing chunk of fur, and a crooked tail didn't bode well for Sweetums's health. Surprisingly, he settled down in Judith's arms as she carried him into the toolshed.

"He's got to go to the vet," Judith declared, carefully resting the cat on Gertrude's plaid settee. "I'll call from here."

"They'll be closed." Gertrude sat down next to Sweetums. Gingerly, she placed a hand on his neck. "Poor dopey little guy. He looks beat."

"He's beat up," Judith replied angrily. "I'm furious with Dagmar, but the truth is, it's all my fault. I should never have let them bring Rover to Hillside Manor."

A recorded voice answered Judith's call to the vet. The office had closed at five-thirty, but there was an emergency number. Judith dialed it. Dr. Jack Smith answered on the third ring. He agreed to meet Judith at his clinic in half an hour.

"This is going to cost me," Judith murmured, gently stroking Sweetums's disarranged fur. "I'll come back here to col-

lect our little warrior at seven-thirty. Don't let him outside.''
She started for the door.

"Hey," Gertrude called, "where's my supper?''

Judith paused to retrieve her mother's meal. The plate was
empty. On the other side of the yard, Rover was doing
something nasty to Judith's dahlias. Judith felt like doing
something equally nasty to Dagmar Delacroix Chatsworth.

Judith skipped dinner. Having replenished Gertrude's supper, she realized there wasn't enough food left for an extra
serving. Judith announced to Joe that she had to take Sweetums to the vet. Her explanation was brief, because she wanted
to confront Dagmar before the Chatsworth party left for dinner.

Dagmar, Freddy, and Agnes were still in the living room.
Freddy was now in the old rocking chair, looking extremely
woozy. Agnes knelt on the hearth, next to a subdued Rover.
Dagmar jumped off the sofa when Judith entered the room.

"You ought to be in jail!" she screamed at Judith. "I
thought this was a reputable establishment! Your wretched
mound of mange has wounded my poor fluffy-wuffy! Rover's
nose is scratched! He'll have to get cosmetic surgery! I'll
sue!"

Judith, who hadn't yet tended to her own wounds, glared at
Dagmar. "I hope Rover has had his rabies shots. He doesn't
act like it." She stuck out her right leg to show Dagmar the
canine bite. "I'll countersue! You never told me your dog was
completely undisciplined!"

"Undisciplined? How dare you!" Dagmar's head—turban,
scarf, and all—swerved in Agnes's direction. "I'm not to
blame. That was Agnes who called you from the Cascadia.''

"I don't give a damn who called." Judith was trying to get
her temper under control. "I was too lenient. Pets are against
the rules, and if you'd read our listing in the B&B guide, you
would have known it."

Dagmar glowered at Agnes, then at Judith. "That was all
Agnes's doing. She exhibited gross incompetence, but that's
not my fault. Or Rover's." She turned back to Agnes. "Call
a veterinarian. The very best this two-bit town has to offer.
Rover must be seen at once.''

Freddy was rocking back and forth, singing softly to the tune of "My Old Kentucky Home": "The sun goes down on our darling little Rover . . ."

Judith tried to ignore him. Agnes had dutifully gone over to the bay window next to the bookcase where the telephone directories were kept. Dagmar, mincing on her high-heeled pumps, was making another pass at the punch bowl. Absently, Judith noticed that it was still almost half full. Her other guests apparently hadn't imbibed too freely, Freddy had his fifth in the paper bag, and Agnes didn't seem to be drinking at all.

Freddy was still singing: ". . . 'tis summer, the poochie got scratched . . ."

Agnes was sitting on the window seat, looking anxious and dialing the phone. Seeing no purpose in continuing the argument with Dagmar, Judith made her exit. She had less than ten minutes to secure Sweetums and drive to the top of Heraldsgate Hill, where Dr. Smith's office was located.

Joe stopped her on the way out the back door. "Do you want me to keep an eye on these goons while you're gone? Or should I go with you?"

Judith considered. "They're out of here for dinner in a few minutes or en route to a gold-plated vet. Why don't you drive and I'll hold Sweetums?"

Joe agreed. They took his aging red MG and arrived at the vet's two minutes ahead of Dr. Smith. Half an hour later, Sweetums had salve, shots, antibiotics, and a bill for one hundred and eighty-seven dollars.

"This Chatsworth crew has impoverished me," Judith groaned as they headed back down the steep section of Heraldsgate Hill known as the Counterbalance. "Why did I ever let them stay here?"

Joe reached over and patted her knee. "You're too good-hearted, Jude-girl. Stop beating yourself up."

Judith gave a faint nod, then assessed her losses: two hundred dollars in deductible, almost an equal amount in veterinarian bills. If Dagmar didn't carry out her threat to sue, Judith was still ahead, if barely. She gazed down at the unusually quiet Sweetums in her lap and smiled faintly. Money wasn't everything, and she was better off financially than she had ever been. But more importantly, she was happy.

Judith rested her hand on Joe's leg. "I shouldn't gripe about things. I've got you."

The gold flecks in Joe's green eyes danced, then suddenly faded. "I wonder if I'll ever stop kicking myself for eloping with Herself."

The reference to Joe's first wife no longer rankled Judith. She had let Joe's betrayal eat at her for more than twenty years. Now that they had been reunited, she had put the past to rest. She wanted Joe to do the same.

"It's now that counts, not then," Judith said softly as they turned into the cul-de-sac. "Maybe we needed to go through the fire to appreciate each other. If there had been no Dan McMonigle and no Vivian Flynn, we might not take so much pleasure from our middle years. This way, it's like being young again. We've been given a fresh start. I cherish that."

Shifting the MG's gears, Joe reversed into their driveway. After he shut the engine off, he turned to Judith. "You've always had a knack for looking at the bright side. I wish I did. Being a cop can make you gloomy."

"You're not gloomy," Judith countered. Indeed, Joe's natural buoyancy was one of the first things that had attracted her to him. That, and his sense of humor and love of adventure and willingness to take a few risks. Despite some similarities, Joe and Judith complemented each other in many ways.

Suddenly Judith recalled Joe's flippant remark to Freddy Whobrey. She put her hands on his shoulders. Sweetums stirred in her lap. "Joe—did you really shoot someone today?"

The green eyes seemed to shut down on Judith, as if Joe had barred the door to his soul. "I had no choice. It was a hostage situation. He'd already killed the tavern owner."

"Is the guy dead?"

"No. But he may never walk again." Joe expelled a breath of air, his usually florid face pale.

Judith gently kneaded Joe's shoulders. "Why you? Where was the special assault unit? Aren't they the ones who handle hostage cases?"

Joe nodded. His color was returning. "The call Woody and I got tagged it a straight homicide—the owner of My Brew

Heaven and his bartender had gotten into a big fight. The bartender shot the owner. Dead. Our understanding from the patrol car was that the bartender was giving himself up. But the circumstances had changed by the time we arrived. The guy had taken the owner's wife hostage. I had one chance, and I took it. Otherwise, it could have been the wife, Woody— or me.'' Joe's expression was rueful.

Judith imagined the scene, with the desperate killer, the ter- rified wife, and the dead tavern owner on the floor. She could picture Joe and his partner, Woody Price, suddenly faced with an explosive situation. Judith knew it wasn't the first time that her husband had been required to fire his weapon. But it was the first time it had happened since they'd gotten married. She leaned over and kissed his cheek. Sweetums made a retching sound, but kept his claws to himself.

"You should have told me everything when you came home," she said. "I thought you were joking with Freddy Whoa. You seemed pretty frisky to me." She gave him a mischievous smile.

He opened the car door. "It takes a while for the bad stuff to sink in. Coming home to you helps. The world doesn't look so off-center when I see you standing at the kitchen sink."

Hanging onto Sweetums, Judith got out of the MG. "I'll try to keep my own perspective while these loonies are still here. But thank heavens they'll be gone tomorrow. Who could ask for anything more?"

Judith could, if she'd known what lay ahead.

When Judith and Joe returned around eight-thirty, the house seemed a trifle cooler and the guests were gone. Breathing a sigh of relief, Judith carried Sweetums out to the toolshed. Gertrude's little apartment felt like a sauna, but its occupant still wore her heavy sweater. Judith immediately began to per- spire again.

Gertrude put the cat on her favorite chair, an overstuffed mohair-covered piece that had been Donald Grover's domain for almost thirty years. Judith could picture her scholarly father reading and smoking next to a floor lamp with a burnished brass stand. When not teaching high school classes the rudiments of the English language, Donald Grover had lived in striped T-shirts, all of which he'd burned with careless ash from his cigarettes, or absentmindedly picked threadbare while absorbed in his book of choice. Judith's smile was wistful as she watched the family cat settle down for a much-needed nap.

"He's tuckered out," noted Gertrude. Despite her obvious sympathy, her small eyes glittered with an emotion Judith could not define. "Say," she went on, "that salmon sandwich wasn't half bad. But why did you put it on hard bread? It's not easy to eat with my dentures."

"You managed, though," Judith noted dryly, wishing she'd had a similar chance at her own meal. The combination of hot weather, ill-mannered guests, lack of food, allergic reaction, and the crisis with Sweetums had worn her down. "I'm heading for an early night. I hope it isn't too hot upstairs."

Gertrude snorted, the spark in her eyes fading. "How can it be anything else, with that shanty Irishman? If they're not drinking like fish, they're . . . never mind." She assumed her most prudish expression.

Judith wasn't in the mood to argue with her mother. "You know how stifling it can get on the third floor in weather like this."

Gertrude snorted again. "I *used* to know. I lived there. For fifty years."

"No, you didn't," Judith countered, feeling a web of contention entwining her. "Until we turned the house into a B&B, you had your room on the second floor. We redid the attic for the family *after* that, four years ago."

Gertrude's eyes narrowed at Judith. "So? Fifty years. That's only counting after I married your father. It was his home from the day he was born."

"I know." Judith headed for the door. The Grover family had lived in the Edwardian saltbox since early in the twentieth century. Judith and her father before her had grown up in the big old house. So had Renie's dad, Clifford Grover. But Cliff and his wife, Deborah, had struck out on their own. They had lived in a small fishing town at first, then briefly with the Grovers, and finally in a bungalow on the other side of Heraldsgate Hill. Judith gave one last look at Sweetums. The cat didn't quite make up for the Grovers who had gone to dust. Especially after a hundred and eighty-seven dollars' worth of vet bills.

"Good night, Mother," said Judith.

" 'Night," Gertrude replied. "Don't forget my eye doctor's appointment tomorrow at eleven."

"Right," Judith answered in a weary voice.

"And my ice cream. Where's my ice cream?"

Limply, Judith nodded. "I'll get it. I'm leaving the door open."

"What for?" Gertrude demanded. "You want more trouble? What if there's a sex fiend loose?"

Judith smiled, if wanly. "Then I'll bring two dishes of ice cream."

Briefly, Gertrude seemed puzzled. Then she edged a bit closer to Sweetums on the sofa and gave a nod. "Swell. I'll eat both of 'em. I won't share ice cream with a sex fiend."

Judith couldn't fault her mother's sentiments.

It dawned on Judith, as she went up to bed, that Rover had been mysteriously quiet. The Chatsworth party was still at dinner. It was not yet ten when Judith ascended the stairs, but there had been no sound from the ill-tempered dog since returning from Dr. Smith's office. Feeling a pang of guilt, she stopped on the second floor and went into the front guest room.

Judith hadn't replaced Grandma Grover's braided rug. Rover lay on the bare floor. The dog was breathing somewhat shallowly, and his tongue was out. He seemed to have fallen in a haphazard manner, with his legs splayed every which way.

Recalling the odd light in Gertrude's eyes, Judith returned to the living room. She hadn't troubled to remove the serving dishes from the hors d'oeuvres hour. The tray was empty; so was the punch bowl. Judith checked the sterling silver receptacle on the hearth. Her mouth curved into a smile.

Rover was drunk. Gertrude had wrought her revenge.

Judith was still laughing when she entered the third-floor bedroom. Joe was already in bed, reading a Western, his genre of choice. He insisted on sticking to an era when lawmen weren't hampered by the necessity of search warrants, the Miranda warning, or admissible evidence. Judith often tried to envision Joe wearing a sheriff's star, a Western hat, and hand-tooled cowboy boots, with six-shooters blazing in the middle of Heraldsgate Avenue. It was not an entirely incredible scenario.

Explaining the reason for her mirth, Judith realized how stuffy the attic bedroom had grown. A large fan stirred the air, but only that which was in its direct path. She was about to take a quick shower when she remembered to ask Joe about the phone call he'd picked up on the kitchen extension.

Joe pushed his reading glasses farther up on his nose. "Some nut. Or else a Third World type who doesn't realize that my Cambodian language skills are pretty rusty."

The trying day and the oppressive heat had sapped Judith's patience. She gave Joe an exasperated look. "Believe it or not, I *do* get foreign guests. And yes, their English isn't always perfect. How's your Japanese?"

Joe arched his red eyebrows above the glasses. "Rusty. Like my Cambodian." He offered his wife a placating smile. "This wasn't a reservation, Jude-girl. I asked. Honest. He didn't even know he was calling a B&B. In fact, he seemed anxious to hang up when I told him he'd reached Hillside Manor. He started talking about 'threats' and 'menace.' I hear enough of that crap on the job."

Judith frowned as Joe turned his attention back to his book. Wrong numbers happened all the time. The B&B's number was one digit off from that of Toot Sweet, the neighborhood ice-cream-and-candy shop. The two establishments frequently got each other's calls. It was an improvement over the misdials at the Thurlow Street number, where Judith and Dan frequently had been mistaken for the local mortuary.

But as Judith stood under the shower a few moments later, the cool water didn't wash away all of her unease. She recalled Dagmar's odd reaction to the earlier phone call. And the columnist's evasiveness about threats.

Not that it mattered, Judith told herself, drying off with a big beige towel. Dagmar and Agnes and Freddy would be gone in the morning. So would the hung-over Rover. Their problems were of no concern to Judith. She slipped into a short cotton nightgown and returned to the bedroom.

It was still stuffy. Joe was still reading. And Judith was still uneasy.

Maybe it was the weather, she told herself.

Then again, maybe it wasn't.

The Chatsworth entourage left Hillside Manor the following morning at ten-thirty. Judith waved them off with a huge sigh of relief. Legal threats apparently had been dropped by both parties. It was just as well; Judith couldn't afford a lawyer. If Dagmar suspected that her precious dog had been driven to drink, she never let on. Indeed, Rover seemed healthy, if passive, when the hired limo pulled out of the drive and into the cul-de-sac.

The phone was ringing as Judith returned to the kitchen. Renie was on the line, sounding imperious.

"I won't take no for an answer, coz. Madge can't go to Bugler because it'll be end-of-month at the insurance company. I've called three other old pals, and they're either already going on vacation or stuck in town. If you don't come with me, I'll never speak to you again."

The threat had been made on many occasions over a period of almost fifty years. It was never intended to be serious, and never taken as such. Still, Judith understood the urgency in Renie's tone. She gazed at her booking calendar for the upcoming week: three sets of regulars, all for two nights each; a honeymoon couple who ought to be able to fend for themselves, and if they couldn't, their marital prognosis was grim; the rest were newcomers slated for one-day occupancies. Judith began to weaken.

"I'd have to talk to Arlene Rankers," she said, referring to her longtime neighbor and friend. Arlene had often leaped into the breach for Judith, taking over the duties of B&B hostess with graciousness and aplomb. She was also Judith's partner in their catering business. "I've been meaning to sit down with Arlene and talk over the extra work, but I've been so busy this summer. Frankly, I'm not sure I can go on catering and running a B&B."

"Let Arlene take over the catering part," Renie said.

"There are several SOTS who'd be glad to jump in and help her out."

Judith knew Renie was right: At least a half-dozen fellow female members of Our Lady, Star of the Sea parish—or SOTS, as they were familiarly known—would be delighted to join forces in a cottage industry such as catering social functions on Heraldsgate Hill. Still, the business was lucrative, and Judith hated to lose her share.

"I really shouldn't go," she demurred, not quite willing to give in to Renie. "This is prime time for me."

"You sound like bird-doo," Renie said. "Are you taking your Benadryl?"

"Yes, but it makes me sleepy. Phyliss is upstairs, cleaning like a madwoman, but it'll be a while before all that dog dander is gone."

"Exactly," said Renie. "So we leave Monday and we're gone until Thursday. The house will be free of Rover and his loathsome stench, or whatever it is that bothers you. How's Sweetums?"

"Stable," Judith replied, somewhat vaguely. She was consulting her calendar, worrying about the guests who would pass through Hillside Manor in her absence. There were no discernible problems, nothing that Judith could foresee. Arlene was, by and large, very competent. And in truth, Judith felt tired. Normally she wouldn't have caved in to fatigue until after Labor Day, when the summer rush was over. But the Chatsworth party had worn her out two weeks ahead of schedule.

"Okay," she said with a sigh. "Two nights won't ruin me. I'll go. But I've got to check with Arlene first."

There was a faint pause at the other end. "Great!" Renie cried, though her exuberance was somehow tempered. "But it's *three* nights. That's why I said we wouldn't be back until Thursday. I misread the brochure."

Judith hadn't caught the slip. She made a face into the receiver, then sat down on the kitchen stool by the phone. "Oh. Well, I suppose that won't matter much."

"Great!" Renie's enthusiasm was now sincere. "Bugler is a wonderful place, even if you don't ski. Which neither of us does, so what's the point of snow? Besides, it's free. My treat, coz. Pack your bags. Monday morning, we'll head north. Lunch in Port Royal at the Prince Albert Bay Cafe. Then on to Bugler. We'll have a hell of a time!''

Renie was right. But she didn't know how or why.

Neither did Judith.

THREE

THE COUSINS PLANNED to arrive in Bugler shortly before three, the appointed check-in time. Renie had cautioned that their wait at the border might take up to an hour, but Canadian Customs and Immigration sped them through in twenty minutes. They'd scheduled the three-hour drive from Heraldsgate Hill to Port Royal so that they would get to the Prince Albert Bay Cafe just before noon. Their early arrival assured them of a window table. In the restaurant's air-conditioned comfort, they lunched on fresh prawns and crab while soaking up the expansive view of the sparkling bay.

For a time, they recalled their previous visit to Port Royal and their stay at the Hotel Clovia, two short blocks from the cafe. The vacation had been marred by the discovery of a body in the hotel elevator.

"Incredible," Renie declared, devouring her crab legs.

"At least we figured out who committed the murder," Judith replied, savoring her prawns.

"Huh?" Renie stared at Judith. "I meant the crab legs. This sauce defies description. It's absolutely delicious, but it doesn't detract from the crab's flavor."

"Oh." Judith's voice was faint. She should have realized that Renie would be more enthralled by food than by a mere murder. Renie's appetite always amazed Judith, especially since her cousin never seemed to put on weight. But even

Renie admitted to flagging a bit in the warm weather.

"When we can shake the kids, Bill and I eat out a lot during the summer," Renie went on, lustily chomping on a sourdough roll. "I do okay when I'm air-conditioned, but at home I sort of fade."

"Me, too," Judith agreed absently. She was watching the hordes of swimmers and sunbathers who occupied the great sweep of beach along Prince Albert Bay. The vista had been very different almost three years earlier, when the cousins had visited Port Royal in November. Rain and fog had obscured the view, and daunted all but the most valiant joggers, strollers, and dog-walkers. Only the big freighters anchored out in the harbor seemed the same.

Still, the sights and sounds and smells of Port Royal were familiar to Judith. But back on the road, she was in new territory. The highway wound west and then north beyond the sprawling city. Within a few miles, Judith found herself in primitive country, with awe-inspiring glimpses of inlets that were carved out of heavily forested granite. The sun sparkled on the calm waters, and an occasional pleasure craft headed for a shady cove. With Renie at the wheel of the Joneses' big blue Chevrolet, Judith sat back and began, finally, to unwind.

"Some ski addicts think that Bugler is the finest resort in North America," Renie said after a long silence. "I'm anxious to see it now that it's been expanded since we were last there."

Judith roused herself from a semi-somnolent state. She had lulled herself into a near nap by recalling the assurances of Arlene Rankers. Arlene would make sure not only that Hillside Manor's guests for the next three nights would have every comfort and convenience, but that Gertrude would be well taken care of. Judith's mother would be the Rankerses' dinner guest for at least one night, and Arlene's husband, Carl, was looking forward to a rousing game of cribbage with Gertrude. In the meantime, Aunt Deb would be waited on hand and foot by Renie and Bill's three children. Not that Deborah Grover would ever demand such attention—but God help the daughter and grandchildren who wouldn't see that it was provided. Renie's mother had raised martyrdom to the status of an Olympic medal event. As for Joe Flynn, Judith knew that her husband could fend for himself and not mind too much. He was used to it, having suffered domestic neglect from his first wife, who had spent much of their marriage in an alcoholic haze.

But Judith wasn't leaving all her troubles behind her. She had vowed to use the time away from Hillside Manor to determine the future of her catering business. She had also promised herself to go over her books. The damages incurred by the Chatsworth party had forced a long-overdue look at debits and credits. Renie didn't know it, but Judith had tucked her ledger and current bills into the side pocket of her suitcase.

"What?" Judith rallied from her stupor. "Bugler's tops, huh?"

Renie glanced over at Judith and smiled wryly. "So they say. You'd never guess it from the lack of development along this stretch of the trip."

Judith had to agree. The road was winding through forests of fir, pine, and hemlock, with no mountains in sight. Occasionally they noted fresh gashes from recent clear-cutting. Now that they'd moved inland, the scenery was less spectacular, though still lovely in its primeval state. Yet Judith sensed a certain desolation, a wild, untamed region that had been left virtually untouched. She knew that British Columbia was vast, reaching almost a thousand miles to the Yukon. Mountains, rivers, and forests covered huge, uninhabited areas. It seemed to Judith that the narrow strip of densely populated land just north of the U.S. border stood as the last buffer between civilization and the wilderness. It didn't seem possible that a tourist resort could exist so far from the amenities of the modern world. Judith wondered if Renie was on the right road.

Then they began to spot dwellings, private ski chalets, some on stilts, some A-frames, some with corrugated tin roofs. Among the trees they could glimpse the cool blue waters of a lake. A restaurant sat off the road, displaying a five-star rating. Oncoming traffic increased, apparently an indication that visitors who had checked out after noon were heading home. Judith sighted a Rolls-Royce, a Bentley, and a white stretch limo. She had stopped counting the Mercedes-Benzes and BMWs.

Clusters of ski condos emerged along the roadside. So did more restaurants and gas stations and various stores. And then, quite suddenly, they saw the great slopes of Bugler and Fiddler mountains, rising above the town. Snow still remained in the deepest crevasses, but what impressed Judith the most was the feeling that she had been whisked off to Europe and dropped down in the middle of a charming Alpine resort.

Nothing in Bugler had been built by chance. The town had been carefully conceived in an old-world mode with New World convenience. Private homes, condos, hotels, shops, restaurants, even the most mundane of services, possessed flair. As Renie consulted the directions to their condo check-in site, Judith's head swerved every which way.

It was late August, off-season, yet there were skiers, sunburned and cheerful, hoisting their equipment after a day on the slopes. Judith realized that there must be snow somewhere on the mountains, other than in the nooks and crannies she could see with her naked eye. There were also golfers and hikers and tennis players and swimmers and skaters and horseback riders. The town was bustling with vacationers, and as the cousins got out of the car, they heard a multitude of foreign languages.

"Wild," exclaimed Judith. "This is unreal!"

Renie also was looking stunned. "It sure is! When Bill and I were here with the kids six, seven years ago, they were just getting started. It was nice, but it wasn't . . . *Techno-Innsbruck*! I don't know how else to describe it."

Neither did Judith. The sun was warm, but the air felt fresh. Cars weren't allowed inside the village. The cousins left the big parking lot, carefully following Renie's map. They crossed a spacious square, where young people skateboarded, dogs drank from water troughs, a mime entertained bench-squatters, artists sketched various subjects, including one another, and three exuberant youths tied multicolored balloons to the patio of a French restaurant. There were flowers everywhere, bright red and yellow and green splashes of color in planters, window boxes, and tiny garden plots. Judith's head swiveled this way and that as she took in the various shops featuring ski clothes, jewelry, sports equipment, designer fashions, leather goods, and the inevitable souvenirs.

Next to the snowboard shop, the cousins found the condo offices. They expected the usual red tape associated with real estate promotions, but instead they were given a map showing them where to find their lodgings, a forty-five-minute sales pitch scheduled for the following day at 11 A.M., and a fifty percent discount for one of Bugler's finest restaurants.

"Wow," breathed Renie as they exited back into the town square, "even if we have to sleep in a broom closet, we're ahead of the game. I paid the tax in advance, and I can get that back from the Canadian guest rebate."

Judith barely heard her cousin. She was too exhilarated by the zestful crowds of every nationality and by the exuberant atmosphere. The informational brochure listed a myriad of off-season activities. The Country & Blues Festival had been held the first weekend in August, followed by a classical-music gala. Summer in Bugler might be warm, but it was stimulating. Judith had a sudden itch to rent a pair of skis and take a run down Fiddler Mountain—except that she didn't know a stem Christie from a telemark.

Back in the Chevy, the cousins carefully studied their map. "We're way up at the top of the town," Renie noted. "I suppose it's a new complex, with rooms the size of your mother's toolshed. We'll probably have to use concrete blocks and packing crates for furniture."

"That's okay," Judith responded as Renie drove out of the parking lot and headed back to the highway. "The family cabin isn't much fancier."

"True," Renie agreed, "but we're going up to the newer part of the resort, the Fiddler section. It didn't even exist when we were here in the mid-eighties."

Still mesmerized, Judith observed the new construction that was under way near the highway. Apparently a huge shopping mall and hotel were abuilding. Indeed, it seemed that everywhere she looked, individual and multiple structures were being added to the Bugler scene. One stood out from the rest: A large red, square edifice with a Canadian flag sat near the conjunction of the road into Bugler and the main highway.

"What's that?" asked Judith. "It looks . . . different."

Renie glanced to her left. "That's the police and fire headquarters. It was already here when we came up the first time. It doesn't quite fit in with the rest of the architecture, but I figure that's on purpose, so that everybody knows where to go if there's trouble."

Judith uttered a strange chuckle. "Trouble? What kind of trouble could there be in a place like this?"

Renie shrugged. "Oh, I don't know. Theft, I suppose. Domestic squabbles. Drugs. This isn't paradise, even if it looks like it. People are still people, no matter who they are or where they come from."

Renie's comments didn't bother Judith. "If this isn't paradise, I don't know what is. Visitors come here to have fun. They aren't in the mood for trouble. I'd guess that shoplifting is the biggest crime in Bugler."

Turning onto the road that led up the side of Fiddler Mountain, Renie slowed the car. "Most of the tourists who stay at Bugler are rich. They aren't prone to the sort of crimes that the lesser classes embrace. You know, people like us, who are getting freebies." She darted Judith a pixie grin.

Judith laughed. "Right. The Broom Closet Condo. Maybe we should have brought sleeping bags and a portable toilet."

"I wonder," mused Renie as they wound back and forth, climbing up the mountain.

And then they were there, at the condo marked "X," high on Fiddler Mountain, overlooking the entire resort complex and the valley beyond. There were other complexes to the right of them, complexes to the left of them, bulldozers and tractors and concrete mixers farther up the road. But their destination, Clarges Court, welcomed them with a discreet sign to approach the underground parking and punch their security code into the machine at the edge of the curving drive.

Renie did so. The steel net gate rose efficiently. The cousins slipped inside, looking for Number 3-A. There were two slots, not just one, available to them. Renie angled the Chevy into the parking place. Removing their luggage, they approached the door. It wasn't locked. Judith and Renie ignored the closed door on their left and ascended the carpeted stairs. They dropped their luggage. They gasped. They squealed with delight.

Number 3-A of the Clarges Court condos was luxurious beyond their wildest dreams. There were two big bedrooms upstairs, a living room, a sunken family room, a kitchen with every efficiency, and a dining room with a table laid out to accommodate an elegant dinner for six. There were three bathrooms upstairs, and when the cousins had charged back down to the lower floor, they discovered yet another living room, a laundry room, a sunken bath, and two more bedrooms. There was a patio for enjoying the scenery. Outside the front door, just off the beautifully landscaped inner garden, were a hot tub and a swimming pool. Although not air-conditioned, the condo was blessedly cool with a soothing color scheme of mauve, teal, and beige. Like children, the cousins clutched each other and jumped up and down.

"The view!" shrieked Renie, overcome by the panorama of mountains, trees, and sky. "We can see all over the valley and the town!"

"The table!" cried Judith, taking in the glass dining room table with its elegant appointments that included mauve linen napkins artistically folded into crystal wineglasses. "I've got to shop! I feel like making a big dinner! Steak and baked potatoes and corn on the cob and fresh bread!"

Hesitating, Renie surveyed the table setting over her shoulder. "Well—yes. It sounds great, but we've got our discount dinner, right?"

Judith settled down, too. "Yes. And we could eat at several really great places. Maybe we'd better save staying in for our last night. Let's check the restaurant guide before we get out of control."

The cousins unpacked first, each taking a separate bedroom with its own bath and TV set. Judith's room was the larger of the two, with a king-sized bed and a view overlooking the inner courtyard; Renie had twin beds, but a panoramic view of the valley to the north.

Still smiling, Judith emerged from her luxurious boudoir. "I can see a pitcher of lemonade out on the picnic table in the courtyard. Why don't we get into our bathing suits, grab a couple of glasses, and have a quick swim?"

"Bathing suits? Swim?" Renie feigned ignorance. She'd never learned to swim, but Judith had spent many hours with Mike in public pools. It was one form of recreation that mother and son could afford—because it was free. Still, the cousins had held a lengthy discussion about whether or not to pack bathing suits.

"Oh, come on, coz," Judith urged. "I brought my suit. You can dog-paddle in the shallow end."

Renie gave in. Ten minutes later, the cousins were relaxing in the small, kidney-shaped pool. For the time being, they were the only guests in the communal patio area.

"This is heaven." Judith sighed, letting the water lap up to her chin.

"Utter bliss," Renie agreed, splashing lazily with her legs.

"I don't feel guilty anymore," Judith declared. "Joe's all wrapped up in that tavern homicide, Arlene's perfectly competent, Mike called last night to say everything was going well with him, and even Mother wasn't too upset about me going away, because the Rankerses will pamper her and she's playing cards tomorrow."

Renie nodded, her not-so-attractive new haircut now plastered against her head. Water hadn't improved it. But then, neither did combing, thought Judith.

"We deserve a break," Renie remarked. "My last two clients nearly drove me nuts. They both kept changing their minds, first about the concept, then about the design itself. And they wouldn't listen to advice. Jeez, I've been a graphic designer for almost thirty years! I swore I'd take up wallpapering after I got rid of those two! But," Renie went on, again growing mellow, "this is even better."

"It sure is." Judith allowed herself to bob around in the water, her face turned up to the sun. "It's so quiet inside the condos, despite all the tourists staying here. It's like a dream."

The dream was shattered by the barking of a dog. Over the fence, across the flagstones, and into the pool jumped the animal, splashing both Judith and Renie. The dog rose to the surface and began paddling toward Judith. She dove under the surface and swam to the deep end.

Judith gave Renie a wry grin as the dog swam in circles. "I doubt that dogs are allowed in the pool. I wonder who owns this thing." Her dark eyes narrowed as the dog again approached her. "Call me crazy, but he looks a lot like that wretched Rover. Is this the year of the Pomeranian?"

Renie remained at the shallow end, inching her way up the steps to poolside. "I thought this season's dog of choice was a Chow. Maybe that's only on Heraldsgate Hill."

The dog in the pool was making great waves, splashing and yapping, destroying the tranquil mood and getting water in Judith's eyes. She swam back toward Renie, trying to keep away from the animal. By the time she reached the other end of the pool, Renie was out of the water, toweling off. The dog was still swimming back and forth, barking intermittently.

"Well, we can't have everything," Judith murmured, rubbing her hair with a fluffy ivory towel. "Let's finish our lemonade and then decide where we're going to eat—"

An apparition was coming through the gate that led to the pool area. Swathed in layers of gauzy white linen and wearing a high-brimmed straw hat and big sunglasses, the figure looked like a Hollywood swami. Judith couldn't help but stare. She just plain gaped when she noticed the two other people who followed at a respectful distance.

Agnes Shay wore a modest brown bathing suit that wouldn't have revealed much of her figure even if she'd had one. Freddy Whobrey's red Speedo was unfortunate in every way: Freddy's skinny body displayed his ribs, his bowlegs, his knobby knees, his puny, hairless chest.

But it was the presence of Dagmar Delacroix Chatsworth, in her mobile linen tent, that shocked Judith the most. Never in her wildest dreams had she imagined that her path would ever again cross Dagmar's. Yet here she was, or so Judith assumed, since it was almost impossible to be sure until Dagmar whipped off her big sunglasses.

"You!" she cried, a finger emerging from the sleeve of her beach costume. "You look like someone! Who is it?"

Judith draped the towel over her wide shoulders. Fleetingly, she wondered if she should lie. But a gossip columnist must have a good memory for faces, no matter how obscure. Judith identified herself, and reluctantly introduced Renie.

"Well!" Dagmar smirked at the cousins. "This *is* a coincidence! What on earth are you doing at Bugler?"

Again Judith considered deceit, but Renie apparently didn't care about saving face. "I entered a drawing at the local fish 'n' chips shop. I won a free stay. How about you?"

Dagmar rolled her eyes, then replaced her sunglasses. "I concluded my book tour in Port Royal over the weekend. My publisher has a condo here in Clarges Court. I'm his guest.

Rover has his own suite. He's letting Agnes stay with him."
She beamed at the dog, who had concluded frisking in the
pool and was now shaking himself all over the cousins.

Renie was making a face at Rover, and looking very much
as if she'd like to give him a swift kick. Knowing her cousin's
unpredictable temper, Judith started to make excuses for their
departure. But Dagmar raised a pink hand.

"Do have a martini. Karl and Tessa are bringing them. They
shouldn't be a minute."

Judith hesitated. She didn't enjoy drinking hard liquor in
the sun. And Renie hated gin. "We just arrived. Maybe later,
after dinner . . ."

But Dagmar wouldn't be put off. "Agnes!" she shouted,
despite the fact that the secretary had just jumped into the pool
with Freddy. "Fetch those drinks! Karl must still be on the
phone." Enthroning herself in a high-backed wicker garden
chair, Dagmar favored the cousins with a confidential smile.
"Karl Kreager is one of the most powerful men in the publishing industry. You've heard of him, I'm sure."

Judith had, but only in the vaguest sort of way. The wealthy
Kreager Klan, as they were known in the press, had been in-
termittent newsmakers for two generations. Judith wasn't exactly sure why, except that they were rich and sometimes
colorful.

Renie, however, was better acquainted with the world of
publishing because of her connections in the graphic design
business. "Midwestern origins," she said, still scowling at
Rover, who had curled up on his own monogrammed beach
towel. "Big family, Nordic good looks, scads of money.
Newspapers as well as books, right?"

Dagmar nodded once, the brim of her straw hat all but cov-
ering her face. "An empire, including magazines, radio and
TV stations, and perhaps a movie studio soon. Karl's wife,
Tessa, is my editor. They're so kind. But, of course, I make
them rich. My book's been on *The New York Times* best-seller
list since it came out last month." She looked up at Renie.
"You've read it, of course?"

Renie stepped aside as Agnes scurried past, carefully balancing a tray with a martini shaker and a half-dozen glasses.

"I read only the classics," Renie replied with a little yawn. "Turgenev's *Fathers and Sons* is really keeping me up at night. I'm just nuts about nihilism."

"Really!" Dagmar shuddered under her folds of white linen. Behind her sunglasses, she appeared to be staring at Renie as if she expected a call to anarchy at any moment. But the sight of the martini shaker seemed to soothe her. "I'll have two olives, Agnes. And give one to Rover."

The secretary dutifully served Dagmar her drink, fed the dog his olive, and offered hospitality to the cousins. They both declined, saying they still had to finish their lemonade. When no further commands were issued, Agnes crept back to the pool.

Dagmar sighed. "Pitiful creature. She needs to create other interests for herself. A hobby, maybe. Like stamps."

Judith felt compelled to linger, if only to make good on her vow to finish the glass of lemonade. She sat down on a metal lounge chair next to Dagmar, but Renie excused herself, saying she had to call her mother. That, Judith knew, was probably true. No matter where Renie had gone or what she was doing, Aunt Deb insisted on at least one phone call a day from her only daughter. Renie swore that if she were stranded at the North Pole, she'd have to commandeer a dogsled and mush to the nearest payphone.

"Did you read my column this morning?" Dagmar inquired, popping an olive into her mouth.

Judith had to confess that she'd merely scanned it. "I was in a rush, getting everything organized at the B&B and packing for the trip up here."

Dagmar waved a languid hand. "It wasn't as scathing as some. There are so many distractions when I'm on tour. Besides, I have to be careful not to top myself while the book is still fresh. It contains so many shocking revelations."

Judith saw Freddy bound out of the pool and make a beeline for the martini shaker. She nodded and smiled. He poured himself a drink and sat down next to her on the chair. There wouldn't have been room for a larger man. Judith was annoyed by his nearness, especially since he was soaking wet and she was almost dried off.

"Hey, sweetheart, isn't fate great?" he enthused. "I never expected to see you again. How about going dancing this evening? Bugler has some terrific nightspots."

Judith was spared a response by Dagmar's intervention. "Now, Freddy," the gossip columnist said sternly, "we have our celebratory dinner with the Kreagers tonight. You can save your partying for another time."

Freddy's ferretlike face puckered. "Oh, Aunt Dagmar, be a sport! We don't have to spend the whole night with the Kreagers. Hey, you're the guest of honor, not me."

Dagmar reached over and patted his knobby knee. "Now, now, Freddy. Karl and Tessa think you're adorable. They'd be utterly devastated if you weren't there for the whole evening. You won't want to miss dessert."

Freddy leered at Judith, showing his pointed teeth. "That's exactly what I was thinking."

Judith drew away from him, almost falling off the metal chair. "My cousin and I plan to make an early night of it. We're both beat. It's a long drive from home."

"Early to bed, early to rise." Freddy glanced down at his red Speedo. "If you know what I mean." He winked and nudged Judith with his bony elbow.

Judith leaped up from the chair. "I really must get back to the condo. Renie will be wondering if I've been . . . kidnapped. Or something. Enjoy your stay." She all but ran toward the gate.

But the Kreagers were just arriving. Or so Judith realized when she heard Dagmar's effusive voice calling out to the handsome couple who were approaching the pool.

"Mrs. Flynn!" Dagmar's tone turned imperious. "Stay a moment! You must meet Karl and Tessa!"

Even in his bathing trunks, Karl Kreager was the portrait of a distinguished businessman. His head of steel-gray hair was still full, his shoulders broad, his physique only marginally touched by time. Judith figured him for around sixty. He was tall, tanned, and had shrewd blue eyes, like agates. His voice was low and cultured, yet still possessed the telltale Midwestern twang. Karl Kreager offered Judith a firm handshake.

Mrs. Kreager's trim but curvaceous figure was encased in a one-piece white bathing suit cut high on the hip. She, too, was tanned, and almost as tall as Judith. Her short blond hair had been expertly cut, with small fluffy curls over perfect ears. Her even features were more striking than beautiful, but her gray eyes conveyed a smoldering sensuality. Judith guessed that she was a second wife, not yet forty, but at ease with a comfortable life-style that she had earned simply by being born with good looks.

"I swear," Tessa said in a low voice that held a trace of a Southern drawl, "Dagmar knows *everybody*. Let me guess— you're a dance choreographer."

For some reason, Judith was flattered. "Well—no. Actually, I'm . . ."

But Tessa had glided over to the umbrella-topped table which held the martini shaker. "I'm perishing of thirst," she declared. "Why do I always make the mistake of an early-afternoon court time for tennis?"

Karl Kreager regarded his wife with a fond expression, then turned to Judith. "Tessa's too hard on herself. She works hard, she plays hard. You'd never guess that her husband owned the company. Isn't that right, Dagmar?" His blue-eyed gaze now concentrated on the bundle of gauze in the lounge chair.

Dagmar's hat again nodded. "Tessa's been a fine editor, though she should have let me name more names instead of hinting at so much. I know my libel law. What's so sacred about Queen Elizabeth and the Pope and all the American Presidents?"

Karl chuckled. "Now, Dagmar, sometimes you can be a bit . . . shall I say, outrageous? Thor Publishing has always avoided hurting anyone unnecessarily. We never object to telling the truth, but we won't cause harm for the sake of sensation."

Dagmar did not take the rebuke kindly. "Harm! Now how can you harm people who behave badly? They ask for it! Movie stars who abuse their families, athletes who take drugs, cabinet members who cross-dress! Where's the *real* harm? They hide behind their celebrity status and break the law and defy morality and scorn ethics! It's up to writers like me— and publishers like you—to expose them for what they really are!"

Karl Kreager's manner was indulgent, patient. "You've

done your share, Dagmar. Your books—not to mention your columns—shake a lot of sins out of the trees. If that manuscript you're working on now is accurate, you'll be getting more than just a few nasty letters.''

It seemed to Judith that what she could see of Dagmar's pink face turned pale. ''Cranks,'' she muttered. ''Nothing but cranks, making idle threats. I've no time for such cowardice!''

Vaguely, Judith recalled that Dagmar had mentioned threats earlier, while staying at Hillside Manor. ''Do you really get threatening letters?'' she asked innocently. ''Are they serious?''

''Of course not,'' Dagmar snapped. ''People like me who tell the truth always receive hate mail. It's an occupational hazard. But it doesn't scare me. Not one bit.''

Judith thought that Dagmar's attitude was very brave. But she noticed that, under the piles of gauzy linen, the gossip columnist seemed to be trembling.

FOUR

RENIE WAS EXHIBITING a fear of her own. "I don't mind heights," she insisted, pouring scotch for Judith and rye for herself, "but I don't like those chairlift things. Remember how I wouldn't go up to the peak of Mount Pilatus when we were in Lucerne?"

Judith could recall their European tour of almost thirty years earlier in amazing detail. "It wasn't a chairlift, it was a tramcar. So you want a *hot dog* for dinner? The gondola that goes up Bugler Mountain holds a dozen people in each car, but there's only a snack bar at the top." She was consulting her visitor's brochure. "Good grief, coz, you said yourself that everything here is efficient and up-to-date. I can't imagine you being a wimp when it comes to *eating*."

Renie pouted a little as she sipped her drink. Having spent ten minutes on the phone with her mother, she had been surprised when Judith had still not returned to the condo. Assuming—rightly—that her cousin had gotten trapped by the Chatsworth party, Renie had driven down to the liquor store in the Bugler village and purchased a couple of fifths of whiskey. She had hoped to get a price break on the Scots import and the Canadian brand. She hadn't. But, she had reasoned, they were on vacation and deserved the best.

"Maybe if I drink about six of these, I won't care if the chair falls off and I get killed," she muttered.

Judith shook her head in dismay. "Forget it, we'll eat someplace else. There are plenty of good restaurants in the area. We've got that coupon for The Bells and Motley. How about the French restaurant out on the highway? Or the Italian bistro? There's German, too. And more French and Mexican and Japanese and—"

"Screw it," said Renie with an air of resignation. "We'll go up to Crest House on Liaison Ledge. I always said I'd die for lobster, and maybe I will. But it'll be worth it, as long as we don't crash until we come back down."

Judith relaxed on the comfortable sofa. She still couldn't quite believe their luxurious surroundings or the spectacular view. She also couldn't believe that they had ended up as condo neighbors of Dagmar Delacroix Chatsworth and company.

"It really is a small world," she murmured, sipping her scotch.

Renie shrugged. "When Bill and the kids and I were here last time, our pediatric nurse and her family were staying next to us. I wouldn't be surprised if there were a dozen people we know from Heraldsgate Hill milling around with the rest of the tourists. This is a popular spot."

Judith wasn't inclined to argue. Idly, she leafed through the weekly tabloid newspaper that was published every Wednesday in Bugler. The edition was six days old, with listings of current celebrity visitors. Actors, ballet dancers, opera singers, and athletes were mentioned. World-class skiers were in training, and several famous golfers were enjoying Bugler's excellent courses.

"Wow," Judith remarked, "this is really the place to be. I have a sudden urge to do something sporty."

"Like eat," said Renie, who was sorting through more restaurant information.

"Listen to this," Judith went on, still reading from the weekly newspaper. "Anatoly 'Nat' Linski runs a school for young ice skaters here. He's on hand for the rest of the summer, and has Mia Prohowska with him. They arrived back in town last week after finishing up the Ice Dreams tour."

Renie finally looked up from her eatery guides. "Really? Anne said the show was terrific. I didn't know that Mia and her coach had a base of operations here, but I'm not surprised. It's a perfect setting for skaters. Linski must be a wonderful coach. He certainly turned Mia into an Olympic champion twice over. I bet he gets his pick of young skaters. He must charge them up the kazoo.''

Judith was gazing at the small photo of Mia Prohowska, poised on one skate and decked out in feathers. ''I don't think I was ever so moved by a skater as when she won her first Olympic gold medal. She was sheer magic. I felt unpatriotic rooting for a competitor from behind the old Iron Curtain, but Mia made politics seem unimportant.''

Under the influence of the mountains, the cousins mused over winter Olympics past, then decided to act on their dinner of the present. Renie phoned in a seven o'clock reservation at Crest House. Judith called Joe.

There was no answer. She heard her own voice on the machine. It was after six. Joe must be working late, probably on the My Brew Heaven Tavern homicide. Or perhaps he'd decided to eat out.

For all of Bugler's glamorous reputation, the resort's lifestyle was casual. The cousins dressed in slacks. Judith added a white cotton shirt with a black geometric print; Renie had delved into her designer wear and come up with a matching cocoa tunic and flared pants. Her hairdo still didn't look very fetching.

Judith and Renie had to drive down the mountain in order to go back up. The lift began above the big new Fiddler Lodge, which was located below the condos. As they approached the little house where the lift tickets were sold, Renie gazed apprehensively at the individual chairs that trundled far up to the higher reaches of Fiddler Mountain.

''I thought they'd be two-seaters,'' she said in a fretful voice. ''We can't ride together.''

''Big deal.'' Judith gave her an ironic look. ''Men, women, and children, too, are making their way up the mountain. If you want to stay here, I'll send your dinner down in a doggie bag.''

Momentarily, Renie's appetite overcame her fixation. ''Don't mention dogs. I just about had a fit when that damned Rover jumped in the pool. No wonder you were so upset with him. Poms are such yappy nuisances. If we ever get a dog, it'll be a Samoyed. Bill thinks they're tops.''

The cousins headed for the lift-ticket office, though it seemed to Judith that Renie was dragging her feet. A fresh-faced young man stuck his head out of the small window. Judith noted that he was cradling a thick textbook in his lap. She figured him for a student working his way through college.

''No skis, no charge,'' he said in a disinterested voice. ''Next chair.''

The lift's pause was almost imperceptible. An eight-year-old hopped off and Judith got on. She glanced back to see what Renie was doing. Another youngster was descending, then a woman and a man. Renie stood there, hesitating. Judith was ascending the mountain, feeling secure as well as liberated. Renie was still on the ground. At least a half-dozen empty chairs had paused, waited, and then continued back up the mountain. Renie appeared to be holding onto her purse as if it were a parachute.

Across the way, on the descending chairs, Judith saw an elderly woman who had to be near ninety. The woman waved. Judith waved back. Then she craned her neck. Sure enough, Renie had apparently been given sufficient courage by the old lady's daring. With an uncertain movement, Renie clambered into the chair. She was a full ten spaces behind Judith.

''Okay, okay,'' said Renie testily when she got out of the chair at Liaison Ledge, ''so we made it up. What about *down*?''

But Judith was too absorbed in the view to listen to Renie's complaints. From this spot halfway up the mountain, the vista was breathtaking. She could see not only the entire resort complex and the valley below, but beyond that to sparkling lakes, the winding ribbon of highway, another valley, and, it seemed, almost the coast. The clear air made her feel euphoric. She smelled evergreens and crystal springs and the hint of fine food.

Judith took in deep, unsullied breaths, pleased to find her allergic reaction to Rover completely cleared up. ''This is just great.''

Finally, Renie's fears seemed conquered by the spectacle.

"This is fabulous. There are helicopter tours, you know. Or horseback rides. And, of course, hikes, if we were the athletic type."

Judith grinned at her cousin. "Let's not get carried away. We are not athletic. Nor are we young. And I imagine all these things cost money."

"The horseback rides aren't too expensive," Renie responded as they headed for the restaurant. "The kids went on them when we were here. They had a great time."

Crest House was busy. Despite their reservation, a brief wait was required. Judith and Renie queued up with a dozen other diners, admiring the restaurant's handsome, rugged architecture and decor. After five minutes, Renie was starting to fidget when another couple entered and the rest of the customers made way as if for royalty.

"Now, wait a minute," Renie growled in annoyance.

Judith poked her in the ribs. "Stick it, coz. That's Mia Prohowska and Nat Linski."

Renie shut up and stared. The lithe, lovely woman with the flaming red hair and the big, burly man with the gray-dappled beard were not only recognizable, but also recognized. Several patrons greeted them by name, if in a deferential manner. Mia and Nat allowed the maître d' to lead them to a table, meanwhile bestowing nods and smiles in their wake. Mia's graceful demeanor made her simple red-and-white polka-dot frock seem as elegant as a ball gown. By contrast, Nat's indigo linen jacket was slightly, if fashionably, rumpled, lending him an air of disdain for the masses.

"She's not as tall as I thought," Judith said in a whisper.

"He's bigger than he looks on TV," Renie whispered back.

"Did they get married?" Judith asked.

Renie shook her head. "I don't think so. Wasn't Mia forced into some sort of liaison with the head of the secret police in her native land? Or was that just a P.R. ploy to get sympathy for her in the West?"

Judith couldn't remember the details. "The guy's name was Boris. Of course, they were all named Boris in those days. But he was a real beast, and had some sort of hold over Mia. Maybe he was hanging her parents by their thumbs, or something. I suppose Boris is now serving up hash browns at a fast-food chain somewhere in Eastern Europe.''

A table was ready for the cousins. To their surprise, they were seated almost directly across from Mia Prohowska and Nat Linski. Judith tried not to stare.

''They're arguing over the wine list,'' she said under her breath. ''At least I think that's what they're doing. They're not speaking English.''

''Surprise. They're not American.'' Renie's tone was wry, but she had already turned her attention to the menu. ''I'm sticking with the lobster, but I want to mull over the salad choices. Let's have a drink and think.''

The cocktails arrived at the same time that Dagmar Delacroix Chatsworth and her party of four were led to a table on the opposite side of the restaurant. Judith was somewhat surprised to note that Rover hadn't been included.

''We can't seem to shed that bunch,'' she remarked, observing Dagmar, who was resplendent in bright green crepe, complete with turban and scarf-cum-shawl. ''I feel haunted.''

''Ignore them,'' Renie said simply, finally choosing a spinach salad with a warm bacon dressing. ''They won't bother us. We're too insignificant.''

But Mia Prohowska and Nat Linski were not about to ignore the Chatsworth party. Or, more precisely, Mia wasn't. She was on her feet, striding angrily toward Dagmar. Nat Linski got out of his chair but remained at the table, watching apprehensively.

Several other diners had now taken note of Mia's stormy descent upon Dagmar. All around the restaurant, heads were turning and conversation dropped to a hush.

Mia gestured in an irate manner; Dagmar half-rose from her chair; at the head of the table, Karl Kreager was acting as either a referee or a peacemaker. The cousins strained to catch what the two women were saying. Mia's excited, accented English was incomprehensible, but Dagmar's shrill voice carried, at least in snatches:

''. . . artistic integrity . . . you've had your day in the sun . . . Americans aren't corrupt like your former Communist bedfellows . . .''

Nat Linski was now stalking across the restaurant, his big

body shaking with wrath. Mia was shrieking at Dagmar, who made a slashing gesture with one crepe-covered arm. The skater shoved Dagmar away. Karl Kreager got to his feet, trying to pull Mia off her prey. A trio of waiters had congregated nearby, their expressions anxious and uncertain. The mâitre d' had been alerted, and was right on Nat Linski's heels.

Nat pushed Kreager aside, no mean feat, considering the publisher's size and physical condition. But Nat was even larger, somewhat younger, and seemingly stronger. Freddy Whobrey chortled with glee while Agnes Shay shuddered with dread. Tessa Kreager seemed more amused than unnerved.

Nat Linski said something brief and hostile to Karl Kreager. He spurned the mâitre d', glared at Dagmar, then gathered up Mia Prohowska and half-carried her back to their table. Mia was crying. She slumped in the chair, her face blotchy and her head down. Nat muttered to her in their native tongue, then sighed with exasperation and reached over to take her hand. Their conversation grew even more intense.

Slowly, the restaurant was returning to normal. Patrons still watched both sets of combatants with curious, if now discreet, eyes. The previously carefree voices had taken on a quiet edge. Peering around her menu, Judith tried to study the Chatsworth group. Karl was brushing lint—or possibly the memory of Nat's touch—off the sleeves of his navy blazer. Agnes was still cringing in her chair, clutching at the high neckline of her plain blouse. A magnum of champagne was being delivered. The gaiety seemed forced. But the party was going on. Judith turned back to the dinner entree listings. Out of the corner of her eye she saw Mia Prohowska leave the table and head for the ladies' washroom.

"I'm having the baby-back pork ribs," Judith announced, trying not to stare at Nat Linski, who was brooding over a frosted glass of vodka.

"Maybe I'll have two lobsters," Renie mused. "They're always so small."

Judith arched an eyebrow at her cousin. "Don't be a hog. They're also rich. You'll give yourself a stomachache."

The arrival of their salads eased Renie's hunger pangs. She settled for a single serving of lobster, then offered to help

Judith eat her ribs. Judith told Renie to take a hike. The cousins enjoyed their food and concentrated on Judith's quandary about the catering business.

"It's a double-edged sword," Judith explained, noting that Mia still hadn't returned from the washroom and that Nat had gone from brooding to fidgeting. She also observed that Dagmar was now absent from her place across the room. "The more outside catering dates I get, the more I'm forced to spend time away from the B&B. Doing receptions and cocktail parties at Hillside Manor isn't a problem. I'm on the premises. But if I need Arlene to help me with an outside job, I have no permanent backup for the B&B."

"Corinne Dooley has pitched in a couple of times," Renie pointed out, spraying herself with lobster, but not seeming to mind. The bib she'd been given didn't quite cover her tunic.

"Those were emergencies," Judith replied. "Corinne's got a big family, and she did it because she's a good neighbor and I was on the spot. Even though some of her kids are grown up and gone, she's still got small children at home."

"Maybe she'd like to get involved in the catering with Arlene," Renie suggested, soaking a large chunk of lobster in melted butter and wearing an ethereal expression that indicated she could see Valhalla somewhere in the mountain mists. "Or what about cutting back on the catering altogether and doing only the in-house stuff?"

"That's possible," Judith admitted. "I figured it out on paper over the weekend. If I did that, I'd lose about forty percent of my catering profits. That's sizable, but now that Joe and I are married, we've got his income. You'd think we'd be rolling in money, but the truth is, I'm no further ahead than I was three years ago, when I was still single and the B&B was just getting on its feet. Where does the money go?"

"Don't ask me. I charge seventy-five bucks an hour, I work an average of thirty hours a week, Bill's salary at the university is decent, he's got his private clients, and we're still broke." Renie paused to motion at their waiter, who was passing by. "Say, do you suppose we could have another couple of these?" She tapped her empty cocktail glass.

"It's baffling," Judith agreed. "Of course, you're still sending kids through college. But Mike's graduated and on his

own.'' She gave a start and put a hand to her mouth. ''Yikes!
I forgot to mail off the monthly payment on his new Blazer!
It's due the first of the month.''

''Send it overnight Friday. You'll still get it in under the
wire.'' Renie wrestled with her lobster, trying to remove the
last tasty morsels.

Judith was having problems of her own with the baby-back
ribs. She decided it would be acceptable to finish eating them
with her fingers. Surreptitiously, she glanced around to see if
anyone was watching. Mia Prohowska stepped into her line of
vision and leaned down to speak to Nat Linski. A moment
later, the couple left the restaurant.

''Dagmar must have spoiled Mia's appetite,'' Judith remarked. ''I wonder what that row was all about.''

''Dagmar's book?'' Renie offered. ''I haven't seen anything
about Mia in the newspaper columns lately.''

Judith's eyes strayed across the room. Dagmar's chair was
still empty. Freddy appeared to have everyone's attention as
he performed some kind of finger show and jabbered his head
off. Even Agnes Shay wore a diffident smile.

The waiter brought the cousins' second round of drinks.
Judith finished her ribs and tried to wipe off her hands. ''I'd
better visit the washroom,'' she said, getting out of her chair.

''The waiter will provide finger bowls,'' Renie said.

But Judith pointed to her scotch. ''I'd still better visit the
washroom. After all that lemonade and scotch, I'm afloat.''

While Judith was in the stall, she thought she heard a
strange sound that was almost a sob. It was not repeated, and
she paid no further attention until she was washing her hands
in the powder room section. Adding a dash of lipstick, she
looked in the mirror and saw Dagmar Delacroix Chatsworth
coming out of the lavatory area. She carried her turban and
its attached flowing scarf in one hand and her purse in the
other. Without the camouflage, Dagmar looked much older.
She also seemed upset, even haggard.

''Mrs. Flynn,'' Dagmar said, her voice flat.

Judith waited for the usually loquacious Dagmar to go on.
But she didn't. The gossip columnist set her purse on the mar-
bleized counter and fussed with her hair. The dark strands with
their red highlights were obviously dyed, and pulled back into

a tight bun at the base of Dagmar's head. Without the scarf concealing her throat, Judith noticed definite signs of wrinkles and sags. She and Dagmar were allegedly the same age, but she honestly thought that the other woman was old enough to be her mother. Not *Gertrude*, of course, but a generic mother, anywhere from fifteen to twenty years Judith's senior.

"This is a nice place for a party," she said at last, to break the awkward silence.

"Is it?" Dagmar's tone was sharp. Then, as swiftly as an avalanche, the gossip columnist unleashed a tumult of angry words: "Celebrities are so self-centered! They live in a narrow little world where no one else exists and they are the entire focus! Today, I write about Mel Gibson; tomorrow, Barbra Streisand; then Ken Griffey Jr. I'm not an encyclopedia of their facts and foibles. I'm interested in *news*, and once it's been printed, I move on. Why can't they *understand* that?"

Dagmar's tone had begun to waver, with an undercurrent of anxiety. Judith wasn't sure how to react.

"Are you talking about Mia Prohowska?" she offered in a kindly voice.

Dagmar threw up her hands. "Mia! Yes, yes, Mia and a hundred others! They're all the same! Mia just happens to be the one who is here. Tonight. In this very restaurant. While I'm trying to enjoy myself. She and Nat Linski are like a plague, shadowing me everywhere. First at the Cascadia Hotel, now here at Bugler! Why can't they go to the Bahamas?" She set her jaw and eyed Judith with a mixture of fury and self-pity.

"You said yourself that stirring up people is part of your job," Judith pointed out reasonably. "I got the impression that you expect these celebrities to react badly." *And*, Judith thought to herself, *that it's part of the payoff*.

But Dagmar didn't look as if she were enjoying the fruits of her labor one bit. With a trembling hand, she rummaged in her big, woven leather purse. "Here," she said, pulling out several folded sheets of paper. "Would you like getting these?"

Judith carefully unfolded the top sheet, which, like the rest, seemed to be standard computer printout paper. It read: YOU

ARE A VICIOUS BITCH AND YOU WILL PAY FOR
YOUR CRUELTY.

"Oh, my," breathed Judith. "That's nasty."

Dagmar snorted, her equilibrium returning. "It certainly is.
Look at the rest. Go ahead, read it all."

There were seven such messages, all short and to the point.
Dagmar's writings had harmed someone—many someones—
and she would pay for her poisoned pen. Possibly with her
life, or so read the final missive:

YOUR SMEARS AND LIES WILL COST YOU MORE
THAN MONEY. WHEN YOU ARE DEAD, NO ONE WILL
MOURN.

"That's definitely not nice," Judith said in a weak voice.
"How long have you been receiving these things?"

Dagmar jammed the letters back into her purse. "A month.
That last one was waiting for me when I arrived at Bugler
yesterday. They come by regular mail, with a New York postmark."

"Have you shown them to the police?" Judith asked, lowering her voice as two young women came into the washroom,
laughing and talking.

"Not yet." Dagmar seemed to fret. "I know what they'd
say—what I say myself. It's a crank, and probably harmless.
No real damage has been done." Her eyes narrowed even as
her mouth curved into an ironic smile. "I have to get killed
first."

Fortunately, the two young women had gone into the lavatory section of the ladies' lounge. Judith fingered her chin.
"I'd definitely show them to the police when you get back to
New York," she said. "I'd consult a lawyer, too. I assume
you have one."

Dagmar tossed her head, the dyed hair threatening to come
loose from its plethora of pins. "Lawyers! They're a leech on
the commonweal! I have an agent in New York with a legal
background. What more do I need? Thor Publishing and the
Kreager chain have a regiment of attorneys, all sucking up
money like vampires drinking blood!"

Judith gave a helpless shrug. "Everybody needs a lawyer
now and then. You know, personal stuff. Property lines, lia-
bility, insurance claims, wills."

Dagmar gave a superior sniff. "I own a Manhattan penthouse, the publishers and the agent take care of my professional needs, I've got enough insurance to cover a Third World country, and I'm too young to make a will. If you knew half the things I do about some of those big-name, grandstanding lawyers, you'd faint with shock!"

Judith decided to risk a pointed question. "The call you got in my living room last week—was that a threat?"

Dagmar avoided Judith's eyes. "It was . . . a crank." Under scrutiny, she squirmed a bit. "Well, yes, it was sort of a threat. But I couldn't identify the caller's voice." Now, almost defiantly, Dagmar did return Judith's gaze.

Before Judith could respond, Agnes Shay slipped into the washroom. When she saw Dagmar, her plain face was flooded with relief.

"Oh! You're all right! I was so worried!"

Dagmar poked at the pins that held her bun in place. "Really, Agnes, you're such a fussbudget! Why wouldn't I be all right? I was merely adjusting my toilette and chatting with Mrs. Flynn. Has dessert arrived yet? I understand the meringues here are divine."

Judith lingered briefly, but it was clear that with Agnes's arrival, Dagmar had assumed her characteristically self-confident persona. Murmuring a word of farewell to both women that was acknowledged only by Agnes, Judith left the ladies' room.

Renie was absorbed in the dessert menu. She glanced up as Judith sat down. "Did you have to wait in line? What do other women do in the bathroom? I've never figured it out. They fiddle around and take forever, and everybody else is practically doing a dance, waiting her turn. Not me—I'm in, I'm out. What's to do, unless you're a graffiti artist?"

Judith explained what had happened. Renie listened closely, pausing only to order a slice of mocha cheesecake. Not having had the opportunity to study the menu, Judith did the same, adding a Kahlúa and cream. Renie requested Galliano on the rocks.

"So Dagmar's scared?" Renie remarked after their waiter had gone off with the order.

Judith nodded. "Her fright seems genuine." She glanced

across the restaurant. Dagmar and Agnes were returning to their table. The Kreagers welcomed them with apparent enthusiasm. Freddy was ogling a platinum blonde who had just arrived with a bronzed male escort in a tank top and tight jeans. Judith ogled the escort.

"Of course," she went on, tearing her eyes away from the handsome young man, "it's hard to tell with Dagmar. She's as much of a show-biz character as the people she writes about. Why would she carry those letters around? And why show *me*?"

Renie shrugged. "Maybe Dagmar feels safer with the letters under wraps. Maybe she's trying to impress you. Maybe, as usual, your sympathetic manner has encouraged her to get chummy. Maybe I'm still hungry." To prove the point, Renie was distracted by the entrees being delivered to other tables. "The prime rib looks wonderful. I could have had that. See, there's a filet mignon with fresh mushrooms. Oh! Salmon! Do you think it's sockeye or king?"

Judith, who was replete and not entirely certain she could down a hunk of cheesecake, eyed her cousin with reproach. "Knock it off. We've eaten like the two little pigs. But we haven't resolved my catering conflict."

Renie waved a hand, almost knocking a tray out from under a waiter who was delivering drinks to the next table. "Yes, we have. No matter how hard you work and how much you make, you'll always be in the hole. So quit killing yourself, give Arlene and whomever else the outside catering jobs, and keep everything else on the B&B premises. End of advice. Where's the cheesecake?"

It was arriving nearly on cue. Judith discovered that she could actually stuff herself just a little bit more. The cheesecake melted on her tongue. She sighed with pleasure.

"Wonderful. And," she added in a more businesslike tone, "I think you're right about the catering. That's sort of the way I've been leaning, and you've confirmed it. Let's face it, coz; people like us never get ahead."

Renie nodded. "Exactly. It's the Kreagers and the Dagmars and that ilk who make it big." She gestured across the room with her fork. "We're the Little Guys, and maybe that's not so bad in the big scheme of things."

Judith gazed over at the Chatsworth table. The group was about to leave. Karl Kreager was embracing Dagmar; Tessa brushed cheeks with Agnes; Freddy leered at the platinum blonde.

Renie grinned at Judith. "Dagmar isn't wearing her turban. What did she do, flush it down the toilet?"

"Maybe it got too warm," Judith replied, arguing with herself whether or not to eat all of the cheesecake. "It feels kind of muggy in here this evening."

Briefly, Renie turned thoughtful. "You're right. Almost every night there's a storm. Mostly lightning, and it doesn't last too long. In fact, it's quite beautiful." Suddenly she grimaced. "Jeez, I hope it doesn't hit the chairlift!"

Judith refused to let such alarmist thoughts spoil her evening. Virtuously pushing aside the last bites of cheesecake, she sipped at her Kahlúa. Toward the front of the restaurant, the Chatsworth party was taking its leave. Idly, Judith wondered if a few bites of Chateaubriand had been reserved for Rover.

The bill jolted her from her comfortable mood. Even with the favorable U.S.–Canadian exchange rate, the cousins owed over a hundred dollars, not including tip. They were thankful that at least they'd taken the time in Port Royal to trade in most of their American currency for Canadian bills.

"It's a good thing we've got that discount for tomorrow night," Judith muttered as they headed for the chairlift. "I brought along only three hundred bucks."

"We got carried away," Renie replied in a subdued voice. "I hope Bill brings back a lot of salmon from Alaska. We may have to live on it this winter."

The exodus from the restaurant had been heavy. The cousins had to wait in line for the lift. As dusk descended over the mountains, spidery streaks of lightning crackled in the sky to the north. The thunder was still faint, and well distanced from the lightning. Judith watched and listened with a sense of awe.

"At least the summer storm is free," she remarked. "Will it rain?"

"Maybe. It doesn't always." Renie was frowning, obviously concerned about their descent on the chairlift.

The line was moving quickly. Judith stood on tiptoe, notic-

ing Dagmar's signature turban up ahead. "Everybody must
have finished eating about the same time," she commented.

"They had quite a crowd when we got here, remember?"
Anxiously, Renie watched the chairlift deposit newcomers to
Liaison Ledge. "People are still coming up to have dinner.
It's not quite nine. They eat later here, like in Europe."

At last it was the cousins' turn to take the lift. Again Judith
went first. Renie didn't dare linger, lest her place be taken by
the dozen or more people behind her in line. As they made
their descent, Judith couldn't resist turning around and grinning at her cousin. Renie was clutching the safety bar and
looking more than mildly terrified. The thunder was louder
now, and the lightning was flashing on its heels. Judith was
enchanted.

Three-quarters of the way down the mountain, the lift came
to an abrupt halt. Judith's chair swayed, but she wasn't concerned. Mother Nature was performing on a grandiose scale,
with the lightning moving closer, creeping across the sky like
slender snakes.

"Help!" The voice caught Judith's ear, forcing her to turn
again. Renie was leaning forward, looking desperate. "Coz!
Is this thing busted?"

Another clap of thunder delayed Judith's reply. "I don't
know," she finally yelled back, trying not to laugh. They
weren't all that far off the ground, though Judith supposed that
if they actually fell, a few broken bones might result. But there
seemed to be no problem with the cable: For some reason, the
revolving mechanism had come to a dead stop. Renie started
to yell again, demanding to know what was going on. Judith
peered into the oncoming darkness. She could see a cluster of
people at the bottom of the lift. They seemed to be grouped
around the chair that was in the arrival position.

Judith turned again. "Somebody's stuck," she called to
Renie. "Maybe the safety bar won't open."

Trying to enjoy the summer lightning storm and the view
of the village with the lights now flickering below, Judith relaxed. But dangling in midair was a bit vexing, and she knew
that Renie's nerves and temper must be badly frayed. Across
the way, in the chairs headed up the hill, people were beginning to grouse.

And then, with a jerk, the cable came to life. Two minutes later, Judith was on the ground, with Renie right behind her. A loud crash of thunder and a blinding bolt of lightning only made them laugh. The cousins were both smiling when they first noticed the sounds and sights that had nothing to do with Mother Nature's summer caprice. Sirens screamed and red lights flashed. They were headed straight for Judith and Renie.

FIVE

BETWEEN THE THUNDER and the sirens, it was impossible to hear anything else. The cousins tried to get closer to a growing crowd which had gathered by the lift-ticket office. With every crack of lightning, the scene took on an eerie, gold-green cast.

"See?" Renie shouted in Judith's ear. "I told you—there's been an accident on the lift. Someone has fallen off, I'll bet."

Judith edged closer, using her height to look over shorter heads. The emergency vehicles had come to a halt just a few yards away. The sirens stopped, but the red lights kept flashing, in garish counterpoint to the lightning. Uniformed personnel spilled out of the fire engine, the police car, and the ambulance. A path was cleared, and Judith tried to see where it led.

"I'm right," Renie went on doggedly, still speaking at the top of her lungs. "They've stopped the lift again."

Judith turned. The lift had come to another halt, and now all the chairs were empty. Their carefree swinging motion struck Judith as macabre.

The emergency crew had formed a circle, urging people to step back. Along with everyone else, Judith and Renie complied. But as the onlookers retreated and shuffled about, there was a brief opening in Judith's line of sight. The lightning crackled again, and the red warning lights illuminated the scene. A figure was lying on the ground. Judith was too far away to see a face or a form. Yet though the colors were distorted, there was no mistaking the turban and the matching scarf. If an accident had occurred on the chairlift, Judith was certain that the victim was Dagmar Delacroix Chatsworth.

In the crowd, speculation was rampant, if hushed. Judith kept her thoughts to herself. She was sure that Renie hadn't been able to see the inert body lying near the lift shack.

The storm was now moving swiftly to the southwest. Darkness had descended on Bugler. Judith tried to hear what the people next to her were saying, but they spoke in Japanese. On her right, the language was German. Frustrated, she grabbed the sleeve of Renie's tunic and led her on an end run around the crowd. They stopped on the far side of the lift office, standing on a knoll.

It seemed that the medics were working on the victim. The minutes dragged by. The police maintained order with polite but firm commands. Judith noticed that the college student who had waved them onto the lift was being questioned by one of the officers.

The fire truck pulled away, its red light now off. The big shiny vehicle lumbered slowly down the winding road, like a tired animal heading for the barn. Then the medics covered the victim and placed the body on a gurney. As if in time to a slow march, the attendants carried their burden to the ambulance and closed the doors.

"Oh, my God," breathed Renie. "Is—*was*—that Dagmar?"

Judith might have been taller than her cousin, but Renie was farsighted. "Do you think so?" Judith asked in a hollow tone.

"I thought I recognized her turban." Renie bit her lip. "Do you suppose she fell? Or maybe tripped on those high heels?"

The big letters on the computer paper leaped in front of Judith's eyes. But it would be impossible to push anyone off the chairlift. Perhaps Dagmar had suffered a heart attack.

"I don't know," she finally answered in an uncertain voice.

The ambulance had left and the crowd was beginning to disperse. The chairlift still wasn't moving. "It had to be something freakish," Judith declared, more to herself than to Renie. "Why else would they stop the lift? They must have started it up just long enough to get everybody safely to the top or the bottom."

The cousins found themselves walking aimlessly. So were a number of other puzzled spectators. The crowd milled around them, eventually drifting toward the road or onto the terrace of Fiddler Lodge.

"Maybe Dagmar had a stroke," Renie suggested as they crossed the flagstones and wandered in through the open French doors.

"That would be less frightening than—" Judith caught herself. What was the point of bringing up the possibility of murder? There had already been too much unexpected violence in Judith's life.

But Renie wasn't so reticent. "Than somebody killing her? Well, you said she got threats. If the police hear about those letters, they'll investigate."

The lobby was huge, a cross between an Alpine chalet and an English hunting lodge. Gleaming wood and shining brass caught the lights of large chandeliers. Big bouquets of wild and exotic flowers were mingled in stoneware vases. The furniture was solid, comfortable, and inviting.

Judith gave herself a shake. "It's so hard to believe that Dagmar's dead. Just a short time ago, she was downing martinis and slurping up meringues. For all her faults and enormous ego, she was so . . . *alive.*"

Renie stopped in her tracks and grabbed Judith's arm so tightly that it hurt. "She still is, coz." Renie pointed across the lobby to a long forest-green divan. "There's Dagmar now, and she's alive and well and drinking brandy from a balloon snifter."

Judith all but leapfrogged across the lobby. Several more decorous guests, who were sipping sherry and after-dinner drinks, stopped to stare. Judith, however, paid no heed. She was staring at Dagmar.

Dagmar was staring at the plush floral carpet. The hand that clutched the big brandy snifter shook, and Tessa Kreager had an arm around the gossip columnist.

Renie had caught up with Judith. Dagmar seemed oblivious of the cousins' presence. Tessa shook her head at them in an apparent attempt at dismissal. But Judith wasn't so easily put off.

"Excuse us," she said, her voice sympathetic. "What's going on? We thought Dagmar had met up with an accident."

"Dagmar's fine," Tessa snapped, her face flushed under the tan. "Please leave us alone. We're waiting for Karl."

Balancing on one foot and then the other, Judith scanned the long lobby. She saw no sign of Karl Kreager. "Is there something we can do?" she offered.

Tessa Kreager's fine features curdled in anger, but before she could reply, Dagmar's head suddenly jerked up. "Mrs. Flynn! Mrs. Jones! Oh, I'm so glad you're here! Please sit!" Dagmar inched closer to Tessa, making room for the cousins.

Clearly annoyed, Tessa shot Judith and Renie malevolent looks, but said nothing. Dagmar took a last sip of brandy, held the snifter out in front of her, then set it down on the leather-topped coffee table. She shut her eyes tight and uttered a pathetic little keening noise.

"I was going to ask Agnes to get me another," she whispered in a shaky voice. "Then I remembered. Agnes can't. She's dead." Tears rolled down Dagmar's wrinkled cheeks, ruining her makeup.

It was Renie who reacted first. "Agnes is *dead*? Oh, no! What happened?"

Tessa spoke sharply. "We don't know. That's what we're waiting for. Karl is trying to find out."

Dagmar was literally beating her crepe-covered breast. "It's all my fault. We left the restaurant in a group, but I'd forgotten my turban and scarf in the washroom. I sent Agnes back to fetch my things."

A waitress strolled by, inquiring if Dagmar cared for a refill. She did. Tessa requested a glass of sparkling Vouvray. Judith hemmed and Renie hawed, but they finally settled on joining Dagmar in a bit of brandy.

"Then what happened?" Judith asked, ignoring Tessa's sour expression.

Dagmar's hands fluttered in a helpless gesture. "Nothing. I mean, the rest of us got on the lift, except Freddy, who'd met some lowlife friend in the bar. We came down the mountain, and decided to come here for a nightcap. The next thing I knew, there was a commotion outside." She waved at the nearest set of French doors. "When Tessa returned from the bar, she went to see what was going on. I waited forever, or so it seemed. Tessa finally told me that something terrible had happened to Agnes." Dagmar held her head in her hands.

The drinks were delivered to the big coffee table. After a sip of Vouvray, Tessa began to relax. "I was one of the first to get to the scene," she said, her Southern drawl more pronounced under stress. "When I saw that turban and scarf, I felt as if I were hallucinating. Then I realized it was Agnes, not Dagmar. I tried to get to her, but there were already some official types keeping everybody at a distance." Tessa slowly shook her head, apparently still shocked. The perfect little blond curls seemed to lack their usual buoyancy.

Judith envisioned the scene. "Was Agnes still in the chair when you arrived?"

"Yes. A couple of men were getting her out. I suppose they thought she was afraid, or maybe sick. They carried her over by that shack where they sell the lift tickets. I tried to follow, but that was when I got warned off with the others." Tessa was not only relaxing, she seemed to be unraveling. Her hand also shook, spilling droplets of wine on her tailored ecru slacks. "I didn't realize that Agnes was dead until the medics or whoever they were covered her up."

Dagmar's fingers flitted at her neck, then her hair. She seemed to be searching for the turban and the scarf that were no longer there, just as, by reflex, she had tried to summon Agnes. "Her heart, perhaps . . . Agnes was never strong. Not that she complained, but what if she had an undiagnosed condition? She almost never saw a doctor." Again Dagmar covered her face with her hands. "Oh, my! I blame myself! For everything!"

Tessa tried to console the distraught Dagmar. Various other

patrons in the lobby were watching, if discreetly. Judith sipped at her brandy, wishing she didn't feel so uneasy.

Karl Kreager's entrance was noted by all. His distinguished figure would have made waves in any setting. But the urgency of his manner caused a stir. Very few would have recognized him on sight, but everyone seemed to acknowledge that he was an important personage.

Karl was taken aback by the presence of Judith and Renie. He squared his shoulders and took a deep breath. Reaching out with both hands, he urged Dagmar and Tessa to come with him.

"We must speak privately. We'll go back to Clarges Court."

But Dagmar didn't budge. "No. Tell me now. I won't be able to walk as far as the parking lot if you don't."

The agate blue eyes flashed. It was clear that Karl Kreager didn't like to be crossed, not over big issues, or over small matters, either. There was no space left for him on the sofa. He stood in front of the four women like an executive conducting a meeting.

"There's nothing definite yet," he said, his deep voice very low. "However, I can tell you this much." Karl licked his lips as if, in having been thwarted, he relished the news he was about to deliver. "The local police suspect foul play. They're going to perform an autopsy."

Dagmar fainted.

The well-trained and highly efficient personnel who worked in Bugler weren't accustomed to handling multiple crises. Emergencies usually involved broken bones on the ski slopes, twisted ankles at the ice rinks, and the occasional celebrity overdose from drugs or alcohol.

But a dead body on the chairlift and an unconscious woman in the lobby of Fiddler Lodge put the staff's usually cheerful poise to the test. The waitress who had served drinks insisted upon finding smelling salts; the concierge tried to summon a doctor; the publisher of the Bugler weekly put aside his mug of Molson long enough to whip out his camera. That was the last straw for the assistant manager, a Tlingit tribal member who utilized his native powers by decking the newspaperman, who fell flat out under the lobby's grand piano.

It was Tessa Kreager who managed to bring Dagmar around by putting the columnist's head between her knees and speaking words of comfort in a soft Southern drawl.

"Writers are notoriously emotional," she asserted in an aside to the assistant manager, who was rubbing his sore knuckles. "Don't worry, we'll handle this."

And somehow, they did. Between them, Karl and Tessa Kreager maneuvered Dagmar out of the lobby and, presumably, from the hotel to the parking lot. Judith and Renie remained on the forest-green sofa, drinking their brandy. Their presence was ignored.

"I don't believe it," Judith said flatly after the hubbub had died away. *"Foul play?"*

Renie smirked. "Hey, coz, it's right up your alley. Murder. Suspects. Motives. Opportunity. A police force that can't find its backside in a small box. Go for it. Otherwise, we have to do wholesome things, like hike and play tennis."

"Aaaargh!" Judith's exclamation was genuine. The cousins differed in many of their interests and personality traits. But neither was athletic, nor ever had been. Renie had given up sports in the sixth grade because she'd been hit in the face with a medicine ball; Judith had surrendered after an ill-fated adventure on a pogo stick. Both preferred more intellectual pursuits, and in Judith's case, her curiosity had often been activated by murder.

"Maybe," she mused, swirling the brandy in the big snifter, "we should go visit the local police."

"What's our excuse?" Renie asked, sufficiently game to find one.

Judith waved a hand. "Bugler. It's a small resort town, barely twenty years old. What—two, three thousand regular residents? This is probably their first homicide. What do they know? They've had no experience; their facilities must be unsophisticated; the personnel is undoubtedly limited. They might actually welcome our help." Abruptly, Judith clasped a hand to her head. "It's going on ten. I've got to call Joe. Afterward, let's drive down to police headquarters."

Joe Flynn answered on the second ring. Arlene Rankers had done a bang-up job hosting Hillside Manor's guests. Or so Joe thought, since they were all comfortably settled in for the night and not threatening lawsuits. As for Gertrude, a light had been on in the toolshed when he got home. Ergo, she must be well.

"Wait a minute," said Judith. "What time did you come home? It doesn't get dark until after eight-thirty."

"I worked late," Joe replied. "Then Woody and I went out for dinner. Sondra was giving a potluck for her day-care co-op."

Judith knew that Woody's wife, Sondra, had been involved in a neighborhood day-care program since the arrival of the Prices' second child. The baby girl had been born in late May; Woody's firstborn, a son, was almost two.

"Are you and Woody still working the tavern homicide?" Judith asked.

"Right," Joe answered. "It's more complicated than we realized."

Judith frowned into the payphone. "I thought it was a show-down between the owner and the bartender. What's compli-cated about that?"

"Oh, there was a classic triangle. The owner, the bartender, and the owner's wife. The bartender, Phil Lapchick, is stable now, and he claims that he was having an affair with Mrs. Bauer. She denies it. She insists that her husband, Les, was the jealous type, and that Lapchick is a pathological liar. Diana is pretty sharp. I think she may have these characters nailed down."

"*Diana*?" Judith's tone was sardonic. "Since when do you call suspects by their first name?"

"She's not a suspect." Joe suddenly sounded irritable. "I told you, she was a hostage. Lapchick was going to kill her, too, if Woody and I hadn't shown up. The problem is that we have to establish motive—for Lapchick. Did he shoot the boss because Bauer had accused him of putting his hand in the till, as was originally claimed, or because he was allegedly hot for Diana? We can't present a case unless we know what was really going on."

Almost three hundred miles from home and enjoying every luxury that a world-class resort could provide, Judith didn't feel justified in making insinuations about how her husband was handling his latest homicide investigation.

"It sounds tricky," she said, "but you'll figure it out. Did we get any interesting mail?" Somewhat guiltily, she thought about the ledger and the bills she'd brought with her. They still reposed in her suitcase. The gas and phone bills had arrived Saturday and remained sealed in their envelopes.

"The usual," Joe replied, then corrected himself. "No, you got a little box from some telecommunications company. Should I open it?"

"Oh, yes," Judith replied with a note of excitement. "That's the thing that goes with the Caller I.D. If you get a chance, can you hook it up?"

Joe agreed that he'd give it a try. "How's it going up at Bugler? Nice digs?"

Judith didn't want to brag about the accommodations. "Nice enough," she answered breezily.

"You and Renie having fun?"

Judith hesitated, on the verge of telling Joe about Agnes Shay. But she didn't know what had really happened. "We ran into some people we knew from—"

"My beeper just went off, Jude-girl. It might be Woody. Or Diana Bauer. Take care. Love you." Joe hung up.

Still holding the receiver, Judith tried not to be annoyed. She considered calling Gertrude. But Judith's mother despised phone calls, even from her daughter. She'd wait until the next day to check in with Gertrude.

Renie was window-shopping in the lodge's boutiques. "Well? How's Joe?"

"Fine." Judith's step was brisk. "Let's drive to police headquarters. Didn't you say it was in that big red building near the main highway?"

Renie nodded, eyeing Judith curiously. But the cousins had built-in antennae when it came to each other's moods. Renie sensed that she shouldn't press Judith for further details about Joe.

Instead, they went to call on the police.

SIX

BUGLER'S CHIEF OF police was in his mid-thirties, with wavy auburn hair, brown eyes, and a muscular build. Rhys Penreddy worked in cramped but up-to-date surroundings. He was more curious than annoyed by the cousins' arrival.

"You were acquainted with the deceased?" he asked after Judith and Renie had been left to cool their heels for almost thirty minutes.

Judith explained how the Chatsworth party had stayed at Hillside Manor the previous week. She told Rhys Penreddy about accidentally running into Dagmar and the others at Clarges Court. She recounted the coincidental meeting at Crest House and her conversation with Dagmar in the ladies' washroom.

"Mrs. Chatsworth showed me some letters she'd received," Judith continued in her most earnest voice. "They were definitely of a threatening nature. She also received a strange phone call while she was at my B&B. I can't help but wonder, if it turns out that Agnes was actually murdered, that the intended victim might not have been Dagmar Delacroix Chatsworth."

Rhys Penreddy's clever brown eyes regarded Judith with amusement. "That might be assumed, of course, since Ms. Shay was wearing her employer's turban. But we mustn't jump to conclusions, eh?"

Judith bridled a bit. "I'm basing the assumption on

72

threats to Dagmar. Agnes Shay was a completely harmless woman. But her employer is a powerful person, a nationally syndicated columnist who knows all the dirt."

Penreddy consulted his notepad. It seemed to Judith that his jottings had been remarkably sparse during the course of his interview with the cousins.

"Anything else?" Penreddy asked smoothly.

Judith glanced at Renie, who was looking blank. "Well . . ." Judith frowned. "I realize you won't know anything for certain until after the autopsy, but what makes you think that foul play was involved?"

Penreddy's brown eyes danced with high spirits. "Really, Mrs. Flynn, I'm not allowed to say. We don't have facilities for a complete autopsy here in Bugler, so the body has been sent to Port Royal. We'll have our results in the morning, and if you're still here on Wednesday, you can read about them in the weekly newspaper."

The police chief's smile struck Judith as condescending. "In other words, your facilities here are primitive." She flinched at the obvious sullenness in her manner.

"Not at all," Penreddy replied mildly. "It's true that we don't have a coroner available, but otherwise, we're very high-tech. Everything at Bugler has been created for the twenty-first century. Being a relatively new resort, we look strictly to the future, never to the past." His smile was now faintly smug.

Stung by the implied reprimand, Judith got to her feet. "I'm sorry to have troubled you," she mumbled. "I just thought that . . . since I knew Agnes Shay from . . . there might be some insight that would have gone unnoticed . . ."

Renie all but dragged Judith out of Bugler's city hall. "Jeez, coz, you blew it!" Renie said frankly. "Penreddy's smart, he's on top of things, he's doing his job. You're going to have to butt out on this one."

Angrily, Judith brushed off Renie's comforting arm. "I feel like an idiot! The Bugler police force needs me like they need ringworm! I'll bet Penreddy thinks I'm some kind of meddling foreign nutcase!"

The cousins drove back up Fiddler Mountain in silence. Judith struggled to quiet her anger with herself. On the surface, it would appear that a small resort town a hundred miles from civilization wouldn't have the resources to handle a high-powered homicide investigation. But Bugler had been built for tourists, especially those who played in the international leagues. The town would have the best of everything, even when it came to crime. In different places, at other times, Judith knew she had been lucky. She had matched wits against incompetents; she had possessed an intuitive understanding of people; she had been the repository of confidences.

But in Bugler, she had discovered a professional police chief who presumably had capable underlings. Rhys Penreddy could also call on up-to-date technology. And, Judith knew from her previous adventures in Canada, the local force could ask for assistance from the Royal Canadian Mounted Police. Judith felt like a fifth wheel, and a foreign make at that.

"I'm going to bed," she announced after the cousins entered their lavish condo a few minutes before midnight. "It's been a long day."

Renie didn't argue. Ten minutes later, they had each retreated to their separate bedrooms. Judith lay down on the comfortable king-sized bed and opened the romantic suspense novel she'd brought along for escapist reading.

But there was no escape from reality. Judith got out of bed and went over to her suitcase. Unzipping the side pocket, she removed the ledger and the handful of bills. Propping herself up in bed, she checked out the unpaid water, light, cable, and newspaper invoices. As always, light and water were huge expenditures. There was no way to cut down on either, unless she started posting annoying little messages asking guests to conserve. Many B&Bs did just that. Judith looked askance at such policies. Her guests came to Hillside Manor to enjoy themselves. They shouldn't be treated like irresponsible children, which, in fact, was how some of them behaved. Like the Chatsworth party. Irked at the memory, she tore open the gas bill. It was mercifully low, since she hadn't turned the heat on for over three months.

The phone bill was another matter. Judith's head reeled as she saw a balance of almost four hundred dollars. Calling back out-of-area guests always brought her monthly charges in at around a hundred, but quadrupling that amount was outrageous. It must be a mistake. She flipped through what seemed like the endless pages of the bill to discover the error.

There were calls to Bangkok, Paris, Geneva, Yokohama, Hong Kong, New York, Sydney, Los Angeles, and other cities Judith had seen only in her dreams. Or, in this case, nightmares. She scanned the dates: All of the expensive long-distance charges had been compiled over a three-day period which coincided with the Chatsworth party's stay at Hillside Manor. In fact, the cutoff date of the bill was the very day that Dagmar and company had checked out. Judith was furious. No wonder she and Joe had heard foreign accents on the other end of the line! Dagmar—or Agnes or Freddy—had been making round-the-world toll calls.

Angrily, Judith bundled up the bills, jammed them inside the ledger, and tossed everything into her open suitcase. She'd deal with her accounting tomorrow. She'd also have to deal with Dagmar. The timing was terrible, given the recent tragedy, but guests were not allowed to charge long-distance calls to the Hillside Manor number. Judith refused to get stuck for three hundred dollars she hadn't spent.

Sitting on the edge of the bed, she peered out through the window that overlooked the inner courtyard. Some of the condos had kept their porch lights on. At least one of those belonged to the Chatsworth party. But otherwise, the complex was dark. Judith wondered if Dagmar was asleep, or if she was still suffering guilt pangs over Agnes Shay's demise. One thing was certain, Judith thought while gritting her teeth— Dagmar wasn't worrying about Hillside Manor's big phone bill.

Judith was about to lie back down in bed when the gate that led to the road swung open. A small figure reeled across the courtyard, then stumbled to the third door down on the opposite side of the complex. Several moments passed before the door was opened. Judith couldn't see who was inside, but she knew that the unsteady newcomer was Freddy Whoa.

Ordinarily, Judith was cheerful in the morning. She had to be, with a dining room full of guests awaiting breakfast at Hillside Manor. But on this particular clear, sunny Tuesday in the coffee shop of the Bugler Village Inn, Judith was glum. Renie, who normally didn't shift into full gear until about ten o'clock, was forced to coax a smile out of her cousin.

"Look—pancakes, pan-fried trout, waffles, farm-fresh eggs, kippers, ham, English muffins, lamb kidneys. These are a few of my favorite things. What'll you have?"

Judith didn't even look at Renie. Nor did she consult the menu. "Coffee and toast. I'm not hungry." Her forlorn gaze stared vacantly at a mural that featured athletic men and women performing all manner of outdoor endeavors from windsurfing to white-water rafting. "Besides, you know I hate lamb kidneys," she finally added. "How can you eat internal organs, especially from a sweet little animal?"

Renie smiled in a faintly evil way. "Easy. I imagine that the lamb who gave up his kidneys was the black sheep of the family." Failing to get so much as a smirk from Judith, Renie slapped the menu down on the table. "Okay, you're pissed off because Rhys Penreddy didn't invite you to hop on the police parade float. Big deal. Are you going to let that spoil our stay at Bugler? I didn't understand that we had come here merely to solve a crime. I sort of thought we made the trip to relax and enjoy ourselves. If I felt that the only way you could have a good time was by finding a dead body, I'd have strangled Ginger at Chez Steve's Salon for giving me this stupid haircut, and saved us a four-hour drive from Heraldsgate Hill."

Renie's diatribe had finally captured Judith's attention. The cousins both had their hair done at Chez Steve on Heraldsgate Hill. Judith went to Steve; Renie was a client of his wife, Ginger.

"Ginger did *that* to you? I thought you liked each other."

Relieved that Judith was returning to normal, Renie raked a hand through her thick, straight chestnut mane. "It wasn't her fault. Bill saw a picture in a magazine that he thought would look good on me. I said I'd try it, but Ginger warned me that the model didn't have as much hair as I do. Plus, she probably combed it once in a while."

"Probably." Judith's tone was dry. Renie was, as Judith secretly phrased it, hair-impaired. She had no knack for styling and not enough patience even to try. "Hasn't Bill figured out that this isn't you?"

Renie's face was genuinely puzzled. "No. He hasn't said a

word. I've been waiting now for almost three weeks."

Judith had to admire Renie's wifely courage. And patience. She also felt compelled to tell her cousin about the huge phone bill. Renie's reaction was mixed.

"You brought *work* with you? What kind of getaway is *that*?"

Judith assumed an appropriately shamefaced countenance. "I thought distance would give me perspective. It would have, too, only now it turns out that my problem is *long* distance. How do I confront Dagmar?"

"Simple," Renie replied. "Present her with the bill. If she doesn't pay it, put it on her bank card. You've got the number, I assume?"

Judith did. She brightened at her cousin's suggestion. "That would be more tactful in this instance. I really feel awkward bringing it up now that Agnes is dead. What if she was the one who made the calls? On Dagmar's behalf, of course."

The waitress came to take their order. Renie went for the French toast, scrambled eggs, lamb kidneys, coffee, and tomato juice. Judith's spirits had picked up sufficiently so that she could allow herself the luxury of blueberry pancakes, panfried trout, orange juice, and coffee. Indeed, as the waitress departed, Judith showed signs of elation.

"Look!" she exclaimed, keeping her voice down and nodding to her right. "There's the kid from the lift shack. He's by himself and just sat down. Let's ask him to join us. We'll treat."

Renie looked dubious, but Judith was already on her feet. A minute later, she was back at the table, the young man in tow.

"This is Wayne Stafford," she announced, signaling to their waitress. "He's from Penticton."

Wayne also appeared to be suffering from hunger. Hurriedly, he ordered waffles, two eggs sunny-side up, a slab of ham, four sausages, a large glass of apple juice, and milk.

"This is really nice of you," Wayne declared, his fresh face glowing with pleasure. "Now, what was it you said about *True Crime*?"

Judith avoided Renie's stony gaze. "Ahhh . . . I said that my cousin and I were interested in *True Crime* articles. Serena—

Mrs. Jones—is a graphic designer who works with a number of publications in the States. And I'm . . . involved with police work. My husband's a homicide detective.'' Having spoken a word or two of truth, Judith smiled and relaxed.

Wayne nodded slowly. ''I see. I think. You wanted to ask about the woman on the lift last night?''

''That's right.'' Now Judith was definitely her usual vibrant self. It was Renie's turn to stare off into space. ''We noticed that the police questioned you,'' Judith went on. ''Were they already suspicious?''

Wayne Stafford wasn't the glib sort who provided pat answers. He fingered his dimpled chin and considered. ''Suspicious? Yeah, I guess. That's probably because the lady was dead.''

''Right,'' Judith said in an encouraging voice; then suddenly she frowned. ''You mean she was dead when she got to the bottom of the mountain?''

Wayne nodded again. ''The chair stopped, like it always does, but she didn't get out. The lift here on Fiddler is very high-tech, operating not only on the opening and closing of the safety bar, but on a weight factor that determines if the chair is occupied. When somebody gets on or off the lift at either end, it automatically starts up again. But this time nothing happened. Now, sometimes kids do weird stuff, especially in the summer when they aren't carrying skis. You'd really be surprised at the stunts they pull.'' Wayne looked very serious, as if his own mischief-making years were a millennium behind him. ''They jump off when they get near the ground or clown around and try to rock the chairs. Then there are the people who are nervous about jumping down or have trouble with the safety bar, or whatever. I have to leave the shack and help them.''

Wayne stopped speaking as the waitress poured coffee for the cousins. ''I saw this lady just sitting there, sort of slumped down, and I thought maybe she was sick,'' he continued. ''I went over to her and asked what was wrong. She didn't say anything. I figured she'd passed out.'' Wayne's youthful face grew disturbed. ''I gave her a little shake, and there wasn't any kind of reaction. I undid the bar and she just sort of fell on top of me. I kind of dragged her over by the shack. The lift started up again. Then I hurried inside the shack and called the emergency number. Sometimes we get people who are scared of riding the lift or have hurt themselves up on the mountain and need help. I thought maybe the lady had passed out from fright. You know—she fainted, or something.''

Judith nodded with understanding. ''You've got a lot of responsibility, Wayne. Do you do this year-round?''

Wayne shook his head. ''Oh, no. Only in the summer. I go to university in Port Royal the rest of the time.''

Juice and milk arrived next. Renie decided to join the discussion. ''Did you think she was dead when you called the emergency personnel?''

Wayne's long face became even more troubled. ''I didn't know. I'd never seen a dead person before. But I knew something was really wrong. People started to come over and see what was happening.'' His expression turned rueful. ''Having somebody lying on the ground will do that, I guess.''

''It's a grabber,'' Renie allowed.

''It seemed like forever before the ambulance and the police and the rest of them got there,'' Wayne said, his hazel eyes faintly misted. ''I felt like I was in a daze, or something. Some other lady came running up to me, but Ivor—he's the security guy who works the lift area—told her to back off. I thought I heard her say she knew the woman who was on the lift.''

Judith hesitated, then asked if the new arrival was a good-looking blonde. Wayne said she was, though sort of old. Judith winced. Tessa Kreager was still in her thirties, but Wayne perceived her as getting up there. The young man probably regarded the cousins as at Death's Door.

Breakfast was served. Wayne stared at Renie's lamb kidneys. ''What's *that*?'' he asked in a horrified voice.

Renie glowered at their guest. ''Kidneys. Your name's Stafford, right? You must be of English ancestry. So are we. My grandfather Grover taught me to love and admire lamb kidneys. They're quite a treat.'' She popped half a kidney in her mouth and sighed with ecstasy.

Wayne looked appalled. He turned to Judith, who was wearing an ironic expression. ''Ignore her,'' Judith urged. ''She also eats bat wings and bird beaks.''

''Do not,'' countered Renie with her mouth full.

Judith paid no heed to her cousin. "So what happened after the emergency personnel arrived?"

Wayne didn't answer until he'd finished pouring maple syrup on his waffles. "I sort of stayed in the background. But then I heard somebody say that the lady was dead. The police came over and started asking me questions. I told them just about the same thing I'm telling you. Except maybe I was sort of incoherent last night."

"No wonder," Judith remarked. There was a silence while the trio ate and, presumably, engaged in deep thought. "Tell me," Judith said to Wayne at last, "did you see anything unusual? Like at the top or bottom of the lift?"

The question seemed to catch Wayne off guard. "No," he answered in a deliberate manner. "No, everything was normal. Of course, I was studying. I'm in the prelaw program."

Judith recalled the scene: Darkness was settling in, with the lightning storm blazing across the sky. Quite a few diners had left the restaurant at roughly the same time, including the cousins and the Chatsworth party. That was natural, since so many of the customers had arrived at Crest House right around seven o'clock. Meanwhile, down below in the lift shack, Wayne Stafford was absorbed in his textbook. His routine was broken only by visitors like Judith and Renie who came to the window to ask if they needed to pay for the ride up the mountain. Or, Judith thought with a pang, Wayne's studies were also disrupted when a dead woman's arrival at the bottom brought the lift to a jarring halt.

"By any chance," Judith inquired with a self-deprecating smile, "do you recall the people who got off the lift just before or after Ms. Shay?"

"Shay?" Wayne's face puckered slightly. "Was that her name? No one told me. After the police showed up, I had to keep out of the way, too." He paused, cutting up a sausage. "Gee, I honestly wasn't paying much attention. Nobody was right behind her. That's not unusual. But I think there was an older man about two chairs back. He got real impatient when the lift stopped and yelled at me, in English and French. I don't remember who was behind him. I was too busy trying to cope with the dead lady." Again Wayne hesitated. "Before she got down—I don't know. I looked up when the lift stopped. Near the shack, I think there was a tall guy in kind of a hurry, and a couple holding hands, all wrapped up in each other. Oh, and a kid in a baseball cap who was doing the hip-hop thing. I suppose maybe he was plugged into a Walkman. But I don't know if any of them came off the lift.'' Wayne's expression was apologetic.

Judith smiled again, this time in reassurance. ''That's okay, Wayne. There's no reason why you should have noticed anybody. I don't suppose you've heard any news about the autopsy?''

Wayne hadn't, and judging from his shudder, he didn't care to, at least not while he was eating. The cousins changed the subject, asking about Wayne's upbringing in Penticton, his choice of law as a career, and his less gruesome experiences at Bugler. He explained that this was his second summer at the resort, and while his job was boring, it gave him time to study. His original desire to become an attorney sprang from his favorite TV show, ''L.A. Law.'' But since starting college two years earlier, he had realized that being a lawyer wasn't all glamour and glitz.

''Lawyers get a lot of criticism,'' Wayne said in a serious voice, polishing off his ham. ''It's not fair. They help people. They fight for justice. They're the bulwark of democracy, and where would we be without them? If it weren't for lawyers, this country wouldn't be a land of opportunity, freedom, and equality. Regardless of race, religion, or national origin, every man, woman, and child is equal under the law.''

Judith was stirred by Wayne's honest, if youthfully naive, speech. She felt like standing up and singing ''The Star-Spangled Banner.''

And then she remembered that she was in Canada.

''Gosh,'' Renie exclaimed in mock surprise as they wandered into the village square, ''how often do we get to spend forty bucks on breakfast? What do we do for lunch, graze in the Alpine meadows?''

Judith tried to hide her chagrin. ''I thought Wayne might be able to give us some helpful information. Unfortunately, he didn't have any.''

''Oh, well.'' Renie was determined to enjoy herself. ''We've got our discount for The Bells and Motley tonight.

Why don't we grocery-shop now, eat breakfast in for the rest
of our stay, and have a steak dinner Wednesday night?''

The plan sounded good to Judith. Somewhat oddly, at least
to her mind, Bugler had only one supermarket. Predictably, it
was crowded. The cousins stocked up on necessary items,
knowing they would have to take any leftovers home. They
were in the lengthy checkout queue when Tessa Kreager got
in line behind them.

Judith couldn't hide her surprise. Tessa hardly struck her as
a typical grocery shopper. Yet the cart she clutched was well
filled, including some of the same basic products the cousins
had selected. In addition, Judith noted she had a dozen cans
of chicken broth, a large jar of what looked like concentrate
for a hot beef drink, two packages of the Canadian cure-all
222, various doggie treats, flea powder, and some sort of pesticide for termites.

''How's Dagmar?'' Judith asked after the three women had
exchanged somewhat stilted greetings.

Tessa's fine features were definitely out of sorts. ''She's
taken to her bed.'' Tessa's slim hand waved over the grocery
cart, as if casting a spell. ''She won't go out and she refuses
to eat properly. Almost all of this is for her or that wretched
Rover. I'm going to be mixing up beef broth in a mug, for
heaven's sake! Good God, in New York I cook only for company! And then I hire help. Why did Agnes have to get herself
killed? Nobody ever told me that an executive editor could
turn into a dogsbody!''

Judith was about to commiserate, but Tessa raged on. ''I
mean that literally. I also have to walk the damned dog! I've
got him tied up outside right now.'' She nodded toward the
entrance. Sure enough, Rover was sitting on his haunches,
panting and looking expectant.

''Let him loose,'' Renie muttered. ''Maybe a moose will
eat him.'' Luckily, Tessa didn't hear her. The cousins and the
executive editor moved up a space.

''Dagmar is absolutely racked with grief,'' Tessa went on,
now lowering her voice and once more allowing the Southern
drawl to creep into the nuances. ''Karl wants to call a doctor,
but I don't think that would help. I've worked with high-strung
authors before. They have to get a grip on themselves. I refuse

to pamper my writers, no matter how much money they bring into the publishing house.''

"It's shock," Judith remarked. "And loss, of course. Personal as well as professional. Dagmar was obviously very dependent on Agnes."

Tessa snorted. "Dagmar treated Agnes like dirt. The same way she's trying to treat me. But, of course, I won't permit it. A lot of good it did Agnes, letting Dagmar push her around!" Tessa now seemed genuinely angry. The three women moved up another notch; Tessa almost banged into the cousins with her aggressive grip on the grocery cart. "Being a subservient little mouse got Agnes murdered, that's what happened!" Tessa's voice now rang out across the checkout stands. Heads turned; scanning stopped; all eyes seemed riveted on Tessa Kreager.

Tessa blushed and hung her fair head. "Sorry. I lost control. But it's not privileged information," she added in a defensive tone. "Rhys Penreddy told us this morning that Agnes was murdered. Her head was bashed in. The police are looking for her killer, and whoever it may be, he or she is probably right here in Bugler. They've put up a roadblock on the highway."

Judith couldn't recall when grocery shopping had proved so interesting. Granted, at Falstaff's Market on Heraldsgate Hill, there was often a piece of intriguing gossip to be picked up in the produce section or a fascinating tidbit about her checkers' personal lives as she passed through the cashier's stand. But learning that the autopsy of Agnes Shay had proved her death to be a homicide diverted Judith from the pain of a sixty-eight-dollar grocery tab. She was even willing to wait for Tessa to emerge from the supermarket.

Renie, however, proved less patient. "We have an eleven o'clock appointment with the condo realtors," she reminded Judith. "It's almost ten now. We've got to go up to Clarges Court, put this stuff away, then come back down to the promotion office."

But Judith was obdurate. "We've got tons of time," she assured Renie. "I've got some questions for Tessa."

Next to them, Rover strained at his leash. Annoyed, Renie juggled her share of the groceries. "Ask her when we get back to Clarges Court. She's headed there, too."

"I want to talk to her alone," Judith insisted. Fortunately, Tessa was now exiting the store. She didn't seem too pleased to see the cousins lingering near Rover.

Judith's manner was diffident. "Mrs. Kreager, I hate to intrude, but—"

Tessa wasn't about to allow Judith an opening. "I'm known professionally by my maiden name, Tessa Van Heusen. Excuse me, I must get Rover and go back to the condo. Dagmar needs her zwieback." Tessa's tone was sarcastic, her manner cold.

Judith refused to surrender. "But I was wondering if you knew that Dagmar had been receiving . . ."

Tessa's attention was focused on Rover. She unfastened the leash and led him away. Judith was left with her words of inquiry fading on her lips.

"Bitch," Judith muttered. "And I don't mean Rover." Angrily, she also began to stride down the covered mall toward the parking lot.

"Coz," Renie said in a pleading tone as she hurried to catch up with Judith's long legs, "give it a rest. The police don't need you, Tessa doesn't want you, and probably Dagmar would ask you to butt out, too."

"Listen!" Judith stopped so abruptly that Renie ran into her. "You don't get it, coz! It doesn't matter what the police and Tessa and Dagmar and the rest of them think! Agnes Shay has been killed, right under my nose, and I feel a personal obligation to help find out who murdered her. I don't give a rat's ass if everybody in this whole fancy, ritzy, glitzy, world-class resort looks at me like I'm some dopey freeloader from Heraldsgate Hill. A woman has been murdered, there's a killer out there, and I'm going to do my damnedest to find out who it is! You got it?"

"I think so." Renie's voice was unnaturally meek.

"Good." Judith started down the three steps that led from the mall to the parking area. Her arms were filled, so she gestured with her head. "You see those mountains?" Renie replied that she certainly did. Judith gave her cousin a tight little smile. "I'm like those climbers. Why do I have to solve the mystery? *Because it's there.* That's why."

Renie waited for Judith to turn her back. Only then did she dare roll her eyes.

SEVEN

THE GROCERIES WERE put away, the door to the balcony had been opened to let in the fresh mountain air, and the beds had been made. The one flaw in the condo stay was the absence of maid service. But the cousins weren't accustomed to letting others do their work. Judith had a cleaning woman, but Phyliss Rackley's duties were restricted to the rooms used by guests. Judith did the rest of the house herself.

Succumbing to the spate of domesticity, Judith went into the courtyard to pick wildflowers for the dining room table. There were red and lavender poppies, white oxeye daisies, and purple valerian. She was pleased with her bouquet, and startled when an eager voice called her name.

"Mrs. Flynn! Yo! It's me, your favorite ex-jockey! Want to ride the horsie?"

Freddy Whobrey was standing in front of the condo that Judith had seen him enter the previous night. She considered fleeing inside her own unit, then steeled herself. She had made a vow, and Freddy might be part of the means to keep it.

Smiling feebly, she stood her ground and let him approach. His step was sprightly, though his eyes were blood-shot.

"That's wild about Agnes, huh?" Freddy said in a confidential manner. "Hey, pretty flowers! You going to get naked and wallow in them on your bed of pleasure?''

Judith tried not to gnash her teeth. "No, Freddy, I'm going to stick them . . . in a vase. How is Dagmar? We ran into Tessa at the grocery store, and she said Dagmar was miserable."

Freddy shrugged. "Dagmar's always miserable. It's part of being Dagmar." He plucked a pair of sunglasses from the pocket of his plaid sport shirt. "Whooey! That sun's bright! How did it get to be morning so early?"

Judith ignored the rhetorical question. "Have the police got any leads?" She felt foolish asking Freddy, but wanted to avoid anything that might lead to more personal matters.

Placing the sunglasses on his nose, Freddy now lighted a cigarette and inhaled appreciatively. "Leads! How bright do you think the cops are in an out-of-the-way place like this? Foreigners, too. But then, cops anywhere aren't exactly brainy, are they?"

Judith bristled. "That's unfair. If you knew any real policemen, you'd know how hard they work and how many obstacles are put in their way and how much of a risk they take every day."

Freddy had the grace to look embarrassed. "Sorry. I forgot your old man is a cop. I thought he just liked to go around shooting people." The ex-jockey sidled up to Judith. "You see, the security guys who work the tracks aren't always the swiftest nags in the starting gate, if you get my meaning."

Judith did. She also got a whiff of Freddy's cigarette. It was a Canadian brand, and very strong. She pretended she didn't regret giving up smoking. She also pretended she could tolerate Freddy's nearness. Indeed, she had to pretend to tolerate Freddy, period.

"Have the police questioned Dagmar or the Kreagers? Or you?" Judith asked, trying to edge a few steps away.

Freddy was gazing at Judith's bustline, which wasn't much below his eye level. "Huh? Oh, the cops. Yeah, right, they talked to the Kreagers this morning. And me. I don't know doo-dah. I'd headed for the bar." He winked at Judith. "I ran into an old chum. Too bad it was a guy. I walked him home about midnight."

Across the courtyard, Judith saw Renie in the doorway of

their condo, apparently wondering what was taking her cousin so long.

"And Dagmar?" Judith pressed on. "Did the police talk to her?"

"Naw." Freddy dropped his cigarette, but didn't bother to extinguish it. "She was too overcome, or whatever you call it. They're coming back this afternoon."

Judith stepped on Freddy's cigarette and ground it out on the pavement. The weather was too warm and the surroundings too dry to allow a cigarette to go unattended. Gingerly, Judith kicked the butt into the flower bed. She ignored Renie's beckoning hand.

"Has anyone asked why Agnes was wearing Dagmar's turban and scarf?" Judith inquired.

Freddy also noticed Renie. He waved in an exaggerated manner. Renie made a disparaging gesture. "Is that your chaperone?" Freddy looked bemused. "She's little, but I'll bet she's tough. Some of those smaller fillies can really put out at five and a half furlongs."

As if to prove the point, Renie charged into the courtyard. "Get a move on, coz," she shouted, not bothering to acknowledge Freddy. "We're due at the condo office in fifteen minutes."

Caught between the peremptory Renie and the uncooperative Freddy, Judith surrendered. She murmured a farewell and hurried to join her cousin. Freddy wandered off in the direction of the hot tub. Judith figured he was looking for unsuspecting teenaged girls. She hoped they would be savvy enough to turn him over to Rhys Penreddy and the Bugler police force.

"Jerk," Judith muttered, arranging her wildflowers in a mauve ceramic vase. "He's completely unhelpful. I wanted to know why Agnes was wearing Dagmar's turban."

Renie admired Judith's bouquet. "Isn't it obvious? She went back to get the turban and scarf from the washroom, where Dagmar had left them."

But Judith shook her head in a decisive manner. "No, no, no. Agnes fetched Dagmar's things from the washroom, yes. But she would have carried them, not worn them. Only a puckish sort would have put on Dagmar's turban. Agnes wasn't the type."

Renie wasn't entirely convinced. "We didn't really know Agnes," she pointed out. "We saw her as docile and eager to please. Maybe she had a mischievous streak we never noticed."

It was Judith's turn to be skeptical. "I doubt it. There was nothing playful about Agnes. And I certainly don't see her joking around with Dagmar. Wearing her employer's turban is almost a sign of disrespect, a sort of mocking gesture. Unless . . ." Judith paused in the act of picking up her handbag and preparing to leave the condo. "Agnes might have wanted to free up her hands to get on the chairlift. She probably had to carry her purse, and who knows what else Dagmar was bringing down from Crest House?"

The cousins descended the carpeted stairs to the garage. At the far end, a family of four was loading windsurfing equipment onto the top of a van. For the first time, Judith studied the other cars that were parked underground. There were no more than a dozen at this late hour of the morning. Some were obviously rentals, and the rest were fairly modest.

"I wonder how Dagmar and her group got here," Judith mused as Renie waited for the automatic gate to go up. "A limo, maybe?"

"Could be." Renie cautiously negotiated the winding driveway. "I figure that most of the people staying at Clarges Court are freeloaders like us. The actual owners probably come for the ski season. Karl and Tessa may be the exception to the rule. But living in New York, they're probably glad to get away to the West Coast during the summer."

Renie's rationale made sense to Judith. But the parking situation at the village was quite different from that of Clarges Court. The cousins couldn't find a space in the big outdoor lot, and after much driving around narrow one-way streets that were under construction, they ended up in a vast underground garage. Confused as to where they were in terms of the village square, they finally emerged near the grocery store and had to backtrack to the real estate office. They were three minutes late for their eleven o'clock appointment.

Marin Glenn accepted their apologies with a toss of her punk-rocker coiffure. She was not much younger than the cousins, but her flared miniskirt, poet's shirt, and Roman sandals winding halfway up her calves indicated that she was fighting middle age every inch of the way. The attire should have looked absurd, but somehow Marin had sufficient aplomb to carry it off. Judith, in her tan slacks and navy pocket-T, felt a pang of envy.

Marin led them into a big, open area with partitioned offices on one side. She offered coffee, which the cousins accepted, then sat them down at a square table not quite in the center of the room. There were at least six other tables with potential customers going over rate sheets and catalogs with cheerful, canny salespeople as their guides.

Flipping open an imitation charcoal leather binder, Marin smiled brilliantly at Judith and Renie. "I'm the Clarges Court rep. Our company owns ten condos in the area. We're building two more. But that's not the best part. We have holdings all over the world—surf, turf, sun, ski. You name it, we've got it. Are you interested in time-share or buying outright?"

Shifting uneasily in her chair, Judith hedged. "At this point, we're just getting the feel of the place. I've never been here before, and in fact, this is my first experience staying in a condo like—"

Impatiently, Renie waved a hand. "Cut to the chase. Mrs. Flynn is married to a city cop; my husband's a college prof. We haven't saved money since the war-bond drive in grade school. Neither of us can afford to pay for staying in a birdbath on a regular basis. You might as well save your breath, Ms. Glenn."

Horrified by Renie's candor, Judith tensed in her chair. She expected Marin Glenn to react with dismay, embarrassment, or even anger. Instead the realtor's smile widened, and she shut her binder with a satisfied air.

"Terrific," she declared. "I love it when people are frank. Now," she continued, leaning toward the cousins and lowering her voice, "tell me everything about the woman from Clarges Court who was murdered. I've been cooped up in this office all morning and haven't heard a word."

Startled as well as relieved, Judith recited the bare bones of the case. Marin was enthralled to learn that not only were the cousins sharing the same condo building with the victim and her companions, but that they had actually been on the lift when Agnes's body had come down the mountain.

"Amazing!" Marin ran a hand through her spiky hair. "Eyewitnesses, as it were. I don't suppose the police know who did it yet?"

Judith shook her head. "We haven't heard anything. But that doesn't mean much. After all, we're basically tourists." She hadn't mentioned her own ill-fated attempt to help with the investigation.

Marin's demeanor grew more serious. "It's an awful thing. I've been working for this company nearly eight years, though Clarges Court was completed only last summer. I'd hate to see a murder scare off buyers." Apparently Marin noticed Judith flinch and Renie blanch at her words. "Excuse me, I don't mean to sound callous. But Bugler is a relatively new venture, and those of us who've been here a while take not only a proprietary but a very personal view of what goes on." She grimaced slightly. "You know what I mean—how would you feel if you owned an inn or a motel and some poor guest got killed?"

Judith felt the color rise in her cheeks. She recalled how upset she'd been almost four years earlier when a fortune-teller had been poisoned at her dining room table. Hillside Manor was barely on its shaky yearling's legs when disaster had struck. Judith had been sure that the adverse publicity would ruin business. But somehow, it hadn't. She, who was credited with a deep understanding of people, was the first to admit that she couldn't always predict their behavior.

To make amends for her rash judgment of Marin, Judith put on her most sympathetic face. "It's true, the full-time residents must be very proud of what's been achieved here. And it's really first-rate. Believe me, if we could afford to buy in, we'd love to!"

Renie looked away. There were times when her cousin's enthusiasm and good heart were too much. This was one of those times. But Marin accepted Judith's peace offering in good faith.

"I've read Dagmar Chatsworth's columns over the years, of course," Marin said in a confidential tone. "But I never met her. I do know the Kreagers, though. I sold them their condo last fall. I got their name through a referral agency.

They were looking for a year-round resort spot, either in North America or Europe.'' The realtor's mouth twisted slightly. ''The commission was grand, but as a rule, once the sale is final, I seldom have contact with the buyers again. Not so with Mrs. Kreager—or Ms. Van Heusen, I should say. Instead of bringing her problems before the condo owners' co-op, she calls *me*. Teenagers playing loud music at poolside, termites in the woodwork, the fireplace not drawing properly! She's a property owner. The problems are hers, not mine, and I'll bet she didn't open the damper in the first place.'' Marin suddenly looked shamefaced. ''Sorry. I sound as if I'm bad-mouthing our clients *and* our condos. I'm not. Most of the people I deal with are wonderful. And the units are amazingly worry-free, especially when you consider our hard winters. But Ms. Van Heusen called again yesterday, to complain about a window that didn't shut quite right. I'm afraid I was rather abrupt with her.''

Judith had now regained her composure. ''Do they come here often?''

Marin's expression was droll. ''Are you asking if they own the condo exclusively? Yes, they do, which isn't as rare as you'd think. I suppose that's why Ms. Van Heusen thinks she has a right to gripe. Some people prefer to make their own arrangements instead of being on a time-share basis. It offers a lot more flexibility.''

Renie was gazing into her Styrofoam coffee cup. ''You'd have to be rich, though,'' she remarked in a slightly wistful voice.

''The Kreagers are that,'' Marin declared, hastily adding, ''Which is a well-known fact. I'm not betraying any secrets.''

Judith, who had drifted a bit, put a question to Marin: ''It looks to me as if the Kreagers have more than one condo. At least their guests seem to be staying in separate units. How does that work?''

Marin's answer came easily. ''Actually, the Kreagers are using two condos at the moment, but they can be divided into separate apartments, like yours. They own one and arrange with their neighbors to lease the other. The Kreagers often bring guests along, usually writers. Wait just a minute.'' With a bounce to her step, Marin hurried off to one of the partitioned cubicles. She returned a moment later with a smaller charcoal binder.

"I keep track of who stays where at Clarges Court. Here," Marin said, opening the binder and moving her finger down a page at the back. "The Kreagers are in the upstairs of the unit they bought, Freddy Whobrey is downstairs, and Dagmar Chatsworth occupies the main floor of the neighboring unit on their left. The poor woman who was killed, Agnes Shay, was in the basement section, below Mrs. Chatsworth. The Kreagers were lucky to find the vacancy next door this time of year. But, of course, they probably made their arrangements well ahead of their stay."

Briefly, Judith reflected. Karl and Tessa Kreager would have known in advance when Dagmar would go on tour for her book. Naturally, Agnes would come along. But Freddy was another matter. Judith wondered if Dagmar's nephew always traveled with his aunt.

". . . it's all a tax write-off or a business expense." Marin was speaking, presumably in response to a question from Renie about the living arrangements. Judith gave a start. She had been deep in her own thoughts and had missed the exchange between Marin and her cousin.

Renie was looking amused. "I asked Ms. Glenn how long the Kreagers originally intended to stay at Bugler. She said eight days. But Dagmar and the others planned to leave Thursday. We were wondering if the police have asked them to remain in Bugler until the murderer is caught."

Judith caught the drift of the conversation she'd missed. "Oh—well, maybe. It probably gets complicated, because officially, they're foreigners."

Marin gave a nod of her punk-styled head. "Exactly. But I was telling your cousin that power and money carry a lot of weight around here. The Kreagers have both. He's a publishing magnate, and she's got wealth of her own."

Judith recalled that Tessa's maiden—and professional—name was Van Heusen. "Shirts?" she asked.

The guess was wrong. "No," Marin replied, "tobacco. No relation to shirts. These Van Heusens are from your Southern states. The Carolinas, I think. Deep roots, old money, new diversification. The tobacco industry has had to move into

other areas, since so many people have stopped smoking.''
Marin looked as if she wished she weren't one of them.

A glance at her watch showed Judith it was going on noon.
The appointment had been scheduled for an hour, and since it
had proved without profit for Marin Glenn, Judith felt that she
and Renie shouldn't impose any longer. Still, she had one
more question for the saleswoman.

''There's never been a problem with the Kreagers before, I
assume.'' Judith spoke casually, almost with disinterest.

''No,'' Marin answered, then frowned. ''Well, not a problem as such, but now that you mention it, there was an incident
last winter.''

Judith presented an encouraging face. ''Oh? What was
that?''

Marin looked a bit pained, as if she weren't certain she
should be revealing her clients' secrets. ''It was in January,
the height of the ski season. A young man broke into Clarges
Court while the Kreagers were up on Fiddler Mountain. The
alarm went off, and he was caught out in the courtyard.'' Hesitating, Marin took a last sip of her now-cold coffee. ''This is
what's so odd about it, and why I almost forgot it happened.
The man insisted he wasn't a burglar, that he knew the Kreagers and was supposed to have been given the security code so
he could let himself in. But Mr. Kreager said that wasn't true.
Yet no charges were filed. I never did figure out exactly what
was going on.''

Judith couldn't figure it out, either, which was hardly sur-
prising, given the sketchy information. The cousins thanked
Marin Glenn for her time; she thanked Judith and Renie for
sharing their personal account of Agnes Shay's demise.

''Whew!'' Renie exclaimed in relief as they got out of the
elevator and headed for the village square. ''I was afraid we'd
end up buying a condo and then spend the rest of our lives in
debtors' prison! Aren't you glad I spoke up?''

Judith was about to express restrained admiration for Renie
when Rhys Penreddy came toward them. Or at least he was
headed for the office building that housed the condo headquarters. Ignoring Renie's tug at her arm, Judith marched
straight up to the police chief.

"Sir," she began, not certain how to address Penreddy, "remember us?"

Penreddy did, albeit with reluctance. His wide mouth turned down at the corners and suddenly he seemed faintly sheepish. "I was going to lunch and thought I'd save a call to the condo office. I wanted to get your unit number so we could request an official statement. Have you time to drop by the station in the next hour or so?"

Eagerly, Judith assured him that they had plenty of time. In fact, the cousins could go now. Or would Rhys Penreddy care to join them for lunch? They'd love to treat him. Judith pretended she didn't hear Renie groan.

Hardened policeman that he was, Penreddy was nonetheless caught off guard by Judith's impulsive offer. "I've only got a half hour," he protested. "I was just going to grab a sandwich . . ."

Judith was nodding with zeal. She had to refrain from taking Penreddy by the arm and steering him across the square past a juggler, two accordionists, and a young woman playing the cello. "You show us where to get a good sandwich and we'll pay for it. It's our way of apologizing for butting in last night. We sure learned our lesson about meddling in a homicide investigation!"

Penreddy's expression was skeptical. Perhaps he noticed Renie, who straggled behind, aiming a kick at her cousin's rear end. Still, Judith paid no heed. She was almost blissful as the police chief herded them into a small, crowded cafe decorated with rock-climbing gear.

Penreddy's status earned them the first empty table. It was round, and not much bigger than a turkey platter. The trio hunched over the Formica top and studied handwritten menus that featured a long list of sandwiches and soups.

Their orders were taken almost immediately. Penreddy seemed to have inured himself to the cousins' company. Certainly he was trying to put a good face on his situation.

"As long as you're here," he said, pulling his hands off the table to make room for their coffee mugs, "you might as well answer a few questions. When was the last time you saw Agnes Shay alive?"

Judith first explained about seeing Agnes in the washroom,

while Dagmar was there. Then she said that she and Renie both had glimpsed Agnes one last time, in the restaurant.

"Did you see her leave?" Penreddy inquired.

Judith thought carefully back to the scene at Crest House. She glanced at Renie, as if at a prompter. But Renie was still looking disgruntled; she offered no aid.

"No," Judith finally replied. "I didn't see Agnes leave. The last time I saw her alive was when they were standing at their table, getting ready to go." Pointedly, she turned to Renie. "Right, coz?"

Renie brightened, though Judith couldn't tell if the mood change was caused by her natural resiliency or by the steaming bowl of French onion soup the waitress was placing in front of her.

"That's right," Renie agreed. "I don't recall seeing Agnes leave with the others. In fact, I really only remember the Kreagers actually going out of the restaurant. They're both tall. Dagmar and Freddy are short. So was Agnes."

Rhys Penreddy jotted information in a notebook. "You saw none of the others afterward? That is, between then and when you came down on the lift?"

Judith confirmed that they hadn't sighted any members of the Chatsworth party—except the unfortunate Agnes—until reaching Fiddler Lodge. As Penreddy made his notations, Judith mentioned the confrontation between Dagmar and Mia.

"Yes, the restaurant staff told us about that," Penreddy responded, looking grave. "Naturally, we've questioned both Prohowska and Anatoly Linksi."

Over her clubhouse sandwich, Judith eyed Penreddy expectantly. But the police chief revealed no more. Just because the cousins were picking up the tab, Judith couldn't pick his brain.

Nor did Rhys Penreddy have any more questions of his own. He ate his roast beef on Russian rye in silence. Judith felt her frustration mount.

"The weapon," she said, no longer able to keep quiet. "Have you found it?"

Wiping a dab of mayonnaise from his upper lip, Penreddy shook his head. "No."

"Can you tell from the blow what was used?" Judith wasn't giving up without a fight.

Penreddy started to shake his head, then gazed at Judith. His brown eyes twinkled. "A blunt instrument," he said. It appeared that he was having trouble keeping a straight face.

In spite of herself, Judith flushed. Renie giggled, spewing cheese remnants onto the tabletop.

"Oops!" Renie cried, now also embarrassed. Hastily, she wiped the table clean.

"Look," said Rhys Penreddy, leaning as far back in his chair as he dared without bumping into his neighboring diner, "I'm not sure why you're so interested in this case. I can understand your fascination because you knew some of these people from their stay with you, but I must emphasize that it isn't wise to make nuisances of yourselves. Homicide is a very serious business. A woman has been killed, and if the killer feels threatened, he or she won't hesitate to kill again. It's a matter of survival."

Even though Judith had frequently heard these words in one form or another, including from her own husband, she still found them daunting. At least temporarily. She also felt that she owed Rhys Penreddy an explanation.

"I'm married to a homicide detective," she explained. "We discuss his cases quite a bit. Plus, my cousin and I have sort of accidentally been . . ." Her voice trailed off. It wasn't prudent to admit that she and Renie had somehow gotten themselves mixed up in murder on other occasions. The acknowledgment could make a lawman suspicious.

Fortunately, Penreddy was nodding in understanding. "I know. You were accidentally thrown in with the victim and her friends, on not one but two occasions. And I appreciate your honesty. I talk about the job when I get home, too, though luckily, this is my first homicide." He caught himself, and gave Judith a hard stare. "That doesn't mean I'm an amateur, Mrs. Flynn. Police work is police work, as I'm sure your husband will tell you."

Judith was trying to cooperate. She nodded and smiled. Both efforts were feeble. "It's just that . . . I feel challenged."

Penreddy arched his eyebrows. "Challenged? Or competitive?"

Judith's jaw dropped. "What? Oh, no! I would never dream of matching wits with Joe!"

"Good." Penreddy took a last sip of coffee and got to his feet. "Thanks for the lunch. Don't forget to drop by the station and sign those statements. And remember what I said—don't act foolishly. Your safety is our responsibility. Enjoy your visit to Bugler." With a brisk step, the chief of police made his exit from the busy cafe.

Judith was brooding. It had never occurred to her that the sleuthing she had done over the years might be an effort to outdo Joe Flynn. In the beginning, when the fortune-teller was murdered and Joe had reentered her life, maybe she had wanted to show him how clever she was. Joe was still married to Herself then. He and Judith hadn't seen each other in more than twenty years. But now she felt no need to impress him, other than with her desire to be a loving wife. Her attempts at crime-solving were virtual accidents, the result of circumstances over which she had no control.

"I'm an ass," she announced to Renie. Tears welled up in her eyes. "I'm a horrible person and a big fraud."

"You sure are," Renie replied, fingering the lunch bill. "You just blew thirty bucks on a lecture. If the killer doesn't get you, I'll do you in myself."

Renie did not look as if she were kidding.

EIGHT

THE STATEMENTS THAT the cousins made at the police station were brief. They were required to state only when and where they had last seen Agnes Shay alive. Already feeling glum, Judith was disappointed with her limited official contribution.

The young policeman who took their statements noticed her downcast manner. "That's all right," he reassured her, his pleasant smile enhanced by a slight overbite. "It's really hard to find yourself involved in a crime, no matter how coincidentally."

Judith genuinely wanted to explain her exact feelings, but she took note of Renie's warning glance. "It's okay," she mumbled. "I just wish we could be of more help."

"You've been wonderful," the policeman asserted. "Now just go back to Clarges Court and relax. We'll catch the culprit. Never fear, eh?"

The young man's official badge stated that he was Devin O'Connor. His flaming red hair also proclaimed his Irish ancestry, and his green eyes reminded Judith of Joe. However, the resemblance ended there. Devin O'Connor was well over six feet, very thin, and retained a faintly gawkish manner. His nose was slightly hooked, and his face was almost gaunt. Yet he had charm. But Judith had always been a sucker for Irishmen. She had, after all, married two of them.

But they were a sucker for her, Judith knew. She gave Devin O'Connor a tremulous smile. "We had lunch with your chief," she said, and saw Devin's green eyes widen in surprise. "He told us you hadn't yet found the blunt instrument that killed Agnes Shay."

"That's right," he replied, still looking impressed at the apparent intimacy between the two female tourists and his boss. "I didn't realize you knew Chief Penreddy."

Judith waved a hand while Renie turned her back and stomped off toward a bulletin board. "It's all very casual, not what you'd call a close friendship." She wasn't really lying; Judith never did. Or so she always convinced herself. "By the way, did Miss Shay have her purse with her?"

"Good question." Devin wagged an approving finger at Judith. "No, she didn't. We found it up on Liaison Ledge, along with a bottle of champagne and a doggie bag full of beef." He moved a step closer and his voice lowered a notch. "The poor lady must have dropped the stuff when she was killed."

"Ah." Judith's black eyes darted swiftly to the stiff figure of Renie and back to Devin O'Connor. "That was just outside the restaurant?"

"No, it was right by the lift." Devin suddenly clamped his mouth shut over his protruding teeth and errant tongue. "Excuse me, I really should get back to my paperwork. There are always so many forms to fill out after a major crime, eh?" With an apologetic gesture, he hurried away.

Judith grabbed Renie by the upper arm. "Stop sulking. I'm the one who's feeling morose."

Renie whirled on Judith. "Dammit, coz, Penreddy's right! One of these days you're going to get us killed! Either that, or we'll end up in the poorhouse! Do you realize we've already spent almost three hundred bucks just on *food*?"

"Since when did you start complaining about paying to eat?" Judith demanded, her own temper catching fire. "I'm the one who feels like a creep. What if Penreddy is right, and I'm competing with Joe?"

"You're competing with Ivana Trump when it comes to spending money on this trip," Renie shot back. "Forget about one-upmanship. You always were a nosy little twit. When we were kids, it was who swiped whose bike or who kissed whom in the raspberry bushes. Now you're into corpses. What's the difference?''

Judith thought the question was rhetorical, but she was wrong. ''Well, I'll tell you,'' Renie went on as they departed the police station. ''Nobody wanted to murder us over a stolen roller-skate key. But this is Murder One, and I don't intend to die in middle age. I'm having too much frigging *fun*.''

Observing Renie's grim expression, Judith burst out laughing. The contrast between word and deed was too much. ''Coz,'' she said, taking Renie's arm, ''*stop*! You haven't been this mad at me since I shot hairspray at your brioche on the steamer up the Rhine in 1964!''

Renie was forced to come to a halt. In agitation, she ran a hand through her short, homely hairdo. Then she grinned at Judith. ''You're right—I'm acting like a brat. But so are you. If you won't stop being an idiot about competing with Joe, at least go easy on this detective stuff.'' Renie paused again, and her brown eyes widened, then narrowed. ''Okay, I get it. For you, chasing killers *is* a vacation. Everybody has to have a hobby. But don't be so damned *obvious*. Let's keep a low profile. Face it, coz, Penreddy's sharp. He may already be on the right track.''

Thoughtfully, Judith nodded. ''You're right. It doesn't pay to advertise. Not in this kind of situation.'' She gave Renie a belated smile of gratitude. ''I'm still an idiot. But you're good enough to forgive me for it.''

Renie shrugged. ''Always have. Fifty years of forgiveness.'' She shot Judith a sidelong glance. ''It works both ways. Big deal.''

Slowly, the cousins walked back to the Chevy, which was parked next to the wood-frame city hall building that housed the police station. Renie was backing out when Judith spoke again:

''You missed hearing the part about where Agnes was killed.''

Renie didn't respond at once. She was concentrating on entering traffic. ''Huh? Where, did you say?''

''You got it—*where*.'' Judith felt faintly smug. ''The police

found her purse and a bottle of champagne and Rover's doggie
bag at the top of the lift.''

Renie's head swiveled. "You mean Agnes was murdered
on Liaison Ledge?"

Judith gave a shrug. "Think about it. Agnes is walking to
the lift. She gets on. The killer comes up behind her and—
bam! Hits her on the back of the head. It's getting dark. The
chairs are spaced at a fairly long interval. Wayne Stafford told
us he didn't think anyone was right behind Agnes on the lift.
So the killer had time to get away. And, of course, Agnes
dropped her belongings. It also explains why she was wearing
Dagmar's things. As we thought, she had her hands full.''

"Gosh." Renie's face was sad. "Poor Agnes. She would
never have gotten killed if she hadn't been wearing that
blasted turban."

Judith didn't respond immediately. "No . . . I suppose not.
The killer came up behind her. He thought she was Dagmar."

Renie had literally reached the fork in the road. "The village or Clarges Court? Do we disport ourselves or shop?"

Judith's black eyes sparkled as she turned to Renie. "We
do neither. Not just now."

Resignedly, Renie headed for the road that led up Fiddler
Mountain. "Okay," she said on a sigh.

Judith didn't say a word. The cousins understood each other
very well. They were headed for Clarges Court, but not to
their own condo. A sympathy call was required, as much by
etiquette as by curiosity.

Five minutes later, Judith was pressing the bell for Karl and
Tessa Kreager's unit. They half-expected a uniformed maid to
greet them, but Karl came to the door. He looked very cool
and comfortable in his white open-neck shirt and custom-
tailored blue jeans. He also looked rather surprised.

Judith explained that she and Renie had come to offer con-
dolences. They had heard that Dagmar was very upset. They
had also understood that Tessa was overwhelmed with unexpected duties. Was there anything they could do to help? After
all, Judith and Renie were their neighbors.

If Karl Kreager believed any or none of Judith's long-
winded introductory remarks, he gave no sign. Instead he gra-

ciously ushered the cousins into the living room. While the condo's layout was identical to the one that Judith and Renie were occupying, the furnishings and decor were quite different. Judging from the period details, the original art, and the color scheme in varying shades of white, the Kreagers had put their personal stamp on the Clarges Court unit.

"Do sit," Karl Kreager urged, indicating a sofa covered with delicate, pale pastel floral upholstery. "May I offer you a drink? Rum, perhaps?"

Renie started to decline, but Judith accepted for both of them. Karl Kreager, she reasoned, couldn't throw them out on their ear if they were drinking his liquor.

After Karl had left the room, Renie made a face. "Rum on top of French onion soup? Gack! I'll be sick as a dog!"

Judith frowned. "Speaking of which, where's Rover? And Tessa? Maybe Freddy is with Dagmar, in the next-door unit. That's where he came from when I saw him in the courtyard."

Renie, of course, couldn't answer Judith's questions. The cousins spent a few moments studying the ivory-colored Louis Quatorze mantel, the Tlingit Indian masks, a Boudin oil painting, and the spotless eggshell carpet.

"Two minutes in our house, and this thing would look like it was one of the major food groups," Renie murmured, moving her left foot over the carpet's plush pile. "Can you imagine anybody keeping a place like this *clean*? Tessa must hire help."

Judith agreed. "I see now why they had to put Rover in the condo next door. He'd have ruined this place." She shuddered, recalling the damage the dog had done to Hillside Manor.

Karl Kreager returned with three rum punches on a tray. They were colorfully decorated with orange and pineapple slices, as well as the inevitable maraschino cherry. Judith congratulated Karl on his bartending skills.

"It's my one talent in the domesticity department," he said in a genial voice as he seated himself on a damask-covered fauteuil chair. "To your health." He raised his glass in a toast.

The words gave Judith an opening. "Speaking of health, how is Dagmar this afternoon?"

Karl's tanned forehead creased. "She's still feeling unwell.

I hope she starts to recover by tomorrow. Dagmar has deadlines to meet, you see.''

Renie set her drink down on a coaster which had already been provided to preserve the bleached pinewood coffee table. Three copies of Dagmar's book were on display next to a nineteenth-century Chinese cachepot. "For the column?" Renie inquired.

Karl nodded, his brow still furrowed. "Yes, she does them two days in advance, though of course we always have to allow for late-breaking news. Dagmar finished Wednesday's piece yesterday afternoon. But the newspapers should have the Friday copy sometime tomorrow.''

Judith made a sympathetic noise. "It'll be hard for her, under the circumstances. She's emotionally distraught, she's lost her secretary, she's three thousand miles from home. By the way, how does she get her information when she's on the road?''

The answer didn't come right away. Karl Kreager was staring off into space, somewhere in the direction of an Emily Carr forest scene. His recovery, however, was smooth, typical of a successful, poised man of affairs:

"Isn't it remarkable how Carr caught the quintessence of British Columbia's raw, natural landscape? In a way, Dagmar is an artist, too. She paints word pictures of celebrities, and captures their core in a few brief lines of copy." He shifted his weight in the exquisite chair. A less graceful man his size might have looked awkward. But Karl Kreager seemed as at home with the eighteenth century as he did with the twentieth. "Dagmar's information is generally culled from a wide variety of sources who phone in on her voice mail. She can access it from anywhere. That's not the problem. It's the writing of it that only she can do, in her customary witty style.''

Judith considered the often scandalous messages that must await Dagmar on a daily basis. The vast range of sources probably explained the long-distance phone calls from Hillside Manor. Judith was scarcely appeased, but at least she understood. Certainly she was justified in billing Dagmar for the toll charges. They must be a tax write-off for the columnist. "These sources must be reliable," Judith remarked. "That is,

Dagmar must trust her informants. Otherwise, there would have to be a great deal of verification.''

"Oh, definitely," Karl agreed. "And occasionally there is an item or a person lacking in credibility. She's always most cautious. Her readers probably wouldn't agree, but as a publisher, I assure you that she's invariably on solid ground.''

Renie had picked up a copy of *Chatty Chatsworth Digs the Dirt* and was flipping through the pages. "Dagmar seems to cover all the bases. Movie stars, singers, models, athletes, politicians, other writers, even business types. I was trying to figure out if the book is a rehash of her columns or new material."

"Both," Karl replied, again looking worried. "In *Dirt*, she uses items from her columns as a springboard, then goes on to update them, or to dig much deeper. That's my primary concern. After all, I'm not responsible for the newspaper columns per se. But the second manuscript is due at the end of September. When we picked her up in Port Royal, she assured me it would be ready, even though she was only halfway finished. Now she says we have to postpone the deadline by at least a month, maybe two. That's not possible, not if Thor is to keep to its production schedule.''

"Can't she hire another secretary?" Judith asked, then winced a little, finding the question heartless.

A faint smile played on Karl's lips. "She'll have to, of course. But she depended so much on Agnes. They'd been together forever.''

Renie exhibited surprise. "Really? Dagmar strikes me as the sort who hires and fires every six months. From Agnes's point of view, I would have thought that working for Dagmar would be difficult.''

"I'm sure it was," Karl allowed. "But when my brother Kurt hired Dagmar fifteen years ago to do a cooking column for his paper in the Twin Cities, she already had Agnes in tow. That's why Dagmar is so bereft. She's never had a different secretary.''

Judith's eyes were wide. "Dagmar started with a cooking column? How odd!''

Karl flicked at a piece of lint on his jeans. "Not really. It wasn't your ordinary cooking column. Dagmar concentrated on recipes from good restaurants—especially the ones that were supposed to be industrial secrets. It wasn't much of a stretch for her to insert gossip about chefs and maître d's and, eventually, customers. Kurt realized that what had started out as a mere filler had become one of the best-read features in the paper. After a while, he asked her to expand and cover the entire Midwest. He ran the columns in all seven of the Kreager dailies. Then, about eight years ago, Dagmar wanted to broaden her horizons, to do an all-purpose gossip column and become nationally syndicated.'' Karl's expression was wry. ''She got her way, and thus was journalistic history made.''

''Fascinating,'' Renie declared, and sounded as if she meant it. ''Your brother—Kurt—he died a year or two ago, right?''

Karl bowed his head, a very formal gesture. ''He did. A heart attack. Untimely, but not unexpected. Kurt did nothing in moderation. Often, his attitude was good for business. But not for his health. Excess has taken many a man too soon.'' The statement was made with a certain amount of satisfaction.

In her mind, Judith was trying to sort out the Kreager publishing empire. It seemed that Kurt had run the newspapers, while Karl had taken over at the book-publishing helm. There were, however, the magazines and the TV and radio stations for which they had not yet accounted. Boldly, Judith asked who was in charge.

''Kirk,'' he replied. ''He's the youngest of us, the one who shuns publicity but carries on the tradition of America First.'' Karl's expression was dour. ''Oh, neither Kurt nor I courted the public eye—that was our father's style. He firmly believed that if you wanted to sell news, you had also to make it.''

Vaguely, from childhood and adolescence, Judith recalled Knute Kreager, a flamboyant man who had made his own headlines by marrying a series of showgirls, grinding the competition under his heel, and, reportedly, holding hands with The Mob. The senior Kreager might have come from Minnesota, but his behavior was atypical. He was material by nature, outrageous by design. The two sides of his character conflicted with standards in the heartland, yet they had worked. Knute Kreager was known for waving the American flag, for beating the drums of anti-Communism, for supporting any national cause whether his country was right or wrong. He had ridden the tide of patriotism and made it pay. Knute Kreager had been a big success, and had thus earned acceptance by his fellow Midwesterners.

"Knute Kreager," Judith echoed. "He was something of a legend."

"Oh, indeed he was." Karl's smile was cynical. "Part of his legend lives today. My brothers and I all had different mothers. A blonde, a brunette, and a redhead. My mother was the blonde."

The statement didn't court comment, which was a good thing, because the cousins didn't seem to have one. Judith was cudgeling her brain, trying to think of a tactful way to ask Karl about the threatening letters, when Tessa burst into the room.

"She's impossible!" Tessa announced, then saw Judith and Renie. "Oh! What are you two doing here?"

Karl saved his guests the arduous task of explaining. "Mrs. Flynn and Mrs. Jones came over to ask about Dagmar and to see if they could help in any way. Would you like to have them relieve you of your nursing duties for an hour or so? We could go for a swim."

The proposal caught Tessa by surprise. It was obvious from her initial reaction that she would have preferred tossing Judith and Renie out into the courtyard. But Karl spoke so smoothly and coaxingly that Tessa was forced into a corner.

"Well . . . why not? I'm getting sick of trying to feed chicken broth to Dagmar."

Judith finished her drink, then got to her feet. "We'd be glad to spell you for a while," she said, trying to tone down the eager note in her voice. "Just point the way."

Tessa did more than that, leading the cousins downstairs, into the parking garage, and over to the door to the neighboring condo.

"She's upstairs, in the big bedroom," Tessa said as Rover ran to greet the newcomers. "Freddy was here for a few minutes, but he's worthless. See if you can get Dagmar to eat a soft-boiled egg."

The door closed firmly behind the cousins. Panting excitedly, Rover adhered himself to Judith as she went up the stairs. The layout was again familiar, yet looked quite different:

Whoever had decorated the unit next to the Kreagers had been partial to Japanese design.

The furnishings were spare and tasteful; the walls appeared to be decorated with rice paper; the smaller windows were shielded by shoji screens; the floors were covered with tatami mats. Rover had chewed up several of them.

Renie had started up the stairs, but Judith hissed at her to wait. "Come here," she whispered, going into the downstairs living room. "This is where Agnes was staying."

"So?" Renie scowled. "We shouldn't snoop. Don't you have any respect for the dead?"

"I do," Judith declared. "I think they should be vindicated." She pointed to a big electric typewriter. "Agnes?"

"Maybe." Renie seemed indifferent.

"Why not a laptop?" Judith strolled from room to room, occasionally giving an ineffectual kick to free herself of Rover's adhesivelike presence. She wondered if the dog could pick up her cat's scent, which must have clung to her clothes.

Renie hung back, impatiently tapping her nails on the rice-paper-covered walls. In her cursory reconnaissance, Judith found the typewriter, a stack of fresh paper, a notebook, and the metal strongbox Phyliss Rackley had mentioned. A quick flip through the notebook showed that a fine hand had written down very small jottings which Judith couldn't read without her glasses. The preponderance of numbers and dates looked more like bookkeeping than juicy gossip items. Judith assumed that the precise penmanship belonged to Agnes Shay.

The rest of the downstairs unit was neat as a pin, except for Rover's various rips and rumples. *Too* neat, Judith thought, returning to the staircase and Renie's sour expression.

"Where are the notes? The copy? The . . . whatever? This doesn't look like the boiler room for a syndicated columnist."

"They're on vacation." Renie resumed climbing the stairs. "Why do you get hung up on trivia? Sometimes you drive me nuts."

"There's no such thing as trivia in a murder case," Judith replied, faintly irritated. "Everything means something. Why, for example, is all the work stuff in Agnes's quarters?"

"Maybe Dagmar didn't want to sully her unit with drudgery," Renie replied indifferently as she rapped on the door to the upstairs unit. There was no answer. She rapped again, then gave the door a hefty kick.

Dagmar's voice was barely audible. Renie stomped into the hallway; Judith tiptoed, with Rover scampering at her heels. Renie headed down the corridor which, she assumed, led to the big bedroom. Sure enough, Dagmar was lying on a futon, propped up by pillows. She wore an apricot peignoir, its lace-edged collar done up to her chin. A faint breeze stirred in the sparsely, if tastefully, furnished room, indicating that although the shoji screens were closed, the windows were partially open. Still, the sun was shut out, and the pervading mood was one of gloom.

"We came to sit with you for a while," Judith said by way of greeting, then glanced around the room. A lacquered bench in front of a mirrored dressing table provided the only seat. There wasn't room for two.

"I'll get a chair," Renie mumbled.

"How kind of you to come," Dagmar said in a lifeless voice. She twisted her beringed fingers on the pale blue down comforter. Rover jumped onto the futon and gazed at his mistress with sad, adoring eyes. Dagmar gazed back. The two seemed to be sharing some deep communion of the soul. "I can't forgive myself," Dagmar murmured, now sounding utterly miserable. "Agnes never harmed a soul. She was selfless, devoted, and without guile." Dagmar was still staring at Rover. Judith wondered if she was mentally comparing her late secretary with the dog. The litany of virtues could have applied to either or both. Except, of course, that Rover was destructive.

"Are you absolutely certain you don't know who sent those threatening letters?" Judith asked, trying to steer Dagmar off her course of guilt.

Dagmar sighed and made a jittery, impatient gesture. "Of course I don't. The local police took them away. Futile, I suspect. How do you trace a computer?"

Judith didn't know. "What about the envelopes?"

Renie had returned, carrying a chair with a bamboo seat that looked as if it belonged to a dining room set. Dagmar rustled around on the pillows, then reached for a glass of juice. "Ordinary Number Ten, no return, the New York City postmark, my address typed by a word processor, and differing only as to destination.''

Judith gave a slight nod. "So whoever sent them knew your itinerary. Surely that narrows the field?"

Dagmar didn't agree. "No. The tour was highly publicized. Anyone with any ingenuity could have gotten hold of where I'd be staying."

"Even here?" asked Judith.

"Certainly. Last month I was silly enough to write about how I looked forward to the Kreagers' hospitality at Bugler. Book tours are grueling. I was already contemplating how I would unwind and recuperate. Plus," she added a bit slyly, "it doesn't hurt to blow Bugler's horn, so to speak. Resorts are sometimes generous to people who can give them free publicity."

Having scarcely broken even on the Chatsworth stay, Judith wondered if Dagmar might spare Hillside Manor a line or two in a future column. She thought not, especially when the long-distance charges showed up on Dagmar's bank card. Judith would be lucky if the columnist didn't allude to her Heraldsgate Hill visit as The Doorway to Death. In her mind's eye she could see the column illustrated with a woodcut of the Danse Macabre, its ghoulish figures beckoning from the sidewalk to the front door. Instead of her own welcoming presence, she glimpsed a gruesome apparition with a rictuslike grin, ready to pitch prospective guests into a fiery furnace. The creature transformed itself: Gertrude in a housecoat, proffering pickled pigs' feet. Judith came back to earth, and was soothed. Sort of. She wasn't entirely convinced that the ghouls were more frightening than her mother.

Renie was speaking, and Judith hadn't heard all of her remarks. ". . . New York with fifteen million people. That eliminates the other two hundred and thirty million in this country, along with thirty million more in Canada."

Dagmar didn't take kindly to Renie's rationale. "So? I could think of two hundred people in Manhattan who might have sent those letters."

"Oh?" Having figured out that Renie was trying to narrow the field of mean-minded letter writers, Judith arched her dark brows. "Then you *do* have an inkling about the sender?"

Dagmar scowled at both cousins, ignoring Rover's sharp little teeth, which were working hard at making holes in the down comforter. "I didn't say *that*. I merely meant that there are quite a few people I've annoyed over the years. Justifiably, on my part. Many of them live in New York City. But I can't think of anyone who would try to kill me."

It was possible, Judith knew, that the letter writer and the killer were two different people. Indeed, it was a stretch to imagine that the person who wrote the threatening letters had come all the way to Bugler to murder Dagmar Delacroix Chatsworth. Why not wait until she returned to Manhattan? Unless, of course, the killer was in Dagmar's own party—or happened to be someone staying at Bugler.

Judith put the question to Dagmar, hoping it wouldn't rile her further. "Where do Mia Prohowska and Nat Linski live when they aren't here?"

"Everywhere," Dagmar replied, the nervous impatience returning. "Switzerland, London, New York." Her eyes narrowed at Judith just as Rover managed to liberate a cloud of down. "Do you think it was *them*? Really, they're impossibly difficult, but I hardly think they're killers! I'm convinced it's a maniac—someone who sees himself—or herself—as an Angel of Vengeance for a celebrity I've criticized. You couldn't possibly understand."

Judith did, however. She realized that there were people—lonely, deranged, and obsessed with famous personages—who wouldn't think twice about murder for the sake of their idol's reputation. History, recent and not-so-recent, proved the point.

Girding for Dagmar's hostility, Judith posed another question: "Were you troubled with threatening phone calls while you stayed at Hillside Manor?"

Dagmar's lips tightened, all but disappearing. "You ought to know. You were there in the very same room when I got one of them."

"One of them?" Judith's gaze was inquiring.

"I must admit, it was the first of the calls," Dagmar said, again growing listless. "There were—what?—two more before I left your hole-in-the-wall. Luckily, I haven't received any since."

Judith ignored the slight of Hillside Manor. "Did you recognize the voice?"

"Of course not." Dagmar's expression showed contempt for the query. "Initially, I thought it was one of my San Francisco sources. But it wasn't. I've no idea who it could be. The voice was disguised, as you might have guessed. What difference does it make—now?"

Briefly, Judith thought about the call that Joe had taken. He had mentioned something about "menace" and "threats." Had the foreign accent been feigned? Would it do any good to press Dagmar further? If she hadn't recognized the first caller, additional questions were useless. Dagmar seemed to have lost interest; Renie was twitching on the bamboo chair; Judith felt frustrated.

Rover, however, didn't give a hoot about human emotions. Bored with decimating the comforter, he leaped onto Judith's lap and licked her nose. "Uh . . ." said Judith, trying to get a grip on the wriggling animal, "can we do anything for you? Something to eat? Egg? Toast? Tea?" The struggle continued as Rover drooled all over her slacks.

Morosely, Dagmar moved about under the comforter. Down floated around the room. Judith stifled a sneeze. Renie got up from her chair and grabbed Rover by the collar, setting him firmly on the floor. Rover clamped his teeth on Renie's shoes. Renie gave him a swift kick. Rover crouched and growled. Renie waved her foot at him.

Fortunately, Dagmar had her eyes closed and didn't notice the byplay. "No, there's nothing I need just now. Nobody can help me." She opened her eyes to reveal tears. "I feel so *alone*."

Judith didn't know how to comfort Dagmar, whose grief seemed genuine. Freddy Whobrey was the only kin Judith knew of, and he didn't strike her as a pillar of strength. The Kreagers were friends of a sort, though Judith sensed that the bond was forged in finance rather than affection.

"Do you have family in Minnesota?" Judith asked, trying to ignore the standoff between Renie and Rover.

Dagmar dabbed at her tears and assumed a vague expression. "Not really. My sister—Freddy's mother—was much older than I. She and her husband have been dead for years. Freddy was born after his parents had given up hope of having children. Then they had Freddy.''

"Instead of a real—'' Renie managed to shut up just in time.

Judith leaped into the breach. "Spoiled, I imagine,'' she put in hastily.

Dagmar nodded. "Pampered, at least. He was small and sickly in his youth. He remained small, but his health improved by the time he reached adolescence. Don't mistake me,'' she went on, wagging a finger. "Freddy is very attached to me. Why, without him and Agnes—'' She choked on her words, cleared her throat, and resumed speaking. "They worked beautifully as a team on my behalf.''

"They got along?'' Judith's voice was casual, despite the distraction of Rover, who apparently had decided that Judith was the less menacing of the cousins and had begun to gnaw on her handbag.

"Certainly they got along,'' Dagmar replied. "Agnes had such a mild disposition and Freddy is always cheerful. As I said, they worked in perfect harmony.''

"They should have made a match,'' Judith said in a distracted manner as Rover sank his teeth into the handbag's leather strap.

Dagmar appeared shocked. "I think not! Really!''

Judith grabbed her bag, trying to wrestle it away from Rover. The doorbell chimes rang, and Renie gave Dagmar a quizzical look.

Dagmar lifted a hand. "By all means, answer it. I suppose it's that Penwhistle person from the police.''

It was. Rhys Penreddy was accompanied by Devin O'Connor, the young Irish officer Judith and Renie had met at the station. O'Connor seemed surprised by the cousins' presence; Penreddy was more appalled.

But the police chief made an effort to be polite. "Excuse me, ladies,'' he said, approaching the futon, "but I was hoping that Ms. Chatsworth was feeling well enough to talk to us. Do you mind?'' He gave the cousins his most appealing smile.

Judith did, but Renie was quick to comply. Resignedly, Judith tugged her handbag away from Rover and bade Dagmar a temporary farewell.

"We'll be back," she declared. "We won't leave you alone."

Dagmar's expression was mixed. She lifted one hand in a desultory wave, then snapped her fingers at Rover, who bounded back onto the futon. The policemen settled in for their interrogation.

Renie got as far as the door to the downstairs unit when Judith grabbed her arm and pulled her in the opposite direction.

"This way," she breathed, nodding toward the front entrance.

"Isn't it closer to go back through the garage?" Renie inquired.

Judith gave her a condescending look. "Closer to what? Do you really think Rhys Penreddy can get rid of me so easily? I'm harder to shake off than Rover."

Renie knew better than to argue.

NINE

ONCE OUTSIDE, JUDITH stepped over the herbaceous border and positioned herself against the wall next to the front bedroom window. With a sigh, Renie joined her, trying to provide some kind of cover by admiring the small garden.

"You eavesdrop, I'll weed," Renie murmured, bending down to inspect the carefully tended beds. Finding no intrusive growth, she contented herself with plucking off a few brown leaves from a dwarf privet hedge.

Fortunately for Judith, the courtyard was deserted. She could hear Penreddy's voice in the bedroom, inquiring after Dagmar's physical and emotional states. Judith wished he'd get to the point of his visit.

At last he did. "We've sent those letters off to the RCMP," Penreddy was saying. "I can't promise that much will come of it, but we'll see. What I'd like for now is to have you go over the last hour or so before you left the restaurant."

Dagmar's voice wasn't as audible as Penreddy's. Her reply faded in and out, like the reception on a shortwave radio. ". . . a celebration . . . such fun, until that awful woman showed up . . . but you know about that . . ."

Penreddy interjected a comment. "We've spoken with Ms. Prohowska and Mr. Linski. They deny having threatened you. Is that true?"

Thinking she'd missed something, Judith strained to

hear. But Dagmar was merely taking her time to answer. "Mia didn't make threats of a physical nature," she said at last in clear, measured tones. "It's difficult to understand precisely what Mia means. Her accent, you know. It becomes more pronounced when she's excited. As I recall, the thrust of her intentions was mainly legal. A lawsuit, I presume." Dagmar now sounded indignant.

"You didn't talk to Mr. Linksi?" Penreddy asked.

"No. At first, he was glowering at us from their table, but when Mia attacked me, he came over and accosted Karl. I've no idea what Nat was saying. He must have been swearing in one of those Slavic languages that make no sense at all." Dagmar's indignation was acute.

Penreddy cleared his throat. "Yes. Well, certainly. But Ms. Prohowska *did* lay hands on you, eh?"

"She was hysterical." Now there was scorn in Dagmar's voice. "If she intended to kill me, she wouldn't have attempted it in the middle of a fine resort restaurant."

"Agnes Shay wasn't killed in the middle of a fine resort restaurant," Penreddy reminded Dagmar. His tone was dry, and Judith could imagine his ironic expression. She could also picture Dagmar's crushed reaction.

Sure enough, the gossip columnist's voice dropped once more. "... forgotten my turban ... Agnes was so solicitous ... never let me lift a finger ..."

Renie was standing up, making a face, and rubbing the small of her back. She gestured toward Judith and the window. "How long?" she mouthed silently. She had to repeat herself three times before Judith understood.

Judith held up two fingers, despite having no idea if the interview was running down. Dagmar was recounting how the group had left Crest House. Though Judith could catch only about half of what was said, the facts jibed with what she already knew.

"So you went down the lift first," Penreddy remarked. "Then Mrs. Kreager—or Ms. Van Heusen, as she prefers—and lastly Mr. Kreager. Were you one after the other?"

"Yes indeed, we were." Dagmar's certainty gave her voice strength.

"And after you got off the lift?" As ever, Penreddy was calm and courteous.

"Why . . ." Dagmar faltered. "Let me think . . . It became so confusing . . . Karl went to the men's room at the lodge. We couldn't get anybody's attention, so Tessa walked down to the bar and asked for a server. Then I heard something going on outside. Tessa finally came back, and I told her to see what was happening . . ." Dagmar succumbed to sniffling.

After a discreet pause, Penreddy posed another question. "How long was Ms. Van Heusen gone? To the bar, that is."

"Oh, forever!" Dagmar now sounded ragged as well as revived. "Editors are the slowest people this side of an ice floe! Do you know how long it took her to read my manuscript? I write faster than she can read!"

Penreddy betrayed the faintest hint of amusement. "Could you be just a little more precise?"

"Precise?" Dagmar was clearly taken aback. "I'm never precise. It's not my style. I'm a writer."

Apparently Devin O'Connor felt obliged to help his superior. "Two minutes? Five? Ten?" His tone was soft, wheedling, and youthful.

"Oh—five, maybe." Dagmar was obviously irked. "What difference does it make? Karl got back before she did, and he saw to it that I got my drink. Or was that after Tessa went outside?" Now Dagmar had become confused. Again her voice sank. "Really, it's so muddled, like a bad dream . . ."

Renie had her arms crossed and was looking like a summer storm cloud. Judith couldn't suppress a smile. It was short-lived: The skies didn't burst, but the automatic sprinkler system went on. Both cousins were caught in its soft spray. Renie jumped back across the herbaceous border and fled to safety in the courtyard. Judith raced away from the condo, fought through the heaviest volleys of water, tripped over the edge of the walkway, and finally staggered to Renie's side.

"Serves you right." Renie grinned; she was merely damp. "Maybe the dog drool got washed out of your slacks."

"Be quiet," urged Judith, gazing from the Kreager and Chatsworth units to their own condo at the end of the opposite row. "What do we do now? We're supposed to be baby-sitting Dagmar."

At that moment, Freddy Whobrey sauntered down the walk from other end of the Clarges Court complex. He was whistling a tune from *My Fair Lady* when he espied the cousins. Ducking down, he beamed at them from behind an upraised arm.

"Jiggers! It's the cops! Let's make a run for it!" Freddy chuckled all the way to the middle of the courtyard.

Judith felt like making a run for it, at least to get away from him. But good manners and a Grover upbringing rooted her to the spot.

"You knew the police were here?" she asked, self-conscious in her clinging clothes.

"Sure," Freddy replied cheerfully. "I came around the other way and saw their car. That's why I'm taking the air, instead of a powder." His eyes raked Judith up and down. "Say, you look real good when you're all wet. Want to take a shower together? I've got a ducky, and it's not rubber. Of course, these days, everybody should use a—"

"Knock it off, Freddy," Judith interrupted, her good manners fraying. Observing his expression of mock horror, she tried to correct herself. "I don't mean that you should knock—oh, never mind. As long as you're here, we're leaving." She turned on her heel.

"Well, thank you very much!" Freddy sounded aggrieved. "Do you think it's fun to whip your pony when you're all alone-y?"

Judith glanced over her shoulder. It was pointless, as well as tasteless, to engage Freddy in conversation. "I'm not being rude, but when the police leave, someone needs to stay with Dagmar until Tessa and Karl get back from the pool. Now that you're here, you can take over. Good-bye, Freddy." Judith forced her voice to sound pleasant.

"Think of me when you're getting out of those wet clothes!" he called after the cousins. "Think of me when you're putting on dry ones! Think of me any old time you like, sweetheart! Freddy's always ready!"

"Freddy's always a jerk," Renie declared, slamming their condo's front door and checking the lock. "Maybe Agnes committed suicide to avoid being around him. It would be worth trying to bash yourself in the head while going down a ski lift. I'd rather spend a day locked up with our mothers than an hour with that creep!''

"Well, now . . .'' Judith lifted one eyebrow. "Let's not get carried away.''

With a smirk, Renie eyed Judith. "Freddy put you off. That's the first time I've ever seen you let a suspect off the hook. You didn't ask him a single question. Thus, he must be particularly repellent, even worse than some of our shirttail relations.''

Judith recalled the unfortunate occasion of a family birthday party she'd catered the previous winter. Renie was right: As loathsome as their uncle Corky's in-laws were, they couldn't match Freddy for vulgar effrontery.

"Okay,'' said Judith, heading down the hall to change clothes. "I can't stand being around Freddy because he's too forward.'' She couldn't help but smile at the old-fashioned phrase. "Crude,'' she added for emphasis. "Sexual harassment,'' she called from the bedroom, trying to move up into the nineties. "I ought to file a complaint.''

Renie, who was already drying out, lounged in the doorway. "Go ahead. Meanwhile, how are you going to find out where Freddy was at the time of the murder?''

Judith paused in the act of pulling a striped tank top over her head. "The same way I'm going to find out where the Kreagers were. And Dagmar.'' Her head emerged and she gave Renie an ironic look. "You didn't hear what Dagmar told Penreddy.''

Renie sat on the bed while Judith finished changing and recounting the interview. "So,'' Judith concluded, brushing her damp hair, "if Karl was allegedly in the men's room and Tessa was allegedly at the bar, then Dagmar was alone. None of them has an alibi. I imagine Penreddy is sharp enough to realize that.''

"Dagmar would have been seen sitting in the lounge,'' Renie objected.

Judith gazed at Renie's image in the mirror. "She wouldn't have if she wasn't there. Nobody paid any attention to them—that's why they couldn't get service. Penreddy will have to check with the other patrons to see if Dagmar left and came back. We'll leave that part to him." Judith turned around, stepped into a dry pair of Keds, and straightened her shoulders.

Renie recognized that her cousin was ready to resume action. She slipped off the bed and sighed with resignation. "Meanwhile, we do—what?"

Judith smiled, displaying more mischief than mirth. "First, we check up on Freddy."

"How?" Renie trailed off down the hall after Judith.

"We start with the bar at Crest House. Isn't that his alibi?"

Again Renie gritted her teeth as she mounted the chairlift. Wayne Stafford wasn't on duty. His replacement was a strapping young woman with curly black hair. She didn't bother to glance up when the cousins reached the lift.

The bar at Crest House had a sports motif, dominated by old hockey uniforms, sticks, skates, helmets, and at least ten photographs of Wayne Gretzky. Other athletic endeavors were represented, however, especially baseball. Sweatshirts, caps, autographed balls, fielders' mitts, and a half-dozen bats showed Canada's pride in its Bluejays and Expos.

Business wasn't particularly brisk in the middle of a sunny Tuesday afternoon. Too late, it dawned on Judith that the evening staff probably didn't come on duty until the dinner service. The bartender greeted the cousins with a gap-toothed smile and a French accent.

"We're looking for someone who was working here last night," Judith began, after she and Renie had placed their drink orders. "Who tends bar in the evenings?"

"I do," the genial man responded, placing a scotch in front of Judith and a rye before Renie. "Today, I substitute. Hilde is having the root canal." He tapped one of his own teeth. "Last night, we are so busy and she assists me, but has the terrible agony, all the way to her toes. She drops a tray of wineglasses, and I think she is going to faint, but no, she takes the 222 tablets for the pain, and I send her home. I manage, I am efficient." His voice was matter-of-fact.

Judith lifted her glass, as if to toast him. "Great. I mean, that you're here," she added hastily. "You're . . . ?"

"Charles," the bartender replied, making the name sound

like one soft caress of a single syllable. "Charles de Paul. Not to be confused with Charles de Gaulle." He chuckled richly at his own humor.

Judith chuckled back; Renie sipped her rye. "I'm trying to track down my cousin," Judith said, ignoring the faint choking sound from Renie. "I got here yesterday and heard he was at Bugler, too. Someone told me he'd been spotted in the bar here last night."

Charles de Paul busied himself with a glass coffeepot. "This cousin—he looks like you?" The gap-toothed smile was flattering, without Freddy Whobrey's lechery.

"Not in the least," Judith answered, trying not to sound aghast. She described Freddy, working hard to keep from making him seem like a hideous little weasel. "He used to be a jockey," she added, lest Charles figure Freddy for a deranged midget.

"Ah!" Charles's broad face brightened. But before he could continue, a young man with a shaved head brought an order for another round of white wine. Judith glanced into the farthest corner, where a middle-aged couple huddled together in apparent misery. Either they were a tryst gone wrong, Judith decided, or else they had been lured into buying a time-share condo.

"This jockey," Charles said after the waiter had gone off with the glasses of wine, "is American? He wears the smart suit, just a little *too* smart?"

Judith nodded. "That would be Freddy." She recalled his dapper attire from the dinner party in the restaurant. "He was here, then?"

Charles nodded as he wiped beer schooners with a towel. "He was here for a long time. Too long, perhaps." His pleasant face grew doleful. "You comprehend? Your cousin, he celebrates a grand event?"

"Yes." Judith nodded some more. "Yes, he was celebrating, actually. He'd been with friends. Was still with friends," she added, hoping the statement didn't come across as the question that it was.

Charles gave a Gallic shrug. "*A* friend." His soulful eyes regarded Judith with sympathy. "This friend is not another cousin, I pray to the *bon Dieu*?"

"Uh . . . no. In fact, I can't think who it might be." At a loss, Judith cast about for a likely prospect. Freddy had said something about meeting an old chum, a man. She glanced at Renie for support.

Renie clasped Judith's shoulder but fixed her eyes on Charles. "Mme. Flynn here has some really strange relatives, especially her cousins. Did this guy have four ears and a hand growing out of the top of his head?"

It took Charles a few seconds before he realized that Renie was joking. He laughed. Judith didn't. "Ah, *mais non*! He had the red nose, the big mustache, the balding head, the hand that shakes. He also has—alas!—the pockets that are empty. Usually," the bartender added as if granting a concession.

"Then you know my cousin's friend?" Judith asked eagerly.

Charles nodded in a sorrowful manner. "Too well, madame. M. MacPherson comes most regularly. Especially if one of his friends pays the bill."

"Where does he live? What's his first name? Will he be back tonight? What time does he come in?" Judith's enthusiasm bubbled over.

Charles laughed in his hearty manner. "His Christian name is Esme. Intriguing, that. Where he lives I don't know. But yes, he will probably come by if he thinks a friend may show up. Perhaps your cousin, eh, madame?"

"Yes, right, great." Judith nodded vigorously and beamed at Charles. She didn't care to encounter Freddy along with Esme MacPherson. "What time does Mr. MacPherson usually arrive?"

Charles cocked his head and screwed up his broad face. "Eight? Nine? He is unpredictable, this M. MacPherson. I suspect we are not the only bar he frequents."

Judith became thoughtful. She didn't want to spend the evening hanging out in a bar, waiting for a man who might not show up. Perhaps the telephone directory would solve her problem. If Esme MacPherson was a regular, he must live in Bugler. She couldn't imagine anyone in the affluent resort town who wouldn't have a telephone.

Just as Judith was about to ask the bartender if he had a phone book handy, he uttered another rich chuckle. "Ah, madame!'' Charles nodded toward the entrance of the bar. ''There he is! The cousin you seek! Your troubles, they are over!''

Judith turned on the stool and saw Freddy Whobrey ambling across the room. One look at his leering face, and she knew her troubles had just begun. Again.

There was only one thing to do, and that was to flee. ''The surprise is on hold,'' Judith gasped at Charles. She slapped what she thought was a ten-dollar bill down on the bar, grabbed Renie, and ran out the rear entrance. The cousins found themselves smack up against the flanks of Fiddler Mountain.

''You idiot!'' shrieked Renie. ''How could you do that?''

Judith glared at her cousin. ''How could I *not* do it? I wasn't about to save face by embracing Freddy and letting him slobber all over me!''

Renie leaned against an outcropping of rich brown rock. ''I didn't mean *that*. I meant the fifty bucks you left for Charles. Who do you think you are, some high-priced PI from an old movie?''

Judith gaped at Renie. ''Fifty bucks? That was a *fifty*? I thought it was a ten!''

Renie started walking along the trail that ran between Crest House and the mountain. ''Tens are purple, fifties are red. You really ought to start memorizing your Canadian currency by color. You sure as hell can't seem to read the denominations.'' Her temper no longer out of control, Renie seemed to have become a bit whimsical. ''Maybe I can write this off somehow. If not a business expense, then mental health. Mine will be gone by the time we get home.''

''*Fifty bucks.*'' Judith was still muttering to herself. ''Shoot,'' she exclaimed as they reached the corner of the restaurant, ''I wonder what Charles thinks. What do you suppose he said to Freddy?''

Renie held out a hand to stay Judith. ''I don't know, but you could ask him. Freddy's out front, looking every which way.''

Her shoulders sagging, Judith swore under her breath.

"Swell. What do we do now? Hide on the mountain until dark?"

Renie was surveying the trail. "We could walk, although I'm not sure where this goes. Hopefully, down."

Judith came to stand beside her cousin, careful not to expose herself to Freddy's view. "I see people," she said, nudging Renie. "Look, about a hundred yards over there."

Renie, whose long-distance vision was much better than Judith's, squinted against the sun. "You're right. Salvation is at hand. It's the police. Let's trot down and see what's happening."

Trotting wasn't quite the method of taking to the trail. Though the cousins guessed that it was probably used for hiking and possibly horseback riding, the route had been gouged out of the mountain with little margin for error. While it was gradual and well maintained, there were scattered rocks and even a few muddy patches. An occasional guardrail marked the sheerest drop-offs. Judith looked down from one of them and gasped.

"I feel halfway to heaven," she said in an awed voice. "Look! The town is so tiny! It's like being in an airplane!"

"Don't talk." Renie's voice was tight. "I hate airplanes. You know that. I'll fly only if the airline promises to hold the plane up with a long stick and run along underneath it."

Concentrating on her footing, Judith ignored Renie. Once or twice she dared to look back over her shoulder to make sure Freddy wasn't following them. There was no one in sight.

Overhead, a blue-and-white helicopter soared to an altitude above Fiddler Mountain. Skiers heading for the snowfields near the summit, Judith guessed, or backpackers being transported to distant Alpine trails.

Back on the ground, the trio of policemen met them halfway. They nodded and smiled, albeit in a tight-lipped fashion. They also waited for the cousins to step aside so that they could proceed up the trail. Judith didn't budge.

"Did you find anything?" she asked, taking an educated guess as to what the policemen had been doing.

"Sorry," replied the older of the three, a rawboned blond in his thirties who was sweating profusely under the summer sun. His official name tag read: VAN DE GRAFF, DEAN. "We aren't allowed to discuss our activities." Dean Van de Graff made an attempt to get around Judith.

"Chief Penreddy and Officer O'Connor are with Ms. Chatsworth," Judith confided, lowering her voice despite the fact that no one else could have heard her. "I'm not sure the interview has produced any results, except the holes in Dagmar's and the Kreagers' alibis."

All three men looked startled. "Excuse me?" Van de Graff stared at Judith. "Who are you?"

She waved a hand in a self-deprecating manner. "We're just witnesses. We were behind the deceased on the lift. We knew the Chatsworth party from a visit to my home. We were with Dagmar when Chief Penreddy and Devin O'Connor showed up. We're nobody. Not really."

Judith congratulated herself, having actually told the truth. Renie was gazing at her cousin with a mixture of wonder and admiration. The policemen all looked just plain puzzled.

Judith didn't give them time to probe further. "You were searching for the weapon, right? That must be an almost impossible task." She lifted a hand, indicating the craggy face of the mountainside. "This is such a vast stretch of territory. For all we know, the killer might have used a rock."

Judging from the bleak expression that Van de Graff gave her, the idea had already occurred to him. "It's possible," he said in a grumbling tone, "but the forensic people think otherwise."

Judith put on her most sympathetic face. "Not the sort of blow a rock would make, I suppose? No dirt particles? No granular matter?"

Van de Graff's perspiring face took on a suspicious cast. "Pardon me, but we can't discuss the investigation with you, witnesses or not. If you've got any comments, put them in writing, eh?" Van de Graff all but pushed Judith and Renie out of the way as he led the other policemen up the trail.

Watching their retreat with thoughtful eyes, Judith nodded. "I was right. They haven't found the weapon. I'll bet they never will." She turned to gaze again at the valley below. The view was virtually the same as the one the cousins had had the previous evening from Liaison Ledge. In broad daylight,

Judith thought she could see even farther into the distance. The lakes looked larger, their cobalt-blue calm disturbed only by the bright hues of sailboats and the occasional wake of a pleasure craft. She envisioned the vast panorama of trees, hills, and village under a heavy winter snow. No doubt it would be breathtaking, a sight she would enjoy sharing with Joe. But for now the summer splendor of Bugler was sullied by murder. Judith began trudging down the trail. "Agnes could have been killed with a tree branch. If the murderer pitched it off a cliff, how could it ever be discovered?"

Renie had no answer, and was too busy worrying about falling down even to make a guess. After another fifty yards, the trail turned a sharp corner and briefly became quite steep. At the next zigzag, it leveled out a bit. Small stands of evergreens grew along the bank, giving a semblance of security.

They were almost to the village when they spotted a lone figure sitting on a smooth brown boulder in a clearing. Renie was the first to recognize Mia Prohowska. The cousins hastened their steps.

"Astonishing view, isn't it?" remarked Judith, and though it was, they were now virtually on top of the town. Judith could have hit the bare beams of new construction below them with a pebble.

Mia Prohowska, however, didn't seem to be enjoying Bugler's beauty. She barely looked up at the cousins. "Umm," she said.

Apparently Renie felt duty-bound to shoulder some of the responsibility for snooping. "Well! I know you! How wonderful!" Her attempts at guile were always heavy-handed. "My daughter, Anne, saw you skate on your Pacific Northwest tour. She was absolutely thrilled." Judith noted that although Renie was telling the truth, she sounded as if she were lying through her teeth. "When will the Ice Dreams company tour again? Anne can hardly wait."

It seemed to cost Mia Prohowska a great effort to respond. "In the west of your country, next spring," she finally said in a hollow voice with its Eastern European accent. "God willing." She glanced away, though her wide-set gray eyes didn't seem quite focused.

"Terrific," exclaimed Renie. "My cousin and I will be

there next time. We wouldn't have missed it before, but she was in prison.''

Judith sighed. She knew that when subtlety failed with Renie—as it inevitably did—her cousin fell back on blunderbuss tactics. They often worked, even if they were at the expense of someone else.

Mia was no exception to Renie's rules of outrage. Her head swiveled and she stared, first at Renie, then at Judith. A flicker of recognition seemed to spark in her eyes, then went out like dying ash. ''Prison? For what? Oh, my!'' She looked genuinely terrified.

Judith started to say something, but Renie cut her off. ''It's a manner of speaking,'' she said with a lame little laugh. ''You know, American slang. She's in the hostelry business, and couldn't leave her guests. It's like being in prison, you see. Locked up. Cut off from the world. Incommunicado.''

To Judith, the explanation was relatively smooth, but Mia didn't appear assuaged. She trembled slightly as she got to her feet. Again Judith was surprised at how small the skater was compared with the lissome, lofty image she presented on the television screen.

''You are very kind,'' Mia said in a quavery voice. ''I am always pleased to hear from admirers of my art. Skating is very hard, very demanding. The reward is to please the audience as well as oneself.'' The words came out as if by rote. Mia's movements were jerky, a far cry from the graceful ice queen. With a bob of her head, she started to move off down the trail.

The cousins were at her heels. Renie gave Judith a dismal look, acknowledging the fact that she had flunked subterfuge. Judith's expression commiserated. She, too, was at a temporary loss for words.

At the bottom of the trail, which led onto a paved road, Judith finally recovered her power of speech. For once, she decided on candor.

''Ms. Prohowska,'' she said, not quite sure how to address an Olympic champion from Eastern Europe, ''why did you let Dagmar Chatsworth spoil your dinner last night?''

Mia halted at the very edge of the pavement. Now her gray eyes finally registered recognition. ''Oh! You were at the restaurant! The table near us. Oh, yes, our dinner was most spoiled! The evening, it was a disaster!'' It didn't seem to occur to Mia that Judith's inquiry was nobody's business. Perhaps the mere presence of the cousins at Bugler automatically gave them a certain cachet.

"She is evil, that Dagmar,'' Mia went on, now walking slowly down the road, which went past the latest spurt of new construction. ''In the West, you boast of freedom of the press. Now in my homeland, it is also considered a boon. What is it really, but a license to spread lies and scandal?''

"It can be that,'' Judith agreed. "There are libel laws, though. Has Dagmar written scurrilous articles about you?''

Momentarily, Mia seemed puzzled, but she translated adequately. "She has, though not yet published. Or so she says. She will ruin all!'' Mia seemed on the verge of tears.

"Is that what she told you in the washroom last night?'' Judith asked, the sympathy in her voice coming through in any language.

Mia didn't reply at once. She was walking very slowly, keeping her eye on a big yellow Caterpillar tractor that was moving along the edge of the road. "There were rumors,'' Mia said at last in a terse tone. It appeared that she had given herself time to consider Judith's questions, and now had one of her own. "How do you know about the washroom?''

"I was there with Dagmar after you left her,'' Judith answered truthfully. "She was upset, too. That's why she left her turban and scarf. Maybe that's why Agnes Shay got killed.''

Mia turned to gaze up at Judith. "The companion? Very sad. What has it to do with me?''

Renie was on the other side of Mia. "I imagine,'' she remarked, "that's why the police questioned you and Mr. Linski. You know, the big scene at Crest House. It couldn't look good for you when, less than an hour later, somebody killed Agnes because she was mistaken for Dagmar.''

With an annoyed gesture, Mia rubbed the tears from her eyes. "Such a waste! The assassin should not have made a mistake.''

The high-pitched words hung on the mountain air as Mia Prohowska turned her back on the cousins and ran off as if the ghosts of the secret police were at her heels.

TEN

JUDITH'S HIP SOCKETS had never been the same since she and Renie had challenged Auntie Vance and Aunt Ellen to a rigorous badminton doubles match at the family cabin some thirty-five years earlier. Renie had never learned to ice-skate because she had weak ankles and impaired coordination. Except for gardening and running up and down the stairs of their multistoried residences, the cousins had no commitment to physical exercise. In middle age, they should have been no match for the twenty-nine-year-old Mia Prohowska. But curiosity could do more than kill the cat: It could turn a pair of menopausal matrons into Olympic sprint contenders. Judith and Renie caught Mia just where the road branched off to Clarges Court.

"You . . . need . . . a . . . cold . . . drink," Judith insisted between gasps for breath.

"You're . . . a . . . nervous . . . wreck," Renie panted. "Come . . . inside." Slackly, she gestured in the direction of the Clarges Court complex.

Apparently drained from the emotional upheaval of the past few hours, Mia offered no resistance. As the three women approached the condo's street entrance, Judith noticed that the police car was gone. Fleetingly, she wondered who was sitting with Dagmar. Freddy had obviously abandoned his aunt. Perhaps the Kreagers had returned from their swim.

Renie tapped out the security code on the handsome wrought-iron gate that led into Clarges Court. They passed the units that housed the Kreagers and Dagmar Chatsworth. All seemed peaceful. The only sign of life in the courtyard was a pair of young boys in wet bathing suits, running out of the pool area and heading for a unit at the opposite end from the cousins' condo.

Mia didn't drink hard liquor, which put her hostesses in a bind. They had purchased only scotch and rye. Fortunately, the skater was willing to accept one of Judith's diet sodas.

The soft drink seemed to loosen Mia's tongue. "I found out about Dagmar's terrible lies just before she arrived here," she said, sitting stiffly on the mauve-and-teal sofa. "Someone phoned and left an anonymous message."

Judith had sat down in one of the two matching armchairs. Renie was in the other. Having cornered their prey, the cousins now seemed willing to give her some breathing room. "What did they say?" Judith asked, keeping her voice on a calm, conversational level.

Mia stared into her tall glass of soda as if she expected to find bugs. Or poison. "This person revealed what Dagmar planned to write in her next book. It was ... *ugly*. And lies. *All lies*." Mia shuddered at the memory.

Judith gave her guest a chance to regain her composure. "Did you recognize the voice?" She was prepared for a negative response.

Mia didn't disappoint her. "No. It was very strange, like a windup toy. Croak, quack, squeak." The imitation wasn't bad. Mia's gray eyes widened and the cords in her neck were strained.

"Disguised," murmured Renie with a sidelong glance at Judith. "What did this person say?"

But Mia refused to reveal the dreadful falsehoods that Dagmar was allegedly putting in her next book. "Nat thinks we should sue now," she said, running a nervous hand through her mane of red hair. "There is a way, he tells me, to stop the presses."

"An injunction, maybe." Renie refilled her own glass of Pepsi. "When did you get the call?"

Fleetingly, Mia looked blank. "The exact date I do not remember. Time runs like a river, especially at the end of a tour. But it was the morning after we returned from your city.''

Judith tried to calculate in her head. ''You came to Bugler right after your last show?''

Mia nodded. ''We never return to hotel. We chartered a plane to Port Royal. Then Anatoly and I drive to Bugler. It is very late when we arrive. I am wanting to sleep in, but no, Anatoly insists I go to the practice. He drives me like a demon.'' Despite the complaint, Mia didn't appear overtly annoyed.

The call had come through Thursday morning, Judith figured. ''You were phoned . . . where? At home?''

Mia shook her head. ''At the rink. It's just outside the village square, next to the driving range for golf.''

''Did you tell the police?'' Renie asked.

Again Mia shook her head. Her poise was returning, and with it, a hint of the regal aura that emanated from her presence on the ice. ''To what end? In this country, it is not against the law to make a phone call. There was no threat. Only the report of Dagmar's vicious calumny.''

''So,'' Judith said in a thoughtful voice, ''it could have been a friend with a warning.''

Apparently the idea had never occurred to Mia. ''A friend? A friend!'' She seemed dismayed. ''No, no, surely not! The unexpected call, the unhappy communication, the secrecy of the voice—is that what friends do? Not in my homeland! In the past, no good ever came from such messages! The next thing, a loved one disappeared, or a stealthy shadow followed, pretending to gaze in shop windows with state-owned goods of dubious quality. Oh, no! This was no friend, Mrs.—'' Mia faltered, then stared at the cousins. ''Forgive me, I know not your names.'' Her uneasiness returned.

Judith and Renie introduced themselves. The formality struck them as both awkward and amusing. But Mia didn't seem to notice.

''I understand there was a small problem with Dagmar at the Cascadia Hotel,'' Judith said, starting for the refrigerator and more soda pop. ''Did you actually talk to her there?'' Her voice was raised as she called out from the compact kitchen.

"No," Mia answered, "I did not. I speak with the poor dead secretary. Except then she was alive."

Judith returned, carrying two cans of diet soda and a single Pepsi. "The discussion was about Rover?"

Politely, Mia refused more soda. "Rover?" Her flawless brow furrowed.

"Dagmar's repulsive dog," Renie prompted.

Enlightened, Mia nodded. "Nasty, that dog. Miss Shay, she is nice. We reach the compromise. There is no serious provocation. Not," Mia emphasized with narrowed eyes, "for murder."

"So you dealt with Agnes," Judith mused. "Nat—Mr. Linski—didn't get involved?"

Mia slapped her hands on her knees and laughed in an ironic manner. "Of course! He is always involved! That is his way!" Sobering quickly, she stared first at Judith, then at Renie. "But this is not perilous. He shouts at Miss Shay, at the funny little man with the bowlegs, at Dagmar Chatsworth! It is of no matter. The dog incident is settled, all is well, my fellow skaters have Band-Aids applied. Then comes the phone call. All is *not* well. And Dagmar comes to Bugler and enjoys herself and is eating the salad with the warm chicken livers and I am desolated! I am looking forward to the long and prosperous career. Skaters age like wine, becoming finer as years go by. But my future, my whole life, is threatened. What should I do? What would *you* do?" Mia didn't wait for a reply. "I accuse her of perfidy! I wish to wring her neck! I try, I fail, Nat stops me! Then I go to the washroom to regain myself, and who comes but Dagmar! So I plead, I beg, I am practically on my knees, but the tile is colder than the ice. She is unyielding, yet I perceive distress in her eyes. She is afraid! But," Mia concluded, suddenly limp, "not of me."

"Huh?" It was Renie, taken aback by the swift change in Mia's attitude. "So who scared Dagmar? Did somebody else come into the washroom?"

Mia turned vague. "I don't recall. I think not. As for the hateful Dagmar, she refused to withdraw her false charges. That shows she was not the least little bit frightened of me, hey? But frightened she was. Yet it does me no good." Mia seemed to wallow in sadness.

In her head, Judith heard the strains of Gypsy violins, their moaning melody filling the lobby of a third-rate hotel in Bucharest. Or some such place where seedy guests with cardboard suitcases and frayed overcoats argued hopelessly with desk clerks who lived off bribes. At Clarges Court, a chipmunk bounded up onto the small deck outside the living room and peered through the sliding glass door.

The chipmunk startled Mia, who reacted as if the little animal were wearing a trench coat and dark glasses. "Oh! Wildlife! They bite, do they not?"

"They do, actually," Renie replied in a matter-of-fact tone. "Years ago at our family cabin, Cousin Sue had one try to take her finger off when she put a small sailor hat on him. Or her," Renie added a bit uncertainly.

Mia didn't seem interested in Cousin Sue's misadventures with the chipmunk. She had just gotten to her feet when the doorbell suddenly chimed. Mia jumped and her eyes grew big.

"Who is it?" she asked in an anxious whisper.

"I don't know," Renie replied, also getting up. "I checked my X-ray-vision glasses at the border."

Tessa Van Heusen Kreager and Anatoly "Nat" Linski stood on the small front porch. Tessa looked annoyed, which the cousins were beginning to think was her standard state of mind. Nat Linski's expression was more difficult to read, not due to any effort at concealing his emotions, but because so many of them seemed in evidence on his bearded face. The cousins discerned anger, worry, frustration, impatience, and, as Nat glimpsed Mia in the living room, relief.

His first words were a torrent of foreign sounds. He bolted into the condo and was at Mia's side in an instant. Tessa uttered a vexed sigh.

"He's been frantic," she said without any trace of compassion. "For some stupid reason, he thought Mia might have come to see us. Or Dagmar. Just to get rid of him, I suggested he try here. The crazy fool wouldn't come on his own, so I had to tag along like a damned duenna. I never thought Mia would actually be here."

"We met her on the trail," Judith said noncommittally.

"Oh?" Tessa's expression was skeptical, but she didn't linger. "Well, the lovebirds are reunited. I'm going to fly the coop.'' Stepping onto the porch, Tessa walked off without another word.

Nat Linksi was already herding Mia toward the door. He glowered at the cousins, his bushy eyebrows uniting above his prominent nose. ''We'll discuss your part in this later,'' he said under his breath. ''Prepare to explain. You are under suspicion.''

''Good-bye,'' Mia called as Nat all but carried her over the threshold. ''Thank you.''

''Jeez!'' Renie stumbled to the sofa and collapsed. ''What was *that* all about?''

Judith retrieved the three unopened soda cans and returned them to the refrigerator. She didn't reply until she had poured serious drinks for herself and Renie.

''Nat's overly protective,'' Judith declared, sitting back down in the armchair. ''Or so I'd guess. His timing stinks, though. We never got to ask Mia about an alibi.''

''Maybe she wouldn't have told us,'' Renie said. ''At the moment, I'd rather find out why Nat Linski said we were under suspicion. Of what, harboring a guest?''

Judith gave a shrug. ''Who knows? He's volatile. Don't you remember the Olympics? Every time they put the camera on him, he was either leaping in the air and shouting with joy or pitching a five-star fit.'' Briefly, Judith fell silent, then glanced at her watch. It was after four o'clock. She went into the kitchen in search of the local telephone directory.

Renie brightened. ''Dinner?''

Judith looked up from the white pages. ''Huh? Oh, right— The Bells and Motley. I suppose we'd better get a reservation.'' She beamed as she found the original object of her search. ''Here—Esme MacPherson, 121 Maple Leaf Lane, Apartment 2B. Should we call him—or call on him?''

Renie tilted her head to one side, her round face pleading. ''Dinner? Reservations? Discount coupon?''

''Okay, okay.'' Judith flipped to the yellow pages. Pacified, Renie sipped her drink while Judith made a reservation for seven o'clock. Hanging up the phone, she consulted the map at the front of the directory. ''Maple Leaf Lane is on the other side of the town, by some of the lodges and pensions.''

''Older,'' Renie remarked. ''By Bugler standards, anyway.

Thus, maybe cheaper.'' She gave Judith a look of resignation. ''Do we go now or on our way to dinner?''

Judith polished off her scotch. ''Now. We don't know how soon Mr. MacPherson starts his evening rounds. He's probably recovered from last night's hangover and may actually be sober this early.''

Renie gave a nod. ''Come on. Let's go waste yet more of our enjoyable vacation time.''

Picking up her handbag, Judith assessed the damage to the strap. Fortunately, Rover had only begun to gnaw. The bag was five years old, had cost almost a hundred dollars on sale, and was dear to Judith. She'd hoped it would last another two years. If Rover could be avoided, that was still possible.

''What other plans did you have?'' Judith asked Renie with a touch of sarcasm.

''Shops,'' Renie replied promptly. ''I honestly thought we might browse, if not buy.''

''We can't afford it,'' Judith replied as they headed downstairs to the parking garage.

''We could afford to browse,'' Renie countered.

Across the roof of the blue Chevy, Judith gave her cousin a wry look. ''We could?''

Renie considered. ''You're right. We couldn't. You'd shell out another fifty for a browsing fee. Sap.'' She got into the driver's seat.

But it was Judith who was leading them on.

In physical terms, they didn't get far. Tessa Van Heusen Kreager came through her condo door and stopped dead when she saw the cousins about to pull away. She seemed to hesitate, then approached the Chevy.

''What happened to you two?'' she demanded as Renie rolled down the power window. ''I thought you were going to stay with Dagmar until Karl and I came back from the pool.''

Renie explained about Chief Penreddy's arrival, adding that the cousins had met up with Freddy in the courtyard. They had assumed he'd gone in to sit with Dagmar after the police left.

"Freddy!" Tessa was scornful. "He came, he sat, he left. Dagmar was alone when we returned. Freddy's a washout!"

Judith and Renie weren't inclined to argue. "I'd hoped," Judith said, leaning across the front seat, "that Freddy would succumb to his family ties. As far as I can tell, he's the only relative Dagmar has."

Tessa snorted. "Is he?"

Judith felt faintly defensive. "Well, we asked if she had any family in Minnesota, and I gathered that Freddy was it."

Tessa smoothed the collar of her black-and-white-striped silk shirt. "Don't be naive. Do you really think Freddy is Dagmar's nephew?" Her expression had turned into a smirk.

Judith was wide-eyed; Renie frowned. "Excuse me?" Judith said in a startled voice. "You mean Freddy *isn't* her sister's son?"

"I doubt it," Tessa snapped. "He's a parasite. And like most women, Dagmar is a fool when it comes to men."

Judith recalled Dagmar's shocked reaction at the hint of a match between Freddy and Agnes. Maybe Tessa was right. Dagmar could be romantically involved with the lecherous little leech. Passing him off as her nephew would explain his otherwise worthless presence. Or so Judith conjectured.

"How is Dagmar?" she asked, anxious to avoid further consideration of Dagmar and Freddy in the throes of passion.

Tessa had started to move away from the car. "The same. She'll give Karl's brother a heart attack if she doesn't pull herself together and come up with Friday's column." Tessa's sour expression dissolved into worry. "To make matters worse, we can't find her files. You didn't happen to see a gray metal box when you were with her, did you?"

Judith and Renie exchanged glances. "It was in Agnes's room," Judith finally answered. "We . . . ah . . . peeked in there to check for Rover."

"It's not there now," Tessa replied, seemingly indifferent to the cousins' prying. "I thought Dagmar might have it upstairs, in her part of the condo. But we've looked all over the place and can't find it. Dagmar can't write the column without it."

Not being conversant with the world of journalism, Judith

threw out a common-sense suggestion. "Can't you run something in the Friday papers to the effect that Dagmar is ill?"

Tessa scowled at Judith. "We're trying to keep the lid on this thing," she said, again leaning into the car. "Bugler is sufficiently isolated that, so far, nobody from the outside has come snooping around. Agnes Shay's name doesn't make any news. But let those vipers on the rival rags hear that somebody tried to kill Dagmar Delacroix Chatsworth—well, you can guess what kind of headlines that would make."

Renie had acquired her aging ingenue's air. "It might help sell books," she noted.

"It might give somebody else ideas," Tessa retorted. "Isn't it bad enough that there's already one murderer on the loose? Karl and I want to keep things under control until the killer is found." Her fine features sagged, and she had to brace herself on the Chevy's dark blue hardtop roof. "I'm starting to wonder if that will happen. The police don't seem to be getting anywhere."

After a few desultory words about the progress of the investigation, Tessa headed back to Dagmar's condo. The cousins waited for the garage gate to go up, then drove out into the late-afternoon sunshine.

"Power," Renie muttered, waiting for a couple of young skateboarders to glide past. "When you stop to think about it, the Kreagers wield enormous power."

Tracing their intended route on the map provided by the real estate company, Judith told Renie to head back to the village. "You're right," she allowed, after her cousin had pointed the car along the road that zigzagged up the first stages of the mountain. "I've been seeing the Kreagers mainly as Dagmar's book editor and publisher. But there's the other Kreager who runs the newspaper chain."

"Kirk? Since Kurt, the eldest, died, Kirk has the newspapers, the TV and radio stations, and the magazines, right?" Renie sensed, rather than saw, Judith nod. "I wonder how closely Karl and Kirk cooperate."

As they came to a three-way stop by the golf course Judith suddenly strained at her seat belt. "Hey—there's the ice rink! And Nat Linksi!"

"Amazing," Renie murmured sarcastically. "A man at his place of work. What next, firemen putting out a fire?"

Judith tugged at Renie's arm. "Come on, coz. Pull up. We have a chance to talk to Nat without Mia hanging onto his frame."

Rush hour in Bugler wasn't exactly like gridlock on the freeway, but parking places were definitely at a premium. Since Renie had never learned to parallel-park properly, she merely drove up onto the sidewalk, scaring the wits out of several pedestrians and two boys on bicycles.

"Coz!" Judith gasped.

"Go on, get out. I'll drive around."

"On the sidewalk? I think that's illegal in Canada as well as the United States."

"Probably." Renie made a face at her cousin. "I'll get back onto the street up there." She nodded at a driveway some thirty feet in front of them. She also ignored a middle-aged man who was yelling at her to get out of the way. "Buzz off!" Renie yelled back. The man pounded on her hood. Renie pressed the accelerator. The man fell back against a lamppost. Judith flew out of the car, barely managing to land on her feet.

Not wanting to see what other mayhem Renie was causing, Judith hurried back toward the ice rink. Nat Linski was getting into a white Bentley. Judith waved frantically. With one long leg still outside the car, Nat rested his chin on the open door and regarded Judith quizzically.

With no time to fabricate an improbable story, Judith smiled brightly at Nat. "Hi, how's Mia? We were so worried about her."

Nat raised his bushy eyebrows. "You? Why should that be?"

Judith leaned against the Bentley. "Well . . . we found her up in the woods, and she seemed . . . despondent. That's why we invited her to our condo. She must be extremely sensitive, since she's such a great artist and all. My cousin and I are just ordinary souls, and heaven knows we were distraught about being in the vicinity when Agnes Shay was murdered. I can imagine how the tragedy must have shattered Mia."

A puzzled expression enveloped Nat Linski's bearded face. "She hardly knew this woman named Shay. Why should it disturb her? We hear later—this morning, in fact—of the tragedy. It is unfortunate, but we are hardened. Murder, treachery, imprisonment, torture—all these are part of our past." He shrugged his broad shoulders, as if listing the sights on the local bus tour through Further Pomerania.

"Oh." Judith ran a hand through her short silver-streaked hair. "Yes, of course." Desperately, she sought an excuse to keep Nat from driving off. A quick glance at the street showed that the goal had already been accomplished. A big blue streak had just made a U-turn and raced off, causing three cars to rear-end each other. The exit to the ice-rink parking lot was effectively sealed.

"That's right," Judith said, gathering her scattered wits. "You and Mia left Crest House sometime ahead of the Chatsworth party. You were probably home by the time the murder occurred."

"Possibly." Nat seemed disinterested. Judith said nothing. He seemed to have forgotten his earlier suspicions of the cousins. He drew his leg into the car and prepared to leave, then noticed the jam-up out in the street. "Good God!" he exclaimed, putting his head out the window. "What's that? An accident? In the village? Incredible!"

All three drivers were out of their cars, arguing in various languages. Onlookers had gathered, and Judith wondered if anyone would recollect the blue Chevy. She hoped that Renie would have the good sense not to return to the ice rink immediately.

"Five o'clock traffic," Judith murmured. "You just can't get away from it." She leaned against the Bentley once more. "You were saying . . . about being home?"

"Yes, yes." Nat sounded testy. He kept his eyes on the street, where two of the three drivers seemed close to blows. "We live on Crystal Lake, west of the town. We walk down the mountain. The lift is for tourists and the lazy."

Being both, Judith gave Nat a limp little smile. "The mountain trail must be lovely at night."

"Lovely?" Nat's tone was uncertain. His attention was fixed on the melee at curbside. In the near distance, the off-key siren of a police car could be heard. "It is evocative, the mountains. I think of my homeland, with the snow-covered peaks, the rushing streams, the eagle soaring overhead.'' He sighed plaintively. "I grow nostalgic. Last night, I stand alone at the cliff's edge and regard the forest primeval. The storm shatters the sky, with lightning dancing in the heavens. In my mind, I can see my native country, I can hear peasant melodies, I can smell the rich, damp earth.''

Judith was moved as well as disconcerted. Nat's imagery had conveyed something else, but the disturbance in the street kept Judith mentally off-balance. "You were born . . . ah, where, exactly?'' she finally asked.

Nat Linski seemed lost in his reverie, now indifferent to the policemen who were trying to separate the irate motorists. "It was the most insignificant of sites, a mere speck on the map. For all that, it was still a glorious place.'' With grave dignity, he drew himself up in the Bentley's sleek leather seat. "I am a Lusatian, and proud of it.''

"Really.'' Judith evinced awe, even as she scratched her memory for Lusatia. Germany, maybe, or Poland. Surely, during her years as a librarian, she had looked it up for some geography student.

In the street, the police had managed to get matters in hand and were taking down information. If Renie showed up in the next few minutes, someone was bound to identify her as the cause of the accident. Judith turned her back on the chaos.

A mental map of Europe came into focus. "East Germany,'' Judith said suddenly. "What used to be, right?''

While the crowd still congregated on the sidewalk, the policemen were moving traffic. The parking-lot exit was no longer blocked. Nat Linksi exhibited impatience.

"Yes, yes.'' He turned on the ignition. "Pardon me, I must go home.''

But Judith wasn't quite ready to give up. "You should,'' she asserted, still leaning on the Bentley. "To Germany, I mean. Now that things are different over there. Is that what you were brooding about last night?''

The car began to move, slowly but smoothly. "No.'' Nat Linksi gave a solemn, definite shake of his big head. "Never. Impossible, that. Good-bye.''

Caught off-balance, Judith staggered, then watched Nat cautiously pull out into the street. Somehow, she had expected the mercurial ice mentor to drive aggressively, heedlessly, even dangerously. Like Renie.

But Renie was nowhere in sight. Judith walked over to the curb, gazing up and down the street. There was no sign of her cousin. Maybe, Judith thought with a little jolt, she'd already been picked up and cited for reckless endangerment, or however the crime would be codified under Canadian law.

Getting her bearings, Judith decided to head for the police station. If Renie wasn't there, then she could try the big parking lot across from the municipal buildings. Surely it wasn't possible for the cousins to lose each other in a town as small as Bugler.

Down the main boulevard Judith went, past the conference center, the elementary school, and the post office. She kept looking in every direction, though the only side streets led to the town square. At the junction of Bugler Boulevard and Fiddler Way, she turned left, by the fire department. The police station was next door, and so was the blue Chevy, parked in the space reserved for Rhys Penreddy. Alarmed, Judith started to run toward the main entrance.

"Psst! Hey, coz!" Renie's head was poking out of the driver's window. "Hurry up, before I get busted!"

A huge sense of relief washed over Judith. Her legs felt shaky as she jogged over to the car. "I thought you were busted already," she said, getting in beside Renie.

"Heavens, no!" Renie seemed to find the idea preposterous. "I figured that the best place to hide from the police was at the police station. You know, plain sight and all that."

The Chevy reversed and was headed for Fiddler Way when Rhys Penreddy drove up in his official vehicle. Judith turned apprehensive, but Renie seemed unperturbed. Recognizing the cousins, Penreddy stopped alongside the blue sedan.

"Giving another statement?" he inquired a bit wearily.

"No," Renie answered blithely. "Just trying to find our way. Isn't Maple Leaf Lane on the west side of town?"

Briefly, Penreddy's tanned brow cleared. "Yes, not far from Lake Paragon and the other golf course. Follow Fiddler Way. It takes several bends after you leave the business area, then turns into Slalom Drive. Keep going until you hit Maple Leaf and . . .'' His expression turned bleak. "Take a left." He floor-boarded his police car and zoomed into the reserved parking spot Renie had just vacated.

Judith sighed. "He knows where we're going. Which means he's already seen Esme MacPherson."

"Well, he didn't try to stop us." Renie waited for the traffic light to change. "Do you suppose that's because it's after five and he's off duty?"

Judith shook her head. "I suppose it's because he thinks we're impossible. At least he didn't have a warrant for your arrest."

"True," Renie agreed. "This place is well planned, but there's not enough parking. I wonder what it's like during ski season. Of course, a lot of visitors probably come by train. Driving might be risky."

The remark caused Judith to raise her eyebrows. "No kidding. I'd hate to see you take any risks."

Renie glanced at Judith and scowled. "You know I won't drive in the snow. It's too dangerous."

"Uh-huh." Refusing to argue with Renie, Judith tried to sit back and relax. They were passing some of the older lodges, already weathered by a dozen winters but appearing comfortable and well maintained. There were condos, too, with sunbathers on balconies and outdoor barbecues sending up trails of charcoal smoke. Plots of bright flowers and window boxes were everywhere, adding a festive, and very English, touch. Along Slalom Drive, the buildings were more modest, possibly geared for students and the economy-minded. When the cousins made their left turn into Maple Leaf Lane, they realized they were in what amounted to Bugler's low-rent district. Here were the pensions and the apartments where the less affluent dwelled. Judith figured that many of the resort's full-time employees lived in this section of town. Esme MacPherson lived here, too.

Still, the complexes were neat and attractive. Judith saw William Tell House on their right. The address was 121 Maple Leaf Lane, and the decor was traditional Swiss chalet. Renie decorously pulled into a spot marked for visitors.

All of the units faced the street, under sheltered walkways.

Esme MacPherson's 2B was reached by a flight of concrete stairs. Judith pressed the buzzer. Nothing happened. She pressed again.

Esme MacPherson flung the door open.

He was holding a walking stick above his head and was ready to pounce.

ELEVEN

"MY WORD," EXCLAIMED Esme MacPherson, lowering the ebony walking stick with its silver horse-head ornament, "I thought you were the police! Again."

"Ah—did you intend to bludgeon them?" Judith asked in a startled voice.

MacPherson ran a thin finger inside his silk ascot. "I suppose not. But I wanted them to know I'm not one to trifle with. These Canadian chaps have some very queer ideas about a man's castle and all that." The gaunt face above the ascot suddenly paled. "I say, who are you? A woman was killed last night, and that's the other reason I've seen fit to arm myself."

Having had time to ready her story, Judith smiled in her most affable manner. "We're crime writers from the States. Canada isn't as violent as our country, or so it seems. We wanted to get the reaction of private citizens to a murder in their hometown. Someone gave us your name."

"The police?" Esme was looking even more alarmed. The hand that still held the walking stick shook rather badly.

"No," Judith answered truthfully. "Charles de Paul, the bartender at Crest House. He said you were a very observant and intelligent person." Honesty was seldom the best policy, as Judith knew well.

Esme MacPherson broke into a smile that made him look

like a malnourished rabbit. He was in his early sixties, perhaps a bit older, with receding gray hair worn a trifle long and a lush, curling mustache. His plaid silk bathrobe hung limply on his slight frame. He was shorter than Judith but taller than Renie, and emanated a furtive air. With a bow, he ushered the cousins into his living room.

Esme MacPherson lived among clutter, with a few solid pieces of aging furniture. Hunting prints, racetrack photographs, regimental mementos, a cricket bat, pieces of harness, and even a horse collar filled the apartment. There was no scheme to the decor, which appeared to be merely an accumulation of items, as if Esme had brought them inside and dropped them wherever there was room.

Which, Judith noticed, left little accommodation for guests. Esme put the walking stick next to the door, then quickly cleared off the old sofa, which was covered with sporting magazines, racing forms, and newspapers. The cousins sat down, hearing the springs creak beneath them. Esme took what must have been his favorite chair, positioned as it was a few feet from a TV set and next to a small table which held a telephone, an ashtray full of cigar butts, an almost empty glass, and a notepad.

"My impressions, eh?" Esme said, gazing at the ceiling where a dusty plywood model of a sulky was suspended. "Sensational stuff, I suppose, is what you had in mind?" He arched his crescent-shaped brows at his visitors. "How much?"

Judith was puzzled, but Renie understood. "We get paid on publication. When that happens, we'll let you know about your share."

Esme's thin face grew sad. "Sorry. I can't remember a bloody thing." His gaze returned to the sulky.

Judith gave Renie a hard stare; Renie tried to look innocent. The silence lengthened, its awkwardness hanging on the air right along with the stale cigar smoke and the scotch whiskey. At last, Judith sighed and reached for her handbag. This time, she carefully checked the color of the bills before handing Esme a twenty.

He took the money, but frowned. "Not much sensation here that I can see."

"We'll settle for the facts," Judith said briskly. "Let's start with where you were at the time of the murder."

Now Esme looked pained. "Oh, no, not again! The police already covered that ground! What about my reaction to a brutal slaying? Do I think it was a sex crime? Is this the work of a serial killer? Are the mountainsides unsafe for even the most casual visitor?" He paused to finish his drink.

"I told you," Judith repeated, "we need facts, not fiction. We'll get to your personal reflections later."

Esme got to the scotch, which he kept in a small cabinet under a big framed photograph showing a group in the winner's circle at a racetrack. He opened one of the two doors just enough to allow him to extract a fifth of whiskey. Esme didn't offer to share it with the cousins.

"I was in a bar," he replied, pouting a bit. "That's not news, by the way." Again he arched his brows, before taking a sip of his fresh drink. "Crest House, same place as the poor cow who got herself killed. I was having a dram or two with a mate of mine from the racing circuit. Later—much later— we heard a rumor going 'round from the newcomers that there'd been a death on the lift." Esme shrugged his narrow shoulders and sat back down in his easy chair. "Pity and all that, but naturally we assumed it was a heart attack or some such misfortune. I didn't know it was foul play until the police came by this afternoon." He brushed at the silk bathrobe. "Tend to sleep in, don't you know? Haven't stepped out yet today."

Judith had been pretending to take notes on a pad she kept for household chores. After consulting the reminder to check on bedspread sales when she got home, she fixed Esme with a serious expression.

"You were with this old friend the entire evening?"

Esme scratched his balding head. "Well . . . no. Freddy— Freddy Whobrey to you, Freddy Fall-Off to me—quite the jockey in his time; pity he came a cropper . . . Where was I? Oh, righto, *Freddy.* He joined me around . . . what? Eight? Nine? Ten? Does it matter?" Esme's confusion seemed genuine. It also appeared to frighten him a bit.

"It'll matter if Freddy needs an alibi," Renie put in somewhat darkly. "We know approximately when he left the dinner party he was attending and went into the bar.''

''Ah!'' Esme clutched at his ascot, as if it were trying to strangle him. ''My word! Then you must know that Freddy was well acquainted with the woman who got killed.''

Judith nodded gravely. ''Oh, yes. We know all about that. This is why you're on our list of . . . uh, fascinating personalities. You know someone who knew the victim. It brings immediacy to the article.''

Esme seemed to relax a little, though whether it was from a change of mood or his intake of scotch was hard to tell. ''Pity I can't tell you much. Freddy and I sat around for some time, tippling and exchanging old war stories. Horse wars, that is. I missed the big show, bit too young, but I served in The Queen's Own Highlanders. Want to see my trews?''

''Pass,'' Renie replied. ''You and Freddy were inseparable last night?''

Esme's blue eyes twinkled. ''Like silks on a jockey. We have quite a time when we get together. Not often enough, but Freddy's quite the lad—here, there, everywhere, is Freddy.''

''Working for his aunt keeps him busy, I gather.'' Judith sounded very casual. Esme said nothing. He was lighting a cigar. ''So you never left each other for a minute.'' Again Judith waited. The cigar was proving balky. ''You never left each other, not even to go to the washroom?''

The cigar finally took off. ''May have done.'' Esme winked. ''Natural function, eh?'' He puffed happily away.

''Okay.'' Judith spoke carefully. ''So you weren't with each other the entire time.''

''Eh?'' Esme seemed a bit startled, peering at the cousins through a haze of smoke. ''Did I say that? Don't recall, actually. Ask Charles. He'd know. Good chap, Charles, even if he is a Frenchie.'' Esme drained his glass, then got to his feet and wobbled back to the cabinet.

''What time did you leave?'' Renie inquired as Esme made another covert attack on the liquor cabinet.

''Hard to say,'' he murmured, squinting into the whiskey bottle. ''Midnight? One? Two? Freddy accompanied me home and we had a nightcap. I must have dropped off. Tiring day, what?''

Noting that their stingy host had been more hospitable to Freddy, and sensing that he couldn't reveal anything of further interest, Judith got to her feet. "Thanks, Mr. MacPherson. We'll let you know when our article is going to come out. If," she added as an afterthought, "it gets accepted."

"*If?*" Esme almost lost his grip on the bottle. "What do you mean, 'if'?"

"We work on spec," Renie answered with a tight little smile. "It's a way of life with freelancers. And don't I know it," she muttered as she followed Judith to the door.

" 'Spec'?" Esme called after his departing guests. "What's 'spec'? Who joined up with the Lancers? What about my personal impressions? What about another twenty? I say!"

Judith closed the door on Esme MacPherson.

"I almost feel sorry for him," Judith admitted as the cousins drove down the winding road that led back to the village center. "How do you suppose he gets by? Makes book?"

"Could be," Renie answered, turning into Slalom Drive. "I glanced at that notepad by his phone. It looked like racehorses. You know—Montreal Marty, Middleground, Counterpoint, Genuine Risk."

Judith nodded. "Taking or placing bets, I suppose. Is off-track wagering legal in Canada?"

Renie shrugged. "I've no idea. It used to be banned at home, but that never stopped Uncle Al's bookies. They were stockbrokers the rest of the time, which as far as I'm concerned is the same thing as being a bookie, only in more conservative suits. It's all gambling."

Passing the condos and lodges, Judith grew silent. At last, as they turned into Fiddler Way, she uttered a discouraged sigh. "The bottom line is that I'm out another twenty bucks, and we aren't sure if Freddy has an alibi or not. Esme was too smashed to remember his own name, let alone the exact events of last evening."

Renie had to agree. "If Freddy went to the washroom—or claimed he did—five, ten minutes could have passed before Esme even noticed Freddy was gone. But Esme might be right about one thing—Charles de Paul would be more observant."

Judith grimaced. "I can't face Charles again. Not after the

big whopper I told him about Freddy being my cousin.''

"We could call," Renie suggested. "I could," she volunteered. "I don't claim to have any weird cousins except you.
What do you think?" They had arrived at the outer reaches
of the main village. "It's not yet five. Shall we browse before
dinner? Shall I call Crest House? Shall we keep driving around
until somebody remembers I caused a three-car accident on
the other side of town?''

Judith had been lost in thought, sorting through alibis.
"Let's not take chances on your immediate incarceration.
We'll stroll the shops and then go to dinner. If I remember
the map, The Bells and Motley is just off the smaller town
square.''

Somewhere after four sportswear shops, three skiing-
equipment stores, two souvenir emporiums, and a crafts boutique, Judith sighted a public phone. She gave Renie a little
push.

"Go for it, coz. See if you can catch Charles before he goes
home. It's almost six, and maybe his shift changes then. That's
the way it was when I tended bar nights at The Meat & Mingle.''

Apparently that was the way it was at Crest House, too.
Charles de Paul was still on duty when Renie called. Judith
leaned over her cousin's shoulder, trying to listen in to the
conversation. The initial exchanges were a bit confused, with
Renie trying to avoid explaining their hasty departure earlier
in the day.

"Family problems," she finally said. "Very complicated.
You understand, I'm sure." She added a couple of phrases in
French which Judith didn't quite catch. Charles, however,
chuckled richly and replied in kind.

"*Oui, oui, c'est vrai.*" Renie laughed lightheartedly. "Anyway, what I really wanted to know was if you remember if
Mr. Whobrey—Mme. Flynn's cousin—left the bar last night.
You know, to make a phone call or something." Renie's voice
took on an air of delicacy.

Charles didn't answer immediately. "No, I think not. M.
MacPherson, he left, somewhat briefly. He also unexpectedly
descended from the barstool two times, but we pick him up

and set him in place." There was another pause. "But M. Whobrey, is it? *Non, non,* I do not recall his absence."

Renie exchanged glances with Judith. "I see," Renie said, sounding disappointed. "You're sure? I mean, did you take a break? *Un petit répit, comprenez-vous?*"

"Ah, oui, mais depuis de le dix heures. I must remain until the dining room grows less busy. Hilde is gone with the aching tooth. One of the waiters comes to permit me the short rest. Then I return until closing."

Thanking Charles in a flowery fashion with a few more stilted French phrases, Renie hung up. "He didn't go on a break until after ten o'clock. He insists that Freddy never budged."

Judith was torn. "Maybe that means we can eliminate Freddy. Darn. It's good to narrow the field, but I'd love to keep Freddy as a suspect. He's such a creep."

The cousins walked slowly past a children's store. "Charles was on his own after Hilde, or whatever her name is, left with her toothache," Renie commented. "Maybe he was too busy to notice. Let's not give up on Freddy entirely."

"Good point," Judith agreed. "The problem is, there may be a dozen other people in Bugler who might have wanted to murder Dagmar. This place is loaded with the rich and famous. Frankly, I wouldn't recognize half the so-called celebrities. What with rock stars and actors and athletes, I'm lucky if I know who Harrison Ford is."

Renie was distracted by the chocolate factory. "Yeah, right, you ought to know the Presidents."

"That was Gerald, from Michigan."

Renie was all but plastered to the window where a young man with slicked-back hair was making truffles. "Sure, the automobile, the Model T, Detroit, and all that." She grabbed Judith's arm. "Let's go in. We can take some candy home to Bill and Joe. Our mothers, too. They can get their dentures stuck and cause us even more problems."

"Yeah, right." Judith sounded unsettled.

"You think I don't know my Fords?" Renie asked wryly. "How about Ford Madox Ford? Victorian writer, produced stultifying tomes about—"

Judith gave an impatient shake of her head. She'd already dismissed the Fords from her mind. "Joe tries to avoid eating sweets."

Renie steered Judith over the threshold, but not without a curious glance at her cousin. "So? Joe isn't the only one who might enjoy chocolates. Your mother will love them and you know it." Judith pretended she hadn't noticed Renie's probing gaze, then she saw the glass cases filled with tempting sweets and forgot about almost everything else. Ten minutes later, the cousins emerged with elegantly wrapped boxes of various chocolate delights. They were also impoverished by another thirty dollars apiece.

"What," Judith asked as they gazed through the windows of an art gallery, "do you suppose Esme meant by Freddy coming a cropper?"

Renie was scowling at a particularly ugly painting that consisted of great green-and-purple blobs. "An accident, maybe? He's not that old, for a jockey. Some of them race into their fifties. Esme called him Freddy Fall-Off. I suppose he got thrown and it ended his career."

"Isn't Freddy Fall-Off a character out of that old card game, Happy Families? You know, Master Daub and Miss Stitch. We used to play it with Cousin Sue."

"Right. She always won. I think she cheated." Renie seemed mesmerized by a sculpture made of macaroni.

"Esme didn't say anything when I mentioned the alleged relationship between Dagmar and Freddy." Judith winced at a series of paintings that seemed to represent a woman with acute gastritis.

"Maybe he doesn't know much about Freddy's personal life," Renie said, stepping away from the gallery and moving past a photography studio and an interior decorator's establishment. "I gather their relationship was professional."

"As in track-rat and jockey?" Judith turned thoughtful as they paused in front of a jewelry store that featured original designs in native stones. "I suppose. But that doesn't help us figure out who killed Agnes, does it?"

"Hey," Renie responded, giving Judith a light jab in the arm, "you're the one who said there was no such thing as trivia in a murder investigation."

"True," Judith allowed, proceeding past another souvenir shop. "We're not focused. That's the problem."

Renie agreed. "Somebody tried to kill Dagmar. What we need to know is why. Who stood to gain by her death? Did she know a secret that was worth killing for?"

The cousins were walking slowly but surely into the smaller of Bugler's two town squares. It was now twenty minutes after six, and the skateboarders were gone, the office workers were home, and the outdoor sports enthusiasts had retired to await a later, more civilized dinner hour. A half-dozen middle-aged tourists, a woman walking her poodle, two enamored young couples, an artist sketching the bell tower that loomed over the square, and a man with a flowing white beard were the only other inhabitants. Brightly colored pennants hanging from lamp-standards rippled on the summer breeze. Flowers of every hue trailed over balconies, sprung up from rugged rock containers, and circled the monument to lost climbers that stood in the middle of the square.

Tucked into a corner between a bike-rental shop and a designer boutique was The Bells and Motley. The cousins were early for their reservation. Judith started to say as much, but Renie interrupted her.

"Well? Aren't you going to say something? Am I on the right track or not?"

From the outside, The Bells and Motley looked like a traditional English pub. A wooden sign depicting a Harlequin figure hung over the entrance, and soft amber lights glowed behind the mullioned windows. The restaurant seemed to offer comfort, safety, and reassurance.

But Judith felt none of those things, at least not in the context of Renie's question. As her cousin had just put it, someone had tried to kill Dagmar. But Agnes was dead. What if . . . ?

"No," Judith answered slowly. "I'm not sure you are on track. I'm not, either. In fact, I think we've got it all wrong." Her oval face set in stern lines as she gazed earnestly at Renie. "The worst of it is that Rhys Penreddy is wrong, too. Unless I'm crazy, this whole case is backward. And that's exactly what the killer wants us to think. If we don't start using our heads, somebody is going to get away with murder."

TWELVE

As ANXIOUS AS Renie was to have Judith explain, a four-letter priority struck first: "SALE," read the sign in the window of a year-round Christmas shop two doors down from The Bells and Motley. They bolted inside, emerging somewhat shamefaced a half hour later with big red shopping bags lettered in gold.

Dazedly, the cousins walked in a circle around the lost climbers' monument. The square was beginning to fill up again, with preprandial visitors. Judith and Renie kept walking; both had grown silent.

At last they stopped. Judith gave Renie a wry look. "How much?"

Renie met her cousin's gaze, then lowered her eyes. "In American money?"

"Yeah."

"A hundred and ten—more or less."

"Piker," Judith said in mock reproach. "Mine was closer to a hundred and fifty." She hesitated, fumbling with her big shopping bag. "Bank card?"

"What else? My cash flow is sort of plugged up."

"Mine, too." Judith started walking again, Renie at her side. "It's almost seven, so we might as well go eat. I hope they have gruel. It's about all I can afford."

Gruel was not on the menu at The Bells and Motley. Prime rib was, however, and Judith ordered the Queen's cut. Renie chose the steak and kidney pie. The cousins congratulated themselves over using their discount coupon.

"We'll save the price of one entree," Judith noted after they had ordered a drink as well as appetizers of crab legs and lox. "I need fortifying. I'm still reeling from summer with Santa."

Renie seconded Judith's declaration. "Let's put our decadent past behind us. Tell me what you meant by looking at the murder from the wrong angle."

But Judith didn't get an opportunity to explain. Karl and Tessa Kreager had entered The Bells and Motley. They appeared to be headed for the bar rather than the dining room. Judith squirmed in her oak chair.

Renie sighed. "Go ahead. I'll hold down the fort."

"You'll eat both the appetizers," Judith countered.

"So? To each his own." Renie smirked. "You grill, I'll guzzle."

The Bells and Motley's bar was partitioned off from the dining area by rough-hewn open beams. Brass warming pans and other homely items hung from the rafters, effectively impairing the view. Unable to resist the Kreagers' presence, Judith left her seat and headed for the bar.

She was halfway across the room when she realized that Tessa and Karl weren't alone. They sat at a small table in the far corner with a third party, a gray-haired man who looked every bit as distinguished as Karl Kreager. Indeed, he looked a lot like Karl in every regard, except that he was younger, and possibly somewhat smaller in stature. Judith shifted uneasily, wondering if she dared to intrude.

A door at the opposite side of the restaurant led to the lavatories. Judith considered feigning confusion and landing at the Kreager table. She discarded the ruse; it would make no sense. Instead she continued on to the rest room. When she returned, she pretended to spot the Kreagers, and evinced surprise.

"How nice to see you," she said, her voice sounding artificial even to herself. "Is Dagmar able to stay alone this evening?"

The trio of faces which were lifted toward Judith did not seem pleased. Tessa, in particular, exhibited hostility.

"Dagmar's asleep," she said in a brittle tone. "We called

a doctor. He gave her a sedative. Besides, we don't intend to be away very long." Abruptly, she turned back to the man who looked so much like Karl.

Judith moved from one foot to the other. "Maybe Dagmar will sleep through the night. That would be the best thing for her."

Karl nodded curtly. "Yes, certainly, of course." He resumed concentrating on the other man.

"I hope the doctor didn't give Dagmar *pills*," Judith said, and the horror in her voice was only part sham.

All three members of the Kreager party again looked up at Judith. "I beg your pardon?" said Karl, his usual affability ruffled.

Judith grimaced. "Well, Dagmar's emotional state is very fragile. She's riddled with guilt. It wouldn't be a good idea to have tranquilizers or sleeping pills at hand. She might be . . . unpredictable."

The man who resembled Karl Kreager spoke for the first time, not addressing Judith, but his companions. "Who is this? Some resort official?" His steel-eyed gaze raked Judith's unpretentious cotton slacks and top.

Tessa's color rose. It was obvious that Judith's presence embarrassed her. "This is Mrs. Finn. She knows Dagmar, if tenuously." Tessa glared at Judith.

"Flynn," Judith corrected softly. Tessa wasn't the only one who was embarrassed. Judith started to back away.

"Hold on." The eyes of steel were now fixed on Judith's face. "What's your interest in all this?"

The authority in the man's voice rooted Judith to the spot. "Well, I . . . Dagmar and her party stayed at my B&B when they were in—"

Karl intervened, putting a hand on the other man's shoulder. "Enough, Kirk. Mrs. Flynn means well. It's just a coincidence that she happened to come to Bugler when we did. Don't be concerned." Karl attempted to placate everyone with his charming smile.

But charm failed with Kirk. "Coincidence? Someone tries to kill Dagmar, Agnes dies, Ice Dreams is melting away, and a strange woman shows up? You call this a *coincidence*? I call it a conspiracy!"

Karl's smile was growing strained. His manner toward Judith was apologetic. "My brother is inclined to find bogeymen under the bed. He used to keep me up half the night when we were children."

"Kirk Kreager," Judith murmured, and started to put out her hand. It was quite clear, however, that Kirk didn't care to be sociable. He picked up his old-fashioned glass and took a deep drink, then glowered at Judith.

"Who do you represent?" he demanded. "The Ice Capades? Tour of Champions? Walt Disney?"

To Judith's amazement, Karl put his hand over his brother's mouth. "Please!" He gave Kirk a hard stare. "Let Mrs. Flynn be. I'm sure," he added with a quick look at Judith, "she wants to get back to her dinner."

Having been mortified and insulted, Judith did. Her unpleasant reception came as no surprise, especially given Tessa's customary hostility. Judith all but bobbed a curtsy in making her hasty exit. By the time she had reached Renie, her knees were weak and she was gasping for breath.

"You're in luck," Renie said, with a fork poised over the plate of crab legs. "The hors d'oeuvres just got here." She tasted the succulent crabmeat and sighed. "Heaven. I'm in heaven."

"*Aaargh!*" moaned Judith, reaching for her scotch.

"Huh?" Renie was chewing away, only now noticing that her cousin wasn't quite herself. "What's wrong?"

With an effort, Judith tried to relax. She also tried to explain what had transpired at the Kreager table in the bar. "Kirk Kreager thinks I'm a homicidal maniac—or a spy for some ice show," she concluded.

Renie seemed unperturbed. "Kirk sounds like a nut. Try the lox."

Judith did. The Nova Scotia salmon was delicious, but it failed to settle her mind. "I don't think Kirk Kreager is nutty. A little paranoid, maybe, but not a nut. Why do you suppose he's here?"

Half of Renie's rye had been consumed, and she was making serious inroads on both the crab legs and the lox. A basket of rolls had also been plundered. Still, Renie paused long enough in her orgy to consider her cousin's question.

"I suppose Kirk lives in the Twin Cities," she said, allowing Judith to get at one of the two remaining crab legs. "Maybe it's easier for him to meet with Karl in Bugler rather than New York. Besides, he's the one responsible for getting Dagmar to meet her column deadlines."

"That's true," Judith allowed, savoring the crab in its delicate sauce. "Obviously, Agnes's murder has precipitated a crisis. Dagmar won't—can't—work, and that's a problem for both Karl and Kirk."

"Right." Renie leaned out of her chair, trying to get the attention of their server. She succeeded, and ordered another drink. "I don't see anything mysterious about all that."

"I agree," Judith said, sipping her scotch and staring across the dining room with unseeing eyes. "I wonder why Kirk mentioned Ice Dreams."

Renie stopped in her assault on the bread basket. "Mia's show? What did Kirk say?"

"That it was melting away, or some such thing." Judith managed to snatch the last roll. "Why bring it up? Why would he care?"

Naturally, Renie had no idea. The cousins' green salads arrived, along with Renie's second drink. Wanting to be companionable, Judith told their server to bring her another round, too.

"I wish we knew what Dagmar intends to publish about Mia," Judith mused. "What could be so damaging that it would cause Ice Dreams to fold?"

For almost a full minute Renie was silent, save for the sound of lettuce crunching and cucumbers snapping. "I'm trying to remember old scuttlebutt about Mia. The only negative press—if you could call it that—is the story from years ago, that she was being pursued by the head of the secret police in her homeland. But so what? Even if the poor woman succumbed, you could hardly blame her, given the old Communist regime."

"A martyr to totalitarian depravity?" Judith gave Renie a wry smile. "It could enhance her reputation rather than ruin it. Except that we all have such short memories."

Renie nodded over a forkful of crisp romaine. "It doesn't take long for people to forget. The Young—including our own kids—have only the vaguest sense of what the Cold War was all about. *Their* kids will think it's something that happened during the Ice Age.''

''And virtue isn't what it used to be.'' Judith sighed. ''As I recall, when that rumor was first bruited about, public reaction was mixed. Some people saw Mia as a pitiful victim of a brutal political system; others thought she had used her wiles to achieve her ambitions.''

''That was what—ten years ago, when she won her first gold medal?'' Renie used the last lettuce leaf to wipe her plate clean of dressing.

''It was after she won the first time, I think.'' Judith made a face. ''It's hard for me to remember. I was kind of wrapped up working two jobs, raising Mike, and keeping Dan supplied with double-stuffed Oreo cookies. Except for the ice skating, the only thing I recall about those Olympics was that Dan said he'd always wanted to be a luge driver, and I didn't hear the 'driver' part and said, 'Why not? You're about the right size and shape.' He threw a rhubarb pie at me.''

Renie, who knew the story by heart, smiled faintly. ''I wonder who started that rumor in the first place.'' She locked gazes with Judith.

''Dagmar?'' Judith voiced Renie's obvious suggestion. ''Karl told us she started writing her gossip column—as opposed to the cooking articles—about eight years ago. It's possible, I suppose.'' She put her fork down, memory triggered by Renie's earlier remarks. ''The Cold War—the Ice Age. Did you read Dagmar's columns from a few weeks ago?''

Renie feigned incredulity. ''Of course. Don't we all, though we hate to admit it? 'Get Your Chat's Worth' is my secret vice.''

Judith nodded, a trifle impatiently. ''Right, like talk shows and call-in radio. But Dagmar was throwing out hints. 'Turncoat' and 'redcoat' and something to do with deep freeze and cold storage. Could she have meant Ice Dreams?''

Renie considered. ''I remember. Cinderella was mentioned, too.'' Her brown eyes widened. ''Mia? But what? Is Dagmar using these innuendos as a lead-in for the next book? It won't be out for almost a year. She hasn't even finished the manuscript.''

The cousins were stumped. Their waitress whisked away the salad plates. Renie requested another basket of rolls. Judith seemed lost in thought until she glimpsed the Kreager party leaving the restaurant. With a nudge for Renie under the table, she tipped her head toward the entrance.

"See? The shorter one is Kirk. I wonder where he's staying."

For once, Renie exercised moderate discretion. "With the Kreagers? They've got enough space."

"Maybe." Judith waited for the presentation of the entrees before she spoke again. "I started to tell you something before dinner—what was it?" Renie had her mouth full of flaky brown crust. She tried to say something, but Judith couldn't understand her. "Never mind, I remember now," Judith went on. "It was about Nat—and Mia. When I cornered him in the ice-rink parking lot, he said that after leaving Crest House last night, they walked down the mountain. They've got a place over by Crystal Lake."

Renie swallowed and nodded. "That's on the other side of town. The trail must traverse the entire mountain face. Maybe both mountains, Bugler and Fiddler. The point, I take it, is that they didn't use the lift."

"Apparently." Judith admired the tenderness of her prime rib. "But there's something else that almost went by me. Nat stayed outdoors—alone. He was brooding and reminiscing about his homeland. He must have been there quite a while, because he mentioned seeing the lightning storm."

Renie looked up from her steaming meat pie. "And Mia?"

"I assume she went home." Judith picked at her fresh vegetable medley. "We saw them leave Crest House right after Mia and Dagmar had their encounter in the washroom. Nat and Mia had—what?—at least a half hour head start on the Chatsworth party. The storm started about the time we left the restaurant. I don't know how long it would take to walk to Crystal Lake, but Nat was still up on the mountain then. Or so he says. Do we believe him? And even if he was, where was Mia? How do we know she was sitting at home, fine-tuning her skates?"

"We don't," Renie said, tackling her steak and kidney pie with verve. "When it comes to alibis, nobody has one. Not really. Oh, Freddy supposedly was in the sports bar at Crest House, but Esme MacPherson's brain is as porous as Swiss cheese, and Charles de Paul was mopping up broken glass along with his barmaid. Karl Kreager visited the men's room, while Tessa went off in search of drinks, thus leaving Dagmar alone. Any one of them could have sneaked out of Fiddler Lodge, ridden the lift up to Liaison Ledge, and cracked Agnes on the head. Ditto for Mia and Nat, who appear to have been apart about the time the murder took place. We're nowhere, coz. If the killer acted as fast as you say, everybody had an opportunity.''

Judith added a dash of horseradish to her prime rib. "The worst of it is that we may not be focusing on the right suspects. Our purview of this case is so narrow. All it would take is one anonymous person with an unknown motive." Judith made a face, partly caused by her feeling of helplessness, but exacerbated by the strength of the horseradish.

"That's Rhys Penreddy's job," Renie noted. "He has the means to find out who else at Bugler had it in for Dagmar. I'll bet he's got quite a list of names." She swallowed a mouthful of gravy and sighed with pleasure. "Mmmmm! There's nothing like real English cooking!"

Judith's expression was tart. "Yes, there is. The stuff that backs up from your sink, for instance. I'm appalled that you're the one member of our generation to inherit Grandpa Grover's taste for English dishes. It's a wonder Bill didn't divorce you the first time you cooked bubble and squeak."

"I served toad-in-the-hole, too." Renie gave Judith an innocent smile. "The doctor insisted that none of those things could have caused Bill's ulcer."

Judith made no comment. Consequently, Renie felt obliged to defend herself further. "I haven't made any of that stuff in years. You got lucky the second time around—Joe likes to cook. Oh, once in a while Bill gets an urge to play gourmet, and he performs admirably, but your husband actually knows all the basics, like sautéing and braising and making a roux."

Still Judith said nothing. She was gazing off into the distance and mechanically eating her dinner. Renie was growing a little desperate. "Sure, sure," she continued, "I realize that Joe had to cook because his first wife was usually passed out by four o'clock in the afternoon. But as I recall, way back when you two were going together in the sixties, he knew his way around the kitchen. He has a knack. And he likes it. When he has time.'' Renie's voice trailed off, lost somewhere in the thick sauce of her steak and kidney pie.

''That's it,'' Judith announced abruptly, getting to her feet. ''I'm going to call him.''

''Huh?'' Renie looked up from her plate.

Judith had grabbed her handbag. ''Joe. It's going on eight. He should be home. He should have been home a couple of hours ago.''

Renie recalled her cousin's somewhat odd reaction at the chocolate factory. She also remembered that Judith had been unusually reticent about discussing her phone conversation with Joe the previous night.

''What's wrong?'' Renie asked.

''Nothing.'' Judith's tone was flat. ''I want to ask Joe if he installed the Caller I.D.'' She avoided Renie's gaze as she headed for the pay phones off the bar.

Joe Flynn wasn't home. Again Judith heard her own voice on the answering machine, inviting would-be guests to leave their name, choice of reservation dates, and phone number. She tried the private line, and heard herself saying she was temporarily unavailable. Angrily, she slammed the receiver back into place. By the time she rejoined Renie, Judith had a rein on her emotions. Or so she thought.

''Now what?'' Renie demanded, putting down her fork.

''Nothing.'' Judith tried to look unperturbed.

''Bunk.'' Renie narrowed her brown eyes at her cousin. ''No Joe?''

Judith gave a single shake of her head. ''No Joe.'' She pushed her half-eaten entree aside.

''Well,'' Renie said in an amiable tone, ''he's working that homicide, right?''

''Right.'' Judith was grinding her teeth.

''Are you worried that he's heard about Agnes?''

Judith frowned. ''No. Well . . . yes.'' She knew that the death of a tourist in Bugler might run in the local papers. Even without the Dagmar Chatsworth connection made public, the resort was close enough and sufficiently popular that foul play on a chairlift would rate a paragraph or two. It was also possible that Rhys Penreddy was in contact with the local police. Agnes Shay, after all, had made her last stop in the United States at Hillside Manor on Heraldsgate Hill.

Renie, however, knew Judith too well to think that her cousin was worried solely about Joe's reaction to his wife's involvement in another murder case. "Competition?" Renie remarked, then snapped her fingers. "No, that's not it. It's something I've missed. Give, coz."

For once, Judith refused to confide in Renie. "Skip it. I'll try again later, from the condo. You having dessert?"

Renie shook her head. As was often the case, she had filled up on what she termed "serious food" and rolls. As for Judith, she had definitely lost her appetite. The cousins requested the bill, and were vaguely horrified to discover that despite the discount and their good intentions, they still owed close to seventy dollars Canadian, tip included.

"Some discount," Renie muttered as they left the cozy confines of The Bells and Motley. "Even the thirty-plus cents on the dollar didn't help much."

"We eat in tomorrow night," Judith replied a trifle vaguely. "At least we've paid for the groceries."

"Now what do we do?" Renie asked as they trudged across the busy square. It was still light out, though the air had grown cooler and dark clouds once again hovered over the mountains.

Judith stopped, staring vacantly up at the lost climbers' memorial. "I don't know. I'm completely befuddled. As I was saying earlier, everybody has this case all backward."

Renie wagged a finger under Judith's nose. "That's it! That's what you were going to tell me! What do you mean?"

Several people turned to stare, more or less discreetly, at the cousins. One of them was Freddy Whobrey. Judith clamped her mouth shut, turned on her heel, and all but ran out of the square.

Freddy was quick. He caught up with Judith and Renie just before they reached the parking lot. "Naughty, naughty!" he cried, grinning and leering. "You two are avoiding me! How about a double date with my old pal Esme? I hear you've been hanging out with him. How come you never told me about your writing career?''

It was Renie who responded, her voice drenched with sarcasm. "It's a sideline, to provide us with luxuries like postage stamps and Scotch tape. Esme didn't exactly make for hot copy. He's not much of a host, either—he didn't even try to get us drunk."

Freddy shook his head in mock dismay. "That Esme! He's forgotten how to have a good time. Stick with me, ladies. How about a little something at Club Cannes? It's early for the show, but we could hoist a few and dance a bit. What do you say?''

Judith was trying to get into the car, but Renie hadn't yet unlocked the doors. "Call Esme. Dance with him. You lead. We're leaving."

"Ohhh." Freddy was chagrined. "Party poopers! It's not even eight-thirty! I misplaced Esme, and I can't go back to the condo yet. Karl's stick-in-the-mud brother is there, and he doesn't approve of me. I can't think why." Freddy assumed a perplexed air.

Renie unlocked the car, but Judith hesitated. "Kirk Kreager? Is he staying with Karl and Tessa?"

Freddy shook his head in an exaggerated manner. "He put himself up at Chateau Arbutus. Mrs. K.—she hates to be called that—doesn't like to have her husband's relatives sleeping under her roof. Maybe it's because they know something about her that isn't fit to print."

Judith gritted her teeth. As much as she loathed being around Freddy, it was difficult to pass up an opportunity for information. "Like what?"

Freddy simpered and drew closer to Judith. "Like her deep, dark past. Mrs. K.—*Ms. Van Heusen*—isn't all she seems." He wiggled his eyebrows at Judith and inched even nearer. Judith could smell his breath, and though Freddy seemed sober, he gave off a distinct aroma of gin.

"Really." Judith tried not to look askance. "What is—*was*—she?"

Freddy snickered. "You'd like to know, wouldn't you? What's it worth, sweet-buns? How about a little romp in the barn with Freddy Whoa?''

''Whoa, Freddy!'' Judith drew back. But she smiled, if tremulously. ''I'm married, remember? To a cop.'' Judith tried not to wince; she wasn't up to thinking about Joe at the moment. ''Whatever Tessa has done, it can't be too dreadful, or Karl wouldn't have married her.''

Freddy attempted to lean on the Chevy's roof, but couldn't quite reach it. His elbow slipped, and he frowned. ''I don't know about that. It's amazing what a man will do if the woman he wants is good in the sack. Tessa may look like she's got a riding crop up her rump, but I'll lay you five to two she can heat the sheets when she puts her mind—and other things—to it.'' Freddy leered.

Renie got into the car and closed the door. Firmly. Judith wanted to join her cousin, but wasn't quite ready to let Freddy go. ''So Karl and his family suppressed the bad news about Tessa,'' Judith said, taking a long shot of her own. ''What was it, promiscuity?''

Holding his small sides, Freddy rollicked with laughter. ''You scamp!'' he cried between gusts of mirth. ''You little dickens!''

Judith held her head. Surely no amount of sleuthing was worth putting up with Freddy Whobrey. ''Well?'' she finally said in a vexed tone.

Freddy got himself under control. ''It was . . . politics!'' He succumbed to another burst of merriment.

Judith stiffened. ''*Politics*?'' Surely Freddy was leading her on. ''What did she do, vote for Nixon?''

Stifling what appeared to be a sneeze, Freddy shook his head. ''No,'' he gasped out, ''no, no. Much worse.'' He didn't notice Judith cringe as he put a hand on her bare arm. ''She went the other way. It was 1972. Tessa was a Spotted Leopard!'' Freddy again fell into convulsions.

From the well of memory, Judith recalled the anarchist group that had started fires, robbed banks, and otherwise committed mayhem in the name of social progress. Their base of operations had been a liberal Midwestern university, though, off the top of her head, Judith couldn't remember which one. Most of the rebels had come from solid, upper-middle-class families; one of the ring-leaders had actually been rich. Some had been caught and imprisoned. Others had recanted and relinquished both their ideals and their co-conspirators' names. A few had gone to law school. Judith remembered nothing about Tessa Van Heusen. Obviously, she had changed her spots.

"Was she . . . indicted?" Judith asked, drawing away from Freddy's touch.

At last he regained his full composure. "Plea-bargained her way out of it. Somewhere along the line she met Karl. He was having some problems with his wife. She probably wasn't giving him any." Freddy shrugged. "You know how it is after twenty years of marriage. The Boredom Stakes. He was fifty, more or less, and raring to run. Tessa caught him in the clubhouse turn. They went wire-to-wire, and it ended in a photo finish—all over the front page of the Kreager newspapers."

Judith was looking thoughtful. "I see. So Karl got her a job with Thor Publishing. What happened to Wife Number One?"

"The also-ran?" Freddy gave another shrug. "He paid her off—big bucks, I'd guess—and put her out to pasture. Palm Beach. The Riviera. Switzerland. Wherever first wives go to die."

"Interesting," Judith remarked, then shook herself. Tessa Van Heusen's colorful background didn't seem pertinent to the murder case. "Say, Freddy, do you know why Kirk came to Bugler?"

Freddy was fiddling with his gold-and-ebony cuff links. "Old Blue-Nose? Business, I suppose. He and Karl are brothers. They have to keep the family rolling in the green stuff, right?"

Judith gave a halfhearted nod. "Probably." Repressing the urge to grab Freddy by the collar and jerk him off his feet, she fixed him with a hard stare instead. "So why is Kirk upset about Ice Dreams?"

Freddy ignored Judith's gaze and lavished a longing look at her thighs. "Huh? Oh, I suppose because he's the money man." He turned his lust-ridden face upward and smiled like a satyr. "Kirk keeps the cash register for the family. The Kreagers own Ice Dreams, you know." He made a dive for Judith. "Or did you?"

Freddy was clinging to Judith's knees.

THIRTEEN

PROFESSOR WILLIAM ANTHONY Jones, Ph.D., had announced his early retirement from the university. Or perhaps it was a mere threat. Either way, Renie was reeling around the Clarges Court condo.

"I don't blame him," she declared, clutching her head with both hands. "He leaves for Alaska in half an hour, and he swears he's never coming back. Months and months of meetings, arguments in the faculty senate, interdivision feuds, entire schools at each other's throats. And now this!" She clawed the air in frustration.

Judith was lying on the sofa with an inch of scotch on the rocks at her side. Separating herself from Freddy had not been easy. Even as he'd held on for dear life and made major attempts to grope various parts of her body, she had tried to elicit additional information from him while also pummeling him about the ears with her fists. At last Freddy had gotten the idea that Judith found his attentions undesirable. Gasping and panting, he had let go, but it was obvious that the skirmish hadn't completely dampened his ardor.

"I'll catch you later in the paddock," he'd vowed, limping off toward a bistro where carefree customers sat outside under big red-and-white umbrellas.

The cousins had returned to the condo, so Renie had called home before her husband headed for his customary early night. Bill's news had dismayed her, and now she, too, poured herself a small drink.

"Math is the only department that's holding out from changing the class names," Renie said, falling into one of the big armchairs. "Imagine, not only lowering the requirements, but renaming courses just to attract students! Bill says he might as well dress up in a clown suit and get himself a bozo horn! Whatever became of academic integrity? What's happened to scholarship? Where did educational standards go?"

The diatribe continued, but Judith only half-heard it. "Boris Ushakoff," she said suddenly. "He was head of the secret police in Mia's native land. The name came back to me just now."

"Bill refuses to have his psych courses called by those stupid names," Renie raged on. " 'Looking Outside At My Insides.' 'Let's See Some ID.' 'Borderline Neuroses or Just Plain Nuts.' 'Gaga 101 and Gaga 102!' Gack! I can't believe the administration would stoop so low!"

"If Freddy's accurate," Judith mused, a hand over her forehead, "the Kreagers invested their personal—as opposed to corporate—money into Ice Dreams. Kurt, the eldest brother, was still alive then. He talked Karl and Kirk into the business venture. But they've insisted on remaining silent partners."

"If you think the psych department is bad, wait until you hear about history and political science. There's a Russian course called 'Freeze Your Borscht Off,' and a Latin American—"

"Coz." Judith pulled herself to a sitting position. "Stop." She spoke very softly. "I think Bill is teasing you. Oh, I don't doubt that the university has made a lot of unfortunate changes, but your husband sometimes overdramatizes. Wait until you see a syllabus before you have a four-star fit."

Renie let her head fall against the back of the chair. "Well . . . maybe. But even so, it's depressing to see a major educational institution pander to the inadequacies of the public schools and the disintegration of the family. Bill says that the real problem is spiritual paucity in today's society, which undermines—"

"Coz." Judith was getting a headache. "Bill may be right." Seeing that Renie was about to interrupt *her*, Judith went on hastily. "*Is* right. No doubt about it. But I'm trying to figure out how the Kreagers' investment in Ice Dreams could provide a motive for Agnes's murder."

Renie's fixation began to diminish. "A motive? For what? Oh, Agnes!" She started to say something, then frowned at Judith. "You mean Dagmar. Nobody really wanted to kill Agnes."

Judith was now sitting up straight, feet firmly planted in the rug's thick pile. "No. That's what I've been trying to tell you all evening. That's why the case is backward. Agnes Shay was murdered. She was wearing Dagmar's turban and scarf, but why would she do such a thing? We wondered about that earlier, remember? The explanation is that she wouldn't. Either someone coaxed her into putting on Dagmar's stuff, or they were planted on her after she was killed. I'm opting for the former. Agnes had quite a few items to carry on the lift. She needed at least one free hand to get aboard. I doubt very much that she would have taken it upon herself to wear Dagmar's turban. I'm guessing that the killer talked her into it—Agnes wasn't the type to argue with anybody. Then she was struck on the head, and the lift went down the mountain."

Renie had become caught up in Judith's re-creation of the murder. "But there were a bunch of people on Liaison Ledge at the time. They were standing in line to get on the lift. How could all this have happened in plain sight?"

The point was well taken. Judith picked up her scotch, considered her incipient headache, and set the glass back down on the coffee table. "I'm counting on two things—as the murderer must have done. First, people in general aren't very observant. They're self-absorbed, and don't notice what's going on around them. Quite a crowd had gathered to get on the lift." She paused to scrutinize Renie. "Where were you looking just before you got into your chair?"

Renie blinked several times. "At the chair. The one coming 'round. I wanted to make sure it wouldn't fall off."

Judith nodded. "Right, and while other people may not be as chicken-hearted as you, coz, they're still watching the on-coming chairs, if only to figure out which one is meant for them. The second big factor is the summer storm, which started about then. According to you, it happens every night this time of year.'' Indeed, as Judith glanced out the window, a distant spike of lightning struck the sky off to the north. ''Clockwork,'' she murmured, noting that her watch said it was nine-thirty-five. ''People would have been distracted. I know I was. After all, we came down not too far behind Agnes.''

Renie was also looking out at the glowering sky. ''That's true. We didn't notice anything unusual. But given all that, why would anybody want to kill Agnes instead of Dagmar?''

Throwing caution to the wind, Judith took a sip of her drink. ''That's the problem. I don't know. There are all sorts of motives for getting rid of Dagmar, but Agnes was so innocuous.''

Renie, however, didn't entirely agree. ''Some of the motives that apply to Dagmar also apply to Agnes. Agnes probably knew almost as much dirt on various celebrities as Dagmar does. Agnes was the secretary who kept the files and took some of the calls. It's possible that she knew something—just one terrible, awful, potentially disastrous thing—that Dagmar didn't. That's all it would take to get her killed.''

The lightning was coming closer, its jagged tendrils flashing at more frequent intervals. The thunder followed, low and deep, like the growl of an angry animal. Darkness hadn't quite settled in, yet the heavy clouds cast a pall of gloom over the mountains.

''So what was it?'' Judith sounded bleak. ''We can't begin to guess. All we can do is consider the suspects we know. The Kreagers. Freddy. Mia and Nat. Dagmar herself.''

''Dagmar!'' Renie seemed aghast. ''No! How could she? She may claim to be fifty, but she's over sixty, more out of shape than we are, and on the small side. At least up and down. I can't see her cracking Agnes on the head, then racing off to . . .'' Renie turned thoughtful. ''Where? Did the killer stay up on Liaison Ledge or ride the lift down behind Agnes?''

Finishing her scotch, Judith got up and took the glass out to the kitchen. ''It depends on who did it. If it was Tessa, Karl, or Dagmar, the killer had to leave the lodge, go up the lift, meet Agnes, get her in one of the chairs, hit her on the head, and then ride the lift back. It would take ten to fifteen minutes, if everything worked smoothly. Dagmar was waiting for her drink—she said. Tessa was trying to find a server—

allegedly. Karl was in the men's room—he claims. But it's possible that one of them could have done it.'' Judith remained in the kitchen, talking to Renie across the dining room. "The same is true for Nat and Mia. Either of them could have gone down the trail half an hour before Agnes left Crest House, doubled back or taken the lift, committed the crime, then headed home. Freddy, too, if we could break his alibi with Esme.''

"Motive,'' Renie remarked. "If you insist that Agnes was the intended victim instead of a big mistake, then why?''

Judith gave a shake of her head before picking up the phone on the kitchen counter. "That's the hard part. We have to ask the obvious—who gains from Agnes's death?''

Renie was left to consider the question while Judith again tried to reach Joe. To her increasing annoyance, she heard only the tiresome recorded messages. Impatiently, she dialed her mother's number in the converted toolshed.

"What now?'' Gertrude's rasp came on the sixth ring.

Judith was startled. "Nothing. I'm checking in. How are you?''

"Almost dead. I've had a stroke. G'bye.''

"Mother!'' Alarmed, Judith tugged on the phone, as if she could force Gertrude to maintain contact. But the loud click signaled that the connection was broken.

"Good grief,'' Judith muttered, starting to redial, "I wonder if she's kidding?'' Before punching in the final digit, Judith hung up. "Are you going to call your mother?'' she asked Renie.

Wearily, Renie got out of the armchair. "Sure, I guess. If I don't, she'll assume we've been stolen by White Slavers.'' Moving with resignation to the kitchen, Renie eyed Judith quizzically. "What now? No Joe? Too much Mother?''

Judith nibbled her thumbnail. "She claims to have had a stroke.''

"She didn't.'' Renie picked up the phone receiver.

"You can't know that.''

"Yes, I can.''

"Sometimes they're very slight. Let's face it, our mothers are old.''

"Uh-huh.'' Renie was waiting for the phone to ring. Deborah Grover answered halfway through the first buzz. Unlike her sister-in-law, Deborah loved talking on the telephone. Her wide circle of friends and relations kept the wires humming from early morning until late at night. Renie was more surprised that the line was free than that her mother had answered immediately. As she engaged in the preliminary opening sallies, Renie leaned over and pulled out one of the dining room chairs. Drink in hand, she sat down, prepared for the long haul.

Judith went off to her bedroom and undressed. She took a shower and brushed her teeth. She went through the small pile of dirty clothes, then checked on Renie's laundry bag. Deciding that they had enough for a load, she went downstairs to the bottom unit and started the washer. Returning upstairs, she fetched her romantic suspense novel from the bedroom and meandered out into the living room. Renie was still talking to her mother.

". . . but Auntie Vance has always been bossy," Renie was saying. "Uncle Vince is basically lazy. Unmotivated, then . . . Okay, okay, so he's downtrodden . . . No, I agree, she shouldn't have set his pants on fire. At least he woke up . . . Oh, he didn't?" Renie's shoulders slumped as she gave Judith a helpless look. "Well, you've been wanting to get a new chair, anyway. The Belle Epoch is having a sale. I'll check it out when we get . . . Yes, of course we're fine. Yes, she's really fine. Yes, I'm ever so fine. Everything is fine. I don't know exactly when on Thursday—you can never tell about traffic at the border this time of . . . In the pewter sugar bowl on the tea wagon. The *tea wagon.* I put it there myself. You must have dropped the earrings out of the pouch on your wheelchair. No, it's the red cardinal, not the yellow canary." Renie was holding her head. Her glass was empty. She was sprawled in the dining room chair, feet splayed. "Really, I have to go . . . Yes, I'm wearing sturdy walking shoes . . . Mother, I've always had flat feet . . ." Renie was actually not wearing any shoes, having discarded her flimsy sandals upon the cousins' return to the condo. "Look, I'll try to call tomorrow . . . Yes, she's right here, reading a book . . ."

Judith gestured at Renie, mouthing the words "*my mother.*" Exasperated, Renie nodded.

"By the way, have you talked to Aunt Gertrude lately? How was she?" Renie's lengthy pause made Judith tense. "What about the second call you made?'' Judith shut her eyes as the silence in the condo went on and on. ''Then the last time you phoned her? When was that?'' Another pause. Judith put her book aside. The heroine of the story wasn't in half the suspense that she was. ''No, no, don't bother calling her again. That's fine. Okay, yes, I love you, too . . . Yes, I will . . . No, I won't . . .''

The cautions, consents, affirmations, and promises continued for another five minutes. At last Renie was able to get off the line.

''Damn!'' she cried, struggling out of the chair. ''Even after all that, somehow my mother makes me feel guilty when I finally do get rid of her. How does she do that? Can I learn that trick? Will I be able to drive my kids insane when I'm old?''

''Probably,'' Judith replied absently. ''What about Mother's stroke?'' A muscle along her jaw twitched, revealing her anxiety.

Renie dragged herself back into the living room and sat down in the armchair. ''My mother didn't mention it. She'd called yours twice this morning, and she was fine, but busy grooming Sweetums. With a saw, she said, but I doubt it. Then Auntie Vance and Uncle Vince came down from the island to play cards with them and have supper at my mother's apartment. They took your mother home before seven. My mother called her around seven-thirty to make sure she'd gotten back safely.'' Renie rolled her eyes. ''Your mother said she wasn't the least bit safe, being, as it happened, menaced by the Hounds of Hell, which, she added nastily—my mother's word, not mine—she would prefer to having her addled sister-in-law call her up every five minutes.''

Judith relaxed. ''Mother sounds normal. I guess she was kidding after all.''

Renie sighed. ''Great kidders, these loved ones of ours. First Bill, now your mother. What about Joe?'' Seeing Judith's face tighten, Renie wished she hadn't asked.

''He's not home.'' Judith's voice was angry.

''He's on a case.'' Renie sounded casual. ''He works overtime every so often, right?''

''Right.'' The truth didn't placate Judith.

The storm had long since blown away and night had finally slipped down over the mountains. Several lights glowed in the nearby complexes. No doubt the village was just beginning to get into its party mode, but it seemed very quiet at the edge of the forest.

Renie announced that she was going to take a bath. Judith pretended to read until she heard water running in the tub, then went to the kitchen phone. This time, she called the private number first. Joe answered on the third ring.

"Hell of a day," he said. "I just got home. How's it going?"

Joe sounded tired, but otherwise cheerful. His innocent question indicated he hadn't heard about Agnes Shay's murder. Judith felt a sense of relief, which was immediately followed by the return of her earlier unease.

"Discount dinner tonight," she replied warily. "A bit of shopping—big sales, huge savings. The exchange rate is very favorable." She paused, and her tone took on an edge. "Where have you been all this time? I was worried."

Did Judith imagine that Joe hesitated? Or that his voice seemed to change? "Trying to wrap up this tavern case. Lapchick—the bartender—is out of intensive care, and his prognosis is better than expected. Woody and I spent about twenty minutes with him this afternoon, and he's sticking to his story about the affair with Diana. We've talked to some of the regulars from My Brew Heaven, and got mixed results. But you know how that goes—they're hammered most of the time and don't know what's going on."

Judith tried to banish her apprehensions. "As in longing gazes between Lapchick and the owner's wife?"

Joe laughed wryly. "You read too many of those gushy women's novels, Jude-girl. As in Lapchick grabbing Diana's ass, or Diana shoving her knockers under his nose. We're talking about a rough crowd. But Diana says it never happened—not with her knockers, anyway."

"Joe . . ." Judith sighed. Basically, her husband was a gentleman. But he was also a cop, and occasionally his language violated good taste. Suddenly Judith's uneasiness spiraled upward. "Are you talking about this stuff with Mrs. Bauer?"

"Sure, I have to. I told you, we need to establish motive.

Shortages in the till are hard to figure, especially if Lapchick was doctoring the bar tabs. It's his word against Diana's. She told me tonight that her husband, Les, knew about the pilfering, but Phil was a longtime pal running out a string of tough luck. Les was trying to get him through the latest bad patch and see if he could get his act together. At first, Diana said Phil skimmed small amounts—ten, twenty bucks a night. Then he got greedy. Last week he—''

"Joe?" There was a plaintive note in Judith's voice. "Joe, where did you go tonight?"

"Oh. I stopped by the Bauers' apartment. Diana hadn't had time to clean the place, so we went out for a drink. And dinner." Joe's voice had dropped a notch.

"You and Woody and Diana, huh?" Judith tried to keep her tone light.

"Uh . . . no, Woody had to get home. Sondra had invited their neighbors over for a barbecue. I told him to go ahead, no big deal, I'd ask Diana a few questions, and we'd brainstorm tomorrow morning, first thing."

Judith calculated. If Woody had gotten home in time to help host the Price family barbecue, he'd probably left Joe no later than six-thirty. It was now almost eleven. Joe had just arrived at Hillside Manor. It appeared that he had spent almost four hours drinking and dining with Diana Bauer.

"My," Judith remarked through stiff lips, "you must have had quite a lengthy session with Diana."

"Oh, you know how it is—she's in a pretty bad place right now. Her husband's been killed, running the business is left to her, she's short a bartender, and the tavern is shut down indefinitely, anyway. It's not as if she's had an easy life." Joe paused, and Judith heard two faint successive thuds. She imagined that he was taking off his shoes. "I've heard it all, but Diana's story is a classic. Abusive father, alcoholic mother, a warped brother who got sent up for child molesting. She quit school at sixteen and married a worthless kid who wouldn't work. Husband Number Two did drugs and beat the crap out of her. She finally settled down with Les, who gets himself killed. Not that he was any great shakes—jealous bastard, the kind who blew his stack if a customer winked at her. But all the same, she loved him."

Joe's voice had grown melancholy, and Judith could almost hear a piano somewhere playing an accompaniment to a husky-voiced torch singer. She thought of Joe's first wife, Herself, who had earned a living between marriages by singing a few bars in a few bars.

"Does Diana sing?" Judith asked, her voice suddenly sharp.

"As a matter of fact, she does. Every Saturday night, she leads the customers in a sing-along." Joe succumbed to a delayed reaction to his wife's tone. "Hey, Jude-girl, what's wrong? You sound pissed."

Renie was coming down the hall, her homely hairdo damp and her face plastered with thick white cream. She arched her eyebrows at Judith, then picked up a magazine and sat in her favorite armchair. Renie pretended she wasn't eavesdropping, but Judith knew better.

"I simply don't understand why you're lavishing all this attention on the Widow Bauer," Judith said in a low voice between clenched teeth. "Lapchick killed Bauer. There's no doubt about that. He's been charged, right? When he gets out of the hospital, you go to the arraignment with Woody and give your testimony. What's so complicated? Let the prosecutor make the case. I don't see why it matters if the motive was a love triangle or offensive egg yolk on Les Bauer's tie. The guy's dead, and his bartender killed him. Don't you have some other cases to solve?"

Judith's voice—and perhaps her blood pressure—had risen. Renie grimaced as she tried to keep her nose in her magazine. At the other end of the line, Joe expressed dismay.

"Hey, I think you're jealous! I'm too beat to be flattered. Besides, Diana is—"

"Don't be silly," Judith broke in, trying to lower her voice. "But you know darn well you don't usually go around holding hands with homicide survivors."

There was a sharp intake of breath at Joe's end before he spoke again. "Knock it off, Jude-girl. I'm just a civil servant, trying to do my job. If you can't find a murder of your own to solve, why not bust some old farts smuggling chess pies into the States?"

Joe had it all wrong. Judith pursed her lips and snarled into the receiver, "I'm not competing with you! I'd never do that! I don't give a damn about solving crimes! I'm talking about you and—"

"Save it!" Joe's usually mellow voice was savage in Judith's ear. It was, she realized, the tone he used with hardened criminals and mass murderers. "I'm bushed, you're unreasonable, and it's late. I'll talk to you when you get your ass back home."

Joe hung up.

Judith was in a state of shock. Immobilized, she sat on the dining room chair that Renie had vacated and stared at the kitchen cupboards. Finally, she replaced the receiver, slowly and deliberately.

"Joe's a jerk," she declared, more in wonder than in anger. "A complete, total jerk." As if in a daze, she walked toward Renie.

"Right, he's a jerk. So's Bill, every now and then. Did you see this article about how to rag your walls? It gives that textured look." Renie shoved the magazine in front of Judith.

With an impatient hand, Judith slapped at the magazine. "Rag, schmag. Don't try to distract me. I'm really upset." She sat down on the edge of the sofa. "First he accuses me of trying to compete with him on a professional level. Then he chews me out for being jealous! And hangs up on me! What kind of a husband is that?"

Renie returned to perusing the article on rag-painting. "The usual kind. The occasional jerk. Remember Dan? The Jerk for All Seasons? Whither trust? Whither self-confidence? You and Joe have traveled too long on lonely roads to let some woman with a sob story upset you." Renie smiled kindly over the top of her magazine.

But Judith refused to be soothed. Getting up, she began to pace the living room. Her bathrobe got caught on Renie's foot. She stumbled just as the doorbell chimed.

"Who's that at this time of night?" she breathed, regaining her balance and momentarily forgetting her wrath.

Renie remained calm. "Go find out. Do you need backup?"

Judith didn't think so, at least not until she'd checked

through the spy-hole. To her astonishment, she saw Dagmar Delacroix Chatsworth standing on the small porch. Judith opened the door.

Dagmar scooted inside, as if Gertrude's Hounds of Hell were on her heels. "It's that awful Lusatian!" she gasped, leaning against the wall as Judith quickly closed the door. "He's trying to kill me!"

Judith peered again through the peephole. She saw nothing. "Was he following you?" she asked Dagmar.

Breathing heavily, Dagmar nodded, then shook her head. "I'm not sure," she said at last. "He threatened me. Oh! I must sit down!"

Taking Dagmar's arm, Judith led her the sofa. "Would you like something to drink?"

Dagmar nodded again. "Brandy, please."

But the cousins had no brandy. They could offer only scotch, rye, or soda pop. Dagmar reluctantly agreed to a bit of scotch, neat. Renie put down her magazine and strolled to the kitchen.

"What happened?" Judith asked, noting Dagmar's pallor and trembling hands.

Dagmar had thrown a lavender summer-weight coat over her peignoir and negligee. She wore beige mules decorated with feathers. Her dyed red hair was in disarray, and without makeup, she looked old and extremely tired.

"I should never have let him in." Dagmar sighed. "I'd been sleeping, and someone rang the chimes, repeatedly. I woke up and realized I was alone. It took a moment to . . . grasp reality. I'm so used to having Agnes there." Her manner was pathetic. "I went to the front door, and it was Nat Linski. He seemed humble, so I let him in. But he exploded into a rage, accusing me of ruining Mia and Ice Dreams! I denied his charges, we argued, we yelled and screamed, which brought the Kreagers on the run!" Dagmar stopped to catch her breath and accept a drink from Renie.

"Take your time," Judith urged in a quiet voice. Her indignation had abated with Dagmar's unexpected arrival. She would worry about Joe later, perhaps far into the night. "Coz," she said in a small voice, "how about a teeny bit for me?"

Renie looked askance, but surrendered. "Why not?" she muttered. "Let's all get stupid and pass out. I haven't had the whirlies since I was twenty-two."

Ignoring Renie, Judith turned back to Dagmar. "Why did Nat think you were ruining Mia and her ice show?"

Dagmar's small, plump body shuddered under the layers of poplin, silk, and lace. "About a month ago, I got a lead that Mia had calcium deposits in her knees. Such a condition could end her skating career. But I hadn't used the information in my column. I wanted to get it checked out with various medical experts first. I was considering it for my next book, in a chapter on athletes who retire early. The whole thrust of the second volume is celebrities as victims, the downside of fame. Very sympathetic stuff. But I told Nat Linski that I planned to include Mia—and he blew up! That's when the argument started, and the next thing I knew, he was threatening me, and then Karl and Kirk and Tessa came rushing in. They all began to argue, and Nat and Kirk actually came to blows! I couldn't stand it, and I ran away. Here." Distractedly, she kneaded the sofa cushions. "Where else could I go at this time of night?"

Renie returned, carrying three glasses. "You mean they may still be across the courtyard, beating each other black-and-blue?"

Gratefully, Dagmar sipped her scotch. "They may be. But Nat might have followed me. He's very big and very strong."

"So is Karl," Judith noted. "And Kirk's no small thing. The Kreagers are formidable."

Dagmar gave Judith a dark look. "Aren't they, though? I hate them!" Her voice shivered with malice.

"But you work for them," Renie pointed out, settling back into her armchair and sipping her rye.

"I have to work for somebody," Dagmar retorted. "Publishers! They're all a bunch of crooks! If I told half of what I know . . ." Her voice trailed off as she took another gulp of straight scotch.

"So," Judith said in a musing tone, "the terrible thing that Nat and Mia said you knew about them was calcium deposits?" Her voice held a note of incredulity.

"Hmm-mmm." Dagmar sagged next to Judith on the sofa.

She took another drink. "Mm-mmm. That's right. Ruinous, if colorless. Mm-mmm . . ."

The cousins exchanged glances. Apparently, the scotch wasn't meshing well with the doctor's sedatives. Or maybe it was, *too* well. Dagmar looked as if she were about to pass out.

"Dagmar . . ." Judith began, then gave up. Dagmar's eyes were closed and the glass tumbled out of her hand. Renie caught it on the first bounce.

"Great," Judith muttered in annoyance. "Now we've got a sleep-over."

Renie stood up. "Let's cart her off to my room. I've got the other twin bed. It'll be easier than taking her downstairs."

Judith tugged at her black-and-silver curls. "Damn. What if Karl and Tessa come looking for her?"

Renie shrugged. "We're asleep. We're innocent. We're simple tourists from the States."

Judith took a swig of scotch, then tried to prop up Dagmar. Renie came to her aid. Together, they carted their unconscious guest off to Renie's bedroom and settled her on the extra bed.

"I hope she doesn't snore," Renie said, watching the irregular rise and fall of Dagmar's coat-covered breast.

"Does Bill?" Judith inquired with a wry look.

"Not much. What about Joe?" Renie asked innocently.

Judith turned away and stomped out of the bedroom.

FOURTEEN

DAGMAR SLEPT IN. At least she was still asleep by the time the cousins had finished their homemade breakfast at eight-forty-five. The groceries they'd purchased would cover them through the morning meals before their leave-taking on Thursday. Judith and Renie managed to save just enough Canadian bacon, eggs, and bread to feed Dagmar, should she desire to eat *Chez Cousines*.

"Should we wake her up?" Judith asked, pouring a second cup of coffee.

Renie was in a merciful mood. "No. She's been through a bad time. Plus, she's had a sedative—and some straight scotch. Let her sleep. She was breathing normally when I got up."

"Good for her." For once, Judith's frame of mind wasn't as benevolent as her cousin's. "I had a lousy night."

"Oh? How come?" Renie was clearing the table.

But Judith still wasn't ready to confide in Renie. "The mattress isn't right," she muttered.

Renie knew Judith far too well to accept a facile explanation. "Wrong, coz." She leaned on the dining room table. "You're out of sorts because of Joe. I'm not exactly sure why, but he ticked you off last night. You can tell me now, or you can tell me later. Either way, by the time we get home, you'll be over it. He'll look at you with those magic eyes, as you call them, and you'll dissolve like jelly.

179

You always do, just the way I melt when I see Bill's chin. They can act like jackasses, make you swear you'll kill them or at least consider divorce, but when it comes right down to it, whatever hooked you in the first place is still there, and it works, every time. The good part is that it's reversible—it works with them, too, which is why we stay married.'' Renie gave Judith an off-center smile.

"Stick it," said Judith.

"Okay, for now. What about Dagmar?"

Before Judith could answer, Dagmar staggered out into the kitchen. She was holding her head and clutching her summer coat around her body.

"I feel terrible!" she exclaimed. "Do you have tea?"

Again the larder was inadequate. "Only coffee," Judith replied. "And orange juice."

"Juice." Dagmar collapsed into a chair. "Why am I here? Did Nat show up?"

Renie was at the refrigerator, pouring a glass of orange juice. "Not that we know of. We went to bed right after you did."

Dagmar shuddered. "Karl must have killed him." She accepted the glass from Renie and drank warily. "I wish I were back in Minneapolis, writing about waiters from North Dakota!"

Judith offered to make toast, but Dagmar declined. She couldn't eat, she insisted. Her life was a shambles. If the police would permit it, she would leave Bugler as soon as possible, fly Agnes's body to the Twin Cities, and make funeral arrangements.

"Does Agnes have family in Minnesota?" Judith asked.

Dagmar seemed uncertain. "She wasn't close to anyone. Except me. Agnes didn't socialize much." Suddenly Dagmar tensed. "Where's Rover? Where's my precious poopy-doo?"

"Rover?" Judith glanced at Renie, whose face was a blank. "He wasn't with you last night. Did you leave him at the condo?"

On unsteady legs, Dagmar got up from the table. "Oh! I must find him! He ran out when I did! Rover would never abandon me in my time of need!"

"Relax," Renie urged, putting a hand on Dagmar's trembling arm. "I'll look for him. I'll start with the Kreagers."

But Dagmar wouldn't relinquish the task completely. "I'll call to him. He'll come when he hears my voice." She leaned on Renie, who led the way to the front door.

Despite Dagmar's shrill cries, Rover didn't show up. Renie steered Dagmar back inside, spun her in the direction of the dining room, and headed out across the courtyard to the Kreager complex.

Dagmar sat down with a plop. "I can't bear this!" She covered her face with her hands. "What if that awful Lusatian did something to my poor Pomeranian?"

"I thought you said Karl had killed Nat," Judith remarked in a reasonable tone.

"What?" Dagmar peeked through her fingers. "Maybe he did. But the police would have come, wouldn't they?"

"Probably." Judith spoke dryly, then took pity on her guest. "Don't upset yourself, Dagmar. Rover will show up. Where could he go?"

Dagmar's hands fell into her lap and her eyes grew enormous. "The woods! There must be wolves and bears and mountain lions! They'll tear my poor precious lambie-pie to pieces!"

Since Rover had almost bested Sweetums, Judith thought that the dog's chances against wild animals would be quite good. She also doubted that there was much danger in the nearby wilds.

"It's summer, Dagmar. The big animals are far away. They probably cleared out years ago, at the first sound of a bank card charge being approved. What with helicopters, private planes, and everybody tromping around the mountains, a couple of deer would be a novelty."

The horror in Dagmar's eyes abated. "Still," she argued feebly, "it's not like him. He never leaves my side."

Judith offered more juice, but Dagmar shook her head in a dull fashion. "Where will you stay in Minneapolis?" Judith asked, trying to pull Dagmar out of her depression.

"Oh—I don't know. In Edina, with Kirk Kreager, maybe. I haven't thought about it." Her agitated fingers traced loopy circles on the teal place mat.

"You lived in Minneapolis a long time before moving to

New York," Judith remarked. "I suppose the area has changed, like most places."

"I suppose." Dagmar had swiveled in the chair, leaning to one side in an attempt to see the front door. She showed no interest in her old hometown.

"It'll be hot," Judith said.

"What?" Dagmar didn't turn around. "Oh, yes, certainly. Mosquitoes, too."

"You don't have mosquitoes in Manhattan?"

"Yes, but not like Minnesota. The lakes, you know."

Renie returned, her round face apologetic. "Tessa hasn't seen Rover since last night."

Dagmar leaped to her feet, but had to lean on the table for support. "Call the police! If they can't find out who killed Agnes, the least they can do is recover Rover!"

Renie gave Judith a questioning look. Judith nodded. "Go ahead, coz. Under ordinary circumstances, missing pets are probably the local constabulary's biggest problem." Too late, she realized the tactlessness of her remark. But Dagmar was too absorbed in her own troubles to notice. She was watching Renie's progress to the phone very closely.

Renie didn't have much luck with the police. A harried voice that sounded as if it belonged to Devin O'Connor took the report but rang off abruptly.

Renie eyed Dagmar. "He said something about missing persons being more important than missing dogs."

"Well, I never!" Dagmar pounded the table. "There are any number of human beings I know who aren't worth one-tenth of—Oh!" She realized that Renie was still staring. "Do you mean—*me*?"

Renie poured herself another cup of coffee. "That's my guess. I suppose Tessa reported you missing. When I went to check on Rover, I told her you were here, but maybe she hasn't called the police back yet."

With a sigh, Judith went to the phone. "It isn't fair to let them continue a search when the problem's solved. The police have enough to do with the murder investigation." She punched in the local number. "Though I notice their officers don't seem to conduct inquiries by taking suspects out for— Yes, is this Devin O'Connor?"

Dagmar was on the edge of her chair. "Don't let them call off the search for Rover! Do you want a description?"

"I already told them," Renie said in a vexed tone. She sat back down at the table, sipping her coffee.

For some reason, it wasn't easy to explain the situation to Devin O'Connor. In fairness to Judith, he seemed distracted. In the background, she heard the word "weapon," and pounced.

"You found the homicide weapon?" Judith was breathless.

But they had not. What they had found was that the champagne bottle discarded near the lift hadn't been used to bludgeon Agnes. Not that they ever thought it was, but all the same, the police had run the bottle through the lab. Did the no-longer-missing Ms. Chatsworth want it back?

Dagmar scorned the champagne. "How could I?" she asked bleakly. "Why would I want to drink champagne now that Agnes is dead and Rover is missing?"

Judith replaced the receiver and sat down next to Dagmar. "They'll do everything they can to find Rover," she said. "Really, he can't have gone very far." The truth was that Devin O'Connor had seemed indifferent to Rover's disappearance.

Dagmar stood up. "I must get dressed and go look for him myself. If you can't trust the police to find Agnes's killer, then you can't expect them to find my goo-goo baby."

Dagmar's logic eluded Judith, but she didn't say so. "I'll walk you home," she volunteered.

The morning was fresh and sunny, with only a few wispy white clouds drifting over the mountains. Judith took a deep breath, savoring the mingled scent of summer flowers and evergreen trees.

"I've never been to Minneapolis," she remarked as they crossed the courtyard. "Was your husband from there, too?"

"My husband?" Dagmar seemed startled. "Oh, yes, he was. Definitely."

"My first husband was from Arizona," Judith said. "His mother still lives there. My second husband is from—" She caught herself before saying something she'd regret. It occurred to Judith that after living with Dan, she could put up with just about anything from Joe. Or could she? Dan had been a horror in many ways, but she'd never questioned his fidelity. She'd never had to. No one else would have wanted him.

"Sorry," Judith apologized. "I lost my train of thought. You were saying that your husband . . . did what? Died?"

They had arrived on the short walkway to the unit occupied by Karl and Tessa. "I wasn't saying," Dagmar replied somewhat testily. "But you're right, he died." She paused, a finger hovering over the buzzer next to the Kreagers' door. "It was very sad. My late husband was a wonderful man. He died too young. He just . . . wasted away." Her eyes became dewy.

"My first husband didn't waste away," Judith responded. "In fact, he didn't have a waist. He weighed over four hundred pounds when he died."

"Really." Dagmar pushed the buzzer; the faint chime could be heard inside.

Tessa came to the door, looking as grim as ever. "Well, there you are. We were worried." She yanked the door open wide, then scanned the walkway with suspicious eyes. "You didn't bring Rover with you, I hope. You know I won't allow him on our white rug."

Dagmar pushed past Tessa. "If I had Rover, would I be upset? I can't believe you're so fussy! What on earth could my poor doggy do on your carpet?"

"Just that, for one thing," snapped Tessa. She turned to Judith, who was still on the porch. "Well? Are you going to come in or what?"

Judith was actually trying to picture Tessa Van Heusen as a revolutionary Spotted Leopard. Only vaguely could she imagine the pristine blond curls hanging long and limp at Tessa's waist, or the crisp beige linen slacks and tailored shirt traded in for battle fatigues.

"I probably should go back to our place," Judith said lamely. "Uh—how's Karl this morning?"

"Fine," Tessa replied, and apparently taking Judith at her word, she slammed the door.

Judith shrugged, then started back down the walkway. She stopped midway and stared in surprise.

Freddy Whobrey was strolling toward the condo with Rover

prancing at his side. In one hand, Freddy carried a newspaper; in the other, he held a metal strongbox.

Despite her eagerness for information, Judith remembered to keep her distance from Freddy. At least he had both his hands occupied. Rover, however, tried to lick her shoes.

"Dagmar will certainly be glad to see you," Judith declared. "Where did you find Rover? And that box?"

Freddy looked puzzled. "Rover? I didn't find him. His howling woke me up this morning. I couldn't get back to sleep, so I went in to Dagmar's condo and found the poor mutt all by himself. I took him to breakfast with me."

It was Judith's turn for bewilderment. "So you reported Dagmar missing?"

Freddy raised his eyebrows in alarm. "Missing? Is she missing? I figured they'd hauled her off to the hospital."

"She spent the night at our place." Briefly, Judith explained about the row between Nat Linski and the Kreagers. "It's fine; we've told the police that she's safe. Now we'll have to tell them that Rover isn't missing, either." Judith pointed to the metal box, which she recognized from the bedroom at Hillside Manor and Agnes Shay's downstairs condo unit. "Where was that thing?" She danced away as Rover renewed his attack on her shoes.

Freddy winked. "You'd like to know, wouldn't you? How about coming to my condo, where I'll explain while we do something even more interesting? Want to stroke my silks?"

"No," Judith replied staunchly, "I do not. But I'll go with you to the Kreagers' condo while you show Dagmar what you found. And who." She flicked at Rover with the toe of her shoe.

Freddy sighed with exaggerated regret. "You don't know what you're missing. There's a lot of fun to be had in the back stretch."

Judith had already started up the walkway, while Rover nipped at the cuffs of her slacks. "Dagmar has had enough tragedy," she asserted. "Come along, ease her mind. She's certain that Rover has been eaten by bears."

"No such luck," Freddy murmured as Judith rang the buzzer. "Hey, I thought you wanted to hear where I found the box. It's pretty weird, sweetheart. You'd never guess."

"Probably not," Judith replied as Tessa once again came to the door, looking no more cheerful than the last time.

"Get that damned dog out of here!" she railed at Freddy. "Downstairs! Now! I'd rather have termites!"

Dagmar was a streak, coming to a staggering stop on the threshold. "Poopy-poo-poopsy-do!" she shrieked, bending down as Rover leaped into her outstretched arms. "My love! My dove! My bovey-wovey-movey . . ."

"Out!" Tessa screamed. "Get that rotten little creature off my white rug or he's toast!"

Author and editor faced off. Both women began shouting at each other, their shrill voices jarring Judith's ears. Karl Kreager came into the entry hall, attempting to assert his publisher's authority.

"Here, here! Stop, both of you!" He grabbed his wife by the arm and gave her a good shake, then turned to Dagmar. "Take Rover downstairs, please. And try to excuse Tessa. She's very high-strung."

Clutching Rover to her breast, Dagmar glared at Tessa. "She can't spell, either," Dagmar hissed, then bestowed several kisses on Rover's furry head before departing with dignity.

Karl unleashed Tessa, whose boiling temper was now at a mere simmer. "Freddy, you'd better explain yourself," Karl commanded.

Freddy repeated his story of Rover's early-morning howls. Judith was distracted by the bruise on Karl's cheek and the bandage on his hand. Apparently Dagmar's account of the quarrel with Nat was no exaggeration. Judith wondered where Kirk Kreager had gone. Perhaps he had retreated to his hotel. She couldn't much blame him.

"And the metal box?" Karl demanded.

Freddy had grown a little woebegone. "Hey, can I sit down? I've been walking all over the damned town this morning. I've been up since six!"

Reluctantly, Tessa led the way into the living room—but not before she'd insisted that Freddy and Judith check their shoes. Judith wondered if hers were all of a piece. They were, though there were distinct small tooth marks on the toes.

"It's like this," Freddy began from his place on a satin-covered, off-white Louis Quinze chair. "I got dressed after I went in to check on Rover, and then I got this bright idea. I knew Dagmar was all upset about Agnes, but she was also in a tizzy about the metal box. So I took one of her scarves and a handkerchief of Agnes's and told Rover to fetch. Or something." Freddy reached into the inside pocket of his houndstooth sport coat, producing both items. "I know horses, but not dogs. Still, I figured Rover could follow a scent. So first thing, before breakfast, we trotted off. You'll never guess where Rover led me." Freddy stopped, leaning forward on the antique chair. "Say, do you suppose I could have a little something? Like gin?"

The request for a bribe worked. Karl went off to fix the drink just as Dagmar reappeared, now wearing a flowing chartreuse caftan. She insisted that Freddy repeat his tale about Rover. By the time Dagmar was exclaiming at Rover's cleverness, Karl had served Freddy a gin fizz.

"And where did my precious fuzzy-wuzzy lead you?" Dagmar asked breathlessly.

"It's pretty weird," Freddy replied, gulping at his drink. "I thought the dog was nuts. We went all over the place—and ended up at my old chum's apartment. The strongbox was in Esme MacPherson's liquor cabinet."

It seemed to Judith that the others had never heard of Esme MacPherson. She listened with growing impatience as Freddy explained. She also tried to figure out why and how Dagmar's metal box had ended up in the old sot's apartment. It didn't make sense, unless Freddy had put it there. But why would he then retrieve it?

Her attention was recaptured when Dagmar announced she had forgotten to bring the key from Agnes's unit. "I can't bear to go in there," she said plaintively, looking at Karl. "Would you . . . ?"

But Freddy snorted. "You don't need a key to the strongbox. Somebody has already broken the lock." He flipped the lid up, revealing a thick set of files.

Dagmar paled with what Judith perceived as relief. "Everything's there! Oh, thank heavens! I was sure the files had been stolen!"

"They were," Freddy retorted. "I mean, how else did they get to Esme's apartment?"

From her place next to Karl on the sofa, Tessa leaned forward and gave Freddy a hard stare. "So why did this old pal of yours take the box?"

Freddy was looking innocent. "He swears he didn't. He told me he'd never seen the thing before."

Judith thought that was unlikely. Esme was into his liquor cabinet several times a day. On the other hand, he seemed to be fixated on his bottles. Maybe he'd never noticed the metal box.

"This is ridiculous," Tessa declared, sitting up straight again. "Dagmar, you'd better make sure everything is really there. You're the only one who knows those files backward and forward."

Dagmar jumped in her eggshell damask-covered armchair. "I do? Oh, I do! But not the way that Agnes did. She maintained them for me."

Karl was nodding. "Tessa's right. There's a reason that those files disappeared, whether this Esme MacPherson took them or not. Someone did. I suggest you go through them. At your leisure, of course."

Dagmar glared at Karl. "I'll do it now." She pulled her chair up to a white drum table with a white marble top. "Give me the box, Freddy."

Freddy obeyed. Dagmar began her methodical search of the files. The room grew very still. Judith wondered if she should leave. Occasionally, Tessa's unfriendly eyes flickered in her direction. Freddy sucked on his gin fizz and gazed longingly at Judith's lap. Curiosity had its limits. Judith stood up, breaking the awkward silence.

"I should go home. My cousin will be wondering what's happened to me. I don't want her reporting me as missing, too." She laughed feebly.

Karl got to his feet to escort Judith to the door. Freddy made a noise of protest, but Dagmar didn't look up. "By the way," Judith said to Karl, "we reported Rover missing. Someone should tell the police that he's okay."

Karl nodded. "I'll see to that. Thank you for taking Dagmar

in last night. We should have realized that she'd seek safe harbor with—''

"Outrageous!" Dagmar's voice spiked the air. Judith and Karl turned in the entry hall. Together, they hurried back into the living room.

Seated at the drum table, Dagmar's face was flushed. About half the file folders were on the floor, the rest still in the metal box. "I got to the L's," she announced in a trembling voice, "and what *didn't* I find? Nat Linski, that's what! Or *who*," she corrected herself. Feverishly, she began to sort through the files that were farther back in the box. She blinked; her shoulders sagged. "Mia's here. How odd!"

Freddy had finished his fizz and was wearing a shocked expression. "You must be wrong, Dagmar. Maybe Agnes misfiled Nat someplace."

Dagmar turned sharply. "Agnes never made mistakes! How dare you!"

Freddy was now chagrined as well as stupefied. "Okay, okay," he muttered. "But it's damned odd. How could it happen?"

Karl didn't agree. "It's exactly as I thought." He pointed to the metal box. "Someone stole those files to purge them of incriminating information. The obvious thief is Nat Linski. Dagmar, what was in his folder that he'd want so badly?"

Her mouth was working, but no audible words came out. At last she managed a squeak. "Nothing." Dagmar rubbed agitatedly at her temples. "Please! I have such a headache!"

Tessa jumped off the sofa and veered across the room to land practically on top of Dagmar's hunched figure. "Rot! You had something damaging on Nat! Why else would he steal the file?"

The columnist shook her head, slowly and shakily. "No . . . I'm sure there wasn't . . . No . . ." She looked not only old, but defeated. The fire seemed to have gone out of her. She leaned away from the encroaching Tessa, her lined face almost touching the marble tabletop.

Judith felt obligated to interfere. "I think Dagmar should lie down," she said in a firm voice. "I'll get her to bed." Wedging in between the Kreagers, Judith reached for Dagmar's arm. "Come, I'll help you to your condo."

Nobody protested. Except Tessa. "Just a minute! We've got one dead woman, missing files, and a lost-and-found metal box! This is dangerous stuff! Why are we fussing over Dagmar's nap?"

"Take care of it," Judith said calmly, getting Dagmar to her feet. "This is your condo; these are your guests. And your author. You're in charge." Her sharp glance took in both Kreagers, but purposely avoided Freddy.

Karl sighed. "She's right. We should contact that Penreddy fellow. He can talk to MacPherson—and to Nat Linski."

Tessa wasn't yet satisfied. "What about the rest of us? We're all involved. We could be next on the killer's list! I want protection! Somebody broke into our condo! We've been burglarized . . ."

Judith shut the door on Tessa. Dagmar felt like a dead weight as the two women shuffled to the premises next door. Luckily, Renie was just coming out of the cousins' unit. She ran across the courtyard to help Judith with Dagmar.

"What's happening?" Renie demanded. "I was about to call over here, and then I saw you through the window."

Judith explained after they had put Dagmar to bed. Again. To Judith's surprise, Dagmar didn't interrupt. Rather, she moved restlessly on the futon, apparently finding little comfort except in Rover's slobbering presence.

At last Judith put a direct question to Dagmar. "When did you discover that the file box was missing?"

Dagmar flung a hand over her forehead. "Oh! I've no idea! Agnes kept the files, as I've said. They were gone yesterday afternoon. That's all I know."

Judith exchanged quizzical glances with Renie. "When did you last see them?"

Dagmar turned sulky. "I didn't. Not here. I remember Agnes carrying them into her downstairs unit when we arrived over the weekend. I never went into her part of the condo. I couldn't bear to, after she . . ." The querulous voice choked and faded away.

Judith's face set. She gazed again at Renie, who was obviously trying not to betray any expression. Judith started to say something, thought better of it, and asked Dagmar if she'd like a sleeping pill. She would, and a couple of the 222 tablets. Judith found the bottle of sleeping capsules and the analgesic packet next to the bed, got a glass of water from the bathroom, and ministered to Dagmar.

"Was there any sign of a break-in?" Judith asked, deciding to put the prescription bottle of sleeping pills out of immediate reach on the teak bureau.

"Not that I know of," Dagmar replied. "The Kreagers didn't mention it."

Something about the Kreagers' twin condos tripped through Judith's brain, but disappeared before she could focus on the stray thought. Instead she recalled seeing the metal box when the cousins had called on Dagmar the previous afternoon. Then Rhys Penreddy had arrived. The strongbox must have been taken after he and Devin O'Connor left. By coincidence, Judith heard a car pull up outside. Peeking through the shoji screen, she saw Penreddy and O'Connor walking toward the wrought-iron gate.

Judith had a final question for Dagmar, who was already showing signs of drowsiness. "Did Mia or Nat come by in the afternoon?"

Dagmar's eyes were fuzzy. "I'm not sure . . . I was resting much of the time. At some point, Nat came looking for . . . Mia . . . or so I heard . . ." Her voice trailed away as her chin dropped onto her breast. Rover tugged at the down comforter.

Renie was watching Judith watch Dagmar. "Now what?" Renie whispered. "Can we leave?"

Rover munched on an extra pillow. Dagmar twitched slightly under the comforter. Judith frowned. "I guess so. The rest of them are right next door if—and when—Dagmar wakes up."

Renie, who hadn't bothered to bring in an extra chair, started for the bedroom door. Judith stood up, but hesitated as Dagmar twitched again, this time more strenuously. Jostled, Rover barked. Dagmar's motions became more jerky, bordering on convulsions.

"I don't like this," Judith declared. "Something's wrong here. She's supposed to be sleeping deeply."

Renie came back to the futon. Observing Dagmar's body

shiver and shake, she, too, expressed alarm. "Do you suppose she has fits? Should we tell the Kreagers to call the doctor? Maybe Freddy knows what's going on."

Dagmar's eyes flew open. She tried to speak, but gasped for breath, then fell back against the pillows, still convulsing.

"Get Karl," Judith ordered. "I'll call 911." She grabbed the bedside phone as Renie hurried out of the condo.

For the next five minutes Judith tried to settle Dagmar down, but failed. The older woman threatened to throw up at least twice. Her breathing was so labored that it was hard to understand her words. Sensing that something was very wrong with his mistress, Rover jumped off the futon and ran to a corner where he sat with his tongue out, panting. He looked not unlike Dagmar.

Frantic, Judith held the older woman by the shoulders. Perhaps it was epilepsy. Judith wondered if she could prevent Dagmar from swallowing her tongue.

To Judith's immense relief, Renie returned with not only Karl Kreager, but Rhys Penreddy. "Oh!" Judith cried, staring at the police chief but still hanging onto Dagmar. "I forgot you were here! I called for an ambulance."

Penreddy took over. Judith backed off, standing near the door with Renie and Karl. Devin O'Connor was in the hall with Tessa and Freddy, apparently waiting to let in the ambulance attendants and medics.

Resenting a virtual stranger's attentions to his mistress, Rover ran forward and tried to take a bite out of Penreddy's leg. Judith made a dive for the animal, picked him up, and carted him down the hall.

"Here," she said to Freddy. "Take this mutt and keep him out of the way." She sneezed twice as she shoved Rover at a reluctant Freddy.

The next few minutes were a blur. The medical team arrived, clearing everyone but Rhys Penreddy out of the bedroom. Devin O'Connor retired to the living room with the cousins, the Kreagers, Freddy, and the dog.

Judith had positioned herself by a window. The gurney carrying Dagmar was moved quickly to the waiting ambulance. Rover strained in Freddy's grasp. Tessa and Karl stared at each other in shock.

"Is she . . . ?" Tessa had gone pale.

On his way out the door, Rhys Penreddy paused. "She's alive," he said grimly. "But we may not be able to save her. Stand by." He nodded once to Devin O'Connor, who stayed on duty with the others.

"The manuscript!" Tessa shrieked as the door closed behind Penreddy, the emergency personnel, and Dagmar. "Karl, Dagmar's up against deadline!"

Karl Kreager put an arm around his wife. He was looking uncharacteristically grim. "She's up against much more than that," he asserted, his blue eyes on Devin O'Connor. "Well? What is it?"

Devin visibly gulped. "I can't say, sir. Not until we know for sure."

Releasing Tessa, Karl took a few steps toward Devin. The two men were close in height, but the older man outweighed the younger by at least thirty pounds. Karl's manner was intimidating.

"Throw out the rules for now," he commanded, with the authority of power and money evident in his voice. "This situation doesn't affect just the handful of us here in Bugler. We're talking about millions of people and millions of dollars. What's going on with Dagmar Chatsworth?"

It would have taken a policeman of much more experience and far more nerve not to be cowed. Devin O'Connor was young, unsophisticated, and naturally given to candor. He licked his dry lips, then met Karl's frosty stare.

"I'm only guessing, sir," Devin said quietly. "Don't quote me, please. But it looks as if Ms. Chatsworth has been poisoned."

FIFTEEN

FREDDY AND TESSA finally agreed upon something: They both needed a drink. They would adjourn to the next-door condo. Karl, who was still looking dazed, went with them. To Renie's surprise, Judith volunteered to keep Rover under control.

"He'll give you an allergy attack," Renie pointed out.

Judith avoided her cousin's gaze. Most of all, she avoided Devin O'Connor, who was uneasily pacing the tatami mats. "I'll put Rover back in Dagmar's bedroom," Judith said, moving quickly down the hall.

She had gotten as far as the door when Devin called after her to stop immediately. "That's a crime scene, ma'am! You can't go in there!"

"But Rover..." Judith protested, inching over the threshold.

Devin was hurrying down the hall on his long legs. "*I'll* take the dog," he said.

Thwarted, Judith tried to hand Rover over to the young policeman. But Rover wanted to stay with Judith. The dog yipped, cringed, and went rigid. Devin tried to pry him loose, but Rover snarled. Judith stifled another sneeze. Again Devin tried to get a firm grip on the dog. Rover snapped at the young man's fingers.

"Okay, okay." Devin sighed. "Just put him down and come right out. I'll stand here and wait."

Rover was perfectly content to snuggle on the comforter. Judith finally sneezed, reaching for a box of tissues on the bureau. In her haste, she knocked over the bottle of sleeping capsules.

"Sorry," she said in an abashed tone. "I honestly didn't mean to do that."

Devin was growing angry. He loped into the bedroom, started to retrieve the bottle, then got a handkerchief from his pocket, grasped the medication, and straightened up again.

"Was Ms. Chatsworth taking this stuff?" he asked.

Judith nodded. "I gave her one of those and a couple of 222s about half an hour ago," she said, mortified at the fact. "Frankly, I feel terrible about it. They're capsules, and if Dagmar was poisoned, the stuff could be inside." Nervously, Judith gestured at the bottle that Devin still held in the cradle of his handkerchief.

"Would it work that fast?" he asked, more of himself than of Judith.

"I don't know," she replied. "It depends on the poison. Dagmar took at least one of the capsules last night, too. The reaction may be a cumulative effect."

Suspicion filled Devin's eyes as he watched Judith. "You know a lot about poison."

"Of course I do," she responded impatiently. "I've had guests drop dead under my dinner table."

Obviously, Devin thought Judith was joking. She wasn't, but there was no need to enlighten the policeman further. Judith exited the bedroom.

She reentered the living room just as Rhys Penreddy returned with two other officers, one male, one female. He swiftly explained that there was nothing more he could do at the medical clinic. Dagmar was being treated, though it was possible that she would be airlifted into Port Royal.

After asking the cousins to remain where they were, Penreddy and his crew went into the bedroom. Judith and Renie sat down on a bamboo couch covered in a deep-blue-and-white-striped fabric. Judith blew her nose while Renie toyed with her unmanageable coiffure.

"You must have been wrong," Renie remarked in a low

voice. "No offense, coz, but it looks as if Dagmar was the intended victim all along."

The same thought had already crossed Judith's mind. "I hate being wrong," she said with fervor. "About murder, anyway. Now I'm really at sea. What's worse, I feel like a criminal for giving Dagmar those damned pills." A light suddenly shone in her dark eyes. "Unless . . ."

Rhys Penreddy reappeared, with Devin O'Connor at his side. "You're going to have to answer some questions, I'm afraid," Penreddy said, signaling for Devin to take notes. "Let's start with why Ms. Chatsworth wanted to go to sleep in the middle of the morning."

Judith explained about the missing metal box and the discovery that Nat Linski's file was gone. Penreddy already knew as much, having just called on the Kreagers.

"That was it," Judith said. "Dagmar sort of fell apart, and I offered to take her over here, to her own bed. She was in a state of nervous collapse and complained of a terrible headache. I asked if she wanted some medication. She did. I gave it to her." Judith sighed and shook her head. "It never occurred to me that someone might have tampered with the capsules. I was so sure that Dagmar wasn't meant to be killed in the first place."

Penreddy bridled. "Pardon me? Why do you say such a thing?"

Judith felt Renie's elbow nudging her in the ribs. "Oh—it was just an idea. It seems to me that when someone is killed in such a daring way, there can't be any mistake about the victim. After all, the killer must have gotten up very close. How could anyone mistake Agnes for Dagmar, turban notwithstanding?"

Squinting at Judith, Penreddy chewed on his lower lip. "You do have a perverse penchant for getting involved in criminal investigations, don't you, Ms. Flynn? Why can't you take up another sport, like mountain biking?"

"It's too dangerous," she blurted, then felt her cheeks grow warm. "I'm sorry, I can't help it. I told you, I'm married to a homicide detective."

Penreddy moved around the living room, gazing at the hanging scrolls, the flower arrangements, the portrait of an ancient Oriental scholar. Devin O'Connor remained at attention, his ballpoint pen poised over his notebook.

"You can't leave Bugler," Penreddy finally said in a flat tone. "Neither of you. I'm sorry, but you knew both the deceased and the intended victim before they entered Canada. You were up on Liaison Ledge when Agnes Shay was murdered. You were here in this condo handing out sleeping capsules when Dagmar Chatsworth was allegedly poisoned. If I could think of a motive, I'd charge both of you on the spot."

"*Both* of us?" Renie exclaimed. "What did *I* do?"

Exasperated, Judith turned to her cousin. "You're guilty of having a bad hairdo. You ought to be locked up for ten years. That way, I wouldn't have to look at it."

Rhys Penreddy didn't see any humor in the exchange between the cousins. "This isn't a joke," he said grimly. "You two are under suspicion as much as the others. I rode in the ambulance to see if Ms. Chatsworth would say anything that might reveal who was trying to kill her." Rhys Penreddy's brown eyes had lost all warmth. "She couldn't say much in the shape she was in, but I managed to catch something about her dog being poisoned at your bed-and-breakfast."

Judith's jaw dropped. "It wasn't poison! It was gin!" She clapped a hand over her mouth. "Oh, dear! It was a . . . prank."

"Some prank," scoffed Penreddy. "Do you always play tricks on your guests?"

"Of course not," Judith responded heatedly. "I didn't do it. It was my mother. She was annoyed because Rover had attacked our cat. I had to take the poor little fellow to the vet. Dagmar blamed Sweetums. My mother got upset, because, for once, it wasn't his fault."

Penreddy snorted. "So you—or this alleged mother of yours—took revenge by trying to put out Rover's lights." He paused, glancing at Devin O'Connor, who began to take hasty notes. "Rover recovered, so *you* went after his owner. That must be some pedigreed pussycat you've got back home, Ms. Flynn."

A vision of Sweetums at his most baleful passed before Judith's mind's eye. "Scruffy," "ornery," and "mean" were the adjectives that danced in Judith's brain. "He's not a cham-

pion cat,'' she admitted. ''But he's much loved all the same.''
She almost choked on the declaration.

Penreddy gave a faint nod, which seemed to dismiss Sweetums. ''The point is, you acknowledge that somebody under
your roof slipped Rover a Mickey. That leads us to think you
might have done the same thing to his owner.''

''Well, I didn't. And Mother isn't under my roof. We keep
her in the toolshed.'' Judith's manner was haughty. ''In fact,
I feel terrible about giving Dagmar the medication. But she
asked for it.'' Seeing that Devin was scribbling as fast as possible, Judith turned to the young man. ''Forget that last sentence. It sounds bad.''

It was Renie's turn to make a disclaimer. ''Hey, forget the
pampered pets, too. They're a side issue. What about Nat Linski? His file is missing. And that old rummy, Esme Mac-
Pherson—how come the box turned up in his hooch hutch?
Unless Freddy Whoa put it there. Have you checked into Tessa
Van Heusen Kreager's background with the Spotted Leopards?
Is Freddy really Dagmar's nephew or just a gigolo? Come off
it, Chief. My cousin hadn't met any of these people until they
barged into her B&B last week. I never met them until I got
to Bugler.''

Penreddy's face clouded. ''Now, see here—''

Judith interrupted. ''My cousin's right. There's much more
going on here than meets the eye. What other celebrities are
staying in Bugler who might balk at some hot item Dagmar
is preparing to write about them? What about Ice Dreams and
the Kreager connection? When did Kirk Kreager arrive in Bugler?''

''That's easy enough,'' Penreddy replied, obviously taken
aback by the barrage of questions put to him by the cousins.
''Kirk Kreager arrived in Bugler by helicopter yesterday afternoon. We've already checked his alibi for Monday. He was
at work in the corporate offices of the Kreager newspaper
chain until after six o'clock, and in the evening he attended a
dinner party at some place called Lake of the Isles. He got
home around eleven, according to his chauffeur, who is still
in Minneapolis.''

''Scratch Kirk,'' Judith murmured. ''What about the other
celebrities in town?''

Penreddy squared his shoulders. "We're asking the questions here, eh?" His severe expression brooked no further argument. "I'm requesting that both of you be fingerprinted. Now."

"Oh, good grief!" Renie reeled around the room, almost toppling a potted bonsai pine tree. "This is stupid!"

Judith, however, didn't agree. "No, coz, it's not. It's procedure. Let the police do their job."

Apparently the male and female officers had finished their task in the bedroom. Moments later, they had fingerprinted the cousins, though their on-site work wasn't done.

"You're free to leave," Penreddy said solemnly. "But don't go outside the village. If Ms. Chatsworth doesn't pull through, we'll want another formal statement."

Renie grumbled all the way back to their condo. She had worked herself into a veritable tizzy by the time Judith reached for the coffeemaker. It was unplugged and almost empty.

"Who needs it? It's lunchtime, anyway," Renie snarled. "Not that I feel like eating."

"You? Not eating?" Judith smiled and sat down at the dining room table, which Renie had obviously cleared earlier. "Relax. Penreddy really doesn't suspect you. And while I was irked when he suggested I might have poisoned Dagmar because of that silly incident with Rover, I know he's got a job to do."

Renie calmed down sufficiently to take notice of Judith's smug expression. "I get it," she said, pulling out a chair and sitting down. "You figure that if you're an actual suspect, you'll get to hear more of what's going on from an official point of view."

"That's right." Judith nodded complacently. "I already have some idea of what the police know—and what they don't know. Or didn't, until we mentioned it just now."

"Such as?" Renie inquired.

"Ice Dreams, for one thing. They would have to get lucky like we did, or do some checking to figure out that the Kreagers own the show. If Dagmar wanted to publish something damaging about Mia or Nat, that gives Karl—and maybe Tessa—a motive."

Renie was looking puzzled. "I know you said that earlier,

but why couldn't the Kreagers simply squelch the item? Kirk could stop it in the newspapers, and Karl and Tessa could prevent it from coming out in Dagmar's next book.''

"Would you like to try to stop Dagmar from printing gossip?'' Judith paused, but didn't wait for Renie's response. "Dagmar's got enormous clout. I'd guess that if she got hassled over her columns—or books—she'd threaten lawsuits galore and find herself another publisher. You can bet she's been sitting on that Spotted Leopard story for years. The Kreagers wouldn't want that to come out in a rival newspaper chain's columns.''

"Journalistic blackmail,'' mused Renie. "I suppose Dagmar has a ton of juicy items she's kept under wraps.''

"That's right. Almost.'' Judith gave Renie an inquisitive look. "Are you thinking what I'm thinking?''

"Huh?'' It appeared as if Renie weren't thinking at all. "About what?''

Judith decided not to tantalize her cousin. "Dagmar seems very vague about those files. I'm wondering if Agnes did far more than maintain them for her. The typewriter is in Agnes's unit, not Dagmar's. Dagmar said she hadn't been in Agnes's part of the condo since they arrived over the weekend. But Karl told us that Dagmar had written her column for today on Monday. How did she do it? Where did she do it? Or did she do it at all?''

Enlightenment burst over Renie. "*Agnes* wrote the columns? The books, too?''

Judith shrugged. "It's possible. If Agnes knew all the dirt better than Dagmar did, it would account for her being killed. The attempt on Dagmar's life may be merely a backup, to ensure that whatever it was the killer wanted suppressed stayed that way.''

Renie considered Judith's theory. "But the killer would have to know that Agnes was the real Chatty Chatsworth. Unless I'm reading the Kreagers wrong, I don't think *they* realize it.''

Judith agreed. "They wouldn't have such a fit about getting Dagmar to finish her manuscript. Or meet her newspaper deadline. Instead they'd be figuring out a way to cut their losses.''

"Nat and Mia couldn't know,'' Renie remarked. "Freddy

is the only real possibility. He was with Dagmar and Agnes all the time.''

"I wouldn't trust Freddy with a secret, though," Judith said, getting up from the table and going to the kitchen counter to consult her tourist brochure. "If our idea is right, I'll bet Dagmar and Agnes knocked themselves out to keep the truth from Freddy. Besides, I don't see what motive he'd have. So he threw a few races, which is about the worst thing I can think of that he'd do. Worst, from his point of view, that is. So what? He's retired. Plus, Dagmar is his meal ticket. Getting rid of her—or Agnes—cuts off his income. Of course, there'll be royalties from the book—Oh!'' Judith smacked her hand against her head. "Dagmar's estate! If Freddy really is her nephew, and he's the only relative, maybe he inherits!''

"So why kill Agnes?" Renie asked dryly.

Judith hesitated in the act of perusing the brochure's food services. "You're right," she allowed. "That part doesn't make sense. Besides, I seem to recall Dagmar saying she'd never made a will. She's too young.''

Renie made a snide face. "Right. The Immortality Factor at work again. That wouldn't matter, though—Freddy would still get everything as her only survivor.'' She waited for Judith to finish scanning the restaurant listings.

"If you're not really hungry, let's go to a deli," Judith suggested. "There's one right by where we parked for The Bells and Motley. We're going to eat in tonight, remember?''

Renie did. Judith picked up her handbag and started for the stairs, but her cousin had yet another uncharacteristic surprise in store.

"Let's walk. It's gorgeous outside, and we could use the exercise.''

"*Walk*?'' Judith was incredulous. "As in one foot in front of the other? Okay, I'm game.''

It was downhill all the way, which, Judith reminded Renie as they reached the halfway point, meant uphill coming home. Renie reminded Judith that Bugler had a bus system. And taxis. She also pointed out the Chateau Arbutus, a tall glass-and-stone structure which shimmered before their very eyes.

"I think there's a deli in the hotel," said Renie. "If not, they must have a coffee shop.''

There was no deli. The coffee shop was surrounded by more rough stonework and tall tinted mirrors which gave the effect of vastness. Coming face-to-face with a smiling hostess, the cousins couldn't refuse the offer of a table.

"Yikes!" Renie exclaimed as she encountered the six-page luncheon menu, "this place isn't cheap. Dinner here would beggar us."

Judith concurred. The least costly item, a watercress sandwich, was six dollars, Canadian. She sighed, pitching the menu back between the condiments and a slim vase with a single white rose. "Oh, well, it's our last full day here. I'm having the pastrami on whole wheat."

"Sounds good," Renie said, also putting her menu away. She scooted forward on her chair. "What I don't get is why Agnes would agree to being Dagmar's ghostwriter. Do you suppose they split the profits? Dagmar certainly got all the glory."

Judith inclined her head. "True, but Agnes was very shy. She wouldn't want the attention. I can understand that part. But the money is another matter. They must have negotiated something between them."

A well-scrubbed young waitress with a coronet of blond braids came to take the cousins' order. "Which," Renie said after the waitress had moved away, "brings up the matter of Agnes's heirs. If she made a lot of money, somebody may stand to gain by her death."

"Dagmar told me Agnes had no family. At least not in Minnesota." Judith's high forehead furrowed. "The trouble with this line of thought is that we don't know a blasted thing about Agnes's finances. And we're really just guessing that she was the actual writer of the gossip columns."

"It's a bollix," Renie said, then stared across the coffee shop. "Here come some suspects now. Mia and Nat." Renie's eyes widened. "They're heading straight for us."

Casting discretion to the wind, Judith turned. Sure enough, the couple was approaching. Nat looked resigned; Mia wore a determined air.

"Excuse, please," Mia said, though there was no sign of deference in her voice. "We are here for a meeting, and saw you from the mezzanine balcony in the lobby. We are hearing rumor about Dagmar Chatsworth being not quite dead. Why is this?''

Judith hedged. "She may have mixed alcohol with sleeping pills. We'll know more later."

The sandwiches arrived. The waitress inquired if Nat and Mia would like to order. At first, they declined; then Nat decided he'd enjoy a plate of kielbasa. Dropping into an extra chair, Mia mulled a bit, then asked for grilled chicken breast and a beet salad. The waitress had already started off when Nat called for her to come back. He requested wine, a Gewürztraminer from Baden-Württemberg.

Nat appeared melancholy. "Dagmar Chatsworth may be ill. That is a minor pity. But she will not print lies!" His voice rose as he banged the menu on the table, rattling china and silverware.

Renie looked up from her sandwich. "My cousin was being tactful. That's probably because we're eating." She gazed innocently at Mia and Nat. "The truth is, Dagmar's been poisoned." Renie took a big, deliberate bite out of her pastrami and whole wheat.

"Aha!" shouted Nat, with obvious glee.

"Ooooh!" cried Mia, but her pleasure was hard to conceal. "Is she dead?"

"Not yet." Judith tried to keep from expressing her dismay, not only at Nat and Mia's reaction, but at Renie's candor. She decided to trot out a ploy of her own. "It happened right after the metal file box was returned."

Judith was disappointed. Nat was still emitting a rumbling chuckle, and Mia swayed in her chair, as if to music only she could hear. Judith tried again.

"The only file missing was yours, Mr. Linski."

This time, Nat did evince surprise, even shock. "My . . . *file*? What is this file? Who keeps it, the police?"

The wine arrived, but Nat rejected the ritual of label and cork. "Pour," he commanded. The waitress with the blond coronet obeyed, quivering slightly as she placed four glasses on the table.

Judith explained that the files belonged to Dagmar. "She keeps information on famous people in them. Like you and Ms. Prohowska. Background data. Or so we gather."

Nat was brooding. "This is not good." He sipped his wine. "This is bad."

Renie was eating a dill pickle. "The wine?"

Nat shook his head. "This file." He drank again. "But if Dagmar Chatsworth dies, it will not matter, hey?"

"True." Judith took a sip from her glass. "The material won't go into her column or a book."

"So who now has this box?" Mia asked as the waitress brought the new orders.

Judith wasn't sure she should tell. Indeed, it occurred to her that she didn't know. Perhaps Rhys Penreddy had confiscated the files. She shrugged, and took another bite of sandwich.

Nat ate and drank with abandon. Judith hadn't seen anybody eat with such verve since the last time Renie had gone for six hours without food and had buttered her eyeglasses.

"We must discover if this Chatsworth creature lives," Nat declared between mouthfuls. "Hurry, Mia. For this time only, disregard your digestion."

Mia complied, devouring beets and chicken with energy. Judith marveled at the young woman's appetite, then reminded herself that Mia was an athlete. No doubt she burned calories every day on the practice rink.

"I don't suppose," Judith remarked after finishing her sandwich, "that you'd care to tell us what awful thing Dagmar was supposed to reveal." She saw Nat's startled face over the rim of his wineglass and amended her statement. "I mean, do you have reason to believe that Dagmar knows something detrimental to one or both of you?"

"She knows too much," Nat replied darkly. He gobbled up the last piece of sausage and drained his glass. "Now we go to the clinic. It is en route to the rink."

Nat and Mia rose from their chairs and departed without another word. Judith sat frozen in place. Renie sank into her seat.

"Oh, no!" Judith gasped. "The bill!"

Even now, the waitress approached with a big smile. "Dessert?" she asked cheerfully.

Judith and Renie shook their heads. The waitress produced the bill. The cousins were speechless. They were out another sixty dollars, American. Capitalism didn't seem to be working for them. But it was doing very well for a pair of ex-Communists. Judith and Renie dug deep into their wallets and barely managed to come up with enough cash to cover the tab and the tip.

They were skulking through the lobby when they spotted Kirk Kreager, surrounded by hotel security personnel. It wasn't until they got a few steps closer that they saw Nat and Mia.

A scuffle broke out; voices were raised. The cluster of people ebbed and flowed, with Nat and Mia now in the center of the melee. It looked to the cousins as if the pair were under house arrest.

SIXTEEN

"Let the woman go!" Kirk Kreager's voice carried no less authority than that of his older brother. One of the four security guards, a statuesque woman with expressionless features, took Mia's arm and pulled her out of the circle.

Mia, however, wasn't going willingly. "No!" She attempted to fend off the woman. "Remove your hands! I stay with Anatoly!"

Nat Linski was putting up quite a fight. His big bearlike body charged the cordon, knocking Kirk off-balance. Nat ran through the lobby like a punt returner, dodging guests, bellhops, and a UPS deliveryman. The three male security guards followed him outside. They were all last seen leaping the privet hedge between the driveway and the street.

A writhing Mia was still in the clutches of her adversary. "Monster!" she screamed at Kirk, then spit in his direction.

The concierge and the desk clerk padded around nervously on the plush lobby carpet. A considerable crowd had gathered to watch the excitement. Mia was recognized by several of the onlookers. She glared as she heard her name, then suddenly became inspired.

"My friends, my admirers!" Mia was playing to the crowd, as if she were performing on the rink. "Is this justice in your fine, free country? The great Anatoly Linski is treated like a criminal! Protest, I beg you! He is innocent!"

Her long red hair had come loose from its French roll and flew around her shoulders. Her gray eyes snapped with anger and indignation, skewering Kirk Kreager. Her free arm was raised, a finger pointing in Kirk's direction. "See him? Attack! Tear him to pieces! Kill!"

Since anyone who could afford to stay at Chateau Arbutus was either personally affluent or on a corporate expense account, Mia wasn't exactly playing to a discontented mob. The Germans were morbidly fascinated; the Americans looked confused; the Canadians were too polite to attack a guest; the Japanese took pictures.

Though visibly shaken, Kirk still assumed command. Warily, he approached Mia, one hand extended. "Please—let's go somewhere and talk this out. I'm doing this for you and Ice Dreams, not just for myself and Karl."

It was clear that Mia didn't believe him. But she was weakening. The security guard finally let go. Mia brushed at her pleated linen skirt and gave Kirk a haughty stare.

"I will not be alone with you," she asserted. "You I do not trust. Nor your brother."

Kirk's brother arrived at that moment, looking unusually harried. Karl Kreager sized up the situation and asked where Nat Linski had gone. Kirk tried to explain.

Mia seemed buoyed by Karl's response that he had seen no sign of either Nat or the security men who had given chase. Still, she refused to go with the Kreagers. Kirk resorted to cajolery. At last Mia's eyes rested on the cousins.

"The prosaic middle-aged American women," she said. "They treat me kindly, with respect. Usually. If they come, I go."

Judith and Renie looked at each other. Judith gave a faint nod. Renie turned to Mia. "That's fine, but the drinks are on you. We're broke."

The cousins, the Kreagers, and Mia didn't go into a bar, but to a small meeting room off the mezzanine. It was Mia who led the way, and apparently it had been there that she and Nat had held their morning conference. Despite the ventilation system, the room smelled of smoke and sweat.

Kirk was regarding Mia's chaperones with distaste. "I'm

not comfortable with this,'' he said in annoyance. He eyed Karl. ''How do you know these women aren't . . . in the other camp?''

Karl exuded impatience. ''They're Americans, for one thing. For another, I've had them checked out. They're exactly what they say they are. They're absolutely nobody.''

''Thanks,'' Renie muttered, picking up a rubber band from the conference table and attempting to shoot it at Karl. She failed, and it fell in her lap. ''Darn,'' she said under her breath.

Kirk remained skeptical, but it was Judith who spoke next. ''*You* checked up on *us*?'' Astounded, she put the question to Karl Kreager.

He waved a hand. ''Yes, yes. Purely routine. You don't think we haven't had people checking on *us*? Nothing's sacred in the world of business these days.'' He grimaced, then made an effort to resume his normal affability. ''We have our own sources in your hometown. Nothing sinister.'' He gave Judith a brief nod. ''The state bed-and-breakfast association.'' His glance took in Renie. ''The local organization for graphic designers.''

Judith relaxed a bit. Kirk, however, still appeared very tense. ''I don't like this,'' he said, again giving the cousins a dubious look.

''Let's get down to it,'' Karl urged his brother. ''I need to know what's going on.''

Kirk composed himself, folding his hands on the table. ''Very well. This morning, Mia Prohowska and Nat Linski met with the representatives of a Canadian consortium which wants to buy Ice Dreams.'' Now Kirk was staring at Mia. She met his gaze without a flinch. ''They met,'' he went on, ''in this very room. Canada's success in the Olympics and the world championships has made skating extremely popular on this side of the border. They've got at least a half-dozen top-notch people who are willing to sign on if the show has Canadian ownership. They're offering Mia and Nat a bigger percentage of the profits than we now pay them. They're promising a world tour every other year, with the Americas in between.''

Karl's expression showed only mild interest. ''So? We could schedule the same thing if Nat and Mia are willing. We might even consider meeting the Canadians' offer.''

Renie, who found corporate meetings the least enjoyable part of her career, showed signs of restlessness. Judith, however, was listening intently.

Kirk's hands tightened; so did his face. "No, we won't consider any such thing. We're pulling out. The Canadians can have them.''

Although Mia said nothing, her cheeks had turned pink. Karl, on the other hand, grew rather pale under his tan. Renie was toying with her hair, which didn't help much. Judith watched everyone closely, trying to make sense of what was happening.

Karl had half-risen out of his chair. "What are you talking about? Ice Dreams has done very well for us. Minneapolis is the perfect home base for the show. Why shouldn't we keep the company?''

Kirk unclenched his hands and sat back from the table. "Because we're Americans, that's why. I don't give a damn whether Communism is dead or not. That doesn't mean we can forget and forgive every Commie swine who brought ruination to Russia and Eastern Europe. Many of them were actual criminals.'' His eyes narrowed as he concentrated on Mia. "Like Anatoly Linski.''

Mia's lips formed the single word "No.''

"Yes!'' cried Kirk, leaping to his feet and raising one arm. "Anatoly Linski, the great figure-skating coach, mentor of the young, idol of millions, *is really Boris Ushakoff, former head of the Lusatian secret police!*''

"You know,'' said Renie in a tired voice as the cousins hiked up to their condo, "I don't give a rat's fandango if Nat is Boris or not. I hate meetings. Especially in windowless conference rooms that smell bad.''

Almost an hour had passed since Kirk Kreager had dropped his bombshell. The ensuing arguments, particularly between Mia and Kirk, had been not only acrimonious, but loud. At intervals, Karl had tried to calm both parties. He'd failed. Kirk had insisted that he had concrete evidence of Nat's dual identity, while Mia had vehemently denied the charges.

"The evidence is in the mail,'' Judith remarked as a trio of young Rollerbladers whizzed past. "Kirk says he'll have it tomorrow from his anonymous, if highly reliable, source."

"Maybe." Renie didn't sound convinced. "Mia swears she did in fact know the man she claims is the real Boris, and that he died two years ago in an alcoholic stupor."

"The bottom line is that Karl isn't ready to give in," Judith noted as they passed several luxurious private residences, built of logs, which reputedly sold for upward of half a million dollars. "He wants to see his brother's 'evidence' for himself. And we're sworn to secrecy by everybody."

The cousins continued walking in silence. The sky was now a vault of blue from mountain crest to forest ridge. The afternoon sun was very warm, with the temperature close to eighty. Judith and Renie were huffing and puffing by the time they reached Clarges Court.

"We're out of shape," Judith announced as they entered the cooler confines of the condo. "We should think about joining a gym."

Renie looked horrified. "What? And ruin our reputations? Cut it out, coz. We get plenty of exercise. We run up and down stairs all day, we work in the yard, we dodge our mothers. Besides, where would we find the time?"

Judith acknowledged that Renie had a point. "I still don't know what to do about the catering sideline," she said, adjusting the pleated window shades and flopping down on the sofa. "Most of all, I don't know what to do about Rhys Penreddy."

"Regarding what?" Renie was in the kitchen, pouring soda pop.

"This new development," Judith replied. "Let's say that Kirk is right and Nat really is Boris Ushakoff. Maybe that's what was in Dagmar's file. Nat could have stolen it, but I doubt it. Do you remember what Marin Glenn at the real estate office told us?"

Renie handed Judith a glass of soda. "About the break-in at the Kreager condo last winter?"

"Right. I'm wondering if whoever broke in wasn't doing a little research for the Canadian consortium. The Kreagers didn't press charges, as you may recall. That's probably because they were doing their own dirty work on the Canadians.'' Judith paused to take a long drink. ''But the point is, they have an alarm system. Marin also mentioned something else that's been eluding me, but I remember it now. In the last couple of days, Tessa complained about a broken window latch. Maybe somebody wanted to make it look like another break-in had occurred. But if there was a second forced entry, wouldn't the alarm go off? Nobody has reported that it did.'' Judith raised her glass to Renie and took another deep drink.

Renie reflected briefly. ''So it's possible that nobody actually broke in, meaning that whoever took the file box had access to both condos.'' She ticked the names off on her fingers. ''Tessa. Karl. Dagmar. Freddy. Kirk. And Nat, who came looking for Mia yesterday and then returned last night. The field's wide open. And how did the box end up in Esme MacPherson's apartment?''

There had to be a logical explanation. Judith was a firm believer in logic. She and Renie had spent so much time the past two days conversing and interrogating that she hadn't sat down just to think about the case. It was now almost three o'clock on a hot, cloudless afternoon. Judith suggested a swim.

''We can sit by the pool and relax and ruminate,'' she told Renie. ''We've already spent too much—''

''Oh,'' Renie interrupted, ''it's awful! I'm cleaned out. It's a good thing Bill's in Alaska. When we get home, I'm going to live on what's in the freezer.''

Judith gave Renie a wry look. ''Actually, I was talking about time, not money. We've spent both, and don't have much to show for either one. Shall we don our suits?''

The pool was empty, though Judith figured it was the lull before the predinner storm. Drying off under a big beach umbrella, the cousins sipped their sodas and rested peacefully. Judith tried to ignore the ledger that leaned against her deck chair.

''Dagmar,'' Renie murmured after the first ten minutes had passed. ''I wonder if she pulled through.''

''I didn't see anybody over at the Kreagers' when we came out to the pool.'' Judith pushed her sunglasses farther up her nose. Like most native Pacific Northwesterners, she suffered from having eyes like a mole, and couldn't stand bright sunshine. ''Maybe we should call the clinic.''

Another silence ensued. The only sounds were the occasional passing car, the chatter of chipmunks, and the blessedly distant noise of children at play. Judith felt herself dozing off.

"Nat," said Renie. "Do you suppose the hotel security people caught him?"

Judith stirred, trying to put her brain back to work. "No. If they had, someone would have told Kirk and Karl."

Bees hummed in the shrubbery that flanked the wrought-iron fence. The hint of a breeze picked up, ruffling the umbrella's fringe. A Caterpillar tractor rumbled down the street, returning from its labors at the nearby construction site. Judith began to breathe deeply.

"The file," Renie said, sitting up straight. "Maybe Nat's was stolen because of what it *didn't* say."

Slowly, Judith's eyes fluttered open. "Huh? Who didn't say what?"

Renie eyed her cousin with amusement. "I thought you were going to sit out here and solve the case. You're *sleeping!*"

Judith smiled weakly. "As Grandma Grover used to say, 'I'm just resting my eyes.' "

"Right, and Grandma would be snoring like a sawmill." Renie smiled, too, at the memory. "What I mean is that if someone wanted to cast false aspersions on Nat Linski, he or she might steal Dagmar's file because there was nothing in it that *would* incriminate him." She paused, waiting for Judith's comprehension. "Dagmar told us that the only gossip she had about Mia was her calcium deposits. If she doesn't know any dirt about Nat, who would?"

"Good point." Judith stroked her chin, temporarily willing to let Renie usurp her sleuthing prerogative on this lazy summer afternoon. "So somebody else who wants to smear Nat—and maybe Mia—dredges up this story about Boris Ushakoff. Who? Why?"

Renie thought hard, her cheek resting on her fist. "The Canadian consortium. They want Ice Dreams to showcase their world-class skaters. They spread a rumor about Nat which they know will anger Kirk Kreager, who has inherited his father's political views. If Kirk dumps Ice Dreams because Nat was really a vicious secret police chief, the Canadians take over."

Renie lifted both hands in an expressive gesture.

Judith nodded faintly. "Yes—that makes sense. But what's it got to do with Agnes's death and the attempted murder of Dagmar?"

Renie's face showed confusion. "I've no idea," she said bleakly. Judith, however, was wide awake, her mind racing. "I think the Canadians were set up. Somebody is using all this as a cover for . . . something else."

Renie turned skeptical. "How can you be sure?"

"I'm not. But I don't think Big Business works that way." Judith's tone was earnest. "There may be some corporate skulduggery at work here, but I don't see how Agnes's murder ties in with it. If somebody wanted those files, they didn't need to kill her. It wasn't as if she were guarding the metal box with her life. Which leads us to the question of what she did know. What does Dagmar know?"

Staring at her bare feet, Renie considered. "Nothing," she concluded. "If Agnes was really the driving force behind Chatty Chatsworth, everything was in that metal box. Agnes was organized and meticulous. She wouldn't trust to her memory. Oh, there are juicy snippets in those files, but worth killing for? I doubt it. Celebrities, including Nat Linski, take legal action first." Renie paused for Judith's agreement. "Well?"

"The columns!" Judith practically reeled in her deck chair. "Cold storage and turncoats and all the rest! Dagmar must have been hinting about Nat being Boris! It makes perfect sense. Mia is Cinderella, the ice queen. Or princess," she amended.

"And somebody called Mia to tell her that Nat was going to be exposed." Renie also sounded excited, but quickly lost steam. "But if Boris Ushakoff died of vodka overload . . ."

Judith had picked up the ledger. Renie watched her curiously. "I've got bills to pay," Judith said in apology.

"I thought it was a big menu." Renie looked disgusted. "I can't believe you really brought work. The Madge Navarre syndrome. Jeez!"

"Never mind." Judith extracted the phone bill. "Call me crazy, but . . ."

"You're crazy. You're guilt-ridden. You're . . . *stupid*." Renie was the soul of distaste. "Vacations are for getting away from it all, for putting work in perspective, for closing the door on . . ."

Judith was scanning the phone bill with a far more exacting eye than she had exercised two nights earlier. "It's here! I should have guessed! Oh, my!"

Renie's expression was incredulous. "What? Dagmar called an assassin?"

Judith was oblivious of Renie's sarcasm. She was grinning at the phone bill and shaking her head. "Not exactly. But," she went on, with a piercing look at her cousin, "somebody from Hillside Manor called Mia Prohowska."

It took Renie a moment to figure it out. "The Nat-Boris thing?"

Judith nodded. "Maybe. One of my guests called Bugler at ten-nineteen last Thursday, just before Dagmar and the others left. What do you bet that the number on the bill turns out to be the ice rink? That narrows the field, doesn't it?"

Renie grinned. "Your logic has finally kicked in, huh, coz?"

Judith sighed. "Finally. Now we have to figure out whether it was Dagmar, Agnes, or Freddy. Which of them would gain anything from making the call?"

"If the charge were true," Renie said slowly, "then it could be blackmail, and I'd bet on Freddy."

"I agree," Judith replied. "But I'm inclined to believe Mia's telling the truth about Nat. For one thing, how could he find time to be a world-class figure-skating coach *and* head the Lusatian secret police?"

"Good point." Renie wiggled her bare toes. "But maybe the caller didn't know the story wasn't true."

"So where did it come from?" Judith asked. "Dagmar and Agnes knew nothing about the story. At least," she added, sounding a little dubious, "Dagmar claims she didn't. Maybe Agnes did and it was in the file, but she never confided in Dagmar." Mildly agitated, Judith shook her head. "No, that doesn't play. Whether Agnes wrote the column or not, she would have told Dagmar everything. Dagmar had to know, because she was the one who met the public. It's possible that Dagmar lied. I can't think of anything else she'd mean by 'deep freeze' and 'turncoat.' "

Renie peered at Judith. "If Freddy called Mia, why didn't he make a blackmail demand?"

Frustrated, Judith tugged at her short, wavy hair. "I don't know. Maybe he was waiting until they got to Bugler. Then Agnes got killed, and Freddy was scared off. But he wouldn't contemplate extortion unless he believed that Nat was Boris."

Though Judith had applied logic, the conundrum remained unresolved. Her brain was going around in circles when three young boys bounded into the pool area, yelling and throwing life preservers at one another. They were followed by a weary-looking woman in her thirties who called for quiet. The boys ignored her and leaped into the pool.

Renie signaled that the cousins should beat a retreat. With a sympathetic smile for the harried mother, Judith stood up, reclaimed her empty glass and towel, then followed Renie back into the courtyard.

Tessa Van Heusen Kreager was strolling down the walk. She saw the cousins and slowed her step.

"Tessa!" Judith made a windmill motion with her arm. "How is Dagmar?"

Tessa continued her unhurried stride. "Upgraded from critical to serious. Is anyone in the pool?"

Tessa's cavalier attitude made Judith wince. Nobody seemed to care about Dagmar's condition—including the cousins. Feeling a sharp pang of guilt, she rushed over to meet Tessa at the entrance to the pool.

"We were going to call the clinic," Judith said in a penitent tone. "I'm glad to hear she's improving."

Tessa gave an indifferent shrug of her unblemished shoulders. "So? She won't make any of her deadlines. I detest authors who fail to meet contractual demands. They put everybody in a bind."

Renie had joined Judith and Tessa. "Try working with freelance writers," Renie said, rolling her eyes. "They're impossible. Change one element of design so that the words don't quite fit the allotted space, and they go to pieces. If I had my way, I'd eliminate the copy altogether. It just screws up the visuals, which are much more important."

Tessa shot Renie a hostile glance. "Designers! Artists! The problem with you people isn't lack of respect for the written word, it's that most of you are illiterate. That's why we end up with cover illustrations that have absolutely nothing to do with—''

Judith intervened, stepping between designer and editor. "Excuse me, is Dagmar in intensive care?"

Tessa grew puzzled. "Ah . . . I'm not sure. I mean, this isn't a hospital, it's a clinic. Why do you ask?"

"I was wondering about visitors," Judith explained. "I still feel guilty about giving Dagmar those pills. I'd like to apologize. Otherwise, she might think I did it on purpose. Poison her, I mean."

"Did you?" Tessa's stare was hard and chilly. She tossed her blond curls. "Somebody did, from what we hear." With another flounce, Tessa walked quickly toward the pool, her espadrille sandals slapping against the concrete.

Judith waited until Tessa had disappeared behind the wrought-iron fence. "Let's go see Dagmar," she whispered to Renie.

Renie, however, had an objection. "They won't let us talk to her. Egad, coz, the woman was almost dead less than two hours ago."

Judith's gaze was enigmatic. "I know. And now she's very much alive, if in serious condition. Doesn't that pique your curiosity?"

The cousins were driving out of the parking garage when Judith changed her mind. She asked that they make another stop first, at Esme MacPherson's apartment on the other side of town. For once, Renie didn't bother to ask why; she was still reeling from Judith's latest theory, which had been elucidated on their return to the condo.

The cousins found Esme MacPherson in quite a different mood from the previous day's post-hangover informality. He wore a tan bush jacket and matching slacks with a white ascot as he met his callers at the door. Just behind him, his walking stick rested against two well-worn leather suitcases.

"I say!" Esme exclaimed, recognizing his visitors. "Don't tell me you've been paid!"

"Not yet," Judith replied, trying to edge over the threshold.

She looked pointedly at the luggage. "Are you taking a trip?"

Stepping aside, Esme beamed at Judith. "Very clever! Yes, yes, I'm off on holiday. My plane leaves from Port Royal tonight at ten-thirty."

The suitcases weren't the only things that were packed. As Judith and Renie entered the apartment, they noticed several cartons and a large crate. While most of the furnishings remained in place, all of the personal effects, from the suspended sulky to the winning-circle photographs, were gone. It appeared that Esme was taking more than just a change of wardrobe.

Judith asked the first thing that came into her head. "Did you rent this place furnished?"

"Why, yes, so I did. Convenient for a bachelor, don't you know." Esme's gaze lingered lovingly on the liquor cabinet. "Just what the doctor ordered."

"You're not coming back." There was no question in Judith's tone.

Esme's eyes roamed the now-bare ceiling. "Excellent point. Bravo. I must attend to some family matters in England. Let's say that my future digs are uncertain."

"Do the police know you're leaving?" she asked.

Esme assumed a shocked expression. "Are you implying that I'm doing a bunk? I say! Why should the police care if I leave Bugler?"

Renie had sidled over to the liquor cabinet. Deftly, she slid one of the doors open. "Haven't you been questioned about the stolen metal box?"

Esme smoothed his thinning hair. "Indeed I have. I knew nothing about it. That Penreddy chap left here not more than half an hour ago. Keen sort, for a Welshman."

Judith had difficulty concealing her surprise. "Did you tell him you were going to England?"

Esme appeared affronted, though he avoided her eyes. "Certainly. I was packing even as he arrived."

Flummoxed, Judith surveyed the stripped-down apartment. Logic seemed worthless. She sensed that something very important, a factor of which she was ignorant, a part of the case that completely eluded her, was preventing a logical solution.

Though the late-afternoon sun streamed brightly through the windows of Esme's apartment, Judith might as well have been standing in the dark.

"Okay," she said in an irritated voice, "so when did you find out that the file box was in your liquor cabinet?"

Esme considered. "I didn't. That is, Freddy showed up at a bloody ungodly hour this morning, complete with a most ghastly dog. Sniff, sniff, bark, bark. Dreadful, and so unrestful. I let them in, though Freddy insisted he was at the door forever, but what could he expect? It was barely *daylight*. The wretched dog pranced over to my liquor cabinet, and I panicked. Did the cursed creature desire a dram? No, it did not. Freddy followed, as if he were the trained animal and this ugly little mutt the master. And then—Freddy produced a steel box the likes of which I'd never seen. Curious-making, said I, and went back to bed. Freddy, the dog, and the box departed. Or so I assumed. Good riddance. Good night. Good grief."

Renie was standing by the liquor cabinet, showing it off as if it were a prize on a TV game show. "You didn't pack your booze," she noted.

Esme gave her a cross look. "Of course not. I can't take liquor into the UK."

Judith eyed Esme skeptically. "You didn't really notice that strongbox? Or look inside?"

Esme sighed with impatience. "No, I did not." A horn honked outside. "Ah!" His thin face brightened. "My taxi. I entrain to Port Royal, and thence to London. Jolly, what?"

Since the police apparently didn't object, the cousins could hardly deter Esme MacPherson. They stood aside as he began hauling out his boxes and luggage. The taxi driver, a buoyant man of Middle Eastern extraction, came inside to help remove the packing crate. Judith and Renie stood by, feeling helpless and confused.

"Ta-ta," said Esme, waving from the threshold. "Do be my guest and have yourselves a farewell drink." He grabbed a pith helmet that had been sitting on a chair. "Oh, lock the door when you leave. Au revoir and all that."

Their host was gone, the taxi pulling away and heading down the street with the packing crate tied on top of the vehicle. Judith and Renie stood on the balcony, watching Esme and his belongings disappear down the curving street.

"He's never coming back," Judith said glumly.

Renie mumbled assent. "We can't leave town, but Esme can? What's wrong with this picture?"

Judith grimaced, then wandered back inside the apartment. "Everything. I wonder if Rhys Penreddy really does know that Esme is fleeing the country."

"Maybe we should tell him," Renie suggested. "He's probably still on duty."

Judith nodded in a distracted manner. Seeing the open liquor cabinet with its collection of bottles, she was tempted to accept Esme's offer. But their host's defection was her priority.

"Let's stop at the police station before we go to the clinic," she said, touching her handbag, where the telltale phone bill was now reposited. "As I recall, the medical center is just a couple of doors from the cops."

Renie nodded, following Judith around the living room. "Well?" Renie inquired. "Are we going to search this place first?"

Judith studied the living room, now devoid of its personality. Sofa, chairs, table, and liquor cabinet didn't seem to offer much evidence of Esme MacPherson. A glance at the notepad next to the telephone revealed only more names of thoroughbred racehorses: Winning Colors, Northern Dancer, Spectacular Bid, Danzig Connection. Vaguely, Judith thought they sounded like winners. Maybe Esme had made enough off his gambling to stake his move. Wandering into the bedroom, the bathroom, and the tiny kitchen, Judith peeked in closets, drawers, cupboards, and even under the bed. She found nothing of interest.

"It's useless," she declared. "Esme's taken everything that might have been helpful. I don't get it. He's cleared out with all his worldly belongings." On a weary sigh, she started for the door.

But Renie had paused. "Not quite," she noted, forcing Judith to turn around.

Lying on the floor, flush with the wall, was Esme MacPherson's walking stick. Judith stared, made a move to pick up the stick, then hastily retreated. She arched an eyebrow at Renie.

"Did he leave us without a clue?"

Renie's expression was uncertain. "I wonder. Did he?"

Judith broke into a grin. "I think not. Let's call the cops."
She moved quickly to the phone and dialed Rhys Penreddy's
number.

SEVENTEEN

RHYS PENREDDY GRUDGINGLY agreed to meet the cousins. Yes, he knew that Esme MacPherson was flying to London. No, he didn't care if the old sot ever came back. What did Esme have to do with Agnes Shay's death and the attempt on Dagmar Chatsworth's life? Esme swore he hadn't met either of the women. Coming out of her stupor, Dagmar had confirmed the statement. Or at least had given a qualified version: *She* had never met Esme MacPherson; she very much doubted that Agnes had, either, but anything in life was possible.

Judith remained in Esme's favorite chair while Renie sprawled on the mohair sofa. "I never thought I'd say this, but I'm glad to hear Dagmar is talking again," Judith remarked as they waited for the police chief. "At least I think I'm glad." She gave Renie an ironic look.

"Are you going to trot out your theory for Penreddy?" Renie inquired, idly leafing through a racing magazine that Esme had left behind.

"Not yet," Judith replied, getting up and going to the window. "I want to see what he thinks about the walking stick." She stared outside for a long moment, then returned to the bedraggled old armchair. "I keep expecting Esme to come back and collect the stick. Maybe I'm wrong." Once more she pulled her fingers through her hair in frustration.

Renie was smiling fondly, if wryly, at her cousin. "Look,

Ms. Logic, try writing down your ideas. That always helps me when I'm putting together a design concept. Contrary to Tessa's belief, graphic artists *can* read.''

Judith decided to humor Renie, and picked up Esme's notepad and a pencil. "I'm still sticking to the idea that Agnes was *not* murdered by mistake." She started to tear off the top sheet of paper, then frowned. "This is strange. I'm no racing expert, but the only social and cultural outings Dan and I attended were at the track. I still have nightmares about the rent money coming in dead last."

Renie put both feet up on the sofa. "So what's strange? Other than Dan, that is."

Judith waved the slip of paper. "These horses. Spectacular Bid goes way back, to the late seventies. I remember, because we had a Happy Hour drink special at The Meat & Mingle called Spectacular Bib. We served it in a dribble glass, and the customers had to wear something over their clothes or they got all wet."

"The Meat & Mingle's clientele spilled their drinks with regular glasses," Renie remarked. "So what?"

Judith ignored Renie's sarcasm. "So nobody's betting on a horse that's been out to pasture for years. Shoot, Northern Dancer won the Derby the year we were in Europe. Don't you remember reading about it in *The New York Herald-Tribune*?"

Renie grew serious. "I do, actually. We were in Rome the first weekend of May."

"Winning Colors is more recent, I think, and Danzig Connection doesn't ring any bells." Judith had become excited. "What were those other names—the ones on the pad when we were here yesterday?"

Renie thought back to her perusal of Esme's notes. "Montreal Marty—I remember that because of Cousin Marty, who is almost but not quite as smart as a dumb animal. Oh, Genuine Risk—that's a famous one. But not very recent, either. I forget the other two. Is there a wastebasket around here?"

There was, in the kitchen. There was also one in the bedroom. But both had been emptied. Judith, however, was undaunted.

"Let's try the old trick of running a pencil over the sheet

underneath to see if we can get an impression," she suggested. "Esme writes with a surprisingly firm hand."

The four thoroughbred names from the top sheet were easy to decipher; the other four from the discarded page were more difficult.

"It's awfully faint," Renie noted. "I can just barely make out Genuine Risk." She put on her teal-rimmed glasses, the lenses of which always seemed to be scratched and smeared. Judith never failed to marvel that Renie's vision wasn't impaired, even with the aid of her glasses.

"Ah!" Renie exclaimed. "I can see Counterpoint. And I remember that the other one was a single name like that, Middleground. I never heard of them," she added in apology.

"Me, neither." But Judith was still animated. "These names aren't for betting purposes. They're a code."

Renie's startled expression changed quickly to appreciation. "Ha! I'll bet you're right! But a code for what?" Her smile faded as she removed her glasses and dumped them haphazardly in her handbag.

"Good point." Judith had now written all of the thoroughbreds' names on a clean piece of notebook paper. "Montreal Marty and Danzig Connection suggest Canada and Eastern Europe. What's the tie-in?" She gazed at Renie, waiting for an answer.

"Ice Dreams? But what's Esme got to do with it?"

"I've no idea. Yet," Judith mused, staring again at the list. "If we're on the right track, Spectacular Bid could refer to the deal itself. Or maybe that could be Genuine Risk." She sighed. "Whatever it means, Esme was in the thick of things. I wonder who—and what—he really is."

"Let's ask," said Renie as the doorbell sounded.

Rhys Penreddy was alone, and wore a beleaguered expression. There were sweat stains on his uniform, his auburn hair had lost its usual crispness, and his broad shoulders slumped ever so slightly.

"It's just after five," he said irritably, "and I'm officially off duty. Make this brief, eh?"

Judith pointed to the walking stick, which the cousins had left exactly as they had found it. "Esme MacPherson bequeathed us a souvenir. What do you think?"

At first, it seemed that Penreddy didn't think much of Esme's memento. Then he leaned down, scrutinizing the heavy silver horse-head and the hard ebony wood. A spark of interest showed in his eyes as he turned back to the cousins.

"What leads you to believe that this might be the weapon used to kill Agnes Shay?"

Judith paused, then glanced at Renie for a sign of support. Renie gave a faint nod of affirmation. "It's hard to explain," Judith said tentatively. "That's because I don't know who Esme MacPherson really is. Look." She produced the slips of notepad paper. "Supposedly, these are racehorses. But we think they're a code. Something to do with Ice Dreams, maybe." She turned a hopeful face to the police chief.

Scanning the list, Penreddy registered no emotion. With a peremptory gesture, he confiscated the three pieces of paper. Then he used a clean handkerchief to pick up the walking stick.

Irked by the police chief's lordly manner, Judith started to object, then realized it would do no good. "I doubt you'll find any useful prints on the stick," she said, still annoyed. "Esme has used it since the murder."

Penreddy remained self-possessed. "If this was the weapon, we might find something else. Hair and fibers, for example. We'll run it through the lab."

Judith was rummaging in her handbag, searching for the phone bill. "I don't know what this means," she began almost shyly as she handed him the sheaf of charges, "but last Thursday morning, somebody from my B&B on Heraldsgate Hill called a local number. Do you know if it's the ice rink?"

Penreddy examined the bill, then took a small address book from his back pocket. He nodded once. "It's the rink, all right." He studied the bill some more, now flipping through the multiple pages. "Your monthly billing cutoff date was last Friday, I see. You must have just received this." His expression had grown thoughtful. "You certainly make a lot of long-distance calls, Ms. Flynn. All over the globe, it seems."

Judith grimaced. "Those aren't my calls. Not the foreign ones. Mine are only to Yakima, Hoquiam, Corvallis, Eureka,

Boise, and Appleton, Wisconsin. Somebody else used my phone.'' Noting that Penreddy didn't look convinced, Judith pointed jerkily at the multipage printout. ''See for yourself— they were all made within the time frame that Dagmar and her party stayed at Hillside Manor. I think one of the Chatsworth people phoned Mia Prohowska with blackmail in mind. Go ahead, ask her about the call she got right after she finished the Ice Dreams tour.''

''Ask her?'' Penreddy was bemused. ''Ms. Prohowska's in seclusion. A nervous collapse, we're told. The next thing we know, she'll also be a patient at the local clinic. You people seem to be causing an epidemic around here.'' Without any farewell gesture, he exited the apartment, taking the walking stick and Judith's phone bill with him.

''Dink,'' Renie muttered. ''The least he could do is thank us for calling him.''

Judith was trying to calm herself, taking one last look around the apartment. ''He evaded the question about Esme MacPherson. Why?''

''Because he doesn't know?'' Renie closed the door behind them, making sure the lock clicked into place.

''Penreddy knows more than he's telling us,'' Judith said, sounding discouraged as well as weary.

''Do we know more than he does?'' Renie asked as they descended the concrete stairs to street level.

''Maybe,'' Judith answered, but she didn't sound very certain. ''Let's go see Dagmar.''

The Bugler Clinic and Medical Center was small but up-to-date. Located across from the municipal hall, which also housed the police and fire departments, the two-story building looked as if the town had already outgrown it. Judith and Renie found themselves in a standing-room-only situation in the waiting area. A trio of parents with cranky children, an anxious elderly couple, and a young man with an ice pack on his knee filled the upholstered chairs.

At the reception desk, Judith inquired after Dagmar Chatsworth. They were told that the patient was resting comfortably.

''Would it be possible to see her for just a minute or two?'' Judith asked in her most plaintive manner.

The woman behind the desk eyed Judith over her half-glasses. "Are you kin?" she inquired with the trace of an accent.

"Yes," Judith replied.

"No," Renie answered.

"We're close friends," Judith amended, stepping on Renie's foot. "We were staying with her when the . . . mishap occurred."

"That part's true," Renie said. "In fact, my cousin here gave her the medicine that . . . ah . . . um . . . Ms. Chatsworth wanted."

The woman was now regarding both Judith and Renie with skepticism. "I'll check with the nurse," she said abruptly, and reached for the telephone.

To the cousins' surprise, permission was granted. Beyond the sturdy steel doors, they were met by a tiny young Asian nurse.

"Your kindness will do the patient good," the nurse declared, leading the way past the examining cubicles and around the corner to the outpatient rooms. "She has had no visitors except a cute little man who came this afternoon."

"Mr. Whobrey?" Judith asked in surprise.

The nurse nodded. "He brought flowers, too. We made room for them. Ordinarily, our patients don't stay overnight. If they need extended care, we send them into Port Royal. But the doctor is making an exception with Ms. Chatsworth. We understand she not only became ill, but has suffered a very recent tragic loss."

Judith confirmed the nurse's statement. A moment later, they were in Dagmar's small but comfortable room. She was hooked up to several IVs and looked very sallow. Her eyes were closed and her breathing was labored. A big bouquet of white and yellow roses stood on the window ledge.

The nurse retreated. Judith cleared her throat. There was no response from Dagmar. The cousins approached the bed, one on each side. Judith called Dagmar's name. Her eyelids flickered open.

"What?" The word was weak. "Oh! You!" She closed her eyes again.

Judith chewed on her lower lip. She had rehearsed her

speech several times in her mind, but now that she was face-to-face with Dagmar, reticence overcame her.

"How are you?" she finally inquired, feeling foolish and inadequate.

Dagmar's polished nails pulled at the plain cotton hospital gown. "Dreadful. I almost died. Maybe it would be better if I had."

"Nonsense." Judith found her tone flat, her own lips dry. She lowered herself into the sole visitor's chair. Renie had moved the bouquet aside and was perched on the window ledge. "You know my cousin and I didn't cause the poisoning." Judith saw Dagmar nod in an indifferent fashion. "Have they learned what kind of poison was used?"

Dagmar shuddered. "I don't know the scientific name, but it's commonly known as Aldrin. It's a pesticide. Or so they think—the tests aren't complete yet. I feel cheated. Imagine, antibug crystals in my sleeping capsules! How unglamorous! Whatever happened to arsenic and cyanide?"

"They're not easy to obtain," Judith noted, wondering if Aldrin was readily available in Canada. "Household poisons are usually at hand and just as lethal. Can you tell us who had a hand in the Aldrin?"

Dagmar's eyes opened slowly. "I don't know," she declared in a querulous tone.

Judith let the protest pass. "You know who sent those threatening letters." She leaned closer to Dagmar, who recoiled. "You know a great deal, Dagmar. Let's start with the letters. Maybe Agnes didn't know how to use a word processor, but I'll bet *you* do. Still, you probably can't be jailed for mailing threats to yourself."

Dagmar drooped against the pillow. "That's right, I can't." Abruptly, she squared her shoulders and thrust out her chin. "Shameless self-promotion—it's not a crime. Authors have to help themselves."

Judith sat back in the chair. "So you figured if you received threatening letters, you could include yourself as a celebrity victim in your next book. What did you do, have someone mail them for you from New York?"

Dagmar turned smug. "I did. I actually managed to coax my publicist at Thor to do it for me. She didn't know what was in the letters, of course. I told her they were memos I'd written myself but didn't want cluttering my busy schedule. I should receive one more before I leave Bugler.'' Taking in Judith's disapproving expression, Dagmar waved a hand, almost upsetting the IV stand. ''Oh, it's not that I don't get my share of hate mail! I do, but usually it's such a mess. People who write bilge like that can't spell or punctuate or put together a coherent sentence. I wanted something quotable. Ergo, I did it myself. It's always the best way.''

The point wasn't arguable; Judith firmly believed it herself. ''What about the phone calls you got at my B&B?'' The question was barely out of her mouth before she realized the explanation.

Dagmar, however, put it into words. ''It was one of my sources. The message was brief and rather pointless. After she hung up, I got the brainstorm to embellish and pretend someone was still on the line, threatening me.'' Her haggard face took on a spark of life. ''Well? You fell for it, didn't you? I was quite convincing.''

Judith had to admit Dagmar was right. There had been no other calls, of course, except the one Judith had overheard. Dagmar had lied about them, and Joe had probably hung up on a billionaire from Tokyo.

''Who used my phone to call Mia?'' Judith demanded. ''Was that you?''

Dagmar's eyelashes fluttered. ''Mia? No, certainly not. Why would I call her?''

Renie was finding the window ledge uncomfortable. She got up and wandered toward the bed. ''Somebody in your party called Mia from Hillside Manor. Whoever it was had some ugly information about her—or Nat.''

Dagmar snorted. ''Oh, that! I've no idea. We've covered this ground before.''

Judith was trying to gauge Dagmar's reaction, which seemed genuine. ''What about Boris Ushakoff?''

''What about him?'' Dagmar was turning sulky. ''There were rumors, but it's old news, going back to before Mia won her first gold medal. I suppose Boris is languishing somewhere in an Eastern European jail cell. Or driving a taxi in Minsk.''

''Mia says he's dead,'' Renie put in.

Dagmar gave an indifferent shrug. "Maybe he is. Who cares?"

"But your columns," Judith persisted. "Those hints about turncoats and cold storage and deep freeze and Cinderella. If you weren't talking about Mia and Boris, what did you mean?"

Briefly, Dagmar looked puzzled, her nose wrinkling. "Oh! That was one of Agnes's ideas! We were heading for Canada, and she thought a hockey item would be appropriate. She loved hockey—it's very popular among young people in Minnesota. The innuendos were to lead up to open criticism of Wayne Gretzky, berating him for defecting from the Edmonton Eskimos to the Los Angeles Kings, or whatever they're called. Red uniforms, ice, Cinderella team, blah, blah. I'm not sure what she planned to say, poor thing, but attacking Wayne Gretzky was guaranteed to garner high readership north of the border. And thus help promote the book."

The cousins exchanged quick glances. Wayne Gretzky was definitely not a suspect. They seemed to be going nowhere with Boris Ushakoff, either. Kirk Kreager appeared to have been taken in, perhaps by some right-wing crank. Or, Judith thought fleetingly, the Canadian consortium, in an effort to lure Mia and Nat away from Ice Dreams. "Does the phrase 'Danzig Connection' mean anything to you?" Judith inquired, wondering if somehow her powers of deduction had failed.

Dagmar arched her thin eyebrows. "What? I've never been to Danzig. Why are you asking these silly questions?" She looked up at the big clock on the far wall. "It's going on six. When do they serve dinner in this ridiculous place? I've had my stomach pumped, and I'm starved!"

Judith was not to be diverted. Despite the detours they had taken since arriving at the clinic, there was monumental purpose in the call on Dagmar Chatsworth. Judith steeled herself and prepared to deliver her body blow. "Rhys Penreddy—and everybody else—began this homicide investigation with the premise that you, not Agnes, was the intended victim. I don't believe that. Oh, the turban and the scarf could have led someone to believe that Agnes was really you. But I don't think that's what happened. There's only one person who could know for certain that you weren't sitting on that chairlift.'' Judith's hand cut the air as she pointed an accusing finger at Dagmar. "That person is *you*, Dagmar. I think you poisoned yourself to divert suspicion because *you killed Agnes Shay*."

In the movies and on TV, the accused killer usually laughs derisively when confronted by the clever sleuth. Judith half-expected Dagmar to guffaw with indignant, outraged mirth. It wouldn't matter, of course. Judith would stand her ground. And Dagmar, hooked up to the IVs and weakened by a self-induced dose of poison, could do nothing except protest her innocence. The police would take over, and eventually, Rhys Penreddy's diligence would pay off in a solid case against Dagmar Delacroix Chatsworth. So Judith—and Renie, standing just behind her—waited for the scoffing laughter. They were prepared, and already wearing incredulous expressions.

What they weren't prepared for was tears. Dagmar shriveled under the light bedclothes and began to sob uncontrollably. Her body shook so hard that once again the IV stand threatened to topple. Renie grabbed it and held on tight. The cousins regarded each other with curiosity and, after a full minute had passed, alarm.

"Should we send for the nurse?" Renie asked in a hushed voice. "She's getting hysterical."

Dagmar was indeed bordering on hysterics. Tears streamed down her face, and she began to choke. Just as Renie reached for the button to summon help, Dagmar began to shake her head.

"Please!" she gasped. "*Please!*"

Renie hesitated, her arm still hovering over the headboard. Dagmar was trying to compose herself, but at tremendous cost. Judith snatched up the water carafe and poured a drink for her.

"Thank you," Dagmar whispered. Her red-rimmed eyes were grateful.

An uneasy sensation was descending over Judith. She writhed on the chair, waiting for Dagmar to regain her composure. Renie was shifting from one foot to the other.

Dagmar took another sip of water, then dabbed again at her eyes with a tissue. "I, as victim!" Suddenly she glared at the cousins, her hands frantically rending the tissue into small, damp scraps. "Why should I make up things? Real life is far worse than sham!" She shook her head in a gesture of despair.

Judith fumbled with the strap on her handbag. She wasn't quite ready to throw in the towel. "Is Freddy really your nephew?"

Dagmar quivered from head to foot. "Of course he's my nephew! Do you think I'd put up with the little wretch if he weren't?"

"Uh . . ." Judith was scrambling for words. "See here, Dagmar, you—er—well, we figured you and Freddy were . . . except Agnes was in love with him, too . . . and then, you haven't been writing those columns and books yourself. Agnes did it for you, but she was too shy to be a public figure. Maybe Freddy goaded her into putting the squeeze on you and the two of them were going to run off together, so you, ah, decided to . . . um . . ." Faced with Dagmar's look of revulsion, Judith let her voice trail away.

"How could you?" Dagmar demanded in a cold, harsh tone. She seemed on the verge of tears again. "*How dare you*?" She swallowed hard, and held her head high. "I would never harm a hair of Agnes's head! How could I? Agnes was my daughter!"

Judith wanted to weep. She felt racked with guilt, embarrassed to the bone, and full of anguish for causing Dagmar such pain. The mistake was monstrous. If Dagmar had possessed the strength, Judith wouldn't have blamed her for inflicting bodily harm on both cousins.

There was only one thing to do, and Judith did it. She offered a handkerchief, clasped one of Dagmar's cold hands in both of hers, and apologized profusely. To Dagmar's credit, Judith only had to humble herself to the level of a common worm.

"All right, all right," Dagmar finally broke in, wiping her eyes with Judith's handkerchief. "You made a reprehensible mistake. Fortunately, you're nobody, so it doesn't matter. But I still can't believe you'd accuse me of such a heinous crime. I hope you don't ever play any of those detective parlor games. You must lose every time."

Judith was blushing. "I thought it made sense," she mumbled. "I'd come to the conclusion by applying logic."

"Oh, bother!" Dagmar dismissed logic with a curl of her lip. "Try facts. That's what I deal in."

Renie, who hadn't made as big a fool of herself as Judith had, rested an elbow on the headboard. "If you're Agnes's mother, that explains why she did all the work and never complained. But why the big secret?"

Dagmar shot Renie a withering look. "Why do you think? I'm much too young to have a daughter in her thirties. I didn't want people thinking I was a child bride. Besides," she went on, lowering her voice and her gaze, "I was never married to Agnes's father. There was no Mr. Chatsworth. Nor was there ever a Mr. Shay. That's my real name—Ingeborg Dagmar Shay. It didn't suit a newspaper byline."

Judith was beginning to recover from her egregious error. She dared to ask a bold question. "Did Agnes always do the writing, or just the research?"

Dagmar lightly touched the wrinkled skin under her chin. "It's a long story, but I'll condense it. I'm good at short copy, and contrary to what you think, I *can* write. My parents died when I was in college. I finished, though it took me an extra year because I had to work part-time. I got a job on a suburban weekly, and met a printer who was ever so handsome. Muscles everywhere. Dimples, too. In several places." Dagmar simpered. "And a wife who appreciated none of the above. I got pregnant. He wouldn't leave the mother of his other children, so I went to Duluth to have Agnes. My sister—Freddy's mother—took me in, and I went back to work, in public relations for General Mills. It got boring, but I stuck with it for almost ten years. Then I decided to strike out on my own. I'd saved some money, and my sister was ever so kind. I went to work for the Kreagers, doing the cooking column, expanding it from helpful hints and recipes to gossipy tidbits.

"Meanwhile, Agnes was growing up, but she had no self-esteem. I suppose that was because she had no father. The Twin Cities are very conservative, and thirty years ago, an illegitimate child was still a target of scorn. I tried so hard to bring Agnes out of her shell. The only thing she enjoyed besides hockey was writing. So when I asked to switch to a regular gossip column, I had her help me write it. She was marvelous. Every frustration, the bottled-up anger, all of her resentment, came out in those scathing accounts of the rich and famous. She was so good at it that after the first year or two, I let her do the whole thing. Oh, I had my sources built up by then, but after a while, she took over that part as well. She wrote the book. She was brilliant. And, of course, she wanted no recognition. In fact, it would have terrified her. Her joy was simple—churning out words, titillating readers, trashing reputations. Who could ask for anything more?''

Judith tried not to look askance. "Yet you still didn't acknowledge her as your daughter?''

Dagmar put a hand to her bosom. "Certainly not! Who would believe it? Why, we were often taken for sisters!''

The bubble of self-delusion was left unpricked by the cousins. Renie was now leaning on the bedside stand. "But Freddy knew Agnes was your daughter?''

"Of course!'' Dagmar threw Renie a reproachful look. "They grew up together. That's why the suggestion of a match between them was so ludicrous. Agnes and Freddy are— *were*—first cousins.'' Dagmar's mouth turned down and her lower lip trembled.

Feeling limp, Judith sat back in the chair. "Do you have any idea why Agnes was killed? Or who tried to poison you?''

Wearily, Dagmar shook her head and gave Judith the rumpled, damp handkerchief. "I'm utterly baffled. Whoever it was, I wish they'd succeeded with me. I told you that, didn't I?'' Her gaze was defiant.

Judith nodded slowly. "Yes, and fool that I was, I thought you'd managed to ingest just enough to make it look as if someone had tried to do you in. You were really lucky, Dagmar.''

Dagmar had turned away from the cousins, staring at the empty doorway. "No, I wasn't.'' She closed her eyes and started to cry again.

"One word,'' Judith said, waving a meat fork at Renie. '' 'Idiot.' If Joe doesn't remember, be sure and put it on my tombstone.''

"Knock it off," Renie said, cutting up a bunch of scallions for green salad. "It was an honest mistake. I thought you were right. You usually are."

"Dagmar may be abrasive, arrogant, and egotistical, but that doesn't detract from her loss," Judith said with fervor. "And there I was, making matters worse."

Renie sliced a tomato. "Enough. Let's forget the whole thing. We leave tomorrow, Rhys Penreddy has Esme's walking stick and the list of horses in code, Nat is not Boris Ushakoff, and Dagmar sent those letters to herself. The case will get solved eventually, and maybe we'll read about it in the newspaper."

Judith had stopped tending the T-bone steaks somewhere during Renie's monologue. "Nat," she said under her breath. "What do you suppose happened to him?"

Renie shrugged. "He probably got away from the hotel security guards and went home to tend to Mia's alleged attack of nerves. What could they arrest him for, other than on Kirk Kreager's word? It was a tempest in a teapot."

"I guess." Disconsolately, Judith checked the baked potatoes in the oven. "I wonder what's happening with Ice Dreams."

"Forget it!" Renie's tone was sharp and compelling. "Come on, coz, it's after seven o'clock, dinner is just about ready, and I'm fainting from hunger. Let's start dishing up and discuss whether or not we're going to stop off in Port Royal tomorrow and hit some of the boutiques."

"With what? Do we barter? I can offer some of my pet homicide theories. They're worth about six cents apiece." Judith's tone was bitter.

"I've got a little room to roam on one of my bank cards," Renie said as she shook up a jar of salad dressing. "We haven't done any clothes shopping, and if we buy Canadian labels, there are bargains to be had."

"*We've* been had," Judith replied with asperity. "This trip has been a disaster."

Renie's eyes sparked. "Thanks a lot, coz! I give you a free vacation to one of the world's snazziest resorts, and you bitch! Next time, I'll bring Madge Navarre if I have to kidnap her!"

The reference to their mutual friend brought a faint smile to Judith's lips. "Madge wouldn't make such a public dunce of herself. She's far too cautious. And smart.''

"You're smart," Renie said, holding out her plate so that Judith could serve the steak. "You just got off on a tangent this time."

"Maybe." Judith took the potatoes out of the oven. She appreciated Renie's kind words, but her ego was still feeling battered. "I guess it serves me right for trying to compete with Joe."

"Stop," Renie said quietly. "Have some salad."

"Of course, Joe is an utter jerk."

"I put the dressing in the cream pitcher."

"I'm not calling him tonight."

"Have you got the butter over there?"

"He doesn't want to talk to me until I, quote, 'get my ass home,' unquote."

"I wonder if Bill's caught any fish yet."

"Maybe I shouldn't go home at all. Maybe I should move into the toolshed with Mother."

"Bill's planning to spend one day with a guide going for steelhead on a river."

"Or maybe I should move Mother back into the house and put Joe in the toolshed."

"The last time Bill went up one of those rivers in Alaska, he saw a grizzly bear."

"I'm not taking this kind of guff lying down, you know."

"The bear ate him."

"It would serve him right."

Renie feigned innocence. "Who, Bill? What did *he* do? My husband isn't the type who carouses on a fishing trip. Early to fish, early to bed. I doubt that he even has a drink the whole time."

Judith glared at Renie; then her mouth opened wide. "Oh! I've been an idiot twice over!"

"Right. I knew you'd come to your senses." Renie blithely chewed her T-bone steak.

Judith gobbled up the last of her salad. "I'm not talking about Bill. I'm not talking about Joe." She whisked her plate off the table and got to her feet. "I'm talking about Wayne Stafford. Shovel the rest of your dinner in, coz. We're going to the chairlift. This time, I know who killed Agnes. Honest, I do."

EIGHTEEN

To JUDITH'S CHAGRIN, Wayne Stafford wasn't on duty. He'd taken a break and had ascended to Crest House, where he was meeting another college student who worked as a waitress.

"Young love," Judith muttered as the cousins waited in line behind a family of four.

"I thought we didn't have to ride this damned thing again," Renie complained. "I had to eat so fast, I've got a stomachache."

Judith clambered aboard, and Renie reluctantly followed. Twilight was coming down on the mountains, with a hint of gold and purple in the western sky. As usual, dark clouds were gathering to the north. Judith realized that she was growing accustomed to the rhythm of life at Bugler. To her surprise, she found herself wishing they didn't have to leave so soon.

Grumbling, Renie alighted on Liaison Ledge. "Okay, okay, so I'm still alive. But I wish you'd tell me what's going on. Keeping secrets doesn't become you."

"Just give me a few minutes," Judith urged as they approached Crest House. "If I'm wrong again, I'll be mortified, even with you."

"Dumb," Renie muttered. "We've been mortified in front of each other for fifty years, more or less. Dumb."

"Bear with me." Judith led the way to the restaurant,

then squeezed past the waiting diners and entered the bar. Wayne Stafford and a pretty young woman with long taffy-colored hair were sitting at a table, sipping what looked like club sodas.

At first, Wayne didn't recognize the cousins. Then he suddenly grinned and put out a hand. He fumbled for names in an attempt to make introductions, but Judith rescued him.

"We won't take a minute," she assured the couple. "I know you're on a break. Just tell me again exactly who you saw coming down the lift the night Agnes Shay died."

Wayne's forehead knit in concentration. The bar was busy, though it was not yet nine o'clock and the evening wouldn't get into full swing for at least another hour. "Gee," he said, mulling over the event, "it seems like two weeks ago instead of two days. So many people go up and down . . . Let me think . . ." The taffy-haired girl smiled encouragement.

But Wayne's memory wasn't tracking well. "I honestly can't say who came down right ahead of the dead lady. The only thing I'm sure of is that the chair behind her was empty, and then the older guy who got real impatient came next." Wayne's earnest face showed disappointment in himself.

Judith wasn't giving up, however. "That's good, Wayne. That part is important, too. Now tell us again who you saw walking past the lift office."

Wayne wrinkled his nose. "Walking past . . . ? Oh, you mean about the time the lift stopped?" He bent his head to give his companion a sly little smile. "Young lovers, hand in hand. They made me think of . . . something." The taffy-haired girl giggled.

Judith kept her smile in place. "And? Anyone else?"

Wayne's face lighted up. "A man, tall, in a hurry, like he had to get somewhere."

It took some effort on Judith's part not to appear overeager. "Good, very good. Did he have a beard?"

Wayne thumped his forehead with the palm of his hand. "Oh, jeez! I didn't notice! I was looking at his jacket. It was really cool, especially for an older guy."

"Describe it," Judith urged.

"A blazer," Wayne replied promptly. "Dark color, blue or black, I guess. It was hard to tell."

Wayne's girl was watching him with pride. "You should be a detective," she said in a soft, sweet voice.

Wayne flushed, but her admiration spurred him on. "And that kid in the baseball cap—the one who was keeping in tune to the music. You know, I told you about him."

Judith nodded. "How old?" Her smile was growing stiff.

Wayne considered. "Oh—thirteen, fourteen."

"What was he wearing? Besides the baseball cap."

Again Wayne furrowed his brow. "I'm not sure. A sweat-shirt, maybe. And pants or jeans. Gee, I just don't remember exactly."

Judith forced her facial muscles to relax. "That's fine. Anybody else?"

"Not then. But as soon as the lift stopped, people began to take notice and come over to see what was going on. Well, you were there. We got quite a crowd." Wayne's grin managed to be both sheepish and engaging.

Judith had one final question. "Did the lovers or the man in the blazer or the kid come back?"

Wayne thought not. At least he didn't remember seeing them again. But on the other hand, with so many people suddenly surrounding the bottom of the lift, he might not have noticed.

Judith thanked Wayne and started out of the bar, then was struck with another inspiration. She grabbed Renie's arm.

"Charles de Paul," she whispered in her cousin's ear. "Let's have a little chat."

"I thought you didn't want to face him again," Renie remarked.

Judith didn't, but had to set embarrassment aside. Or so she thought, though it turned out not to be necessary. Charles de Paul wasn't on duty behind the bar. A plump blonde was mixing drinks with a sleight of hand that would have done a magician proud. The cousins commandeered a pair of empty stools.

"I'll bet you're Hilde," Judith said brightly.

"I'll bet you're not." The blonde burst out laughing. "Hilde, that is. Because you're right, I am. What will you have?"

Judith and Renie ordered Drambuie. "Is this Charles's night

off?'' Judith inquired as Hilde served them each a small snifter of the pungent amber liquid.

Hilde nodded. "He likes a midweek break." Her round, pleasant face expressed puzzlement. "Sorry, I don't know you. I don't think you've been here on my regular shift."

"We're simple American tourists," Judith replied. "We talked to Charles the other day. He told us about your tooth troubles. How is it now?"

Hilde put a hand to her cheek. "It's fine, except that I have another appointment. I've got a temporary now." She turned as a bald man at the far end of the bar called to her. "Excuse me. I'll be back shortly."

Renie leaned closer to Judith. "What are we doing?"

"Drinking." For emphasis, Judith sipped her Drambuie.

"Besides that. Charles isn't here. What's the point?" Renie swirled the liqueur in her glass.

Judith let out a small, exasperated sigh. "I'm not sure. But as long as we're here ...." She shrugged and took another drink.

Having served up a vodka martini, Hilde returned. "Dentists!" she lamented. "I can't believe what they charge. It's a good thing we've got decent coverage in Canada."

Briefly, the cousins commiserated. Renie asked a few questions about Canadian health care in general. Judith bided her time, though she was growing impatient. Hilde was interrupted by a server who had a trayful of orders. Almost five minutes passed before she returned. Judith and Renie were nursing their drinks.

"Say," Judith said before another topic could be broached, "do you know a man named Esme MacPherson? English, or maybe Scottish. Older, a regular."

"Esme?" Hilde laughed good-naturedly. "I do indeed. Quite the caution. Harmless, though." Her expression changed. "Come to think of it, I haven't seen him tonight. He must be making the rounds elsewhere."

Judith didn't enlighten Hilde. "He had a pal with him Monday. A little guy, ex-jockey. Do you remember?"

Hilde's eyes rolled back in her head. "Do I! What a lecher! There I was, absolutely miserable with my tooth, and this pint-sized twit is driving me crazy with his corny come-ons! Not that I don't hear my share in this job, but he was outrageous! He even pinched me as I was coming back to the bar with a tray of wineglasses. I felt like taking Esme's walking stick and cracking him over the head. In fact, I went to reach for it, just to threaten him a little, and I couldn't find it. That's when I dropped the tray. Never try to do two things at once.'' Regretfully, Hilde shook her head.

Judith stared hard at her. "Freddy was there but the walking stick wasn't? Where was Esme?''

Hilde blinked, frowned, and acknowledged a patron who wanted a refill for his schooner. "I don't know. I don't remember seeing him at the time.'' Turning toward her thirsty customer, she laughed mirthlessly. "I suppose the walking stick wasn't there because Esme took it with him.''

Judith carefully sorted through her few remaining Canadian bills and put her last ten on the bar. "Let's go,'' she said to Renie out of the side of her mouth.

The sky was threatening by the time they emerged from Crest House. It was growing dark, and the expected lightning storm was about to break. A long line had queued up for the lift. Judith judged that the early diners had finished eating and were heading back to the village for their nighttime revels.

Renie was not in a good mood. "It's bad enough to ride that damned thing, but waiting for it makes my stomachache worse,'' she groused. "I don't see why we had to come up here in the first place. Especially since you won't tell me anything.''

Judith gave her cousin a placating smile. "Then let's walk. We can go the other way, and end up at Crystal Lake. Come on, coz. We need the exercise.''

"Phooey,'' said Renie, but she followed Judith.

"It beats the chairlift.'' Judith began the descent, noting that the route leading away from the village was as precarious as the one they had taken the previous day.

"Okay, okay, so I'm a wimp,'' Renie conceded. "But I trust my feet more than a bunch of cables suspended over Certain Death. We've made five trips up and back. I figure the odds are against us.''

Lightning struck just beyond Fiddler Mountain. Judith gave a start and Renie stumbled slightly. The trail was deserted at this time of night, but after the first turn of the switchback, the grade leveled off. Both cousins gained confidence.

They had reached what Judith judged to be the halfway point when a second bolt of lightning illuminated the landscape. Crystal Lake shimmered briefly beyond the evergreens. The scenery was magnificent. Judith was enthralled; Renie's mood improved.

"How far is it from Crystal Lake to our condo?" Renie called as they rounded a sharp corner in the trail.

"I'm not sure. You're the expert. You've been here before." Judith spoke over a rumble of thunder.

"Crystal Lake wasn't developed when we were here," Renie shouted back. "For all I know, it's halfway to the Yukon Territory."

The lightning was closer, turning the landscape an eerie shade of green. Below, the cousins could see scattered lights. The lake grew larger, its waters pale as a shroud. Judith plunged ahead, her eyes on the darkening sky.

That was a mistake. She didn't see the depression in the trail. Her ankle turned on her and she fell, striking her right knee. She swore and winced with pain.

"Jeez." Renie was at her side. "What did you do, hit a gopher hole?"

Judith swayed back and forth. "A washout, I think. Or something. Damn!"

"Is it broken? Sprained? Or just a turn?" Renie's voice was full of concern.

Gingerly, Judith tested the ankle. "It's okay. I mean, it's nothing serious. But it hurts."

The lightning jolted both cousins, striking directly above them. Renie squatted beside Judith. "No hurry. We'll wait until you can go on. It looks as if we're almost down the mountain."

Distractedly, Judith followed Renie's gaze. Through the trees, there were lights no more than a hundred yards away. At the side of the trail, a small waterfall trickled into a gully, then flowed on, probably into Crystal Lake. As another bolt of lightning struck, the cousins saw two smaller lakes, almost at the edge of town. Inching toward them was a train, lights glowing in the passenger cars.

"I wonder if Esme is waiting on the platform," Judith said, tenderly rubbing her ankle.

"I doubt it," Renie answered. "That train is coming from Port Royal. He probably left hours ago." Spying a boulder next to the trail, Renie sat down. "As long as we're here, why not tell me what's going on? I don't mind being your stooge, but I hate to be stupid as well."

Judith expelled a sigh. "If I'm wrong, don't mock me, okay?" Taking in Renie's bemused but sympathetic expression, Judith continued. "The chairlift is the key. Why was the seat behind Agnes empty? There had been people waiting, as you may recall. The only reason I could think of for a vacant place was because it *was* occupied when it left Liaison Ledge. The killer was in it, having already whacked poor Agnes over the head."

Renie let out what passed for a whistle. "Good thinking! So what did the killer do, fly down the mountain?"

"No, it was much simpler than that. The killer jumped off the lift just before it got to the bottom. Once you're approaching the ticket office, it's only a five-foot drop to the ground. Wayne Stafford said the lift stops only when a chair is empty or the safety bar is released. Agnes couldn't move the bar because she was dead. So whoever was behind her must have gotten off to make the lift come to a longer-than-usual stop."

Renie was skeptical. "That's a big risk—for a lot of reasons."

"Not really. Wayne Stafford was studying, the lightning storm provided a distraction, and apparently kids do goofy things on the lift."

Renie started to ask for a clarification, but an odd sound made her pause. Judith also cocked an ear. The noise was coming closer, seemingly moving down the trail. It sounded very much like the clip-clop of a horse.

Renie was quizzical. "Riders at this time of night? Doesn't lightning spook horses?"

"I don't know," Judith replied. "I'm a city girl myself."

The storm was actually beginning to move off over the village. The horse and rider, however, were coming closer at a walk. As they rounded the bend in the trail, Renie dragged Judith out of the way to let the animal pass safely.

But the horse, a sleek chestnut Arabian, was reined in. Judith recognized the outline of Freddy Whobrey, looking less like a jockey and more like a trainer in his flannel shirt, denim vest, and blue jeans.

"Two babes! Too much!" Freddy cried, his pointed teeth gleaming as the lightning flashed. "Hey, isn't it a little late for a picnic, or did your dates stand you up?"

Standing up was what Judith tried to do, leaning on Renie. "We hiked down from Crest House," Judith said, rubbing her ankle. Every ounce of her energy seemed to be invested in the throb of pain. "I took a tumble."

Freddy evinced shock. "Without me? Hey, climb aboard Starbird. I'll take you home and bed you down."

Judith put her full weight on the ankle. The pain shot up through her entire body. "No, thanks, Freddy. I'll walk." She gave him a strained smile and sat back down again. "My cousin will lend me a hand. It's not that far."

Freddy was skeptical. "It's not that far to the end of the trail, but it's almost a mile back to your condo. You can't go the distance on a game leg."

Judith glanced down over the edge of the trail. She could see nothing but a dark void. Freddy was right, of course. Crystal Lake was now hidden by the forest. The two smaller lakes were farther away, where the train was whistling as it came to a stop. While lights shone through the tops of the evergreens that clung to the side of the cliff, the village itself lay behind them. Yet nothing would induce Judith to ride with Freddy Whobrey. Perhaps it would be possible to call a taxi or catch a bus.

Renie had sat down again, too, precariously close to the drop-off. She was completely caught up in the exchange between her cousin and Freddy. Her round face showed worry and bewilderment. "Maybe you can send someone up to get us," she suggested to Freddy.

"Can do," Freddy replied. "Freddy Can-Do, that's me."

Judith put on her bravest face. The initial shock of pain was receding. "Then go ahead, Freddy. We'll wait." She waved halfheartedly, before her hand paused in midair. "By the way, where are you going at this time of night?"

Freddy tugged on the reins as his mount began wandering

off to crop at some of the tough grasses that grew along the edge of the trail. "Oh, just keeping in practice. I miss strad-dling a pretty filly now and then." He leered, but for once, his heart wasn't in it. Indeed, having had his offer rejected, he seemed anxious to be off.

Judith nudged Renie, trying to move her away from the drop-off. "Where do you rent horses around here?"

"Huh?" Freddy's gaze was fixed on the distance, somewhere in the vicinity of the railroad station. "Oh, a cou-ple of places." His voice was vague.

Another sound, faint but persistent, caught Judith's atten-tion. Not footsteps, she thought, squinting up the trail. The noise was being made by something lighter than a hurrying human or even a fleet-footed deer.

They all heard, rather than saw, Rover. Barking his head off, he had careened in front of Starbird and planted his paws in the trail's soft edge. The horse was startled, rearing her front hooves and whinnying in fright. Rover didn't budge, but kept barking, a harsh, relentless sound.

Freddy tried to gain control of his mount, but the terrified horse continued to shy. Rover didn't give ground. Freddy swore, brandishing his riding crop. The nervous mare skittered out of the dog's path, heedless of the cliff's edge and kicking Renie's shoulder with an errant hoof. Rolling away from Star-bird, Renie felt her knees skid in the loose dirt. Losing control, she fell into what seemed like oblivion.

"Coz!" Judith screamed as Renie disappeared over the edge of the cliff.

Freddy flicked the whip, and the frightened horse took off at a gallop. "I'm going for help," he shouted. Rover was in hot pursuit, yapping fiercely. Scrambling to the spot where Renie had fallen, Judith felt tears sting her eyes. She was afraid to look. The mare's hooves and the dog's bark grew fainter, but Judith's only concern was for Renie. She was cer-tain that her cousin had fallen at least fifty yards into the black chasm below the trail.

"Coz!" Judith's voice was hoarse. Her legs shook as she groped for something solid beneath her feet. "Where are you?" Her cry grew louder, echoing across the valley. The tranquil mountain setting now seemed vast and uncivilized.

Danger was almost palpable on the night air, making Judith suddenly go cold.

"Get me out of here!" The voice belonged to Renie, and it was irate. "I'm stuck in some stupid gorse bush!"

Now Judith peered over the edge. Her vision was blurred. Dimly, she saw Renie, no more than ten feet away, a furious, fighting ball, trying to free herself from a large thicket.

It was anguish for Judith to make the descent, but she tried. She failed. The cliff was too steep, at least in her crippled condition. By the time she had found the first foothold, Renie was on her knees, swearing like a sailor.

"Stay put. I can climb up now," Renie finally called. "Jeez, I've wrecked my blouse and I've got a hole in my pants."

"I don't care if you've got holes in your head," Judith said in relief. "I thought you were dead! I was sure you'd gone all the way to the bottom!"

"That *is* the bottom," Renie answered testily. "This isn't the Grand Canyon, it's just a little drop-off." She gained purchase on a rock and hauled herself back onto the trail. "What about you? I didn't think you could stand on that ankle."

"It's numb," Judith said, retrieving their handbags, which had fallen by the wayside. "You scared the pain out of it. Let's see if we can find Freddy."

Judith had fibbed about her ankle, but walking was bearable. Renie had suffered various bumps and bruises, including Starbird's kick in the shoulder. The cousins began hobbling down the trail. After two more turns, they met pavement. Freddy was nowhere to be seen.

"He and Starbird are long gone," Renie asserted. "So's Rover. Do we care?"

Miraculously, Judith's step didn't falter. Pushing all thoughts of pain aside, she concentrated on her goal. Indeed, she willed herself to move briskly now, following smooth, new blacktop that ran past the far end of Crystal Lake. As they hurried by a sprawling Spanish-style villa, Judith realized that the thoroughfare was too narrow for vehicles but was intended to accommodate horseback riders, bicyclists, and unadventurous hikers.

"I wonder where Nat and Mia live," she remarked to Renie over her shoulder.

"Are we trying to find them?" Renie asked.

"Not really," Judith replied, sounding anxious.

"We've passed Crystal Lake," Renie said, catching up. "Are we looking for Freddy?"

Judith gave a sharp turn of her head. "Yes. If we don't, there may be another death. Just concentrate on—"

Judith froze in place. A horse and rider were standing some twenty yards ahead of them. It was Freddy, and his back was turned. There was no sign of Rover. Another man stood next to Starbird. He was speaking to Freddy and held something in his hand. The cousins approached cautiously. After the first ten yards, they recognized Esme MacPherson. Judith and Renie took a few more steps. Esme was holding a gun, and it was pointed straight at Freddy.

Renie turned to Judith. "What do we do? Rush him or run for help?"

Judith staggered slightly, then put a hand on Renie's shoulder. "We do nothing. Don't move."

"But . . ." Renie was utterly confused.

The nervous horse must have sensed the cousins' approach. Starbird bolted, catching Freddy completely off guard. He was thrown, crashing into Esme MacPherson. The gun clattered to the pavement as the mare galloped off down the bridle path.

Judith and Renie took off at a run. The two men wrestled on the ground, with Freddy appearing to have the upper hand. As the storm faded over the ridges to the west, the moon peeked behind scudding clouds. The gun's bluing shone in the pale light.

"Grab it!" Judith shouted at Renie, who happened to be closer to the weapon.

But Freddy had landed a solid blow to Esme's jaw, leaving him dazed. Diving for the gun, Freddy snatched it away from Renie. Still bewildered by the turn of events, Renie glanced at Judith.

"Should we tie Esme up?"

Judith started to answer, but Freddy broke in with a burst of laughter. "Why not? I've got a rope on my saddle."

"No!" Judith cried, then cringed as she saw Esme writhing

on the ground near her feet. ''Coz, get back! Esme isn't the killer! It's Freddy!''

''Why, you frigging broad!'' Freddy raised the gun and released the safety. He was aiming it at Judith even as Renie let out a horrified squeal. And then Freddy was falling backward, yelping with surprise and pain. Esme MacPherson pounced, and wrenched the gun from Freddy's hand. Freddy still howled. He reached for his leg and rolled over.

Rover had attached himself to Freddy's calf and didn't seem inclined to ever let go.

NINETEEN

THE INVITATION FOR drinks had been declined by all. Esme MacPherson was still huddled with Rhys Penreddy at the police station, Karl and Tessa Kreager were tied up on phone calls to New York, Kirk Kreager was sending faxes to Minneapolis, Dagmar was spending the night at the clinic, and Freddy was in jail.

Judith and Renie had one guest, however. Rover was out on the balcony, gnawing on the T-bone remnants. It appeared that the cousins were stuck with him until Dagmar was released in the morning. Tessa refused to let him near the Kreager condos without proper full-time supervision.

"I don't know why you didn't tell me it was Freddy," Renie said for the sixth time since she and Judith had returned from giving their statements at the police station. "What if I'd grabbed the gun and shot Esme?"

Judith, sipping her scotch, was wide-eyed. "But I thought you knew. I kept trying to tell you, and when I got to the part about mischievous kids jumping off the lift, I assumed you had it doped out."

"Dope is right." Renie glowered over her rye. "But which of us is the bigger dope, I'm not sure. Oh, the motive is clear—I should have seen that. Dagmar had no will, which meant everything would have gone to her daughter. Agnes had to die so Freddy, as the next of kin, would inherit. He swiped some of Tessa's termite pesticide to put in Dagmar's sleeping capsules. But he miscalculated on the amount of Aldrin necessary to kill her. He would have tried again, though.''

Judith nodded. It was almost midnight, and exhaustion was setting in. Her ankle, which was propped up on the coffee table, throbbed so hard that it made her head ache, too. Dagmar's 222 Canadian painkillers hadn't yet kicked in.

"Freddy could bide his time with Dagmar," Judith noted, stifling a sneeze. "Having failed on the first try, he might have waited months or years. Still, I think he got scared, and I'm almost sure he intended to catch that train and head off into the northern reaches of British Columbia until things calmed down. If Dagmar refused to admit she was growing old and wouldn't make a will, he'd still inherit."

"I never would have figured the part about the baseball cap," Renie mused. "And sweatshirt. How did Freddy take those things from the Crest House bar without anybody noticing?"

"That wasn't hard." Judith blew her nose. "They've got sports memorabilia hanging all over the place. When Freddy pinched Hilde and she dropped the tray of wineglasses, everybody's attention was focused on her. Then she threatened to pass out from the pain in her tooth. The scene was pretty chaotic. No wonder Charles de Paul didn't notice anything amiss. Freddy had already swiped Esme's walking stick. In the confusion, he probably grabbed a cap and a sweatshirt and dashed out of the bar. Esme wasn't there, as you may recall."

"He'd gone to the men's room," Renie said. Both cousins were still trying to sort through the snatches of information they'd gleaned at the police station. "Freddy hadn't been in the bar for more than five minutes, but Esme had arrived much earlier."

"That's right," Judith agreed. "Freddy left the rest of the dinner party and made his plans. He knew Agnes had to collect Dagmar's things from the washroom, so he waylaid her before she got to the chairlift. She was carrying Rover's doggie bag, the champagne, the turban, the scarf, and her own purse. Freddy probably suggested she lighten her load by wearing Dagmar's belongings. It wouldn't have been easy for Agnes to get aboard with so much gear. I suppose she was grateful for Freddy's thoughtfulness. As soon as she climbed into the chair and put the bar in place, he cracked her on the head with Esme's cane. Then he got into the chair behind her, put on the sweatshirt and cap, jumped off, and scampered away. Or hip-hopped, as Wayne Stafford would say.''

Renie was looking dubious. "I don't get it. I mean, I know hip-hop is something too cool for my middle-aged understanding, but what's it got to do with Freddy?"

Judith smiled through her aches and pains. "Nothing. He had that walking stick stuck down his pant leg. It made him walk funny. Wayne thought he was dancing or something. Freddy's so small that in the dark he could pass for thirteen or fourteen."

Renie leaned back in the big armchair. "Lord, I'm tired! I feel like I was hit by a bus! And I'll never know how you figured Esme MacPherson for somebody out of MI-5 or MI-6 or whatever they call it in London."

"I don't know what they call it and I didn't." Judith looked faintly chagrined. "But when Esme left that walking stick in the apartment, I knew he was trying to tell us something. Or leave a message for the police."

Judith rubbed her sore ankle. Neither Rhys Penreddy nor Esme MacPherson had been clear with her about the latter's occupation. Judith wasn't entirely sure that Esme *had* an occupation, except that in his past, he'd worked for the British government and had established a convincing cover. He'd been semiretired in Bugler for several years, ostensibly drinking heavily but, in fact, never getting drunk. Judith guessed he'd been hired by the figure-skating consortium to get the goods on Anatoly Linski and to investigate the Kreager brothers' Ice Dreams involvement so that the Canadians could make a viable counteroffer. Industrial espionage, even in show business, wasn't unknown.

But whatever Esme MacPherson was, he was no fool. Judith figured he'd suspected from the start that Freddy had killed Agnes Shay. Not wanting to blow his cover, he'd kept a low profile, but had leaked information to Rhys Penreddy after Dagmar was poisoned. Esme had great faith in Penreddy.

"So Esme's really going back to the UK?" Renie asked, checking the black-and-blue marks on her arms.

"I guess," Judith answered with a yawn. "He'll have to wait a day or so until Penreddy and the Royal Canadian Mounted Police have everything under control. I overheard Devin O'Connor say something about a wedding."

Renie arched her eyebrows. "Esme's family?"

"Esme." Judith grinned. "Confirmed bachelors don't always stay that way. I gather he's had a pen pal."

Renie smiled. "And those horses *were* a code."

Judith scanned the sketchy notes she'd taken at the police station. "Esme wouldn't answer me directly, but my guesses came close. Montreal Marty is the consortium itself, Spectacular Bid is the offering price, Genuine Risk refers to Ice Dreams, Winning Colors means Mia, and Northern Dancer translates as Nat. The Brothers Kreager are Middleground and Counterpoint. You guess which is which."

Renie chuckled. "That could go either way. Danzig Connection was Boris Ushakoff, right?" She stood up, offering to refill Judith's scotch.

Judith hesitated, then agreed. "We might as well polish it off. We can't take it through customs." She raised her voice slightly as Renie headed for the kitchen. "Esme had known Freddy from the Canadian racetracks. Freddy was spreading rumors, including the call he made to Mia from Hillside Manor. The more people who seemed to have a reason for killing Agnes and Dagmar, the better. He probably started the story that Dagmar wasn't really his aunt, just to throw everybody off. Nobody outside of Freddy, Dagmar, and Agnes knew for sure. Then he pinched the metal box. No alarms went off, because there wasn't any break-in. Freddy was trying to make it look as if somebody wanted to find out what was in the files. Having had access to the box all along, he knew there wasn't anything, at least not on any of the suspects in Bugler. Retrieving the files made him look like a hero."

Renie had returned with their refills. "Dagmar would never print anything about Tessa's spotted past, not as long as she's with Thor and the Kreager syndicate. But I thought Freddy seemed genuinely surprised when Nat's file came up missing."

"He was." Judith shifted her legs on the coffee table. At last the pain pills—and maybe the scotch—were taking hold.

"Dope that I am, I didn't suspect Freddy at that point. And he didn't suspect Esme of being other than he seemed. Freddy stashed the box at Esme's, figuring he was too befuddled to notice. That was a weird coincidence. Esme opened it and pulled Nat's file, presumably to show the Canadian consortium that their Ice Dreams king was definitely *not* Boris Ushakoff."

"So Mia's doing fine and Nat's not in trouble," Renie mused. "Kirk Kreager's rumor mill was a dud, it seems. I'll bet Karl talks him into keeping Ice Dreams as is."

Judith inclined her head. "That's up to the negotiating skills of the Kreagers—and their ability to soothe Nat's and Mia's ruffled feathers."

"Well, now." Renie was bemused, contemplating the jumble of events. "So Rover didn't actually find the metal box. But how did he find us?"

Judith reached into her handbag and pulled out the bedraggled handkerchief that she had lent to Dagmar. "I honestly don't know. I suspect that Tessa threw him out of the condo, and he's been running all over, looking for his mistress. Maybe he went to the clinic. They wouldn't let him in. Eventually he followed Dagmar's scent to the trail—and to us. Freddy must have scared him off after they reached the bottom of the trail. But Rover's persistent." Seeing Renie's skeptical expression, Judith amended her statement. "Of course, it's possible that Rover was following Freddy instead of us. If animals have a sixth sense about people, Rover never liked him, either."

Renie wasn't inclined to argue that point. "Freddy took a great risk killing poor Agnes. He had to count on so many different things going his way. I almost have to admire his nerve."

"Hey, he's a jockey," Judith countered. "In his prime, he was big stuff. You don't win races without taking chances, making split-second decisions at sudden opportunities, using every trick of the trade to your advantage. If he could pull it off, Freddy was riding into the winner's circle, big-time. Of all the suspects, only Freddy had the personality and the daring to make it—almost—work."

Rover, having finished his bones, was whimpering outside the glass door that led to the balcony. Renie and Judith chose to ignore him. He started to howl. Renie got up and let him in. The phone rang just as she was sliding the door closed.

Judith jumped. "Joe!" she breathed, and couldn't suppress a smile. Who else would call after midnight? Her heart raced as Renie picked up the receiver.

"Yes, she's doing fine ... I know, she realizes you forgive her ... Well, we all react strangely under pressure ... Talk to ... ? Of course—here."

Judith had struggled to her feet and was halfway to the phone. But Renie was on her knees, holding the receiver to Rover's ear. Rover listened, barked, and sat up on his hind legs. Judith collapsed against the dining room table. Renie put the phone back to her ear.

"Don't worry, your floofy-woofy is doing fine. You get well. Good night, Dagmar." Renie hung up.

"It wasn't Joe." Judith's voice was flat. She felt drained and depressed.

Renie grimaced and avoided Judith's eyes. "Uh ... no. It was Dagmar. She's shocked about Freddy, of course, and says her sister raised him all wrong. Spoiled. Selfish. A brat." Anxiously, Renie finally met her cousin's gaze. "She forgives you for the bum guess, though. Maybe she'll mention Hillside Manor in a column someday. Assuming she gets around to writing them again."

Rover was sniffing at Judith's slippered feet. Judith felt like kicking him with her good leg. "Beat it. You make me sick. Literally."

Recognizing that Judith's ire wasn't really intended for Rover, Renie put on a sympathetic face. "You're exhausted. Go to bed. Everything will look better in the morning."

"Like fun it will," Judith muttered, still glaring at Rover. "What if I get home and find that Joe's moved out?"

Renie didn't dignify the remark with a response. Instead she pushed Judith in the direction of the hallway. "I mean it. Hit the hay, or whatever Freddy would call it. And don't pick on Rover. We owe him," she reminded Judith. "I'll take him downstairs and give him some water. Come on, you wretched little mutt. You're going to sit and stay and fall down and go to sleep."

Rover trotted along, his pink tongue hanging out and his

tail wagging. Out of sight, Renie bent down and scratched him behind the ears. "Good doggy," she whispered. "Wenie woves Wover."

"I heard that," Judith called from the hallway.

Renie and Rover didn't reply.

The full force of the late-afternoon sun was hitting the front of Hillside Manor when Renie dropped Judith off the next day. The big windows, with their rows of diamond panes, reflected the houses and shrubbery from both sides of the cul-de-sac. A slight breeze stirred the maple, fruit, and evergreen trees that shaded the neighborhood. All appeared peaceful, though there was no sign of life at the B&B.

Limping around to the back door with her suitcase and parcels, Judith panicked. Off the top of her head, she couldn't remember who was booked for Thursday night. Californians, maybe. A repeat couple from east of the mountains. Four attendees of a conference on something or other. Judith's mind was a quasi-blank.

Dumping her burden on the back porch, she hurried down the walk to the converted toolshed. Despite the heat, Gertrude had the door and the windows firmly closed. Judith knocked and called to her mother.

Gertrude allowed the door to open only a slit. "Hunh," she growled, though the sparkle in her eyes betrayed her. "You're back. Finally. I thought you'd be here by noon."

"We stopped in Port Royal," Judith replied, waiting for the door to swing wide. It didn't. "Besides, it's almost three hundred miles from here to Bugler."

"Bugler? I thought it was called Bassoon. Or Baboon. Speaking of which, he isn't home yet." Gertrude moved just enough to allow Sweetums's exit. The streaking blur appeared to be in fine fettle.

Judith had already checked the garage. She knew Joe's MG wasn't there. "I know," Judith said, trying to wedge the door open with her good foot. "It's just a little after five. I gather he's been working late." She almost choked on the words.

Gertrude stuck her head outside, staring in the direction of the porch. "What's all that stuff? Don't tell me you and your dim-witted cousin bought up Canada."

"I got you some chocolates," Judith answered with a big, artificial smile.

Briefly, Gertrude brightened. "Good. Leave 'em on the doorstep." She started to close the door.

"Mother!" Judith grabbed the doorknob just in time. "What's going on? Are you hiding a man in there?"

Mother and daughter tussled with the door. Judith won, though the battle wasn't easy, especially on a bad ankle. Marching into the little apartment, she surveyed Gertrude's domain. At first glance, nothing seemed amiss. The hot, airless room smelled of liver and onions.

"You're eating?" Judith asked, still suspicious.

"Just going to sit down. You know I like my supper on time." Gertrude glared at her daughter, but her movements were nervous.

The adventures of the past three days, the long drive home, the physical battering, and the uncertainty about Joe had taken a big toll on Judith. She was too tired to hassle with her mother.

"I'll come back after dinner with your chocolates," she said in a tired voice.

"Fine," Gertrude retorted. "G'bye."

The phone rang. Judith's eyes automatically darted to the green Trimline on the small table by the davenport. A gray box sat next to the phone. The ringer sounded a second time, but Gertrude didn't budge. Her eyes narrowed and her mouth set in a hard line. The phone rang again.

"Aren't you going to answer it?" Judith demanded.

"No." Gertrude advanced toward Judith on her walker. *"G'bye."*

Circumventing her mother, Judith moved swiftly to the phone. She started to pick it up, then stared at the little box, taking in the small screen and the logo.

"That's my Caller I.D.!" Judith exclaimed. "What's it doing here?"

"Rats!" Gertrude banged her walker on the carpeted floor. The phone kept ringing. She sighed and her stooped shoulders sagged. "The stupid thing won't register phone calls from outside the city. So it's worthless to you, right?" She paused as Judith took in her mother's meaning. "That current lummox you married let me try it out.'' The phone was still ringing. ''I won't get one of those dopey answering machines, but this works just fine for my purposes.'' At last the phone was silent. Gertrude hobbled over to the small table. ''Ha! It was Deb! See, her number comes up on this little TV-screen thingama-bob. Now I can avoid talking to her more than six times a day.''

Judith held her head. ''Mother—that's mean.''

''No, it's not. It's sensible. It's not necessary to listen to her yak my life away. Short as the rest of it may be.'' Gertrude seemed to shrink behind her walker.

Judith started to upbraid her mother, then moved swiftly to give her a hug. ''Don't say things like that. You'll make a hundred, easy.''

Almost shyly, Gertrude looked up at her daughter. ''You'll be sorry if I do,'' she warned, but her raspy voice shook.

Judith hugged her tight. ''No, I won't. I'll throw you a party like this town has never seen. If I have to, I'll cater it myself.'' Lightly, she kissed the top of Gertrude's head.

''You better cater it yourself, kiddo.'' Gertrude returned the hug. Or maybe it was a little shake. ''Your hot-water heater went out while you were gone. The dishwasher busted. The microwave blew up. I'm glad I don't have *your* bills.''

''*What?*'' Suddenly in shock, Judith released her mother. ''Are you serious? Why didn't you tell me? Why didn't Joe say something?''

Gertrude shrugged, making her heavy cardigan sweater bag even more than usual. ''Why worry you? You and my goofy niece were over the border, *having fun.*'' The note of reproach was only a trace more subtle than usual. ''Hey, take a hike. My liver and onions are drying up!'' She made a shooing gesture with her walker.

With dogged steps, Judith retreated to Hillside Manor. Her first duty was to check her guest list. She had come close to cataloging the evening's visitors: All five rooms were full, though the Californians were actually Floridians. There was no sign of occupancy upstairs. Apparently everyone was still out playing tourist or conferee.

Swiftly, Judith put the boxes of candy in the refrigerator. She ran down to the basement to throw in a load of dirty clothes. She also stored the new Christmas decorations with the rest of her holiday finery. Then she climbed the three flights of stairs to the family quarters, where she dumped her suitcase and hung up the blue-on-blue crepe de Chine dress she'd purchased earlier in the day at a chic Port Royal boutique. Regrets were useless: Her bank cards were at the limit, her cash reserve was down to eighteen dollars and forty-three cents, and whatever was left in the savings account would go for household repairs. Disheartened, she returned to the main floor to fix appetizers and punch for her guests.

As Judith worked in the kitchen, she listened to the staggering number of messages on the answering machine. Most of them were for upcoming reservations. There were also three requests for catering social events, including a wedding reception at the B&B in January. Since business seemed to be booming, Judith tried to console herself. Maybe she would be forced into keeping the catering sideline going, at least until the bills were paid. That, she knew, would probably take forever. Having insulted Dagmar, Judith was having second thoughts about transferring the phone charges. Three hundred dollars was cheap penance for accusing a bereaved mother of killing her daughter. Of course, she'd have to ask the phone company for a copy of the bill; Rhys Penreddy hadn't remembered to return it. For all she knew, the Bugler Police Department was using her number to make calls to Zimbabwe.

Having thawed three dozen prawns, Judith was unwrapping a package of Brie when the back screen door slammed. Only family and close friends entered the house from the rear. Judith peered into the passageway. Joe was slinging a rumpled cotton jacket on a peg. His face was very red and he was perspiring. He still wore his shoulder holster.

Seeing Judith, he rocked slightly on his heels. "You're home," he said in a voice devoid of emotion.

"Of course I'm home," Judith answered stiffly. "Why wouldn't I be?"

Joe came into the kitchen, but made no move to embrace Judith. She held her ground by the tiled counter. They stared at each other for a long moment; then Judith lowered her eyes and went to get a platter from the cupboard.

"Tough day?" she asked in a cool tone.

"Tough. Satisfying." Joe moved uncertainly about the kitchen, going between the stove and the table. "Say, are you limping?"

"It's nothing. Renie and I went on a short hike. I fell in a hole. No need for you to worry." Judith's air smacked of Aunt Deb at her most martyred.

Joe glanced at Judith's legs. Luckily, the swelling had gone down while Judith kept one foot propped up during the drive home. "They look okay to me. They always do."

Judith ignored the hint of appreciation in Joe's green eyes. "Dinner may be a little late. I haven't stopped for a minute since I got home."

"No problem. I need to unwind." He removed a beer from the refrigerator. "The arraignment in the My Brew Heaven homicide is set for Monday. Phil Lapchick should be out of the hospital by then. I hear he's going to plead not guilty. He's threatening to sue the city and his lawyer is demanding that we drop the charges."

"Really." Judith's interest was minimal.

Joe took a couple of steps closer to Judith. "He's claiming self-defense. He says Les Bauer had a gun in a cupboard behind the bar."

"Oh?" Judith sidestepped Joe to get at the microwave, then remembered that it was broken. Except that it wasn't. A sleek new model sat on the shelf next to the stove. "Joe!" Judith turned to face her husband, her jaw dropping. "Did you buy this?"

"What?" He glanced at the appliance. "Oh, right, I got it this morning after I let the gas company in to install the new hot-water heater. I had to hurry, though, because the dishwasher repairman was coming at one o'clock. Phyliss Rackley didn't show up until two, because she had to help get ready for her church's Pentecostal Follies."

"The dishwasher's fixed?" Judith could hardly believe her ears. She dropped the plastic plate for the Brie, then bent down to pick it up. "I thought you worked all day."

Joe shrugged. "I put in a few hours this afternoon. The Bauer case is pretty well wrapped up. Except for Diana, of course. She's still going to need somebody to help her get through the next few weeks."

Judith's rush of good feeling faded fast. "Oh. Well, certainly." She turned her back on Joe and popped the Brie into the new microwave. "By all means, make time for Diana."

"I will." Joe sounded casual. "I told you, it's tough. The tavern hasn't been doing well lately, Les didn't have much insurance, and they bought a new car last month. Diana's thinking of selling My Brew Heaven, investing the profits, and living off her Social Security."

Judith opened a box of sesame crackers. "How nice for her." Sarcasm oozed from her voice. "Is her home paid for or is she—" Judith dropped a handful of crackers. She whirled on Joe. "Her *Social Security*? Why does she get that? Is she disabled?"

"No." Joe's face showed no expression. "Diana's seventy-three. She's been drawing it for eleven years, but so has Les. Now she'll only get her own, or his, whichever is greater."

Judith dropped her guard. She didn't care if she stepped on the fallen crackers. Throwing herself at Joe, she started to laugh and cry at the same time. "Oh, Joe! I thought Diana was a gorgeous young girl! I had visions of her fawning all over you and gaining your sympathy and coaxing you into . . ."

"I tried to tell you she wasn't exactly a kid," Joe said on a note of reproach. "But you kept blabbing away at me. Screw it, I figured. Let Jude-girl stew. It might be good for her."

Judith started to say she thought otherwise, but Joe's kiss stopped her rampant speculation. She held him tight, choking on tears and laughter. Renie was right: Judith hadn't trusted Joe; she hadn't trusted his love for her; she hadn't trusted their marriage. Instead she'd thrown herself into solving Agnes Shay's murder. She did have faith in her ability to solve problems. Not her own—eighteen years of marriage to Dan had been an exercise in futility. But Judith could help other people, whether their needs were related to hospitality or homicide. Maybe, she thought vaguely, it was time to let Joe help her be herself. And to trust in each other.

Dimly, she heard the front door open. The guests had their own keys, and several voices were making merry noises in the entry hall. Over Joe's shoulder, Judith peeked at the old schoolhouse clock. It was two minutes to six. Reluctantly, she pulled free.

"The social hour," she gasped. "I've got to get this stuff out for the guests." Hurriedly, she removed the Brie from the microwave, arranged more crackers on a tray, and placed the prawns on a bed of ice. She was putting the ladle in the punch-bowl when she unleashed her grievance.

"You were awfully mean on the phone the other night," she said, though the anger in her voice was subdued.

Joe was taking off his holster. "You were awfully unrea-sonable. I was awfully tired. And it was awfully hot here this week, especially in the attic bedroom. Besides," he went on as he hung the holster over the back of a kitchen chair and moved to get the appetizer tray, "I kept worrying about you, Jude-girl. I couldn't help thinking how you and Renie get into all kinds of trouble when you leave town. I'm glad as hell that you managed to kick back and relax on this trip."

Judith blinked. Giving Joe a sidelong look, she was almost certain that he was quite serious. Perhaps the local media hadn't covered the murder of Agnes Shay or the attempt on Dagmar's life. The Kreager factor might be keeping a lid on the story. And maybe the Canadians hadn't made an inquiry into the Chatsworth party's stay on Heraldsgate Hill. Or, if any of those things had happened, it was possible that Joe had been too busy to notice.

Judith let Joe elbow open the swinging door that led to the dining room. They greeted their guests warmly, delivered the punch and the appetizers, then retreated to the kitchen once more.

"Bugler's a beautiful spot," Judith remarked noncommit-tally. Casting about for a change of subject, she dropped the empty fruit-punch can. It rolled almost to the sink.

Joe was scanning the evening newspaper's sports page. He looked up from the baseball scores as Judith threw the can in the recycling bin. "How did you and Renie amuse yourselves? Neither of you is exactly what I'd call athletic."

Judith was searching the freezer for dinner ideas. "Oh, as I said, we hiked. We swam. We shopped. We ate. We drank." She found four small lamb chops and avoided Joe's gaze as she defrosted them in the microwave. "There were horses and dogs and all sorts of interesting people. Mostly, we just sat around and enjoyed the scenery.''

Joe was now leafing through the front section of the newspaper. "Sounds great. By the way, the mail's in the basket by the phone. Nothing much except bills." He grinned over the top of the paper. "I half-expected us to get a summons from that Chatsworth woman. She was pretty riled about her dumb dog. I wonder what happened to that crew."

Judith took a deep breath. She should tell Joe the truth, of course. That was part of the trust they must forge between them. But would she be bragging? Did she want to top Joe's latest homicide arrest with her solution of Agnes Shay's murder? Was she really competing with him or merely an innocent victim of circumstances?

Old habits die hard. Judith turned to Joe and gave him her most beguiling look. "I don't know," she said. Judith would never mention Dagmar again; she would keep her mouth shut about Bugler; she would drop no hints of any kind. But she almost dropped the chops.

Joe continued reading the newspaper. Judith lined the broiler rack with aluminum foil. From the living room, the guests could be heard laughing and talking. Sweetums managed to claw open the back-door screen. He ambled into the kitchen and dropped a dead starling at Judith's feet. If it had been a crow, Judith would have felt like eating it. She scolded Sweetums, who seemed to sneer at her. Judith wrapped the dead bird in a paper towel and threw it in the garbage can. Sweetums yawned.

"Hey," Joe noted, glancing at the cat, "he looks pretty good. Frisky, too. I wonder what happened to Rover."

Judith came over to the kitchen table and sat on Joe's lap. "Who knows? Who cares?" She kissed Joe on the lips. He returned the kiss.

They dropped the subject.

TAMAR MYERS'

DEN OF ANTIQUITY MYSTERIES

STATUE OF LIMITATIONS
0-06-053514-8/$6.99 US/$9.99 Can

Antiques dealer Abby Timberlake Washburn's friend Wynell Crawford has renewed their strained relationship with one phone call . . . *from prison!* If bad taste were a capital crime, Wynell would be guilty as sin—but she's certainly no killer.

TILES AND TRIBULATIONS
0-380-881965-1/$6.99 US/$9.99 Can

For all her extraordinary abilities psychic Madame Woo-Woo didn't foresee that she herself would be forced over to the other side prematurely. Suddenly Abby fears there's more than a specter haunting her friend's new house.

SPLENDOR IN THE GLASS
0-380-81964-3/$6.99 US/$9.99 Can

When Amelia Shadbark—doyenne of Charleston Society—meets a foul, untimely end before she can let Abby broker her pricey glass sculpture collection, Abby is left to piece the shards of the deadly puzzle together.

NIGHTMARE IN SHINING ARMOR
0-380-81191-X/$6.50 US/$8.99 Can

Not long after an unexpected fire sends her Halloween costume party guests fleeing from her emporium, Abby discovers an unfamiliar suit of armor in her house. And stuffed inside is the heavily siliconed, no-longer-living body of her ex-husband's current unfaithful wife.